Cropredy Capers

ANOTHER PEOPLE'S HISTORY OF FAIRPORT CONVENTION

First published in Great Britain 2024
by Spenwood Books Ltd
2 College Street, Higham Ferrers, NN10 8DZ.

A CIP record for this book is available from the
British Library.

ISBN 978-1-915858-16-0

Hardback printed & bound by Sound Performance Ltd,
3 Greenwich Quay, Clarence Road, Greenwich, London, SE8 3EY

Design by Bruce Graham, The Night Owl.

Front cover image: Danielle Croft
All other image copyrights: As captioned.

spenwoodbooks.com

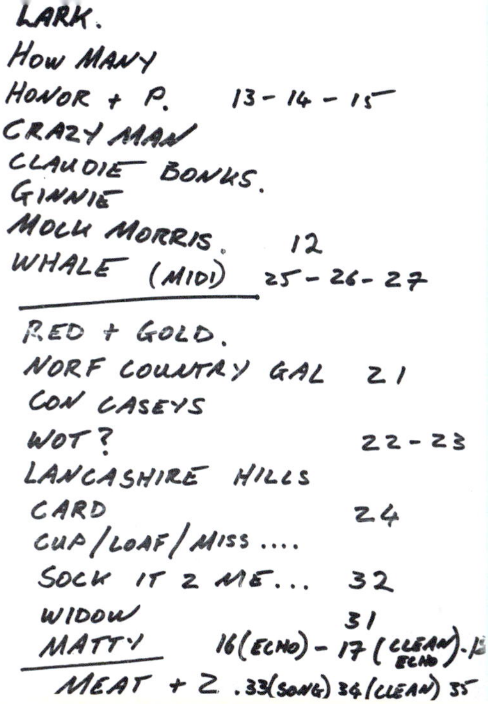

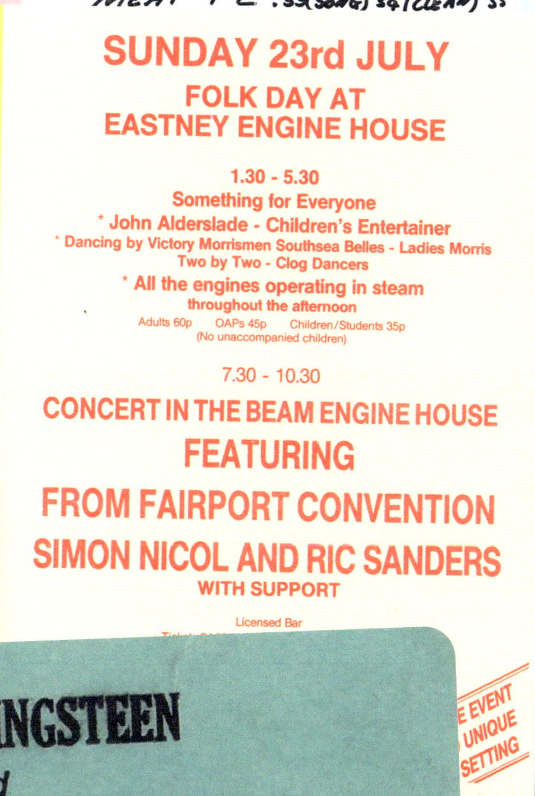

REVIEWS

Fairport perform the old favourites

FAIRPORT CONVENTION at St David's Hall, Cardiff

FOLK MUSIC is often misinterpreted as being humdrum and dull, evocative of a bygone era, and out of touch with current trends. However, with the advent of electronic keyboards, guitars and other modern instruments, a new dimension has opened up for composers, instrumentalists and singers to exploit.

At St David's Hall last night, the supporting act to Fairport Convention was Beryl Marriott, the leading folk keyboard player. She opened with two Scottish dances, *Devil in the Kitchen* and *Dream of Tulagh*. Her adept keyboard skills were admirable even though all four of her numbers, two of which were accompanied by her husband Roger, on harmonica, were lacking in potency.

Their inadequate stage presence was completely overshadowed by Fairport's entrance and subsequent performance. Their up-beat jigs, juxtaposing folk-idiom with rock rhythms and harmony, were catching to say the least.

Walk a While With Me, sung by Simon Nicol, was a most powerful ballad, although the group's acoustic balance in this song, and several others, was questionable.

Ric Sanders's song, *Black Briony*, contained dubious utterances by other composers, and one could not help but perceive fragments of the group, Dire Straits, throughout the concert, and Eurythmics' *Here Comes The Rain Again*, in *The Beggar's Song*.

As Fairport is celebrating its 25th year in the music industry, many songs from the 1960s were played, such as *The Deserter*, a slow waltz, calling upon more traditional folk expressions. The most traditional of all their songs, *Tripping Up The Stairs*, was performed by Martin Allcock, on folk guitar, and proved the most popular with the audience which, incidentally, was only a quarter of the hall's capacity.

The lasting impression of the evening is that the volume of the music was too high. Practically every melody played by the electric violin, unless it was a solo was drowned by heavy bass and booming drums. In parallel, Sanders's rendition of *The Dove*, accompanied by Marriott on keyboards, was praiseworthy.

For a group that has enjoyed the experience of a sell-out concert at Carnegie Hall, it is a shame the concert was marred by meaningless conversation by members of the band between numbers.

MEURYN REES

Cropredy Capers

ANOTHER PEOPLE'S HISTORY OF FAIRPORT CONVENTION

Richard Houghton

Spenwood Books
Manchester, UK

ABOUT THE AUTHOR

Richard Houghton is the author of more than 20 books about music. He lives in Manchester, UK with his wife Kate and his pomapoo Sid. He can be contacted at iwasatthatgig@gmail.com and is always interested in hearing people's memories of seeing classic rock bands in live performance.

INTRODUCTION

NIGEL SCHOFIELD

The *Cropredy Years* account for forty-five of Fairport Convention's fifty-seven year history. This is the story of a band now approaching what was 'retirement age' when it first started out but which remains forever young and continues, as the age range of contributors to this volume reminds us, to attract new fans, though it still has no idea where the time went.

Lack of easy access meant Cropredy avoided becoming a commuter town. With a unique ambience and low property prices for the region, it instead became the home of two members of the world's greatest folk-rock band in the mid-seventies. Other band members lived reasonably close by. The village hall, two minutes' walk from the homes of Dave Pegg and Dave Swarbrick, became their rehearsal space. They were booked, with little fuss, as the local band to play at the local village fete in the late seventies.

In 1979, at the end of a farewell tour which saw them, for the first time, revisit and play again material from their back catalogue, Fairport decided to hold their final (UK) gig on home turf.

Simon Nicol: 'We opened for Led Zeppelin at Knebworth in the afternoon and then came back to what we all regarded as home turf for a chance to say goodbye to friends and fans of the band.'

Swarb: 'We'd played at the village fête for the last three years, so we more or less took it over and brought it all back home for one last gig, with Fairport and friends who had been in the band previously.'

Peggy: 'The Zeps said they would fly us back by helicopter, but it looked strangely like a transit van! We had strong ties with the village. Swarb and I both lived there. We knew everyone and everyone knew us. It was a local thing, but anyone who loved Fairport could come along.'

Future members were there – Chris Leslie on stage with Steve Ashley, Maart and Ric in the audience. It was the end of Fairport. 'We'd been together, in various permutations, for a dozen years, which is longer than The Beatles managed!'

The event went well. Everyone enjoyed it. A small profit was made. Picking up on the mood, Simon Nicol coined a Cropredy catchphrase and jokingly suggested 'same time next year?' A roar from the audience confirmed mutual approval. So, the following year was a Reunion. The next the Second Annual Reunion (what a welcome muddle word that was!). And so on, through various names – a weekend in the country, Cropredy Festival, Fairport's Cropredy Convention, etc. It didn't matter. Whatever name they gave it, to fans it was always just Cropredy, to locals it was simply Fairport.

Audiences grew, up to the maximum allowance of 20,000. It expanded from a one-day event with parking, to two days with camping at the top of the field (Home Field became its base after a couple of years and has remained so), to three days, with tents and camper vans filling the panorama around the natural amphitheatre at the base of which sits the Cropredy Stage. On that stage, Fairport always ended the weekend with a mammoth set, reconvened line-ups, special guests and lots of surprises (from specially made videos to a literal secret Santa!). Eventually, the band's acoustic version (an innovation predating the 'Unplugged' era by nearly half a decade) of the band opened proceedings. Between, over the years, came some of the biggest names in pop, rock, folk, skiffle, country and almost every genre of music you can think of.

In the mid-eighties, I asked Simon Nicol to describe Cropredy: 'I take it you mean the annual event, not the village? It's certainly not a folk festival, though a lot of people call it that. It's not even just a music festival, though that's at the heart of it. It's a gathering of like-minded people, a peaceful coming together. A chance, as the song says, to see all our friends. It's also the occasion when people from across the country… across the world in fact – because we have visitors from Europe, Australia, America, Africa and Asia – who for three or four days became part of a small and very special community in North Oxfordshire. It is unique and very special.'

That uniqueness and the way it developed, the people it involved and the way it affected their lives is what this book is all about: their experiences, their impressions and most of all their memories. Enjoy being part of it.

VARIOUS ADDRESSES
SUMMER 1966, MUSWELL HILL, LONDON, UK

ANN TULACZ

I have a kaleidoscope of memories from the very early days of Fairport. I remember many coffees at Fairport House; listening to early band practices; Richard Thompson patiently trying to teach me to play 'Bobby Shaftoe' on the guitar in Richard Lewis's garden, near Fairport House; Simon, very young, skinny and confident and around all the time; being at the party when Richard Lewis suggested the name Fairport Convention; begging Richard Thompson to play 'Season Of The Witch' at every early gig I went to; and visiting The Angel, which was messy in the extreme, but such fun and freedom.

The summer of 1966 was really good, just hanging out with a group of friends and doing everything together. I lived in New Barnet and they all lived round Muswell Hill. I was going out with someone in Muswell Hill who was very best friends with Richard Lewis's brother, Danny and a friend of Richard, Simon, Tyger and Richard Thompson and all the rest, so I was round there all the time.

Simon was the one I knew most. It wasn't until I read my diaries again that I realised just how much Simon was around. He'd be at Richard Lewis's house. He'd come to my house. We'd go up to the pub. I think Simon had quite a lot of freedom because his father had died. He was quite grown up and advanced in what he was doing. And then he lived in Fairport, where Tyger lived, which was the corner of the next road along from my boyfriend then.

What's so amazing is how very young Simon was when they first started. There's a photo of him in Richard Lewis's garden. My friend and I are sunbathing and Simon's parading around in his swimming trunks and he looks so young. He was 15 or 16, a couple of years younger than me, but he seemed the same age as everyone else. He was just very, very mature for his age.

I do remember Richard Thompson coming over and sitting on the step in Richard Lewis's garden and trying to teach me 'Bobby Shaftoe' and being very patient with me. I wrote in my diary that I learnt to play it that day but I don't think I did.

Tyger was a lot older and much more sensible and grown up. He lived in Fairport House so we would go round there a lot for coffees and to mess round after school, to go out to pubs and things. They (the band) would rehearse there. It all seemed quite casual. They'd be doing a lot of rehearsing at Fairport and there'd be a lot of people coming and jamming. I never thought it was anything big. It was just people playing the guitar and getting started. I wasn't particularly a fan of American West Coast music before I heard them play it. I was probably more into traditional folk. It was all very casual, in church halls and things like that. You could stand by the stage and ask them to play what you wanted.

Their parents were very liberal, so I often would stay over there if their parents were away rather than take the bus there and back every day. They were able to have parties and things like that there. And it was at a party with just a whole group of friends that I think Richard Lewis said, 'Well, you rehearse in the house called Fairport. You all convene there. So why don't we call it 'Fairport Convention'?' And it started up from there, from a pretty ordinary party they were playing at.

Simon had just married his first wife, Roberta, and they lived in this old pub out in Hertfordshire called The Angel. I lived on the edge of Hertfordshire and I had just started driving so I drove my friend Andy out there. I can remember it just being such a mess, and Roberta saying she wasn't going to open any of the wedding presents. She was going to keep them under the bed because she didn't want anything spoilt at all. Because everyone was mucking in together and it was just a whole group of boys living in squalor. Nothing much would be washed up or the bathroom cleaned or anything. It was pretty bad. It seemed so other worldly to me, because my father was a vicar and I lived in a neat and tidy vicarage. And you went out there and it was so wild and free and easy. It was just something I had never really known before. It seemed like the start of something completely different, with no parents around or anything. It seemed like such an exotic thing to do.

I went to see them perform a lot. One of the first times I saw them was when they played on a barge on the Thames when Richard's sister had her 21st birthday. There was a party and we all went along to that. Once was at the Saville Theatre. But it was mainly halls and training colleges. And when I went to college in Birmingham, they came up to Birmingham University as they'd obviously moved into the university circuit then, and I saw them there.

I was at college when the crash happened. Richard Lewis was at the same college and came and told me he'd just heard it on the radio. It was a huge shock and we just sat and talked about it.

The whole thing is a bit odd looking back, because it wasn't anything at the time. You never realised how big it was going to get. We had a little get together at Cropredy on the fiftieth anniversary. That was nice.

LEASIDE AVENUE
APRIL 1967, MUSWELL HILL, LONDON, UK

RICHARD LEWIS

I grew up in Muswell Hill, living in the next street to the Fairport house where our family doctor, Simon's dad, had his practice. I knew both Simon and Ashley and, later on, Richard and Judy. A very early version of what became Fairport played at a party in my house in Leaside Avenue in April 1967. I was by then at teacher training college in Birmingham and later that year I spent the 'Summer of Love' in America, returning home with albums by Jefferson Airplane, Eric Andersen, Tim Buckley and Jim & Jean, all of which provided songs for Fairport's early setlists.

Whilst staying at my American pen friend's home on Long Island, I received a postcard of a London policeman with a text that read:

Having super time in London, weather is not too grand, rain everyday so far. Went to see the Tower of London & Changing of the Guard yesterday. These National Costumes are really something. National dish - bangers and mash is delicious – very tasty. Tomorrow, we visit Fortis Green, a place of great antiquity I'm told. Wish you were here.

Love Tyger, Simon, Richard, Martin & Judy

ST MICHAEL'S CHURCH
27 MAY 1967, GOLDERS GREEN, LONDON, UK

CHRIS DRINKWATER

Martin Lamble, Fairport Convention's first proper drummer, was my eldest cousin. His mother, Wendy, was my father's younger sister. In the early 1950s, his parents bought a terraced house in Christchurch Avenue, Wealdstone, near Harrow in north London, where they lived until 1966 before moving to another house in Radnor Road, Harrow. My father, Peter, was a meteorologist and in 1961, following a tour of duty in Gibraltar, was posted to Heathrow Airport. My parents ended up buying a house in Kenton, about a mile from where his sister and family lived. This gave Martin – who was two years younger than me – and myself the opportunity to meet up, which we did regularly. It enabled us to get to know each other better and we became good friends, sharing the same interests in cycling, model railways and music.

Martin Francis Lamble (to give him his full name) was the eldest of three children – all boys – born to Donald and Wendy Lamble (nee Drinkwater). He was born on 28th

SUTTON MAN JOINS FAIRPORT CONVENTION

First, years ago, it was Susan Maugham . . . then, a little later, Steve Winwood . . . and now a third Sutton musician, Dave Pegg, from 77, Gibbons Road, is in with a chance of making the big time.

This week Dave, his wife Chris and their two years-old daughter Stephanie, will be leaving the council home where they live with Chris's parents and moving to a large house at Bishop's Stortford, where 22 years-old guitarist, Dave, will begin practice sessions with the internationally-respected Fairport Convention.

He has been invited to join the Convention since the departure to other fields of singer Sandy Denny and bass guitarist Tyger Hutchins.

LAST GIG

A professional musician for five years, Dave plays bass guitar, string bass and mandolin. He has played with Roy Exception, Jimmy Cliff and the Uglys', and is currently a member of the Ian Campbell Folk Group. His last gig with Campbell is at the Jug o' Punch, Digbeth Civic Hall, on New Year's Eve.

It was through the Campbell group that Dave got his invitation to join Fairport Convention, a job which he regards, not surprisingly, as at least the makings of a very big break. He was recommended by a Convention member, Dave Swarbrick, who used to play with Ian Campbell.

After audition in the hall of a London school, Dave was selected, and his first appearances with Fairport, whose latest album "Liege and Lief" was released earlier this month, are scheduled for the new year.

In March, he leaves with the group on a tour of the U.S.A. America is about the only country he has not so far visited as a musician. One

Germany, and he h[...] been round Scandinav[...] gium and France.

A former pupil of [...] Grammar School, Dave [...] in an insurance office [...] I didn't like it much" [...] turning pro. He came [...] in Sutton Coldfield [...] married tax office cler[...]

STEP

How does he fe[...] joining a top-line o[...] Fairport Convention [...] I'm pleased, of cour[...] think Chris is, too. I [...] red them for a long [...] used to play electric [...] liked it. To go from [...] Ian Campbell play t[...] folk like Fairport [...] natural step, it seem[...]

His musical tastes are very wide, thou[...] fondest of progress[...] "The only thing I'm [...] on is reggae."

Will Fairport b[...] even bigger name [...]

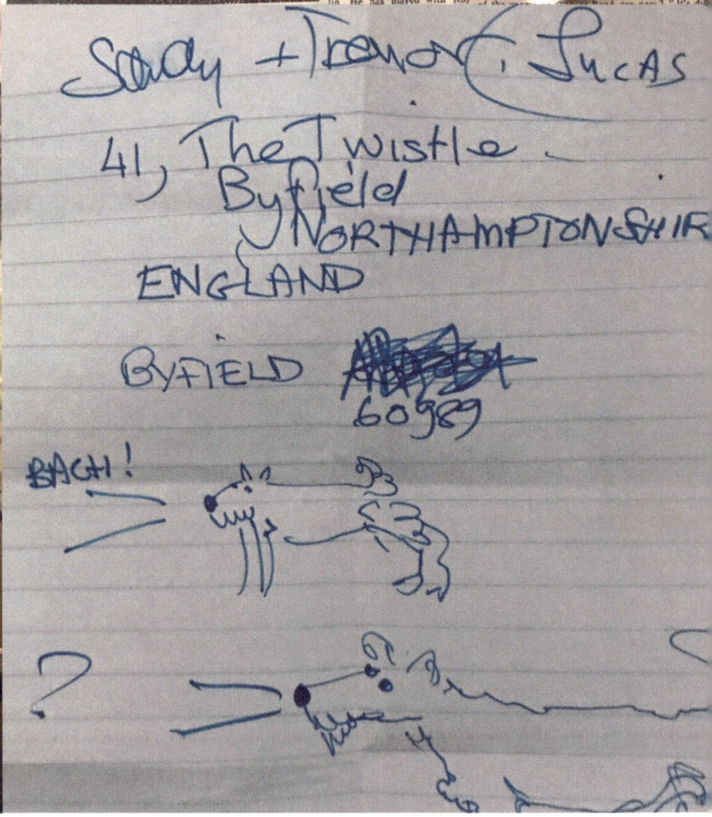

Sandy + Trevor Lucas

41, The Twistle
Byfield
NORTHAMPTONSHIR
ENGLAND

BYFIELD ~~[illegible]~~
60989

BACH!

?

(clockwise from top left) Dave Clemo was there at the Saville in 1967; Mike Dillon in the white trousers; Peggy joins Fairport; Sandy Denny's contact information as given to Denyse Anger; Ann Tulacz with Simon Nicol; Ann Tulacz; Mick Monk was at the Isle of Wight Pop Festival; Denyse Anger as drawn by Joen Swan

(clockwise from top left) Ann Tulacz with *Friends of Fairport* at Cropredy, 2017; Martin Lamble's drawing of The Pheg; Chris Drinkwater drove a Bond Mark D minicar; Ann Tulacz; Simon Nicol at Leaside Avenue with Ann Tulacz & Richard Lewis; Martin Lamble performing on 'Time Will Show The Wiser'; Scott Bernie's family were regular Cropredy attendees, and Fairport fans going back to 1968; Martin Lamble's drawing of Chris Drinkwater's Bond minicar

August 1949 in London, his middle brother Robin in 1952 and his youngest brother, Graeme, came along in 1957. Their father, Don, was musical. He played the piano and when they were older, he encouraged his three children to learn to play a musical instrument, starting with the violin. Soon their terraced house in Wealdstone, north London, was reverberating to the sound of strings being scratched as they took it in turns to practise.

As Martin approached his teens, his interest in playing an instrument turned to percussion. He liked both the sound and the rhythm that drumming offered. In the absence of a proper drum kit, he would improvise by drumming with his fingers on a table top or banging a teaspoon against the side of a sugar bowl whilst tapping with his feet to learn the various different rhythms.

Martin went to the local Priestmead Junior School before, in 1961, having excelled in passing his eleven-plus exam, he was offered a place at the prestigious University College School (UCS) in Hampstead. Later, he managed to buy a proper drum kit, and together with some other musically-minded school friends in his class who played guitars, he formed a band called The Pheg. Later on, they changed the band's name to Captain Rudgely's Blues Band. It was through playing the drums in his school band that Martin developed his percussion skills. He was entirely self-taught and seemed to have a natural sense of rhythm and timing.

Although extremely intelligent, he wasn't particularly academically minded, preferring the arts and music to science and mathematics and other subjects. He had no real desire to go on to university after finishing his schooling. He was also skilled at sketching and drawing on paper. A few months before he was due to leave school in July 1967, he told me that he was thinking of applying to London Transport to work in their advertising department. Then, suddenly and by chance, something came about that would change his future for good.

One day in April of 1967, Martin and I met up and he said that a girlfriend of his had told him a band that called themselves 'The Fairport Convention' were playing their first public gig at a church hall in Golders Green one Saturday evening in early May. She asked if he would be interested in going to see them and he asked her what sort of music they played. His tastes in music at that time, like mine, were mainly the blues and folk and country music rather than mainstream pop. She said they did covers of songs by The Byrds and Dylan, West Coast and Blues-oriented stuff. Martin liked the sound of this and said, 'Yes, I would like to come and hear them.' I said to him that I would like to come too. He also told a few of his classmates.

So, on the evening of May 5th, we met up and made our way to St Michael's church hall in Golders Green, where he also met a few school friends. The band set up their equipment and then began playing. I can't remember anything of what was on their set list that night but I do remember that I enjoyed their playing. At the end of the evening, while the band were packing away their equipment and Martin had gone to talk to his school friends in another part of the hall, I approached their bass guitarist, then known (as I found out later) as 'Tyger' Hutchings, to have a chat with him. I told him that I understood that it was their first proper public gig and that whilst I enjoyed their playing, I wondered how he thought of the gig. He said he thought it had gone quite well but they were not very happy about the playing of their drummer, someone called Shaun Frater, and that they were looking for a new drummer who was a lot better than him. Immediately, I pointed to Martin and said that he – my cousin – was an aspiring drummer who had played in a blues band at school.

Tyger asked me to ask Martin to come over for a chat, which I did. Afterwards, Martin told me that Tyger had invited him to an audition with the rest of the band one afternoon the following week in the upstairs flat of a house called Fairport in Muswell Hill. So it was that the following week I collected Martin and his drum kit in my only means of transport, a Bond Minicar three-wheeler, and drove him to his audition.

They put Martin through his paces as a drummer as he accompanied them on some of their numbers. They obviously liked his drumming because, afterwards, he told me that they wanted him to perform for a trial period on their next few gigs to see how it went. Well, a few gigs later, he told me that they now wanted him to stay on as their replacement drummer. They obviously liked both him and his drumming and felt he would fit in well with the band personality-wise. That was great news for both Martin and the band.

Soon they had a new manager, Joe Boyd, who managed to get a recording contract for them with Island Records and the more they gigged, the more the popularity of their type of music grew, leading them to play more gigs in lots of clubs and universities.

SAVILLE THEATRE
1 OCTOBER 1967, LONDON, UK

DAVID CLEMO

I was a latecomer to seeing live groups. I grew up in Cornwall in the 1950s. My family didn't get a TV until 1958 and the radio was a virtual desert for pop music. We were far more likely to hear a brass band than a band with guitars. This changed when my family relocated to West London in the summer of 1962, a few months before The Beatles released their first single and changed the world.

My father was a railwayman. We lived just off Ladbroke Grove in a rented house that backed on to railway sidings beside the main line into Paddington. This part of West

London was an incredible melting pot of cultures, with Irish, West Indians, Africans and Londoners living together. I was just a 13-year-old country bumpkin with a thick Cornish accent. My schooldays were spent in a state of perpetual penury, with no money to spend on buying records of going to gigs. Indeed, I couldn't even afford the 19/11d for a set of Black Diamond guitar strings for my cheap plywood guitar.

I left school in the summer of 1967 and went to work for a bank. The salary was £370 a year plus £150 London weighting – an incredible £10 a week. I have never had as much disposable income since!

In October 1967 my friend Dave and I decided to go to a Sunday night concert at the Saville Theatre in Shaftesbury Avenue. The top of the bill went to The Pink Floyd, with support from Tomorrow with Keith West (featuring a pre-Yes Steve Howe on guitar) and The Incredible String Band. The opening slot went to a band I'd never heard of – 'The' Fairport Convention. We took our seats on the balcony. The curtains were drawn. When the compere introduced the first act, the curtains opened and three guitarists and a girl clad in a long flowing dress stepped forward. She (Judy) was playing what I later discovered was an electric autoharp. I've never seen another one played live. The first song was their cover of Donovan's 'Season Of The Witch', which I think was sung by RT. The hairs stood up on the back of my neck. I was mesmerised. I'd never heard anything like it. All too soon, their set was at an end. The rest of the evening was an anticlimax.

MIDDLE EARTH
28 OCTOBER 1967, LONDON, UK

DAVID CLEMO

A few weeks after seeing Fairport at the Saville Theatre, I persuaded my parents to let me go to an all-nighter at Middle Earth in Covent Garden. It didn't begin until 11pm. We paid our entrance fee (about a pound) and went inside. It was a dimly-lit room. There was what looked like a concrete blockhouse in the centre of the room. I looked through the door at a tangle of wires where a blond and bespectacled Jeff Dexter was playing records between the live performances.

The stage was very low, no more than a foot or so off the ground. I was able to stand right at the front. Fairport were still a five-piece band. Iain Matthews was yet to join them. They opened the evening, and then I'm pretty sure we had sets from Tyrannosaurus Rex (Marc Bolan and Steve Peregrine Took) and The Incredible String Band before Fairport played a second set to close the evening. I was once again transfixed by their sound. What was it? Was it the interplay between bassist Ashley (Tyger) Hutchings and drummer Martin Lamble? They were a really tight outfit. Richard Thompson was extraordinary. He could (and did) solo all night without repeating himself. It was in some ways a chastening experience. How could someone who was only six months older than me be that good? Fiftyseven years on, I still ask myself the same question.

Fairport's second set seemed to consist of one extended piece. I stood at the front of the stage, midway between Richard and Judy Dyble who sat on a chair looking cool while RT noodled away. Judy kept her fingerpicks on the frame of her horn-rimmed glasses and took her time getting them off and onto her fingers before it was her turn to play her autoharp. After the set finished, I plucked up courage to speak a few words to the bass player, and he smiled and thanked me.

The following spring I was eagerly awaiting the release of Fairport's first album. Every Saturday I called into Musicland record shop in Portobello Road and every Saturday they told me why it hadn't been released. I remember one excuse. Apparently, the sleeves had been laminated before they were folded. I have no idea if that's possible. I'd already bought their first single 'If I Had A Ribbon Bow'. It was a strange choice for a first release. It bore no resemblance to their stage sound. That's not to say I didn't like it, but if I'd heard the record before seeing them live, would they have had the same attraction? Eventually the LP was released and it stayed on my record player for weeks.

SPEAKEASY
21 DECEMBER 1967, LONDON, UK

ANDREW LAUDER

I saw them at the Speakeasy in 1967 or '68, by accident. I was taken by a friend and it just happened to be the Fairports that were the band that night. I really enjoyed them and bought the first album as a consequence. I was a fan of the Merry-Go-Round single 'Time Will Show The Wiser' and had a copy of the 45. Fairport put me in mind of Jefferson Airplane, whose first album I had acquired a copy of in 1966, and who I became a big fan of.

THE BARN BBQ CONCERT & BARN DANCE
2 JUNE 1968, WHITTLESEY, UK

ROSE PRENTICE

I saw Fairport Convention at a festival in Peterborough. I think they introduced Sandy Denny as it being her first time joining them on stage. Fleetwood Mac played too, and

I knew Peter Green from the Marquee. Fairport also played at Dacorum College in Hemel Hempstead. I remember them playing Leonard Cohen's 'Suzanne' at that one. I knew Dave Swarbrick's parents because they retired to the village where I lived. I absolutely love *Liege & Lief*. And Cropredy is okay… some years!

MIDSUMMER NIGHT'S DREAM BURTON CONSTABLE HALL

21 JUNE 1968, BURTON CONSTABLE, UK

MIKE DILLON

I saw Fairport many times from the late sixties, starting when I was a very young art student in Scarborough, going frequently to the Candlelight Club in the town from late 1967. The Candlelight was an amazing place, putting on many bands that now are recognised as part of a golden era in contemporary music. As well as Fairport in their early guise as a sort of English Jefferson Airplane, my fellow students and I loved seeing Peter Green's Fleetwood Mac, The Herd, Spooky Tooth, even Slade when they were a skinhead pub band. If only I'd kept the flyers printed on cheap paper and scattered on every beer-stained table advertising the following week's band.

Of all the wonderful bands we saw, Fairport Convention absolutely blew us away. Sandy Denny's voice was spellbinding, particularly alongside the super-cool Iain Matthews (whose fringed suede jacket was the envy of our entire year group at the art school). Iain's lead vocals on Leonard Cohen's 'Suzanne', with Martin Lamble's haunting drums, remains the most potent memory of my musical awakening. Richard Thompson's guitar playing simply mesmerised us on every song, with everything held together by Simon Nicol, Tyger Hutchings and Martin Lamble.

I remember one evening (perhaps the second time they played the Candlelight) someone on the balcony overlooking the stage spilt a glass of beer during the interval which went all over Martin Lamble's drum kit. He didn't make a fuss but carefully cleaned his drums ready for the second set. Not too long after that gig, we were devastated to hear about the tragic car crash that killed Martin and Bradford (the dog that we'd seen at gigs). We felt a personal and deep loss on that dreadful day.

Whenever we got the chance, we'd go to see Fairport at places such as the Railway Institute in York, Redcar Jazz Club, the Burton Constable all-nighter in 1968 and (I think) Lincoln Folk Festival. Although we loved the West Coast-influenced stuff, it was when 'A Sailor's Life' was first in the set list, with the magical combination of Richard Thompson and the guesting Dave Swarbrick, that we first saw the magic interplay of these two geniuses. Of course, this signalled the transition from West Coast-influenced music to their own interpretation of English traditional folk music, a move that initially fanned the flames of our interest but ultimately diluted our devotion as the band migrated to a different, yet still wonderful land.

COCKPIT, HYDE PARK
24 AUGUST 1968, LONDON, UK

DAVID CLEMO

The summer of 1968 was memorable for a series of free concerts held in Hyde Park. I missed the first but went to the second on August 24th. It was a lovely summer's day with a great vibe. This was by far the best festival I ever attended, and while the ice cream van had a long queue all afternoon, there was a Coca-Cola lorry parked nearby under the trees where you could buy a warm can of fizziness for an eye-watering two shillings (about two pounds in today's money). That was the sum total of the catering facilities.

I arrived in good time before the music started. The stage was on the path with the Serpentine behind. The Cockpit was a sloping area of grass with shade provided by overhanging trees. About ten thousand of us sat in the sun and were royally entertained all afternoon, with performances by Ten Years After, Fleetwood Mac, Family and Peter Sarstedt.

The Fairports were amazing. Sandy had only been with the band for a matter of weeks, but it was a match made in heaven. They played just a few songs including The Farinas' 'Reno Nevada', Tim Buckley's 'Morning Glory' and Leonard Cohen's 'Suzanne'.

1ST ISLE OF WIGHT POP FESTIVAL
31 AUGUST 1968, GODSHILL, UK

MICK MONK

I first heard Fairport Convention on John Peel's *Night Ride* on the inaugural BBC Radio 1 in early 1968 and bought the first album on the strength of those broadcasts. Little did I know I would get to see them play live a couple of months later. I was on a camping holiday in Hampshire/Sussex with two school friends on the August bank holiday weekend. We had been driving along the coast from Bognor Regis to Southsea and were walking along the promenade when I spotted the Hovercraft, a novelty to us landlubbers from Hertfordshire. We headed over to it for a closer look where we came across these very exotic folk standing around waiting to board. They had the appearance of a contemporary band with their Afghan coats, crazy hats and long hair. Then I recognised Roy Wood of The Move and, shortly after, John Peel. My two friends were reluctant to go up and say hi but being more precocious, I wasn't. I waltzed up to John Peel and asked what was going on. He replied, 'We, that is myself, The Move and T. Rex, are heading over to the Isle of Wight for a music festival that is happening over there this evening. You should come.' 'Yes, we should!' I replied. 'I hope to see you later then,' he concluded.

I had read somewhere that Jefferson Airplane were playing. I had no idea who else was on the bill beyond them and now The Move and Tyrannosaurus Rex. I certainly didn't know Fairport were playing. I went back to my friends and told them that we should go. They were reluctant but I could be quite persuasive. We collected our camping gear and drove to Southampton to catch the ferry.

I remember we got to the Isle of Wight around teatime but missed the special festival buses, so we walked. There were other people like us. We fell in with them. When we got close, we heard the music. We followed our ears, reaching the festival site about 7pm. Although it was supposed to have started earlier, it hadn't. We arrived to witness The Pretty Things on stage with Twink, their drummer, clambering around precariously on the scaffolding that formed the stage superstructure on two flat back trailers.

They were followed by the spectacular Crazy World of Arthur Brown and then The Move, who were headlining with Jefferson Airplane. The Airplane were on stage from about midnight. They were touring the rather stark *Crown of Creation* album and were very good, though their music didn't engage me as much as it should have.

But then I heard that Fairport were playing later. The music press had made a big deal about them being the English Jefferson Airplane, because up to that time they had played mostly covers of songs by American folk singers, notably Joni Mitchell, Dylan and Leonard Cohen, plus they had male and female lead singers like the Airplane.

By now, however, Sandy Denny had replaced Judy Dyble, introducing a whole new dynamic to their sound including her own distinctive songs like 'Who Knows Where the Time Goes'.

Fairport arrived on stage at about four in the morning following two or three other acts, including the uniquely characteristic Tyrannosaurus Rex. By this time, the audience of 8,000 had dwindled down to a few hundred stalwarts which allowed me to get really close to the stage. I remember that it was very cold but as the Fairport's set progressed, the sky began to lighten and a red glow from the stage lights mirrored the gathering dawn, which cast the band half in shadow and half in light. I was awe struck and transfixed from the very beginning of their set, which included early favourites 'It's Alright Ma, I'm Only bleeding', 'Jack O' Diamonds', 'Reno Nevada' and Leonard Cohen's 'Suzanne'.

They were such a contrast to the earlier acts, and especially Jefferson Airplane. Their music was so appropriate for that calm time just before dawn. As Sandy began to sing, Ian harmonised and Richard, almost hidden at the back of the stage with a shock of hair covering his face, played the most beautiful lyrical guitar that complemented the songs. The lead voices and Richard's guitar were seamlessly linked by Simon's rhythm guitar and underpinned by Ashley's bass and Martin Lamble's drumming. The music just drew you in. It was a very special performance. The memory is as vivid today as it was for days afterwards. The Airplane with The Move may have been the headliners, but it was Fairport that left the lasting impression. It was magical. I have been a fan ever since.

I drifted away with the remnants of the audience. I was in a dream-like state for the rest of the day and for days afterwards. And no substances had been taken!

Later, Fairport came to live in Little Hadham, a village close to the one where myself and my younger brother, Dave, were raised. Dave's initiation into Fairport live was with me at the first Hadham Fete. He was lucky enough to see them at the next one too. I also saw them twice at Sheffield University where I was a student, at least once more with Sandy, and then with Swarb, Peggy and Dave Mattacks. In advance of that particular gig, and to publicise it for ENTS, which I was then a member of, I wrote 'a bit of bio' for the Students Union newspaper, DARTs.

Dave and I have been to Cropredy several times. Each time I see them it's a new experience but also always linking back to that very first time in the dawn of 1st September 1968 on the Isle of Wight.

PARLIAMENT HILL FIELDS
5 SEPTEMBER 1968, HAMPSTEAD, LONDON, UK

SCOTT BIRNIE

I first heard Fairport on the radio with 'If I Had A Ribbon Bow' on the John Peel show on Sunday afternoon and first saw them live at a free concert in London with the American band Jefferson Airplane one weekday evening. They did 'Reno Nevada'. As she'd been a few years previously, my partner suggested we go to Cropredy and we took the kids each year from 1999 to 2014. We'd hope to be camping in a field with posh toilets, we'd look for shooting stars and, when they were really little, we'd take blankets over to the music field of an evening so the kids could sleep whilst we listened to the music. We stopped going because of myriad problems (kids getting bigger, more tents, same small car, partner's health and mobility problems) but me and my partner continued to see them once a year on their spring or winter tours, as they would invariably play one of the local theatres in a nearby town.

FAIRPORT CONVENTION

LIVE AT MAIDSTONE

1970

Full House Line-up

and

MATTHEWS SOUTHERN COMFORT

VHS

32 MINS APPROX

MF01

Limited Edition

Each Copy Numbered

Only £10.00

inclusive of post & packing (UK only

MUSIKFOLK

Remittances payable to 'MUSIKFOLK'. Please send you application to 'MUSIKFOLK', 18 Ferndale Road, South Norwood, London, SE25 4QP.

Please allow 28 days for delivery.

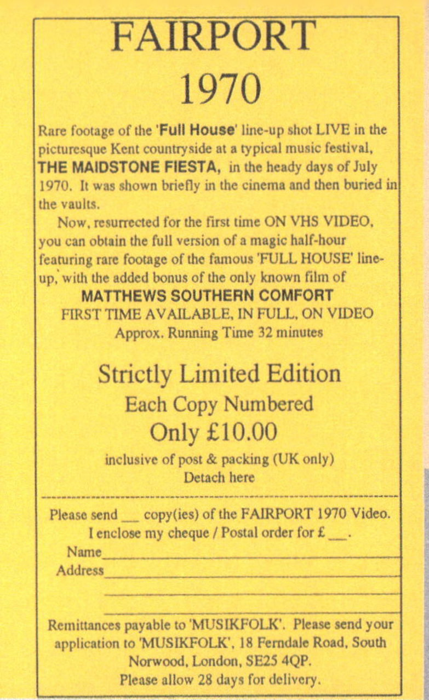

FAIRPORT

1970

Rare footage of the **'Full House'** line-up shot LIVE in the picturesque Kent countryside at a typical music festival, **THE MAIDSTONE FIESTA**, in the heady days of July 1970. It was shown briefly in the cinema and then buried in the vaults.

Now, resurrected for the first time ON VHS VIDEO, you can obtain the full version of a magic half-hour featuring rare footage of the famous 'FULL HOUSE' line-up, with the added bonus of the only known film of

MATTHEWS SOUTHERN COMFORT

FIRST TIME AVAILABLE, IN FULL, ON VIDEO

Approx. Running Time 32 minutes

Strictly Limited Edition

Each Copy Numbered

Only £10.00

inclusive of post & packing (UK only)

Detach here

Please send __ copy(ies) of the FAIRPORT 1970 Video.

I enclose my cheque / Postal order for £ __.

Name ____________________

Address ____________________

Remittances payable to 'MUSIKFOLK'. Please send your application to 'MUSIKFOLK', 18 Ferndale Road, South Norwood, London, SE25 4QP.

Please allow 28 days for delivery.

FAIRPORT CONVENTION:

A continuing story of country folk

Six albums every one a different line up

So Fairport have done it again, or, rather, had it done to them. The continuing story of country folk, as followers of this extremely rewarding but frequently depressing serial will doubtless be aware, took its periodic turn towards despair earlier this month with the shock announcement of lead guitarist Richard Thompson's immediate departure from the group.

By NICK LOGAN

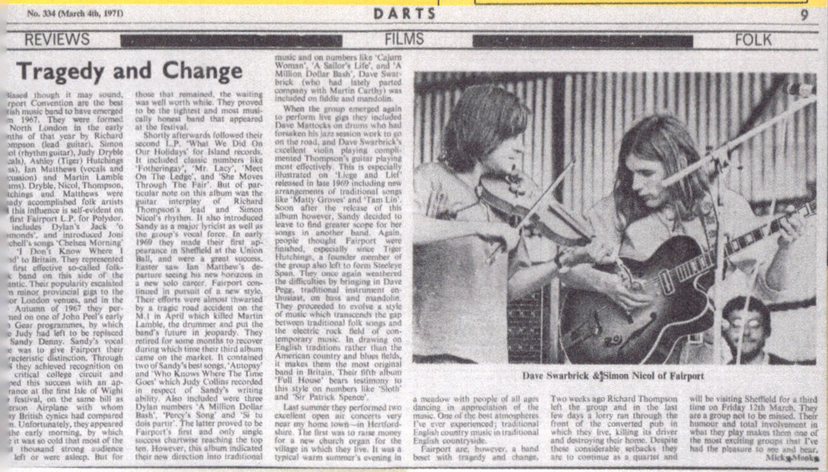

No. 334 (March 4th, 1971) DARTS 9

REVIEWS FILMS FOLK

Tragedy and Change

Biased though it may sound, rport Convention are the best tish music band to have emerged m 1967. They were formed North London in the early nths of that year by Richard ompson (lead guitar), Simon ol (rhythm guitar), Judy Dryble cals), Ashley (Tiger) Hutchings ss), Ian Matthews (vocals and cussion) and Martin Lamble ums). Dryble, Nicol, Thompson, tchings and Matthews were eady accomplished folk artists l this influence is self-evident on first Fairport L.P. for Polydor. includes Dylan's Jack 'o monds', and introduced Joni chell's songs 'Chelsea Morning' 'I Don't Know Where I nd' to Britain. They represented first effective so-called folk- k band on this side of the antic. Their popularity escalated n minor provincial gigs to the or London venues, and in the Autumn of 1967 they per- ned on one of John Peel's early Gear programmes, by which e Judy had left to be replaced Sandy Denny. Sandy's vocal e was to give Fairport their racteristic distinction. Through they achieved recognition on critical college circuit and ped this success with an ap- rance at the first Isle of Wight festival, on the same bill as erson Airplane with whom ny British cynics had compared m. Unfortunately, they appeared the early morning, by which e it was so cold that most of the t thousand strong audience left or were asleep. But for those that remained, the waiting was well worth while. They proved to be the tightest and most musically honest band that appeared at the festival.

Shortly afterwards followed their second L.P. 'What We Did On Our Holidays' for Island records. It included classic numbers like 'Fotheringay', 'Mr. Lacy', 'Meet On The Ledge', and 'She Moves Through The Fair'. But of particular note on this album was the guitar interplay of Richard Thompson's lead and Simon Nicol's rhythm. It also introduced Sandy as a major lyricist as well as the group's vocal force. In early 1969 they made their first appearance in Sheffield at the Union Ball, and were a great success. Easter saw Ian Matthew's departure seeing his new horizons in a new solo career. Fairport continued in pursuit of a new style. Their efforts were almost thwarted by a tragic road accident on the M.1 in April which killed Martin Lamble, the drummer and put the band's future in jeopardy. They retired for some months to recover during which time their third album came on the market. It contained two of Sandy's best songs, 'Autopsy' and 'Who Knows Where The Time Goes' which Judy Collins recorded in respect of Sandy's writing ability. Also included were three Dylan numbers 'A Million Dollar Bash', 'Percy's Song' and 'Si tu dois partir'. The latter proved to be Fairport's first and only single success chartwise reaching the top ten. However, this album indicated their new direction into traditional music and on numbers like 'Cajum Woman', 'A Sailor's Life', and 'A Million Dollar Bash', Dave Swarbrick (who had lately parted company with Martin Carthy) was included on fiddle and mandolin.

When the group emerged again to perform live gigs they included Dave Mattocks on drums who had forsaken his jazz session work to go on the road, and Dave Swarbrick's excellent violin playing complimented Thompson's guitar playing most effectively. This is especially illustrated on 'Liege and Lief' released in late 1969 including new arrangements of traditional songs like 'Matty Groves' and 'Tam Lin'. Soon after the release of this album however, Sandy decided to leave to find greater scope for her songs in another band. Again, people thought Fairport were finished, especially since Tiger Hutchings, a founder member of the group also left to form Steeleye Span. They once again weathered the difficulties by bringing in Dave Pegg, traditional instrument enthusiast, on bass and mandolin. They proceeded to evolve a style of music which transcends the gap between traditional folk songs and the electric rock field of contemporary music. In drawing on English traditions rather than the American country and blues fields, it makes them the most original band in Britain. Their fifth album 'Full House' bears testimony to this style on numbers like 'Sloth' and 'Sir Patrick Spence'.

Last summer they performed two excellent open air concerts very near my home town—in Hertfordshire. The first was to raise money for a new church organ for the village in which they live. It was a typical warm summer's evening in a meadow with people of all ages dancing in appreciation of the music. One of the best atmospheres I've ever experienced; traditional English country music in traditional English countryside.

Fairport are, however, a band beset with tragedy and change. Two weeks ago Richard Thompson left the group and in the last few days a lorry ran through the front of the converted pub in which they live, killing its driver and destroying their home. Despite these considerable setbacks they are to continue as a quartet and will be visiting Sheffield for a third time on Friday 12th March. They are a group not to be missed. Their humour and total involvement in what they play makes them one of the most exciting groups that I've had the pleasure to see and hear.

Mick Monk

Dave Swarbrick & Simon Nicol of Fairport

(clockwise from top left) 1970 video; press cutting; Pete Turner saw Fairport in 1970; Phil Secretan first saw Fairport 54 years ago; Pete Turner promoted Fairport in 1998; Mick Monk's 'bit of a bio' for the Sheffield student newspaper

Savoy Brown

Fleetwood Mac

Fairport Convention

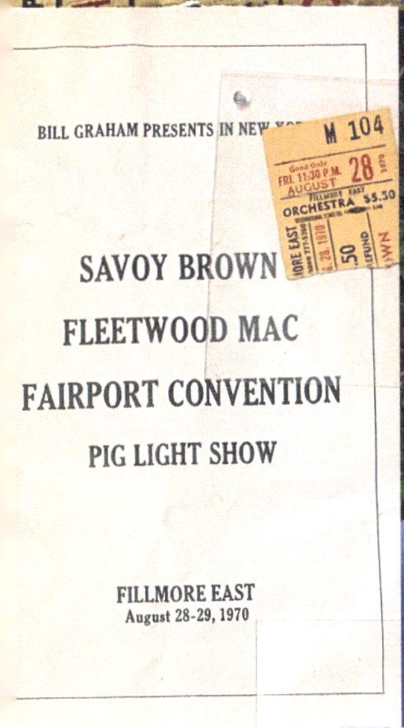

(clockwise from top left) Michael Murray was at the Krumlin Festival; Mitch Weingand's Fillmore East programme; Stephen Pegum listened to Fairport on the John Peel show; Gloria Hiscock got lost on the way to Solihull; Sal Desiano's Fillmore East programme; Mitch Weingand's Fillmore East ticket; Pete Turner saw Fairport again in 2024

LONDON SCHOOL OF ECONOMICS
30 NOVEMBER 1968, LONDON, UK

DAVID CLEMO

I was walking past the London School of Economics in Aldwych with a couple of friends, when I heard the familiar sound of Fairport Convention coming from within. We blagged our way in and sat at the back listening to Sandy Denny and Fairport singing Dylan's song 'I'll Keep It With Mine'. It was as awesome as it was unexpected. Island released Fairport Convention's 'Meet On The Ledge' as a single at around the same time. It was a buzz to hear it played on the radio, although it never troubled the compilers of the Hit Parade.

'SHE MOVES THROUGH THE FAIR'
RELEASED JANUARY 1969

BOB MACKRETH

Thank you for the opportunity to express what Fairport Convention has meant to this American fan from Wisconsin over the years, from 'Meet On The Ledge' and 'Fotheringay' to 'Red And Gold' and 'Lalla Rookh' and beyond. I discovered Fairport by chance one afternoon in the spring of 1970. Goofing off in my teenage bedroom while I should have been writing a term paper, I heard a haunting song on the local progressive rock station, with the most beautiful voice I'd ever heard singing a strange tale about her dead sweetheart. She said something about a fair, and how her father wouldn't mind something or other, and... well, I wasn't quite sure what. The song was not the sort of thing I was used to hearing on the radio back then, and it riveted my attention immediately. I waited, transfixed, to the end of the cut, fervently hoping that the DJ would identify the song before moving on, and much to my delight, he came through.

'That was Fairport Convention with 'She Moves Through The Fair',' he announced and moved on. 'Fairport Convention?' I'd never heard the name before and vowed to find out more about the band, little knowing that this chance encounter was a life-changing moment for me, the start of a love affair that has now lasted fifty-four years.

Thanks to Simon and Peggy and every other member of the band that has celebrated life's high points with me, and has offered comfort in times that I needed it. They have stood above all others as number one on my personal chart for my entire adult life.

UNIVERSITY OF SOUTHAMPTON

18 JANUARY 1969, SOUTHAMPTON, UK

JOHN CLARE

Aaah, Fairport Convention, the band that became and still are, one of my all-time Top 10 favourite bands. I came across them first via John Peel's *Top Gear* on BBC Radio One, who I had been listening to since he was a DJ on the pirate radio station Radio London (The Big L), where he presented his wonderful *Perfumed Garden*, which had been the soundtrack to my fourteenth year in 1967, as I studied through the long summer school holiday in my bedroom for my mock O levels. He always played stuff out of leftfield and Fairport's 'If I Had A Ribbon Bow' was one of them on that *Top Gear* show sometime in 1968. I'm guessing it would have been in February, when the single was released.

After that, I forgot all about them until that lightbulb moment towards the end of the year, thanks to John Peel again – 'Meet On The Ledge'. What a single! I had to rush out and buy it with my Christmas money and I still have it and it is still one of my most treasured singles. And I made a mental note that it had been written by group member, Richard Thompson. But it was that voice that beguiled me, singing the second verse, 'The way is up, along the road, the air is getting thin.' The voice of an angel, Sandy Denny. Both Richard and Sandy were destined to become a lifelong hero and heroine of mine respectively and I still rate Sandy Denny as the finest female singer that ever lived. Somehow though, I bypassed the *What We Did On Our Holidays* album from whence it came, but that didn't matter because something even better happened next.

As a fifth year student at one of Southampton's top grammar schools, Richard Taunton, the Southampton University Student Union, in their infinite wisdom, decided that both fifth and sixth year students from our school (and a couple of others) would be granted access to any of their concerts in both the Old Refectory and the Lecture Theatre. I'd already been to quite a few since my 15th birthday in June 1968, but on January 18th, 1969, Fairport Convention were appearing. This was not to be missed! I seem to remember that Ian Matthews was still in the band (just) and hadn't been ousted yet, but if he was, I don't really remember him doing much. But the most mind-blowing experience was that they opened with a song called 'A Sailor's Life', with Sandy's voice soaring and a riveting Richard Thompson guitar solo, after which he was firmly cemented in my mind as one of my three all-time favourite British lead guitarists, alongside ex-John Mayall and now Rolling Stones guitarist, Mick Taylor, and Pink Floyd's David Gilmour.

More gems followed, particularly from the silver-throated Sandy and included her mesmerising version of 'She Moved Through the Fair', as well as 'Autopsy' and 'Fotheringay'. Plus, of course, there was 'Meet On The Ledge'. The only downfall of the night was that we had to suffer the horrendous cacophony of support band Van Der Graaf Generator first!

Fast forward five months to June 1969 and I'd landed a prized job at Henry's Records in Southampton. I'd only been there a matter of weeks before *Unhalfbricking* was released. Now most people will rave on about *Liege & Lief*, and I agree that it was a pioneering album and probably the precursor of the folk-rock movement but I have always preferred *Unhalfbricking*. In fact, it is still one of my top ten favourite albums of all time. Why? Because the amazing 'Sailor's Life' had now become not just a mind-blowing guitar solo from Thompson, but a riveting duel between him and violinist Dave Swarbrick. Because it had their amazing French language version of Bob Dylan's 'If You Gotta Go, Go Now', plus two other great Dylan interpretations. And because it had two more beautiful Sandy Denny songs, the aforementioned 'Autopsy' and the song considered by myself, to be *the* greatest song written by anynody anywhere, 'Who Knows Where The Time Goes?' That song sends me into raptures every time I hear it. It will be played, as my wife Linda well knows, at my funeral and as I said earlier, it features the voice of an angel!

Yep, *Liege & Lief* is a great album too. It has another great Thompson/Swarbrick duel on 'Matty Groves' and it does have two more beautiful Sandy Denny vocals on 'Farewell, Farewell' and 'Crazy Man Michael', but it doesn't have anything remotely in the same league as 'Who Knows Where the Time Goes?'

We all know what happened next. Ashley Hutchings left and continued the folk-rock revolution with first Steeleye Span and then The Albion Band. And Sandy left too, and although I have always been a lifelong fan, her solo albums never really soared the same heights of 'Who Knows Where The Time Goes?'

But Thompson was still there and the next album, *Full House*, featured another epic, 'Sloth', with a guitar solo so incendiary that it was to become the blueprint for all future Thompson marathon workouts, from 'Night Comes In' to 'Shoot Out The Lights'. But even though the album has no Sandy or any female replacement, it is a fine album with standouts, the two Swarbrick/Thompson co-writes, 'Walk Awhile' and 'Poor Will And The Jolly Hangman' (they also wrote a fine single together, 'Now Be Thankful', which sadly wasn't included on the album until the 2001 reissue), plus the Dave Swarbrick instrumental fiddle wig-out, 'Dirty Linen'. But of course, that was the last Fairport album with Richard Thompson on it as well and the first golden era of Fairport was over, sad to say.

I also attended some of other great Southampton University gigs, including Eclection, another outstanding folk-rock band that featured future Fairport Conventioner and husband of Sandy Denny, Trevor Lucas, an amazing black female singer in the style of Odetta called Dorris Henderson, drummer Gerry Conway (who went on to work with Sandy in Fotheringay) and John 'Poli' Palmer, who would become a future key member of Family.

UNIVERSITY OF BRADFORD
6 FEBRUARY 1969, BRADFORD, UK

STEVE PUGH

I saw an early incarnation of Fairport with Sandy Denny singing (not Judy Dyble) at Bradford Uni just before the accident that killed drummer Martin Lamble. I've been a Richard Thompson fan ever since. I went to another Bradford Uni gig (not Fairport) shortly after the accident and BBC Radio 1's John Peel was doing the intro spot. We 'met' in the gents and I said 'hi' and asked if he'd heard how Fairport were doing. He said 'doing OK but obviously really sad about Martin, etc.' I said 'please send my best wishes' and he said 'I'll be glad…'. I didn't get a name check on air but he mentioned the gents meet up, saying that he'd met someone who'd asked about Fairport! He just seemed so normal and unassuming. I used to love his radio show.

Richard drew fans from all over New England to a little theatre in Lebanon, New Hampshire in 2023 and I saw him again in Derry, New Hampshire in March 2024. He was just great, with amazing guitar playing, and in good voice and fine humour. He was reminiscing about the Marquee Club in London and bands he'd seen there in his youth. He had a Vincent Black Lightning on stage courtesy of the local bikers and Dave Mattacks joined him for the encore!

MIDDLE EARTH, ROYALTY THEATRE
15 MARCH 1969, LADBROKE GROVE, LONDON, UK

RICHARD LEWIS

I was home for the weekend from college and went in the Fairport van to Middle Earth, which was in a temporary home at the Royalty Theatre in Ladbroke Grove. It was here that 'Si Tu Dois Partir' was born. My memory is much the same as the quotes from Simon and Richard in Patrick Humphries' biography. The only addition is that I am pretty sure that whilst we were hanging out backstage between sets, they asked me, as their resident Dylan expert, to write out the English lyrics for 'If You Gotta Go, Go Now' before asking for others to translate it into French.

Another memory I have is of Ashley telling me that some of Fairport were invited to a pre-release listen of Dylan's *Nashville Skyline* in April 1969. Ashley told me that whoever was playing the album said that, as the first track featured Johnny Cash and the second was an instrumental, they would start with track three as 'you won't want to hear those!'

M1 MOTORWAY
12 MAY 1969, LONDON, UK

CHRIS DRINKWATER

They made three albums and all was going well with them when, just after they finished their third album, *Unhalfbricking*, and only two years after Martin had joined the band, tragedy struck. While they were returning from a gig at Mothers Club in Birmingham, in the early hours of 12 May 1969, their road manager fell asleep at the wheel of their Transit van. The van crashed just a few miles from the end of the M1, rolling 40 feet down an embankment, sadly killing both Martin and Richard Thompson's then girlfriend, Jeannie Franklyn, and injuring the other three members of the band.

Despite the shock of the accident, once they had all recovered, the band later decided to continue, recruiting Dave Mattacks as a replacement drummer for Martin and then releasing their seminal album, *Liege & Lief*. The band continues to perform to this day, following several personnel lineup changes, with only Simon Nicol left as an original band member. Martin was only nineteen years old when he died. Who knows what would have happened to him and his career as a drummer had he not died in the accident? All I can say is that I lost a very good family member and friend and Fairport lost a very talented drummer. Still, his legacy and his contribution to Fairport in their early years lives on in the three albums he made with them. He would be proud of that achievement, as I and his family are.

ROUNDHOUSE
25 MAY 1969, LONDON, UK

DAVID CLEMO

In January 1969 Fairport Convention released their second album. I must have played *What We Did On Our Holidays* continuously for weeks. The band was on a roll. They went back into the studio to record *Unhalfbricking*, but on May 12th Fairport Convention's van crashed on the way back from a gig in Birmingham, killing Richard Thompson's girlfriend Jeannie Franklyn and drummer Martin Lamble and putting the rest of the band in hospital. When the news broke everyone rushed to offer their help.

A benefit concert was quickly arranged for at the Roundhouse. A huge crowd turned out to see performances by The Pink Floyd, The Pretty Things, Family, Blossom Toes and Eclection (featuring Trevor Lucas and Gerry Conway). It may have been the first time I saw David Gilmour, the Floyd's new guitarist. It was a great evening despite the sad occasion.

One abiding memory of this time was that there were no house PA systems. Every band had their own PA and on occasions when there was more than one band playing, the back and sides of the stage would be filled with amplifiers and speakers. The headline band would set up first. Their amps were right at the back. The support acts would set their amps in front according to the order that they were performing, so that the opening act would invariably have but a tiny space to work in.

Most bands were using WEM PA speakers. They were the 'must have' at that time. The *Stones in the Park* event, the 1970 Isle of Wight Festival and the early Hyde Park festivals all featured WEM systems, and the firm's founder Charlie Watkins could often be seen working a mixer at the side of the stage, his bald head and white lab coat in stark contrast to the long-haired hippy types all around him. The sight of all those identical speaker cabinets, each one stencilled with their owner's name, was a familiar one to me and my musician friends.

9B ARTHUR ROAD

SUMMER 1969, WIMBLEDON, LONDON, UK

ERIC HAYES, PHOTOGRAPHER

I like to think that as a Canadian, my gentle nature and the folky ways of Fairport were a good match. We took a liking to each other and I spent a lot of time with them in the studio and at gigs. One day, they asked me if I'd like to shoot the cover for their new album, the one that ended up being entitled *Unhalfbricking*. We had no concept, no idea what we would do, so I suggested that we should get together and see what might happen. So one morning the band and their van picked up me and my wife, Sharon, and all of us drove around London looking for inspiration. It was Sandy Denny who eventually said, 'Why don't we go visit my parents in Wimbledon? They have a nice house and a lawn and maybe we can shoot something there.' And we all thought that was a great idea.

I don't know how Sandy's mother felt about the entire band, complete with a photographer and his wife, showing up unexpectedly, but she very graciously served us tea on the lawn. That may have been my idea, actually, thinking from my Canadian perspective, that something as quintessentially English as tea on the lawn would give us a theme and some pleasing compositions. I recall working on that idea for a while, with Sandy in the foreground pouring a cuppa and the rest of the band as supportive compositional elements behind her. At some point, I must have tired of that and backed away entirely when the idea came to put Sandy's parents in the foreground and the entire band taking tea on the lawn behind the lattice work fence. People have asked me how hard it was to get each person's head in a different hole of the fence, but in truth it was a lucky accident.

The cover was shot on 35mm Ektachrome slide film and cropped to fit the square format of the vinyl album cover. I don't know who did the graphic layout, nor do I know who chose that particular frame as the cover shot. I'm just very pleased with the results. The photograph on the back of the album came when Sandy's mother, not content to just serve us tea, generously invited us to stay for supper. We had just started eating when I noticed that the long table and the light in the house echoed some of the elements of classical paintings such as 'The Last Supper'. So Sharon and I backed away from the table and I asked the band to continue the conversation they were already deeply into while I photographed the tableau. Once again, I am grateful to the album designer for choosing that shot. The two extra plates were for me and Sharon, which we hungrily dug into when we rejoined the table.

'SI TU DOIS PARTIR'
RELEASED JULY 1969

MARTIN CROPP

My earliest memories of Fairport are of being in my local pub when I was about 17. On the jukebox was a track by Fairport, the French version of a Bob Dylan song ('Si Tu Dois Partir'). A few years later, I rekindled my interest in Fairport by seeing them at Cropredy which is an amazing festival. I have been several times, and met many members of the band, but unfortunately, not Sandy Denny, much to my disappointment. Some years on, at Bridlington Spa, I was chatting to Peggy about the price of a pint! I've seen them in various concerts – York, Scarborough and Bridlington – and most of their albums on CD and vinyl. I guess I'm a collector of FC. I love Simon's singing now. He seems to have matured from the older days. His voice is quite unique, especially on my favourite song, 'The Hiring Fair', and of course the anthemic 'Meet On The Ledge'. It's a classic!

ROYAL FESTIVAL HALL
24 SEPTEMBER 1969, LONDON, UK

ROBIN DENSELOW

I first met the Fairports in a pub in Chiswick, down by the Thames in London, back in August 1969, and I wasn't quite sure what to expect. After all, the band was something of a mystery at that stage. Their drummer Martin Lamble had tragically been killed earlier in the year when their van crashed on the M1, they had notched up a singles hit with 'Si Tu Dois Partir' (a Dylan composition they sang in French), and they had rightly received some great reviews for their last album, *Unhalfbricking*. Since then they had acquired two new members – drummer Dave Mattacks and fiddle-player Dave Swarbrick – and had been out of sight in the countryside, working on new material. From what I had learned, they were planning to follow-up the folk-rock track 'A Sailor's Life', one of the highlights of the *Unhalfbricking* album, with a new project devoted to matching traditional music and rock.

The band were rehearsing in the back room of the pub, where a pile of faded ballad sheets rested somewhat incongruously between the amps. Guitarist Simon Nicol launched into the sturdy melody of 'The Deserter', and then drums, bass, fiddle and lead guitar joined in, as Sandy Denny re-worked the old story of the young man who has too many drinks, finds he has been enlisted, deserts, is re-captured 'and the sentence passed upon me that I was to be shot'. The British folk scene was gloriously experimental in the late sixties, but I hadn't heard anything quite like this.

I had been asked to write about the new-look Fairports for *The Guardian*, and decided that the focus should not be on Sandy, even though she would soon become my favourite female British singer, or even on that extraordinary long-haired guitar Richard Thompson. I would talk to them later. Instead, I decided to concentrate on Dave Swarbrick, now a full-time member of the band after guesting on 'A Sailor's Life'. After all, he was a folk scene celebrity thanks to his years with the Ian Campbell Group and then playing as a duo with Martin Carthy. He was also in his late twenties, and far older than the other Fairports. So why had he decided to go amplified and join the band?

'I'm still a folk fiddler,' he said. 'And maybe this is the folk revival. Or maybe it is the story revival, which comes to the same thing.' He said that 'at least half' of the Fairports' songs were going to be traditional, and he would change none of the words on 'all those fantastic stories, that would be taboo' (if they weren't folk songs). He stressed that the story in each song should not be lost because of the amplification. The lyrics had to be clear, and there had to be what he called 'separation'.

A few days later, the new line-up made their triumphant debut at the Royal Festival Hall, and I got to hear their thrilling treatment of 'Matty Groves' for the first time.

'This,' I wrote excitedly in *The Guardian*, 'is English folk music for the seventies.'

(clockwise from top left) for Graham Somers, the Fairport journey has been worth every penny; Johnny Carlsen with Peggy; Fairport have made an indelible mark on David Johnson; David Wraith saw a very giggly Sandy; Nigel Banks has been following Fairport since 1970; Johnny Carlsen with Simon

(clockwise from top left) Katy Averill (now Rhodes) helping clean up at Cropredy; Robert Plant playing footie with Jerry Donahue (Roger Averill); the first show on Richard Crossman's lawn (Roger Averill); Dave Hughes wiring up a job; the 1980s electric crew (left to right) Wayne Averill, Tim Sharpe, Paul Sisman, Mick Peters, Dave Hughes & Roger Averill, with Peggy sitting on Mick Peters' Harley; the record shop where Pat McGurk discovered Fairport

ZIGZAG BENEFIT CONCERT, CIVIC HALL
14 OCTOBER 1969, DUNSTABLE, UK

ANDREW LAUDER

The next time I saw the Fairports live was in Dunstable for the *ZigZag* benefit with Mighty Baby, who I also enjoyed, having been a fan of The Action. They'd had a change in lineup by then, with Sandy Denny now in place. It was a great night but I have no recollection of how I got there or how I returned to London! I loved the first copy of *ZigZag*, which was issued with Sandy on the front cover, and contacted John Tobler and Pete Frame at *ZigZag* and soon became friends with them both. I ended up writing for *ZigZag* in the early days under the name Alan Lord, mostly about San Francisco bands.

MOTHERS
2 NOVEMBER 1969, BIRMINGHAM, UK

ROGER GOULD

They played the *Liege & Lief* album. It was a brilliant evening and the last time the six from that album played together. It was Dave Pegg's 22nd birthday and he was in the audience that night. He joined the band shortly afterwards, as Ashley Hutchings and Sandy Denny had left. It was the first time I'd seen an electric fiddle. Swarb was superb. And Sandy is the greatest female singer I've ever seen, and I've seen Dusty, Hazel O'Connor and Heather Small.

LIEGE & LIEF
RELEASED DECEMBER 1969

PHIL LAMBERT

It was Christmas 1967, just a few weeks before my twelfth birthday, and I was given a Cathy McGowan Dansette record player with four LPs. One of these was *Sandy and Johnny*, an album she recorded that year as part of the Johnny Silvo Folk Four. Her voice blew me away. I had been exposed to much American folk and country music from my Canadian grandfather – Burl Ives, Jim Reeves, Roger Miller, Pete Seeger and even Woody Guthrie. For this reason, I was not one of those kids who idolised the Stones or the Beatles.

Move on three years and I am now fifteen years old and over six feet tall, with the obligatory mass of hair. Thanks to the *Melody Maker* I am aware of the 'scene' and beginning to get to gigs in the Kingston (The Barge), Putney and Wimbledon areas. Getting in didn't seem to be a problem. And then it happened! I heard *Liege & Lief*, and Sandy's voice once again, this time with the backing of the boys that have stayed with me through all the line-ups and taking me off in all different directions as members come and go and forge their own way, but always returning to the core.

We have grown up together, albeit I am only just a few years younger, and I have loved all the albums for many different reasons. Over the years, I have been fortunate to see them at (amongst others) Putney, Wimbledon, Fairfield Halls at Croydon, Guildford and of course Broughton Castle and many of the early Cropredy festivals. Highpoints? Anything involving Swarb (aka 'The Little Master'), Sandy singing at full voice, Richard and Jerry Donahue's guitar playing, Maart standing centre stage making all the hand and arm movements to 'London River', and Swarb singing and playing 'Yellow Bird' and Simon singing 'Woman', both at Wimbledon.

I remember a lady in a red dress completely out of it at Fairfield Halls, and in recent years the fabulous tones of Simon's vocals which I always have enjoyed. And I haven't even mentioned the fabulous line-up of drummers, the difficult job Ric has had and done so well in following Swarb, and the multi talents of Chris Leslie. Let alone all the guests and the early bass of the Guv'nor, the later bass of Peggy and vocal tones of Iain Matthews, especially with Sandy. Wait a minute… there are no highlights… it's just been a blast!

CHRIS REVIE

A few years ago, I did one of those internet memes – ten favourite vinyl albums – and here are my thoughts on *Liege & Lief*.

So, I'm going to start with this, as it was one of the first records I ever heard crawling around on the floor (no, I was not drunk, I was about two, so stop sniggering at the back). Little did I know back then the profound influence this album would have on my life [working at Cropredy since the mid-eighties], *starting with the really strange experience of rediscovering it as a teenager – putting this, so I thought, unheard album on the turntable, only to realise with the first note that I could instantly recall every word and note, and had a flashback of the rug my parents had in the living room. Who needs drugs!*

And over the years watching played live 'John Gaudie', the Lord Randall version of 'Matty Groves' and most recently 'Cider Rain' and thinking each time, 'Yeah, they've still got it!'

DENYSE ANGER

I was a Judy Collins fan, listening to the *Who Knows Where the Time Goes* album with its' compelling cover photo, and wondering who 'S. Denny', the writer of the album's title song, was. I had moved to Canterbury in the UK in November 1969, and then to London, where I heard *Liege & Lief* playing as I passed one of the shop stalls in Kensington Market. I asked the owner 'what is this?'. She nodded toward the album cover, propped up to be plainly visible as you entered her shop. I'd never heard a voice like that or traditional English folk played at great speed with a terrific rock 'n' roll sensibility. I was hooked.

Working as a cleaner, I was sent by London Domestics to the door of photographer Linda Fitzgerald Moore. Asking if I'd be interested in a new client, Linda told me about her upstairs tenants – 'they're musicians' – which led me to being invited upstairs to meet Trevor Lucas. Imagine my surprise when I found myself in Sandy and Trevor's flat one morning.

I cleaned house for Sandy and Trevor for six months, until I moved back to Virginia. I didn't see them again until 1974, at Washington DC's Lisner Auditorium. Sandy hugged me and it felt as though no time had passed since I worked for them. I wasn't used to seeing them onstage, despite already being a fan when I went to work for them. It was a bit of an out-of-body experience, a culmination of something, and hearing 'Matty Groves' brought me back to myself and to that heightened moment. Sandy seemed especially appreciative afterward when I told her the song made my heart 'rush'.

As I immersed myself in the music, I understood what someone described as an essential part of Fairport's appeal. Sandy was more than an interpreter, instead fully embodying the history and drama depicted in whatever she sang. As I once wrote, Sandy was like 'a disembodied force crashing into elements of *The Golden Bough*, *The Exeter Book Riddles* and *The White Goddess*.'

A few years later, I was a student at Naropa (Institute) in Boulder, Colorado, studying poetics with Allen Ginsberg, William Burroughs, Anne Waldman, Gregory Corso and others. A chance conversation at a party with another student resulted in the discovery that we both had an uncanny connection with Sandy Denny and the various iterations of Fairport. My friend, Jim Cohn, and I (at his suggestion) plied our separate 'Fairport journeys' into the creation of a long (and ongoing) work – a masque was the form he believed it should take. It was the beginning of a long friendship where Sandy's life and myth is elaborated and revisited and allowed to take its own shape.

I gave a draft of *The Masque of Sandy Denny* (as it was at the time) to Linda Thompson during her last (*Shoot Out the Lights*) tour with Richard Thompson, at the Blue Note in Boulder, Colorado. She said she was happy to read anything about Sandy.

JIM COHN

I'd fallen for Judy Collins' cover of Sandy Denny's 'Who Knows Where The Time Goes' when it hit the US charts in 1968, but to hear Sandy's version the following year was like falling in love. The song had an ancient feel to it. The singer was talking about time passing as if she was a world-weary ghost, not someone in their early twenties. I only knew of Denny at this point in relation to being this song's writer and singer, and I was enchanted by her voice that touched me more deeply than any other singer I've ever known.

Then, in the late summer of 1972, I was hitchhiking one evening from Amherst to Northampton, Massachusetts as I didn't own a car and had been visiting with some friends at Hampshire College, including Ken Burns, who would go on to make many award-winning documentary films. I was amidst my first psilocybin trip, having just left these college friends, and was on Route 9 at the edge of Amherst when a VW Beetle pulled over. The first thing that struck me as I approached the car was the music coming out the windows. It was Fairport Convention's cover of Bob Dylan's 'Percy Song', and I was blown away by the quality of the arrangement, the mesmerising narrative and the song's utterly notable refrain, 'Turn, turn, to the wind and the rain', and, more so in my very high state of mind, with the vocalist whose voice was captivating, hypnotising. 'Who is this singing?' I asked the driver. And then I learned that the singer was Sandy Denny. I became enraptured with the track. It remains one of the finest pieces of music I have ever heard.

From that point on, I collected every Sandy Denny record I could find, up to and all her solo work post-Fairport and the box set of recordings after her death. She was in many respects the greatest vocalist I've ever heard, especially in relation to the British Isles and the folk tradition. She is, to my way of thinking, the greatest ballad singer of the entire twentieth century, connecting then-modern-day American listeners to a musical tradition that was hundreds of years in the making, and certainly a folk tradition going back to the Child Ballads.

Later, while a student at the Jack Kerouac School of Disembodied Poetics, in Boulder, Colorado, I met another young poet named Denise King (now known as Denyse Anger) at a party. What was crazy to me at the time was not only did Denyse know of Denny's work and appreciate as I did as well, but she'd *worked* for the woman in her *home* for six months while in England. To our mutual shock and pleasure, we learned that we both loved the work of Sandy Denny, and over time, we began a collaborative poem that was created through the mail that Denyse named 'The Masque of Sandy Denny', and we bonded over this connection for the rest of our lives.

When Denyse wrote to me about how, out of the blue, she'd 'met' Georgia Rose Lucas, Sandy Denny's daughter, in a Facebook group, I was way beyond stunned by the news. I wasn't even sure I was still alive, learning that Sandy and Trevor's daughter had surfaced online with the purpose of meeting and communicating with this Facebook group.

PHILHARMONIC HALL
5 FEBRUARY 1970, LIVERPOOL, UK

JOHN DAWSON

I was in the Upper Sixth and my best friend at the time promised me I would not regret spending money on tickets to see two bands on consecutive nights at the Liverpool Philharmonic Hall, Fairport Convention and Pentangle. The venue was full to capacity on both nights. Much as I loved Pentangle, it was the Fairport *Full House* lineup that completely blew me away. Opening for them was a very nervous, but clearly amazingly talented, Nick Drake. He walked on to the stage carrying his guitar. Wearing his jacket with its leather patches, he sat on a stool, played about six beautiful songs without introductions and walked off with guitar and stool.

Onto the stage came Fairport who were brilliant and played songs mainly from *Liege & Lief* ('Deserter' was the one that stood out for me on the night) and the yet-to-be-released *Full House*. How impressive they looked and sounded, with DM at the back providing amazing rhythm to the now all male lineup as they stood in an imposing row towards the front of the stage. The following day I bought *Liege and Lief* and waited, impatiently, for the release of the new album the following year. My musical interests were changed forever that night!

Subsequently, I saw the band at Newcastle City Hall (with Allan Taylor opening) and Newcastle University Students' Union, where I was now a student. It was also there, sitting in a friend's room in our Hall of Residence, that later we heard on Radio Luxembourg that Richard Thompson had left the band. It was, at the time, devastating news. That lineup remains my favourite but it has been a joy to see them over 50 times since then and they are still an invaluable and highly significant part of my life. Thank you for then… and for now, Fairport!

ROUNDHOUSE
23 APRIL 1970, LONDON, UK

DAVID ALLAWAY

A few months after my first Fairport gig, at the Fairfield Halls, Croydon in late 1969, I saw them again a few months later as part of a week of 'Pop Proms' being held in the wonderful Roundhouse in Camden, London, a building formerly used as a railway turntable and now converted into a fine venue for live events.

The date coincides with the birthday of my now-wife, Jane, who I would eventually meet some 15 years later, but who had just turned eight years old on that day. I have been to a great many Fairport gigs in the 50-odd years since then, enjoying each one of them, along with all the various lineups in personnel, but the Roundhouse one was a bit special.

Between the Croydon gig and this one, both Sandy Denny and Ashley Hutchings had left the band (Iain Matthews had left before I first saw them). They had replaced Ashley with Dave Pegg, but had chosen not to replace Sandy. I suppose she was as near irreplaceable as you could get. However, for this particular show, Fairport Convention were the headline act and they had Matthews Southern Comfort opening the show and then Sandy's new band, Fotheringay, on the same bill. If Steeleye Span had been there as well, it would have been a complete reunion of all the six Fairporters I had seen in Croydon.

Matthews Southern Comfort were very accomplished and professional, and their brand of American-influenced, harmony-based folk rock was very pleasing on the ear. But there was an even louder cheer when Sandy appeared on stage, and she and her band had me (and pretty much everyone else there) spell-bound from their very first song. Although possibly a little under-rehearsed, the sounds they produced were wonderful, and with Sandy's voice soaring above it all, I would have gladly bought the ticket and gone there just to hear that set alone. (I was lucky enough to see Fotheringay play again at the Queen Elizabeth Halls in London before Sandy decided to take up a solo career.)

Then Fairport came on, and as usual it was a great little set, including a lot of new material from their soon-to-be-released album, *Full House*. Even then, I could see some really good chemistry between Peggy and DM; they were so tight, as indeed they always would be together. Swarb, Richard and Simon seemed to be taking turns at lead vocals, but the harmonies were every bit as good as they ever were.

But unsurprisingly, it was Mr Mattacks that held my attention the most, with even more subtlety and invention on the drums than when I'd first seen him, and now he had even more cymbals around his kit, somehow attaching two cymbals onto one stand, one on top and one just over halfway up. It was around this time that, inspired by DM, I went out and bought my first little Premier kit. Alas, my capabilities behind it were destined never to be more than a fraction of those of the master!

I have recently discovered via Facebook that there is a Dave Mattacks Appreciation Society, which naturally I now subscribe to. In the mid-Seventies I seriously considered forming a Dave Mattacks fan club. I even had a name for it, 'The Mattacks Fanattacks'. I never quite plucked up the courage to ask him what he thought of the idea.

BOSTON TEA PARTY
7 & 8 JUNE 1970, BOSTON, MASSACHUSETTS

FRED JEFFERY

I saw them at the Boston Tea Party on the *Full House* tour, opening for Traffic who had just put out the *John Barleycorn* album. Fairport were great! I was a big fan from the *Unhalfbricking* album forward, and the song off *Full House*, 'Walk Awhile', was one of many favourites they played that night. They were on fire. I saw them again at the Sanders Theater in Cambridge, Massachusetts on May 10, 1974, when Sandy Denny was back with the Trevor Lucas version of the band. They were very good but a very different band than what I had seen at Tea Party.

RONALD ZWICKER

I saw the *Full House* lineup of Fairport Convention, opening for the *John Barleycorn* trio version of Traffic in Boston, MA. I'm afraid I don't really remember much, except being fixated on Richard Thompson's guitar playing. This tour was vividly captured on the *House Full: Live at the LA Troubadour* album. I did see a later version of Fairport when Sandy Denny returned, in neighbouring Cambridge in, I think, 1974. Richard and Simon Nicol were gone by then. I'm really glad I got to see Sandy. Oh, to have seen Fairport when both she and Richard were in the band.

LEWIS ATHANAS

I saw them open for Traffic at the Boston Tea Party. This was without Sandy Denny. Then they peeled off from the tour temporarily and three days later played at an acoustic club in Ipswich, Massachusetts called Stonehenge, a 1700s inn and tavern that had been redone as kind of a hippie folk venue. It was much more intimate than the 350-seater Boston Tea Party, although they packed some more people in there, but I did see The Who and Led Zeppelin and a variety of others there in that very, very small venue. There were maybe two dozen people at Stonehenge for Fairport. I also saw Sandy Denny solo acoustic, just her with a 12-string guitar, at Jordan Hall in Boston. It was a very interesting concert. She spent a long time playing her music, and then Randy Newman came out – just him at the piano – and he played his music. I was really fortunate to see all of this.

BATH & WEST SHOWGROUND
27 JUNE 1970, SHEPTON MALLET, UK

PETE TURNER

I have followed the fortunes (perhaps not the best word to use) of Fairport from when I first heard them on a Sunday afternoon in 1968 performing on John Peel's *Top Gear* radio show. Precisely what date that was escapes me now, but that was it – I was hooked. It was such a shame that I missed their performance at the 1968 Isle of Wight Festival. The first time I saw them was at the Bath and West Showground in June 1970. The weather had been appalling but the lineup more than made up for it. My distinct memory is of Dave Swarbrick playing his violin so fast that he almost fell into the audience!

I followed their lineup changes but never saw them again until I actually booked them in 1998. A couple of friends, Vic King and Mick Plumbley, and myself had written a book about the Isle of Wight music scene from the 1950s to the mid-nineties. We self-published the book and it sold out. With the money we thought we'd put a gig on. The other two left it to me, so when I told them I'd booked Fairport Convention they were over the moon. Their euphoria didn't last long when I told them that their fee (including VAT) came to the exact amount we had in the bank from the sales of our book. It transpires that even the band thought we were mad! Nevertheless, the gig was a huge success and no financial damage was done.

My most recent gig was on 9 March 2024 at the Union Chapel in London. 54 years of following one of the best bands in the country and 'Sloth' was performed superbly, as it was in 1970 all those years ago.

LONDON PALLADIUM
26 JULY 1970, LONDON, UK

PHIL SECRETAN

I must have been 16 or 17 when I first heard Fairport Convention. The track was 'Cajun Woman', one of the tracks on the fabulous Island sampler LP *Nice Enough To Eat*. I was away at boarding school in Bedford at the time and hating it. I was very homesick and all of the cross country running, rugby and cadet training didn't suit me at all. Music was the only thing that kept me going and I was mad on the groups of the day like the Stones, The Beatles, Cream, The Kinks, Hendrix and Dylan. This was a very magical period for 'pop music', and the boundaries were being pushed

Swarbrick & Co. have re-activated Fairport

FAIRPORT CONVENTION is being re-formed with a new line-up, little more than a month after the break-up of the original outfit. The split came about because Sandy Denny and Trevor Lucas decided to leave the group to operate as a duo, and Jerry Donahue was finding it difficult to commute to and from Britain, having now settled in America.

At the time, the three remaining Fairport members — Dave Swarbrick, Dave Pegg and Bruce Rowlands — decided to continue functioning as a trio. But they have now decided to augment and to retain the name of Fairport Convention. They have already taken on ex-Wizzard keyboards player Bob Brady a fiddler Roger Burridge, and th are now seeking a guitarist complete the new line-up. T new-look band will make their but with two performances London Victoria Palace on J 6, and a British tour will follow the autumn.

15-MAN BLUES BAND

GONZALEZ member Gordon Hunt has formed his own part-time 15-piece r-&-b band, called the North Side Rhythm and Blues Ensemble. He told NME this week: "I'm not leaving Gonzalez, and I've got this outfit together strictly for fun. We shall be playing occasional gigs which don't conflict with my work with Gon-

Elton add Apollo gig

ELTON JOHN has added an er performance to his British c cert tour itinerary, which start the end of next month and is ready a virtual sell-out. There no tickets remaining for his c certs at Glasgow Apollo Ce on May 24 and 25, and co quently an extra show has b added at midnight on May and tickets for this are now sale. A spokesman for Ro Records commented: "This

(clockwise from top left) Ad for Fairport's *Nine* (Ian Burgess); press cutting about the 'reactivated' Fairport (Ian Burgess); Kenny's Kemp's autographed poster is his pride & joy; Kenny had seen Fairport previously at the Caley Picture House; Springsteen didn't show for the Glassboro gig – too much competition from the support? (Vince Farinaccio);

(clockwise from top left) Evan Smith saw FC with Sandy back in the line-up; Hans Henrik Francke (left) first saw the *Nine* line-up; Trenton, New Jersey ad (Vince Farinaccio); Vince Farinaccio saw FC again when they returned to New Jersey every day. John Peel was the DJ everyone listened to and he featured this new group Fairport Convention several times on his *Perfumed Garden* radio show. I was saddened when I read in *Melody Maker* about the M1 crash which took the life of young drummer Martin Lamble.

By this time, I had started to buy LPs and I bought *Liege & Lief*. I was totally blown away by the fantastic sounds emanating from my record player. Everything about the sound was special – Dave Mattacks' drumming, Sandy's fabulous vocals, Richard's guitar licks, Ashley's bass, Simon's guitar and Swarb's fabulous fiddle playing. It all meshed together in a fabulous new sound. The choice of songs and the lyrics drew you in. I was hooked on Fairport from that moment.

The first time I saw them was the *Full House* lineup at the Royal Festival Hall, shortly after the release of said album. They were supporting the Incredible String Band. I don't remember much detail of Fairport's performance, apart from how tall Richard seemed to be and Swarbrick's fabulous fiddle playing. That was 54 years ago now. I've seen them about ten times since with various lineups, with Simon the one constant member in the shows I've seen.

YORKSHIRE FOLK, BLUES & JAZZ FESTIVAL
14 – 16 AUGUST 1970, KRUMLIN, HALIFAX, UK

MICHAEL MURRAY

I became a fan in 1969 when a friend brought round a copy of *Unhalfbricking*. I immediately liked the whole album but especially 'A Sailor's Life', a superb long track. I went and bought *What We Did On Our Holidays*, which I also thought was really good. I bought both *Liege & Lief* and *Full House* on the day they were released (which back then was always a Friday). I remember being excited at work in the morning and nipping out to buy them during lunch. I couldn't wait to get home and listen to them. When I did, they were even better than I had hoped.

I could often listen to Fairport on *Folk on Friday*. 'The Lark In The Morning Medley' was the show's theme tune. I listened to anything Fairport that was available. I played the albums constantly, and I still get a thrill from 'Matty Groves', 'Sloth', 'A Sailor's Life' and many more, despite having listened to them loads of times.

Living on Britain's east coast made it almost impossible for me to see them live. The first opportunity was the Yorkshire Folk, Blues & Jazz Festival in 1970. My friend Mark and I had been camping and we decided to leave early and go to this festival. We arrived on the Friday and had a good day, but Mark was feeling unwell and we went back to our tents early. I got up on Saturday morning, excited to be seeing Fairport at last, but Mark was still ill. I persuaded him to at least stay until we'd seen Fairport. Sadly, things went downhill. The weather deteriorated, people were crashing onto the site over the fence, without paying or using forged tickets, and rumours were spreading that bands hadn't been paid.

Mark was feeling worse and I reluctantly agreed that we should leave. The site was chaotic by then. Fairport did play, I gather, but the weather and atmosphere were awful and their set was forgettable. The promoters ended up owing £30,000 and hundreds of fans were treated for hypothermia.

I eventually did get to see them at Cleethorpes in the mid-eighties as part of the *40 Nights In The Wilderness* tour. This set was so exciting for me!

LITTLE HADHAM FETE
22 AUGUST 1970, LITTLE HADHAM, UK

GERARD BOUMAN

My mother was English and my dad was Dutch. I was born in Amsterdam and grew up in Holland but had family in England too. In 1970, we went to stay with my grandparents in Bishop's Stortford. One day I went to see my cousin who lived up Scott Road. She told me there was a band playing in a nearby village and asked if I would like to come. So we went to the gig that appeared to be Fairport Convention. They played outside on the village green. I didn't quite know what to think of them then. I was 17 and heavily into Led Zeppelin at the time. I remember I was impressed by the guitar player, Richard Thompson, and even more with this guy in his leather jacket playing a blue fiddle. Peggy later once told me that it was a charity event for the local police and that they got paid with a washing machine.

Back home in Holland I never gave it much thought anymore until 1973. A friend was playing the double album *History of Fairport Convention*. When the record got to the 'Lark In The Morning Medley', my skin went all tingly. I thought, 'This is music that I want to play!' Later that year, I bought the *Rosie* album. After hearing 'The Hens March Through The Midden & The Four Poster Bed' and 'Peggy's Pub', I bought myself a mandolin and got an old fiddle from the loft and started to practise. I also formed a folk band with a mate from school. (I'm playing in a band with him again nowadays and we play some Fairport classics.) The first time we saw Fairport live in Holland was when they played the Paradiso in Amsterdam. Colin Blunstone also played that night. When Fairport came on stage, Peggy took a microphone and said 'hello,I'm Sandy Denny'. My friend next to me said, 'Did you hear that? Sandy Denny is also playing with the band.' He didn't have a clue who Sandy was.

FILLMORE EAST
28 & 29 AUGUST 1970, NEW YORK, NEW YORK

MITCH WEINGAND

Fairport were on the bill with Savoy Brown and the Peter Green version of Fleetwood Mac. My friend had gone to the box office to buy these tickets and got mugged around Astor Place by the Cube! They took his money but he begged them not to take his Fillmore tickets. They agreed and thus we were able to see a great, great show. We got there early, before the show had started, and I distinctly remember looking at this guy in the first row, really dressed like a hippie with long hair, and leaning back in his seat with his feet up on the stage. A couple of minutes later there he was onstage with Fairport – Richard Thompson!

Fairport opened the show but I wasn't familiar with their music and so they just seemed like a warm-up act. It was the loudest show we were ever at, and we were there a lot. Savoy Brown were greasy and loud and Fleetwood Mac finished their show with an Elvis medley which had the place going nuts.

I didn't see Richard again until 1999, when I went to see Wilco open for him at the Beacon in New York doing their Woody Guthrie set. RT came on and looked completely different! And I saw him some years back (in 2013) with the Richard Thompson Trio on Dylan's *Americanarama* tour, outdoors in Memphis. He sounded fantastic. He is a master of the guitar. I was staying at the Peabody when he pulled up in his bus and that was thrilling.

SAL DESIANO

I remember seeing them at a show at the Fillmore East in 1970. Pretty good band. Their bass player was pretty impressive. I found out years later after seeing him in Jethro Tull that he was in Fairport Convention.

SOPHIA GARDENS PAVILION
17 OCTOBER 1970, CARDIFF, UK

MIKE MURPHY

Back in the late 1960s, my girlfriend Margaret (later my wife) used to frequent the Jug 'o' Punch folk club in Digbeth, Birmingham. I never did go to any of the gigs, but she used to tell me about the musicians and her friendship with Ian Campbell and Dave Swarbrick. She would go out for a Chinese with them after the club finished for the evening, and on one occasion in 1967 Joni Mitchell performed at the club and she also joined them afterwards. Swarb's incredible fiddle playing was well known in purist folk circles at that time (but alas, not to me until the Sophia Gardens gig.)

Then, by chance I just happened to hear *A Sailor's Life* on a friend's record player. By this time, I was a first-year economics student at Cardiff University, and I couldn't believe the juxtaposition of traditional English folk and rock music. I was lucky enough to see Bob Dylan in May 1966 at the Birmingham Odeon, but at the time Dylan appeared to be making electric versions of his own compositions. (It was still an astonishing concert). Fairport were delving into the past for material, so their muse was clearly different and more eclectic (as well as electric).

With *Unhalfbricking* in mind, my wife and I went to Sophia Gardens in Cardiff, curious to see this group. She was interested in seeing how Swarb handled playing in a rock group and I wanted to explore their unique sound. We were sitting about three rows back and it was just mind-blowingly different from anything we had heard before. The lineup of Swarb, Richard, Simon, Peggy and Dave M just about says it all.

After university I lived in El Paso, Texas for a few years and was invited to play some of my favourite tracks on KLAQ 95.5 FM radio station one Sunday night. I had the pleasure of including the *Liege & Lief* track 'Matty Groves'. This certainly stimulated some interest as people were phoning the radio station from El Paso and Juarez while I was on air, pleading to hear more Fairport music.

Over the years I have seen Fairport many times in concert, including the *Rising for the Moon* lineup (with Sandy Denny, Trevor Lucas and Jerry Donahue) at St David's Hall, Cardiff. Each new iteration of the band seemed to inject new musical influences. I have tried to determine the lineup I liked best and have concluded (with difficulty) that the original *Full House* lineup from 1970 and the *Liege & Lief* line-up from 1969 were exceptional. The former because I never recovered from that initial blast of *Full House* Fairport magic and the latter because of its' groundbreaking impact on traditional music.

Finally, in October 2023 I drove up to see my son Chris in Sheffield and we both went to a Fairport gig at Crookes Social Club. There I had the genuine pleasure of meeting and chatting to Dave Pegg. Talking to Peggy brought back so many memories. He is a very modest man who is arguably the best folk bassist in the business as well as being the glue that held Fairport together for so many years. Incidentally, the current lineup easily perpetuates the Fairport music genre, as the band has always attracted very talented musicians, so long may it continue. Thank you, Fairport, for many years of great music.

MCILROY'S BALLROOM
20 OCTOBER 1970, SWINDON, UK

GLORIA HISCOCK

I've been a fan since I was 15. The first time I saw them was in 1970 at Mac's in Swindon. I've seen them at Wimbledon Theatre, in Banbury and as many times as I could at Cropredy Festival. After Covid the first concert I could get to was in Solihull. We had moved to Warwick but soon after moving there my husband died with cancer. So, alone, I set to Solihull but it was a fruitless journey. I couldn't find the effing venue. I was in tears after eventually turning around and going home. I posted on the fan page to this effect and asked that no-one tell me how good the gig was! Next thing I knew, Simon messaged me and offered me two guest list tickets for whichever venue I would be able to get to on their tour. What a gent! They really value their devotees and we all love them. They are superb musicians, every one.

COLSTON HALL
7 NOVEMBER 1970, BRISTOL, UK

STEPHEN PEGUM

To summon up my very earliest memory of Fairport Convention, I have to go all the way back to the early months of 1970 and the John Peel show on Radio 1. I used to listen to his show in bed on my German pocket radio! All these years later I cannot now recall exactly which Fairport song first drew the band to my attention, but I can say with absolute certainty that it was Sandy Denny's angelic and unique voice that had me immediately transfixed. (John Peel's show also introduced me to the music of another folk-rock band around that time. One Saturday afternoon I visited the famous Spiller's Record store in Cardiff, asking whether they stocked any albums by the 'Steel Iced Band'. The shopkeeper quickly corrected my misheard band name with a laugh at my expense!)

In July 1970 I started working as a trainee-chartered accountant earning the princely sum of £6 per week. With my first week's wages I spent more than 50 per cent of my take-home pay buying the then newly-released *Full House* album. Rather naughtily, I told my parents this was a welcome gift from my new work colleagues. I first saw Fairport live at the Colston Hall in Bristol in late 1970. After *Full House*, I quickly added *What We Did On Our Holidays*, *Unhalfbricking* and the legendary *Liege & Lief* albums to my burgeoning record collection. I may have seen the band in concert on other occasions, but no specific dates come to mind these days. It's a source of lifelong regret to me that

I never saw Sandy sing with Fairport, even after her brief return to the band in 1974.

Having been a huge fan of FC throughout the 1970s and early 1980s, for reasons that I simply cannot really explain my enthusiasm cooled somewhat thereafter. This period of my life I guess could be called 'Fairport – The Wilderness Years'!

Fast forward to the year 2000, by which time I was working as a civilian staff member at a military barracks in Mill Hill, North London. That summer there was a staff barbecue to which partners/spouses were invited, with casual dress being the order of the day. I noticed quite quickly that Brigadier Barry (the senior officer in camp) was wearing a Fairport t-shirt. (He was also showing off the massive scar from his second knee replacement surgery.) It was an hour or so before I got the chance to tell him that that t-shirt he was wearing was of one of my all-time favourite bands. We got chatting about FC generally and then Barry asked me if I'd heard of their Cropredy festival. I replied that I had (through the regular FC newsletters), but that I didn't know enough about it to decide to attend. He strongly recommended that we go as a family, which we duly did that August.

My family and I quickly became totally enamoured of the very special (dare I say magical?) atmosphere in that North Oxfordshire field, so much so that we only missed two years between 2000 and 2017. These special weekends rekindled my passion for FC and we made sure that we saw them on many of their winter tours over the same time period. We mostly saw them at the Alban Arena in St Albans, but on one occasion at the Union Chapel in Islington, North London (where I spotted the actor Alun Armstrong in the audience). On another visit to the Alban Arena, we were privileged to get invited backstage through our mutual friend Simon Hart. I distinctly remember the presence of almost no alcohol – not very rock 'n' roll, Fairport! – although I did have an interesting chat with Simon's son Henry.

That's a fairly comprehensive run-through of some of my memories of Fairport Convention covering the last 50-odd years. As the song title so aptly says – who knows where the time goes?

UNIVERSITY OF EXETER
12 DECEMBER 1970, EXETER, UK

BRIAN NEW

I first heard Fairport's music around the end of 1967 from listening to John Peel's radio broadcasts. Even though I was studying for A-levels, I still managed to hear most of them. 1968 brought even more radio sessions and I was soon entranced by the range of songs they played. The first album I heard was *…Holidays* in early 1969, when a friend who had seen the band in London over the holidays (!) brought a copy to school to play at a Music Appreciation Society some friends and I had set up (the school had an amazing hi-fi set up). I was hooked for life.

I left school that summer and my first month's money was spent on *...Holidays* and *Unhalfbricking*. *Liege & Lief* was a revelation. Sandy and Ashley leaving was all a bit worrying but *Full House* allayed any fears.

I saw the band in 1970 at Exeter University and they were amazing, though the speed of the instrumentals was a bit overwhelming. I carried on getting all the band's albums (as well as those from Sandy, Richard, Ashley and Iain) and loved them all. It wasn't until 1976 that I saw them again. It was the lineup with Dan and the version of 'Sloth' was the highlight in my memory.

I was really upset when they broke up in 1979, though sporadic live releases kept the flame alive. My first Cropredy was 1984 and I continued going every year until 2004 when camping became too much. I have so many Cropredy memories of wonderful friendships (renewed every year) with people from Netherlands, Germany, Norway, Canada and the USA as well as homegrown. Two that stay in the mind are a full moon coming over the stage during 'The Hiring Fair' and, in a different year, having a long chat with Trevor about the band and Sandy. Thankfully, the occasional live release and more recently Radio Oxford have meant I can at least still hear them at Cropredy, and YouTube has also meant we can now watch them and the amount of archive footage is astounding. Thanks to all concerned for putting this year's online.

1984 saw the arrival of the 'Friends of Fairport' group and *The Ledge* fanzine from Martin Kenney and later Ian Burgess (to whom many thanks). This was soon followed by *Hokey Pokey* from Colin Davies and friends and similar minded publications from USA and Australia. These provided all the information needed on current news (as well as archive material). Contacts from these soon led me to the murky world of bootleg tapes and I was astounded at the number of old live/radio recordings there were of Fairport and friends (thanks mostly to the late Dave Healey and Jim Lee). I soon realised that the only way to get these was to have recordings of your own to trade, so I went out and got a Walkman and for the next 20 years or so I recorded just about every concert I attended, as well as festivals. Some of Fairport's four hour sets in the past were a real labour of love! It was always fun at Cropredy after Saturday night's set to sit outside the tent listening to the recording – weather permitting!

Sadly, time and technology have moved on and these recordings now have a new home and I only have a few on CD. Many of the radio sessions have been released, as well as a few live shows.

1985 saw the band back with a vengeance. Ric and Maart brought their own blend of magic and I was finally able to see them live regularly. I have managed at least one show from every tour since and they always leave me wanting to see them again. DM left, Gerry joined and has sadly now left and DM is now back! Maart left and is much missed, but Chris joined and it seems as though it was meant to be.

A string of excellent studio albums always allowed them to play new songs as well as the old favourites and the various projects, eg. *'Babbacombe' Lee* and *Full House*, have added extra interest. All my old worn vinyl has long been replaced by CDs with extra songs, and the various box sets add even more wonderful music to listen to. I think every Fairport fan has their own favourite song they would like to hear again and maybe some of mine will pop up sometime.

Thanks to all the lineups over the years for enriching my life with your wonderful music. And especially now to (in alphabetical order) Chris, Peggy, Ric and Simon for being such wonderful human beings. And to the backstage folks who make the live shows so good. Keep on trucking…

UNIVERSITY OF MANCHESTER
13 MARCH 1971, MANCHESTER, UK

DAVID HENDERSON

I went to my first folk club, aged 15, in 1967, in my home of West Cumbria (Barbara Dickson, since you ask.) 'Old boys' took me under their wing and suggested things I should listen to…

In 1969 in the sixth form, we used to share albums – 'have you listened to this?', etc., etc. I sat on my bedroom floor with my trusty second hand green Dansette, with a borrowed album listening to 'A Sailor's Life'. To call it a Damascene moment sounds horribly pretentious but it was… a way into music that I just instantly loved. That led to exploring so much more.

I went to uni in Manchester, saw Fairports in March '71 (when it was 50p for a gig), and saw everything and everyone I could, from Steeleye and Lindisfarne to Free and Arthur Brown. Being of an age, *Liege & Lief* was the album played to death in my halls of residence on my new Amstrad amp, Garrard deck and Wharfedale Denton speakers – the positives of a summer job pouring concrete.

I saw many Fairport lineups in the intervening years, plus RT and Ashley doing *Candleford* and *'Mysteries* at the National Theatre. Skip to 1995 and I had just met Sheena, who is now my second wife. Looking for a local, we were sat back-to-back with a couple we didn't know. Their conversation was Fairports and Cropredy. I turned round and the conversation then lasted an hour and a half, as the bloke and I realised we had followed similar musical tastes and epiphanies!

Gareth and Ce became very close friends, and Gareth my best male friend. With

(clockwise from top left) Swarb's back (Ian Burgess); Swarb's front (!) with Peggy & Simon at Chorley Wakes (Stephen Brightman); the 'first Cropredy' in 1977 (Andy MacLeod); Staffan Wennerlund travelled to Cropredy in '77 (three images); Cropredy 1977 (Andy MacLeod); Ian Ashleigh with grandsons Jack and Harrison

(clockwise from top left) Cropredy '77 (Staffan Wennerlund); **Cropredy** '77 (Staffan Wennerlund); Cropredy '77 (Staffan Wennerlund); Mike Ball was there in 1977; Staffan Wenner**lund's 1977** ticket; Graham Warren is a Cropredy stalwart; Bruce Rowland in 1977 (Staffan Wennerlund) a bunch of other friends, in a convoy from Gareth's village of Glooston, we did over 15 Cropredies. (We later ran a festival called Gloostonbury – sorry!) Magical times, many stories. Gareth and I used to just stand and watch different Fairport lineups. Our erudite conversation would often extend to:

'They're playing well.'

'Yup.'

Gareth and I ran small festivals together, finding acts we loved and could afford and which we had seen at Cropredy or the Brase. Gareth died in 2011, aged 59. He was seven days younger than me.

My wife Sheena, Gareth's widow Ce and I scattered his ashes during 'Meet On The Ledge' at Cropredy in 2012. I had had the honour of reading his eulogy and we sang 'Meet On The Ledge' and taught the congregation the words. Shortly after his funeral, Ce gave me Gareth's copy of the 'Group Disbands Sensation' poster from Cropredy '79 that he had liberated from outside the Brase. The holes for string are still in it! I cannot express how special it is and my emotions when Ce gave it to me. It encapsulates a world of memories. It is now framed and hangs beside a Fairport poster featuring Swarb.

I went to see the Fairports at De Montfort Hall in Leicester in 2013. At the interval, I was behind Simon in the queue for the bar and I told him (I couldn't help it, sorry) that it was the best I had ever heard him sing 'Who Knows Where the Time Goes'. 'Did you notice I sang the first verse twice?' he said. I hadn't.

In 2023, I went to see them in Stratford-upon-Avon. DM, a hero of mine, was back on the stool and he brought power and drive. I sat and went back 50 years. I looked round and thought 'bloody hell, this audience is aging', and realised I am part of that audience.

I organise festivals and folk clubs and still play original songs in an acoustic band. It may never have happened except for that Dansette, and Swarb and RT swapping licks...

REDCAR JAZZ CLUB, COATHAM HOTEL
14 MARCH 1971, REDCAR, UK

GRAHAM SOMERS

It seems, and is, an awfully long time since my introduction to Fairport, back around 1970, when the BBC radio programme *Folk on Friday* used 'The Lark in the Morning' as its intro music. A school chum advised me that I should listen to 'The Asian Leaf' as the source album for this wonderful piece of music. Eventually, this mishearing was clarified and I went looking for *Liege & Lief*, only to find there was an even newer album out... *Full House*. I got them both, although I can't remember in which order, and then had to get my head around the ever-changing lineup theme.

I got to see them live for the first time a year or so later, at our local venue, the Redcar Jazz Club. Yet another lineup change, as Richard had left by then. I'm sure I remember Swarb sitting and strumming a couple of solo songs mid-set, possibly to appear later on *Rosie*. Anyway, I was hooked.

I've seen them regularly over the years, with myriad lineups, although I only saw Sandy with them once, after she rejoined. I saw them supporting Lou Reed at the Hard rock in Manchester, but had to leave before Lou's set, as we had a lengthy walk back to our uni digs.

One memorable gig was their appearance at the July Wakes festival in Chorley in 1977. It was a big natural bowl of an arena with a small lake in front of the stage. My mind may be playing tricks, but I'm sure I remember Simon announcing during the set that Swarb would donate his jeans to the first person to jump into the lake. Somebody did, Swarb duly obliged and he played the remainder of the set in his underpants.

On another occasion, a long hitchhiking trip from Manchester to Southampton (don't ask) was timed to coincide with a trip to the fabled Roundhouse in London on the way back to see the chaps. We arrived outside the venue, perfectly timed… except we were a week early. You can't win 'em all!

Moving forward to 1979 and the tragic news of the end of the band. And a farewell gig at somewhere called Cropredy. We duly ordered tickets and set off to a much smaller festival than it is nowadays. It was wonderful, if a little basic, with a great atmosphere and even a campfire sing-around at the end of the day. Since then, I've only missed two Crops over the years, and I've seen some amazing and diverse acts, from Lonnie Donnegan to Alice Cooper, Pet Clark to the Buzzcocks.

One year I even got a pair of free tickets and a signed copy of Peggy's solo album as a reward for naming said album. When the album was finally released on CD, I cheekily messaged Christine to say it would be lovely to hear it in its pristine digital glory, and duly received a copy by return. I did have to buy my tickets that year.

All in all, it's been a long, glorious and a tad expensive ride, with LPs, cassettes, CDs, box sets, books, gigs, Cropredys, t-shirts and maybe a pint or two. But it's been worth every penny.

GARDEN PARTY II, CRYSTAL PALACE BOWL
31 JULY 1971, LONDON, UK

JOHNNY CARLSEN

I am one of a group of Norwegian friends who used to travel to Cropredy (I've been twelve times). We were known as The Crazy Norwegians. We behaved ourselves – we just got that name because we are all musicians. I have seen Fairport live a lot of times, and I've met them twice in my hometown of Bergen. But the first time I saw them was in Crystal Palace Park in London in 1971. Elton John was warming up for them!

The first time I met Peggy was in Bergen in 2009. Fairport had played a concert in the Ole Bull theatre. Me and my friend, another Crazy Norwegian, had a beer at the Hotel Norge before going to the theatre, each with a glass of beer in our hand. I saw a man sitting alone. I said 'he looks like Dave Pegg'. It was Peggy and he must have heard what I said, because he said to us 'come here and sit down'. He was going to be interviewed by Norwegian TV. We sat and talked with him, watched him being interviewed and then went to the theatre and saw a fantastic concert. After that, we had a glass of beer with Peggy. Although, believe it or not, Peggy drank red wine.

I have met all of the current and many former members of Fairport many times, including Iain Matthews, Judy Dyble (RIP), Richard Thompson, Maartin Allcock (RIP), Jerry Donahue, Dave Swarbrick (RIP), Bruce Rowland (RIP) and Ashley Hutchings. As they say, Fairport is not a band it is a family. I used to stay at the same hotel as Gerry Conway. I last sat and talked with him and his wife at Cropredy in 2022. He was one of the best drummers ever. He did not beat the drums, he *played* drums.

'BABBACOMBE' LEE
RELEASED NOVEMBER 1971

IAN JOHNSON

I was first introduced to Fairport Convention by my brother when he brought this new record home called *'Babbacombe' Lee*. I liked the music. When I played it for the first time, I read the story about John Lee which came with the record. Then the first side had finished and I had to put it on again to listen to the music. I was concentrating on the reading so much that I had not heard the music. After that, with not very much money in those days, I bought *Liege & Lief* and *What We Did On Our Holidays* secondhand. They were closely followed by *Rosie* and the very first album. After many years, I bought some cassettes and graduated to CDs. I now have more Fairport vinyl, cassettes, CDs, VHS tapes and DVDs than any other band that I like. I also have seen them live over the years more times than any other band.

APOLLO THEATRE
12 NOVEMBER 1971, GLASGOW, UK

JIM MCGRATH

I saw Fairport three times in Glasgow in the early seventies, at the City Halls on 30 October 1970, at the legendary Apollo in November 1971 and at Glasgow University in February 1973. My memory is a bit hazy, but I think Richard and Sandy were still there at the first of these Fairport gigs in October 1970. Either that or I saw Fairport at a concert pre-October 1970 of which I have no record. They were, of course, well worth seeing, hence the fair number of attendances. The Apollo gig was to promote the *Babbacombe Lee* album and I seem to recall leaflets or even small souvenir booklets on our seats. I also recall Swarbrick being very loud and dominant on the stage.

I was also at the Lincoln Festival on 24 July 1971 so saw Sandy Denny plus Swarbrick and Martin Carthy. More recently I've seen Fairport in Glasgow in January 1994 at the Royal Concert Hall, presumably part of that year's *Celtic Connections* festival, and in January 2006 at The Garage. And I've seen Richard Thompson lots!

CECIL SHARP HOUSE
3 DECEMBER 1971, LONDON, UK

NIGEL BANKS

After my introduction to the band in November 1970 at Oxford Town Hall, I was to follow their fortunes in various locations throughout the ensuing decade through good times and bad, and with many personnel changes. I saw the *Angel Delight/'Babbacombe Lee'* lineup at a special charity gig held at Cecil Sharp House in December 1971. Due possibly to contractual reasons, the band didn't appear as Fairport Convention but by their individual names. The only other acts I can remember appearing that night were Harvey Andrews and Dave and Toni Arthur. Having purchased *'Babbacombe' Lee* when it came out earlier in the year, I was hoping the band would play the album live, but they were clearly not in the mood for that and treated us to a real mash-up of a set, which culminated in Trevor Lucas, who was in attendance, being called up onstage by Swarb to sing an Aussie folk song or two, followed by some rock and roll standards. Simon was clearly not well-versed in playing classic Chuck Berry-type intros, so Peggy shouted across 'oh, for goodness' sake, give it 'ere' and relieved him of his lead guitar whereupon Peggy relived his old Brummie pub-rock days with some classic rock 'n' roll riffing. Simon didn't look best pleased and so the announcement a few weeks later that he was leaving the band didn't come as a surprise.

It was sad, though, to think that within four years of being in existence, there wasn't a single original member left at that point. But as Richard Thompson famously said, FC is like Hotel California, so Simon would be back! As would someone else who was there that night – Sandy Denny. She'd obviously come along with Trevor Lucas, but sadly didn't perform on that occasion. I did overhear her voice, however, on my way to the loo past the makeshift dressing room having one of her legendary strops about something or someone and thinking, 'I wouldn't want to get on the wrong side of her!'

CAMDEN FESTIVAL, ROUNDHOUSE
2 MAY 1972, CAMDEN, LONDON, UK

NIGEL BANKS

I saw the next lineup of Pegg, Swarbrick, Roger Hill and Tom Farnell on two occasions during 1972, once at the Roundhouse in Camden supported by Quiver with the excellent Tim Renwick on guitar, and then at St Catherine's College, Oxford. It seemed an uneasy, Brummie-centric combo with no clear musical direction and giving the drummer a solo signalled time-filler. I thought DM would be dead against that idea if he were still in the band!

Then came the abortive David Rea interlude followed by the issue of the *Rosie* album, which was fairly panned by the critics. Although I still have a soft spot for some of the tracks such as 'Matthew, Mark, Luke and John', 'The Plainsman' and the title track.

CITY HALL
10 MAY 1972, NEWCASTLE, UK

DAVID WRAITH

I remember a couple of solo Sandy concerts when she had obviously over-indulged and was very giggly. However, her voice was like an angel. The one where she supported Hawkwind and a three-piece Doors in 1972 was something else. Stacia danced and then on came Sandy. She did about 40 minutes and then The Doors. For one concert, Sandy had Richard Thompson with her and for the other, she supported John Martyn. I think it was shortly after the release of *Solid Air*.

I am disappointed that I never saw the original lineups of Fairport as I am a big fan. I have seen the later incarnation but still wish they had a female singer. I saw them live in December 1974 but unfortunately the concert is a blur and I can't remember anything about it!

BANBURY FOLK CLUB
1972, BANBURY, UK

CHRIS LESLIE, FAIRPORT CONVENTION

I would have been 16 at the time, and I went down to Banbury Folk Club to do a floor spot with my fiddle, which I had recently got from a friend of my mum. I don't remember what I played that night, but the main guests were Dave and Toni Arthur who were brilliant. Half way through their second set, who should come in and take a seat but Dave Swarbrick!

I couldn't believe it. He was one of the main reasons I took up the fiddle, I loved his playing so much. After the show was over, I plucked up the courage to go and say hello, fiddle case in hand… Swarb could not have been more lovely. He chatted about playing and took a look at my fiddle and played a bit on it… wow! I was gob smacked! Little did I know what would drop into my future life… getting to know Swarb and Fairport as very dear friends and a huge part of my musical journey… still on-going as a member of Fairport for 27 years now. Here is that same fiddle – the one I always pick off the wall and play at home… 'It all comes round again.'

WEALDSTONE FOOTBALL CLUB
15 JULY 1972, WEALDSTONE, UK

NIGEL CHITTY

I first saw Fairport at Wealdstone Football Club. Stone the Crows topped the bill, along with Vinegar Joe, but it's Fairport I remember. It was a scorcher of a day, and being a typically under-prepared teenager, I spent the following day recovering from heat stroke. Fast forward thirty odd years and I was travelling through France with my late wife Paula, who had taken the first two hour stretch behind the wheel. We stopped at some services where I took over for the second half of the journey.

Now, we had an arrangement whereby whoever was driving would have their choice of music on the stereo, so Paula said, 'I'll put on your new Fairport CD.' (Note she didn't say she'd put on the Pink Floyd CD containing the track 'One of these days I'm going to cut you into little pieces,' which for some reason she found a little creepy!)

Whatever, she fed the disc into the player as I accelerated onto the main carriageway and with impeccable timing it began, 'Forever, forever, the road goes on forever.' Paula just glanced at me and quietly said, 'Sorry!'

Long may Fairport's road go on… and on…

RAINBOW PAVILION
6 AUGUST 1972, TORQUAY, UK

ROGER AVERILL

My family and myself have a record which I doubt very few people can match. My wife, Jane, and I have attended every Cropredy Festival right from the first, on Richard Crossman's lawn, up to the present day. Our daughter, Katy, attended her first in 1984 at nine months old and our son, James, was eleven months old when he attended in 1992. None of us have missed a Cropredy since.

I was born and brought up in the village of Wollaston in Northamptonshire which, despite only having a population of around 4,000, has a couple of claims to fame, being the birthplace of Doc Marten's boots and also the home of the Nag's Head pub, whose landlord, a guy called 'Big' Bob Knight, was good friends with the legendary DJ John Peel. That connection resulted in bands like Free, Black Sabbath, Rod Stewart and the Faces (and, a bit later, U2) playing at the Nag with up to 400 people in a room that now would be restricted to a maximum of 100.

So my friends and I regularly saw up-and-coming bands live, and on a camping holiday to Devon around 1972, we noticed that Fairport Convention were playing at the Pavilion in Torquay and tickets were purchased. I hadn't really heard a lot of Fairport before this evening but it was a really good show with a mammoth version of 'Sloth'.

The next involvement with Fairport was when my elder brother, Wayne, started to attend a folk club in the Northamptonshire village of Islip, where Simon Nicol lived and helped at the club. They became friends which eventually resulted in Wayne and I doing some electrical work at a cottage that Simon had bought near Huntingdon. After this, we got to know most of the band, doing jobs for Swarb, Trevor and Sandy and also Peggy. When the first 'Cropredy' happened in Richard Crossman's garden, we were the on site 'sparks'.

We continued to be the sparks for the festival, seeing it grow from a few hundred to 10,000 plus, and our crew expanded to cope with the extra work. A certain Mick Peters was a mechanic in the local Wollaston garage and Wayne got him involved in maintaining the generators. Mick is now the Cropredy Site Manager!

I recall going into the marquee backstage to get some equipment. I was walking out when I met a guy coming in. There was a quick 'how you doing mate?' and I carried on with my job. I was then thinking 'where do I know him from? Is he one of the sound crew or the bar staff?' Then I remembered the face: it was Robert Plant!

In those days, Wayne and a couple of others would start work on Monday morning with the rest of us joining on Thursday to get the festival ready to open at Friday tea time. The whole thing was put together in less than a week and all the electrics were stripped out and stashed away by early Sunday afternoon. And in those days, we powered up all the stalls and the bar as well as the toilets out in the camp sites, so it was a hectic but enjoyable few days!

My wife often says one of her claims to fame is that when we were camped backstage, she took the children out for a walk around the arena field before it opened that day and Procol Harum were playing 'A Whiter Shade Of Pale' as a soundcheck, and my family were the only ones in the field. Their own personal gig!

Over the years, we've seen Fairport at quite a few different venues. We were invited to Island Studios in London and finished up singing backing vocals on one of the tracks on the album *Bonny Bunch of Roses*. If you listen closely, I'm the out of tune one.

We continued to provide the power for Cropredy for well over a decade, our last year being in 1993. After that, the job became too big and Cropredy then employed a full-time company to do it. I think they might have charged a few pounds more than we did…

Since I stopped working, our Cropredy weekend routine has remained pretty much unchanged. We live just under an hour away, so it's usually a 7-8am Thursday morning departure to meet up with friends in the layby in Charwelton to drive in convoy and try to camp together in Field 5. We get the tents and gazebo up, have a few cups of tea and then head to the cricket club for a few beers to get into the Cropredy spirit and meet up with our daughter and son-in-law and their friends.

Like everyone else, we are finding the camping harder to do, as is everything when you get past 70! In 2022, my wife and I decided to travel back home each night rather than wake up at around 7am with the sun at just under 40 degrees. After returning from Cropredy 2023, all our crew agreed that it was one of the best for a few years, with some really good bands and Fairport on top form.

It is still a great feeling to walk into the arena field and 'see all my friends' again, and to look around to see what has evolved from that gig on Crossman's lawn. I like to think I've played a very small part in the success of the Cropredy Festival. Of course, every year when it closes with 'Meet On The Ledge', I just hope we're all there again the next year.

THE HISTORY OF FAIRPORT CONVENTION
RELEASED 10 NOVEMBER 1972

PAT MCGUIRK

The first indication I ever had that Fairport Convention existed was in 1974. Every Saturday I would go to a tiny secondhand record shop called Caroline Records', located at 42 Richmond Road South in Rathmines in Dublin. One time I came across a copy of *The History Of Fairport Convention* and back then it was the cover

Cropredy in 1979 (all photographs by John Hendy, by kind permission of Simon Hendy

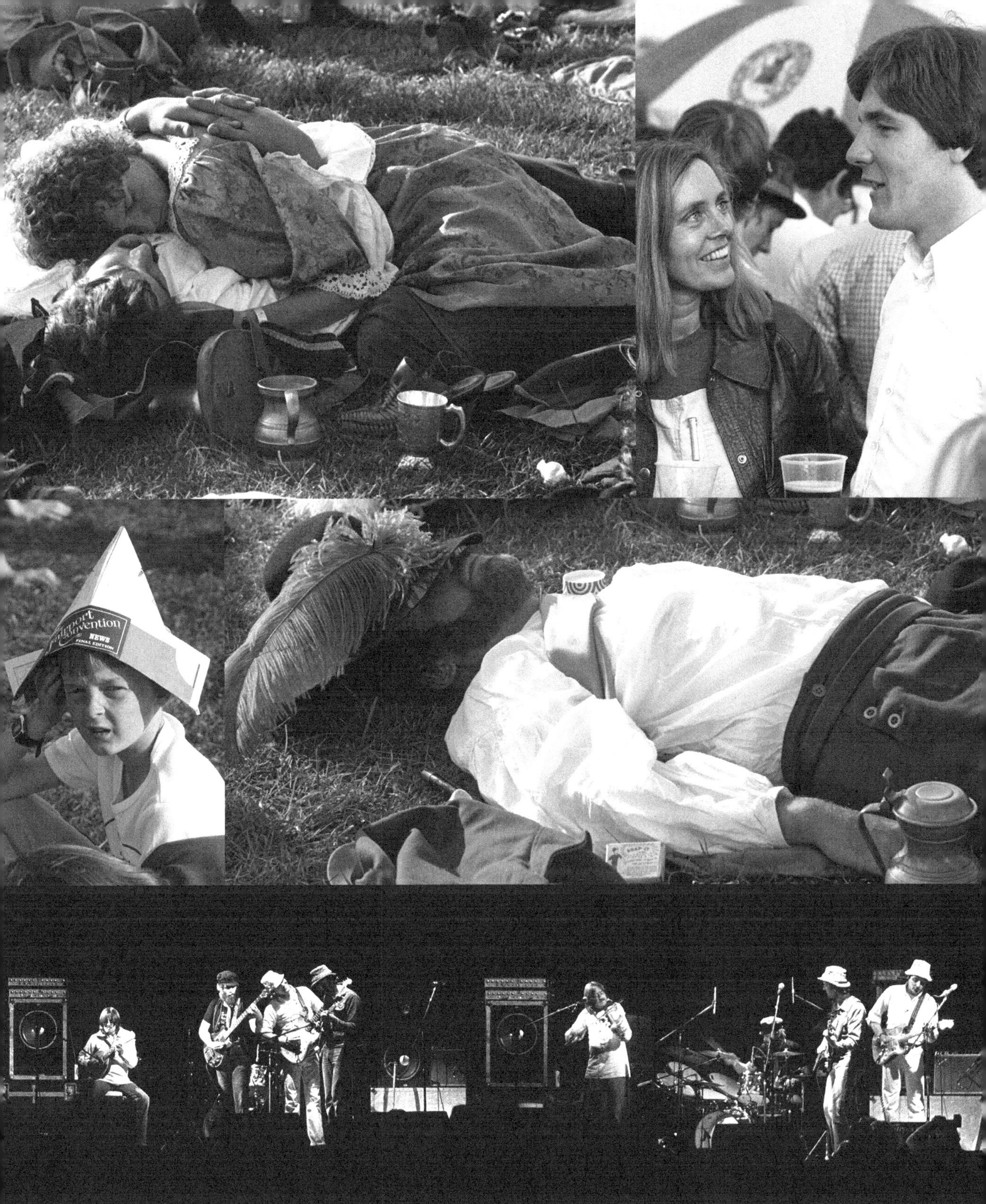

Cropredy in 1979 (all photographs by John Hendy, by kind permission of Simon Hendy that would hook you in to a new band you had never heard of before. The detail on it – the history in the family tree, the ribbon, the inner booklet and a double LP – I had to have this. I got home, put it on and instantly fell in love with them. This was the sound I had been listening out for all my life and I didn't even know it... until that point. My God: Sandy's voice, Richard's guitar, Swarb's fiddling... I was absolutely stunned by the album, and I'm still shell-shocked 50 years later. Quite a few times when Fairport play in Dublin, they would play within 500 yards of that record shop, which was run by a husband-and-wife team and which has long since closed (2003). The man's name was Anthony Sage a gentle soul who often reduced his prices so I could afford a record. I've been attending Cropredy since 1997.

LADY SPENCER CHURCHILL COLLEGE

16 FEBRUARY 1973, WHEATLEY, OXFORD, UK

CLIVE PHILLIPS

I can't remember a thing about it… except that Dave Swarbrick was excellent!

IMPERIAL COLLEGE

17 FEBRUARY 1973, LONDON, UK

NIGEL BANKS

Reading the announcement in *Melody Maker* in 1973 that Trevor Lucas and Jerry Donahue were to join the band gave fresh hope, so I duly caught the coach to London to see this new incarnation (nicknamed Fotheringport Confusion by some) at a gig at Imperial College and was not disappointed. With the reassuring return of Mr Mattacks to the drum stool, a virtuoso lead guitarist and a strong vocalist the band had regained a lot of its confidence and swagger. I saw them again in the December of that year at Preston Guildhall along with my younger brother Alastair, to whom I had introduced the band's music back in 1970 via my copy of the *Full House* album. I had purchased the *Nine* album when it came out in the October and it has remained one of my all-time favourites.

GUILDHALL
4 AUGUST 1973, PLYMOUTH, UK

CLIVE ALLEN

It was the first gig I ever went to. I was about 14 and my older sister took me. (I'm pretty sure it was a tour promoting the *John Lee* album.) My sister, who I didn't get on with at the time, asked me if I wanted to go, for reasons lost in the mists of time. I think our mother let me go because Fairport have always been a band with a well-behaved audience. I loved Dave's fiddle playing and thought he was very cool. My main lasting impression of the evening was the power of a live band. It was a life-changing event, probably in some way contributing to me being a semi-pro bass player for 45 years. I have seen hundreds of bands since, including Fairport in Ivybridge in Devon a few years ago. They were really good then. I tried to chat to Peggy but he got bored very quickly and disappeared!

I have played in all sorts of bands, from social club bands to rock bands. Until five years ago, I was playing 100 gigs a year in a Classic Rock band. And I was in a duo with Flamenco guitarists. That was fun. At the moment, I am in a folk band and a Blues-rock band. And I play bass for Beltane Border Morris.

CALEY PICTURE HOUSE
14 NOVEMBER 1973, EDINBURGH, UK

KENNY KEMP

I still have my ticket from my first concert, at the Caley Cinema. My diary tells me I went with a school friend called Michael Hook, who became a history teacher. I loved Swarb from the moment I saw him. (I went on to play fiddle in a ceilidh band and ended up once jamming with Jerry Donahue in Edinburgh.) When *Rising For The Moon* came out, I was blown away again. Jerry and Trevor were both immense. In October 1975 I went to the show at the Glasgow Apollo, when the guest was David Lewis, and the following night I was at the Usher Hall in Edinburgh, where I went back stage and met Sandy Denny. I was really star struck and couldn't really say much. Both shows were amazing.

In 1978 I was Vice President of Strathclyde Students Union and I instructed the Ents Officer, who was into punk by then, to book Fairport. They played there on Thursday 11 May 1978. I was 21 and I remember being very nervous. I went backstage to give my condolences to the band about the passing of Sandy a few weeks earlier. I think it went down like a lead balloon. The guys all signed my Fairport music book, but they were all still in shock. For several years after I was quite traumatised. It sticks with me to this day.

I've now been to Cropredy almost ten times and will be going again in 2024. I get an annual selfie with Simon Nicol. He's such a great human. This music and the musicians who play it have been a central core of my life. Fairport Convention have been the changing thread... sometimes I've lost touch or missed them for a while, but I've returned to those familiar and comforting musical geniuses.

CARDINAL LANGLEY RC HIGH SCHOOL

1974, MIDDLETON, UK

MIKE KELLY

I went to school with Maartin at Cardinal Langley in Middleton, Manchester. He'd been absent from French A-level classes for a while and when he returned the teacher (Jock Crawford) asked him where he'd been. Maartin replied, 'Sorry sir, I've been on tour with Suzi Quatro.'

ESBJORSON GYMNASIUM

12 MAY 1974, GLASSBORO, NEW JERSEY

VINCE FARINACCIO

Fairport made ample visits to the Garden State in the early 1970s and their music could be heard by South Jersey residents on radio stations like Philadelphia's WMMR (New York City's WNEW served the same for North Jersey listeners). Electric arrangements of folk songs like 'Matty Groves' and 'Tam Lin', as well as original material like 'Sickness And Diseases', were a staple of playlists. Before her concert at the Main Point in Bryn Mawr, Pennsylvania, Sandy Denny dropped by to chat at the WMMR studios with Richard Thompson in tow and Fairport's syndicated performance at the Howff Folk Club found its way into weekday evening programming.

But the music industry was changing by the mid-1970s, and British folk music had nearly run its course with most radio stations and record labels who had dabbled in it. That's the world in which Fairport chose to launch its biggest tours in the US, playing colleges, theatres and even Carnegie Hall twice along the way. Its 1975 album, *Rising For The Moon*, was produced by the noted Glyn Johns, whose ear for commercial product didn't quite mesh with the band's ties to jigs, reels and folk songs of the British Isles. For the first time since the group's 1968 *Unhalfbricking*, there would be no traditional music included on an album.

But live shows in this period didn't forsake the traditional ballads or the instrumentals and featured plenty of Denny's songs, old chestnuts and even an array of cover songs. The concerts were never leashed and always permitted the musicians to exhibit the abilities that had established their place in contemporary music as songwriters, players or vocalists.

Fairport carried its reputation into the US through April and May 1974, beginning with shows in upstate New York at Syracuse and Ithaca before moving through Pennsylvania with stops in Philadelphia, Wilkes-Barre and Allentown. April 27 included an afternoon festival slot in Storrs, Connecticut and an evening performance in Worcester, Massachusetts. There are six known recordings from this spring tour, three of which are radio broadcasts, beginning with the Worcester concert. Fairport played My Father's Place in Roslyn, New York on May 8, 1974, and part of the night was broadcast on radio by WLIR. The band's appearance for two sets at Ebbet's Field in Denver, Colorado on May 23 was also professionally recorded and features the earliest live version of a new Denny composition, 'One More Chance', which would take its place as a highlight on *Rising For The Moon* the following year.

Previously, the closest Fairport had come to South Jersey while touring was Philadelphia's Electric Factory in July 1970 when founding members Richard Thompson and Simon Nicol were still in the lineup. By 1974 colleges and universities were regularly booking musical acts. The concert at Glassboro State College was the second New Jersey stop on the spring tour that year, with Parsippany the site of a show on May 4.

The headliner at Glassboro was Bruce Springsteen, a popular draw in the area but still a year away from beginning his candidacy for superstar status, with Fairport as his opening act. That's how the concert was advertised until the doors to the college's Esbjorson Gymnasium opened on the night of May 12. Greeting ticket holders was the announcement that Springsteen had cancelled. Attendees were told refunds could be obtained at one of the tables in the foyer. Some availed themselves of the offer, but those who stayed witnessed Fairport perform a ninety-minute set that had both fans and non-believers on their feet dancing by the end of the show.

Fairport's arrival that night was evident to anyone observant in the slowly filling gym. Pegg and Swarbrick walked through the crowd, deep in conversation with a Student Activities Board representative, no doubt discussing the band's new headlining status. Before long, Mattacks was onstage setting up his drum kit in full view of the growing crowd.

Because Fairport were suddenly the headliner at the Glassboro show, the band's set list could offer a wider array of the lineup's repertoire, which had been reshaping itself since Denny had rejoined the group. Several songs from Fairport's recent album *Nine* appeared less frequently as the spring tour progressed, replaced by some of Denny's solo material and new compositions such as 'Like An Old-Fashioned Waltz', performed by the songstress alone onstage. She confided to the audience that the other musicians always abandoned her when this song came up in the set. Another new tune, 'Solo', summoned the band back to the stage in the Glassboro gym. And 'Rising For The Moon', a regal composition which would become the title track of the band's next album, was yet another of Denny's new songs to whet fans' appetites for future releases.

Fairport standards performed included 'Sloth' in an arrangement that added a bass solo for Pegg along with Donahue's and Swarbrick's improvisations. And there were additional workouts by Donahue, Swarbrick, Mattacks and Pegg on traditional songs like 'Dirty Linen' and 'Matty Groves', which served as the concert opener and soundcheck, with Denny still in her street clothes before exiting during an instrumental to change into her stage attire.

A defining moment of the show was the first encore of the evening, Denny's 'Who Knows Where The Time Goes?' which was delivered as a delicate performance that politely demanded and graciously received the audience's reverence and quiet. The song, last performed at the February LA Troubadour shows, had been recently reinstated to the set, probably in Cambridge, Massachusetts on May 10.

Glassboro was among the last stops on the spring tour before appearances in Atlanta, New York City, Washington DC, Denver and Long Beach, California.

The set lists in the final round of gigs in the spring formed a template for a 1974 fall tour, which would commence on the East Coast on October 10 and conclude on the West Coast November 10, during which Fairport would play at three more New Jersey locations: New Brunswick, Trenton and Parsippany.

LISNER AUDITORIUM

18 MAY 1974, WASHINGTON DC

DENNIS HOELSCHER

My dad worked for the CIA and we lived in Taiwan, Khartoum, Thailand, Japan (where I bought my first 45, by the Kinks) and Hong Kong. But Dad was also a musician and he encouraged us kids to play. In late 1969 we moved back Stateside and I freaked out as it wasn't anything like living in Asia. I eventually made some friends and was turned onto Fairport Convention's *Unhalfbricking*. It was late in the year and immediately went out and purchased *Liege & Lief*. I cut class when I heard *Full House* was down at the local record store. I just love *Full House*, and Swarbrick's violin.

I was living in Virginia then, where CIA headquarters was, and I turned a lot of the kids at school onto Fairport. I still get calls from people asking me Fairport queries even now. I was lucky to catch Iain Matthews with Richard Thompson touring with him to promote Plainsong. They played at a community centre, at one end of a basketball court. There was a small group of big fans listening intently, and at the other end of the court was a guy with a Nazi symbol on his jacket. Richard was making comments about the jacket. They were excellent but it was a strange venue.

I saw Fairport then in 1974 with Sandy Denny and I somehow got backstage and met her. It was during the instrumental break. She was very friendly and offered me a beer and we talked for a bit and I offered her a joint and she took it. That was a really incredible moment in my life. I can't believe I met her. I remember when she died. I had just moved to the Pacific North West and they were playing Sandy on the radio. And they never play Sandy here. I thought, 'Oh no, something's happened.' It was so sad.

The first time I saw Richard around this area was 1980. He did the Vancouver Folk Festival. Simon and Dave Swarbrick were on the tour also, but not with Richard, and I think it was the first time they had got together in a long time. I taped it but it's not very good quality.

Then in 1984 I heard about Festival Tours and I went to Cropredy in 1984 and 1987. I have caught Fairport a few times since then and enjoy Chris Leslie as a member. I was sorry to hear of the news about Gerry Conway. I love his perfect deft touch and how it doesn't get any better than Pat Donaldson's bass playing alongside him.

Having lived in Khartoum for three years and being a history buff, it is eerie how well Fotheringay captured that moment with 'Banks Of The Nile'.

BOROUGH HALL

21 JUNE 1974, GREENWICH, LONDON, UK

DAVE CHICK

I was very fortunate to see Sandy solo a couple of times and also twice with Fairport after she rejoined. On 21 June 1974 I was in Borough Hall at Greenwich. Among the audience was a couple with a very young child. The person in the next seat to mine mentioned that they were local councillors. Sandy started to sing 'Solo':

Good morning, good afternoon,
And what have you got to say?

With absolutely perfect timing, the baby let out a loud cry!

The last time that I saw Sandy was at the Fairport gig at the Royal Albert Hall on 10 June 1975. I have lots of clear memories of all four occasions when I saw her, but a particular highlight was Sandy standing alone on stage for 'The Quiet Joys Of Brotherhood'. She sang beautifully but was visibly, and not surprisingly, very nervous. I had the strange sensation that everybody in the Albert Hall was holding their breath and willing her on. As the song finished the tension was broken by Swarb walking on to play the coda.

BIRMINGHAM UNIVERSITY
22 JUNE 1974, BIRMINGHAM, UK

MIKE LOCKWOOD

I've seen Fairport quite a few times. A memorable gig was at the Students Guild at Birmingham Uni about the time of the *Rising For The Moon* album. My old school mate was a cameraman for TV Guild and another schoolfriend, Chris Drinan (a singer and flautist), was the support act. We were in the green room with the band after Chris' set. Swarb was really kind. Sandy was drunk and not very pleasant (there was a big atmosphere between her and Trevor Lucas) and Jerry Donahue was practising new licks on his guitar and smiling a lot. Another life-changing event for me was to see them at Reading Uni on the *Full House* tour (Swarb and Thompson were astounding – I'd never seen anything like it). I also saw them at Croydon on the *Angel Delight* tour and we put them on at Exeter Uni (I was on social committee there) during the *Nine* tour. I've seen them a few times recently as well. I also saw Fotheringay in the Assembly Rooms when they came to my home town of Tunbridge Wells, just before the album came out. I also went to the first ever Cropredy Festival and I really enjoyed it – but I've never been back!

THE GREYHOUND
30 JUNE 1974, CROYDON, UK

CHRIS HARDING

I was introduced to Fairport by my older brother when he played 'Walk Awhile' on an Island sampler called *Bumpers* and I loved the song and added it to my cassette of favourite music. I must have been around 13 and hearing this song changed so much for me. I started to collect their music, and I saw them for the first time at The Greyhound in Croydon on a Sunday night. They were excellent and from that night I started to see them quite often, in Greenwich, Croydon and Gravesend.

They were really the soundtrack of my life from 13 years old and their winter tour t-shirts and programmes have been collected over the years. I don't think I have missed a winter tour since 1987.

Each gig continues to be a warm enjoyable night with musicians I consider as friends. I was lucky enough to have chatted with Maart over the years and miss his warmth and musicianship. I feel blessed to have been born musically at such a fantastic time and wait eagerly for the winter dates to come along and get my ticket(s) for Canterbury. I have made new friends on this musical journey and shared stories. It goes back to my brother and my introduction to the great band. I was lucky that it was Fairport that my brother introduced me to.

CARNEGIE HALL
25 OCTOBER 1974, NEW YORK, NEW YORK

MARK ALESSIO

I saw Fairport four times in New York City. The first was the *Rising For The Moon* lineup at Carnegie Hall in 1974. Seeing Sandy Denny onstage was a wonderful thing. She had a very self-effacing manner, even poking fun at herself during one song introduction. The audience was much taken with her. And Dave Swarbrick was so animated, of course. I was hoping his violin cord wouldn't wrap around his legs! And what a thrill to see Jerry Donahue in person (I would see him again years later with The Hellecasters).

The second was the *Angel Delight* lineup at the Lone Star Cafe in 1984. It was a small venue, so how nice to be so close to the stage. I'm pretty sure it was the Swarbrick-Nicol-Pegg-Mattacks lineup, although I've read that also Bruce Rowland played with them in the US. I guess you can clear that up with Mr. Pegg!

The third and fourth times were at the Bottom Line and the *Expletive Delighted!* lineup, a nice venue. I remember being blown away by Maartin Allcock's playing. The band sounded so good, with Nicol's singing as strong as ever. One very strong memory remains from one of those shows. When they played 'Meet On The Ledge', a palpable feeling came over the entire audience. It was as though everyone there was reliving the old days and remembering. You could feel it. Eyes closed, people gently moving to the song. A spell had been cast for those few minutes. I will never forget that.

I was (and remain) a big Fairport fan, so getting to see those different lineups four times meant a lot to me. I was in paradise every minute of those shows.

Fairport Convention's mourning glory

LIKE all good wakes, it was a joyous occasion, with a hint of tears at the end. Fairport Convention was finally laid to rest after 11 years and eight months of life (and 14 changes of personnel) in a farmer's field in Cropredy, Oxfordshire — 60 or so miles northwest of Fairport, the Muswell Hill doctor's house where a group of friends started jamming together in the spring of '67 before emerging later that year as a significant force on the London underground circuit under the name which changed the meaning of folk-rock.

As far as I could see, none of the 16 or so ex-members attended as pallbearers. Their first drummer, Martin Lamble, and Sandy Denny, their second female vocalist, are both dead, the first in a traumatic motorway crash in June 1969 — out of which nevertheless came their most influential album, "Liege And Lief," the second of brain haemorrhage in April 1978.

Richard Thompson, for whom a few unreconstructed optimists were still calling after the last number, was putting the finishing touches to his latest album in London, with the man who achieved almost "fifth Beatle" status with the group, engineer John Wood, producing. Ian Matthews, too, was somewhere else finishing his new album.

Trevor Lucas was presumably back home in Strine-land with his new wife of a month or so. Guitarist Jerry Donahue is a leading light in a new band of Arista hopefuls, Thieves, and Dave Mattacks was no doubt playing a session somewhere; I had seen him at the QEH two nights before, playing for ex-Stealer's Wheel member Joe Egan at his come-back concert. Stivell guitarist Dan Ar Bras, a brief Fairport member in 1976, now has his own electric band.

I had no news of Ashley "Tyger" Hutchings — presumably resting between the umpteenth versions of his Albion Band — nor of any of the other Fairport alumni, Judy Dyble, Roger Hill, Tom Farnell, Bob Brady, or Roger Burridge.

It was in the low-key nature of the event that, though they had spoken of hedge-hopping in by helicopter from a gig supporting Dave Pegg's old Brummie mate John Bonham at Knebworth earlier in the day, they abandoned the superstar trip and talked Zeppelin into letting them go on first, so they could journey back by road, melting into the crowd of Thakestone-quaffing Fairport fans listening to a collection of folk club hopefuls at about mid-afternoon.

Musically one began to wonder uncharitably if they had deliberately chosen weak support acts to throw their own last performance into a more favourable light, for Fairport were never one of the tightest of bands. Compere Johnny Jones was having his work cut out thinking of nice things to say about each successively more dire guest, until a group called the Rollright Stones brought the crowd to its feet with some lively concertina-based music.

But it was Steve Ashley who struck exactly the right note, with a set of songs that was shambolic but inspired, joined at the end by Fairporters Pegg and Rowlands.

By now the crowd was getting restless. They gave short shrift to a sound-plagued Bert Jansch, and were prepared to jeer at Earl Okin's zany mix of camp nostalgia and excellent vocals, but they stayed to cheer, and Jones had difficulty getting him off.

Eventually, at about the time the concert had been planned to finish, the four loped on: original member Simon Nicol (1967-1971 and 1976-9) in whose garden the band originally started playing together, longest-serving member Dave Swarbrick (ten years, almost to the month), bass-player Dave Pegg (1971-9), and drummer Bruce Rowlands (1975-79).

Though none of the expected ex-members materialised, a rather joiced Ralph McTell made the only reference to Sandy when he sang "White Dress," and Maddy Prior captured everyone with an acapella version of her own "Mother And Child."

The band played basically the "farewell" set they have been touring around Europe since their retirement was announced in February, when Swarbrick was warned that electric music was driving him deaf: the requisite supersonic jig-tunes, the old favourites like "Walk A While" (but no "Sloth"), a few surprises ("Journeyman's Grace," "John Lee"), rounded off by "Matty Groves."

It was two in the morning, and encore time had come round at last. Would it be "Flowers Of The Forest," which a Scots guy in the front row had been begging for all night? No, they'd done that at Sandy's funeral.

Inevitably, then, it had to be the Richard Thompson song which sums up Fairport in its late sixties' heyday — and which, incidentally, they never played in public again until this tour after doing it at Martin Lamble's funeral in 1969: "Meet On The Ledge," with its images of parting and hopes of ultimate reunion. They did it much slower than the original, and Simon Nicol hasn't the voice of either a Denny or a Matthews to get round its jagged, rather plaintive tune, but who was taking critical notes at this point in the game? I guarantee there wasn't a dry eye on the field.

We all went our separate ways: Pegg to play bass with Jethro Tull, Swarbrick to the cottage he's going to renovate in Scotland, the other two no doubt to session work and record production, the crowds to the roads back to civilisation.

Johnny Jones had held out a vague hope of an annual reunion starting next year, but I hope not. What does it say in "The Unquiet Grave" about excessive mourning not allowing the dead their well-earned rest?

With 18 albums behind them, including US and European compilations and the final live "Farewell," Fairport had certainly earned theirs. Time, at last, to move on to something new. — KARL DALLAS.

(clockwise from top left) 1979 gig review (Ian Burgess); in action at Sunderland Poly, May 1979 (all photos, Ed Wallage)

SUNDERLAND POLYTECHNIC STUDENTS' UNION

Fairport Convention

plus BERT JANSCH'S CONUNDRUM

and DISCO

Saturday, 19th May, 1979

No Re-admission after 10.30 p.m.

№ 363

Members £1.50

CHRIS LESLIE

Chris Leslie from Banbury, is a young fiddle and mandola player who is destined to become a household name. He started playing in 1973 in folk clubs with his brother John. The brothers Leslie recorded their debut album in 1976 and also played on Roy Bailey's 'New Bell Wake' album. Chris and John disbanded their partnership in 1978 and the following year Chris teamed up with Steve Ashley.

FAREWELL FAREWELL FOR ONLY £4.00 FAIRPORT COMMEMORATIVE ALBUM AVAILABLE FROM WOODWORM RECORDS, CHAPEL ROW, CROPREDY, Nr BANBURY, OXON. RECORDS

THE Fairport Convention NEWS FINAL EDITION

PRICE £2.50 (£3.00 on the day) | AUGUST 4TH 1979 | Vol No1 (FINAL)

THE LAST FAREWELL

FAIRPORT COMES HOME TO SAY GOODBYE

CROPREDY VILLAGE

Once again we would like to welcome you to the picturesque village of Cropredy, which nestles [...] and we sincerely hope that the weather will be kind and show it off to its best advantage, enabling you to enjoy your day to the full.

Cropredy has probably existed for 900 years, as it is mentioned in the Domesday book as Cropelie, and has, down the stony path of time, also been spelled Cropperia (Henry I), Crapridden, Cropridy (Richard III) and Cropperidge, among about fifteen variations.

To the casual visitor, Cropredy may seem to be hidden away in the north of Oxfordshire, and give the impression that little has changed since the days of Charles I, but nevertheless, we look at our past with pride and our future with anticipation.

On the 29th June 1644, Cropredy was the scene of a famous Civil War battle widely described in history as 'The Battle of Cropredy Bridge'. King Charles was present, and his force of several thousand horse and foot soldiers under the command of several Generals, was shadowed by a similar force of Roundheads, under the command of General Sir William Waller, who had a superior armament of cannon pieces. In order to lure the Roundhead forces to a suitable place of battle, the Royalists split their forces, and sent a small decoy group in front. Waller fell into the trap by following and was caught between two forces. The ensuing battle raged for many hours before the Royalists routed Waller's men and forced them to retreat in disorder across Cropredy Bridge, leaving approximately 700 dead, wounded and deserters as well as many cannon pieces.

History has it that during the battle a messenger boy jumped through the Church window into the vestry for sanctuary. He was promptly killed by a Roundhead, and the stain on the vestry floor, which is still visible, is said to have been made by the boy's blood. We

Turn to Page 2 col 3.

Fairport Convention

Today marks the end of a countrywide tour of farewell concerts, which have been both successful, and at times emotional. It will be a day of many mixed feelings. Some of sadness, in the knowledge that this is the farewell concert of a group that has given so much to the world of folk music, both in this country, and in many other far flung parts of the world. Still there will be feelings of gaiety, in the knowledge that Fairport Convention, and a host of their friends, will give their many fans a day of entertainment, the memory of which will linger for a long time, and be savoured like the taste of vintage wine.

A measure of Fairport's popularity can be gained from the long list of friends and fellow Artistes, many of whose names are bye words in the folk world, who will be attending and participating in the concert. Unfortunately, it is not possible to specify individuals, but, it is sufficient to say that they are stars in their own right.

The response to the groups offer to play some of your requests at this concert has been phenomenal, and I can tell you now that "Sloth" and "Rosie" are certainties, but that many other of the more popular requests will be played once we have extracted them from your many letters.

Few bands have already covered as much ground as Fairport. Since their formation in 1967, Fairport Convention have shown the ability to assimilate countless influences. In addition, they have literally written the book on British electric traditional folk music, blending timeless balladry and dance tunes with consumately modern musicianship in a sound which has reverberated around the world for the last twelve years.

In spite of a number of personnel changes over the years, they have maintained a gratifying continuity which keeps the band rich in both tradition and talent. The original Fairport Convention coalesced around guitarists Richard Thompson and Simon Nicol, and bassist Ashley Hutchings; they added drummer Martin Lamble, vocalist Judy Dyble, and later another vocalist, Ian Matthews.

The initial Fairport Convention style combined unusual and original material with a tasteful approach to playing American-rooted "Folk Rock". The replacement of Judy Dyble by Sandy Denny on the band's second album added extra strength to the song writing axis. This configuration produced chart

Turn to Page 2 col 1, 2

WARNING!

THE FIELDS SURROUNDING THE SITE WILL BE FULL OF RIPENED CROPS AWAITING HARVESTING. PLEASE DO NOT ENTER ANY FIELDS OTHER THAN THE SITE AND TAKE PARTICULAR CARE IN FULLY EXTINGUISHING ALL CIGARETTES AND MATCHES.

THIS IS YOUR TICKET OF ADMISSION TO THE CONCERT AND WILL HAVE TO BE STAMPED ON ENTRY. DON'T FORGET TO BRING EITHER THIS SECTION OR THE WHOLE PROGRAMME WITH YOU TO AVOID DISAPPOINTMENT. THIS TICKET ADMITS ONE

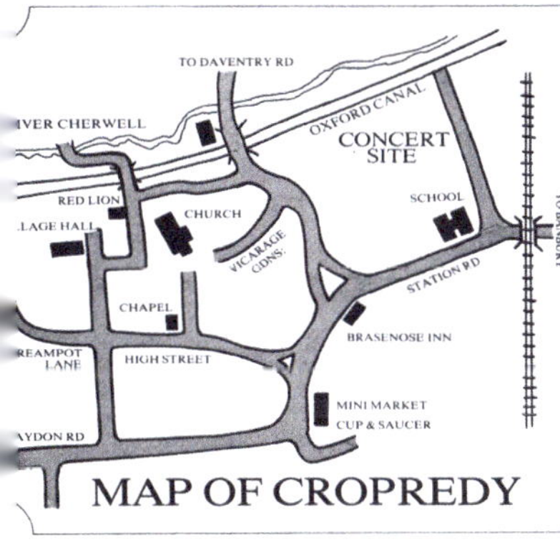

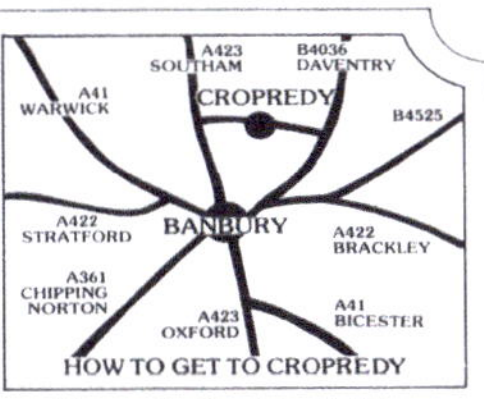

When approaching Cropredy from the Banbury — Southam road through Great Bourton, the concert site will be found up the first lane on the right under the railway bridge and past the school. The site is called Pewet, pronounced "Peewit" and if you get lost, any of the village residents will be able to tell you where it is.

If you approach Cropredy from the Banbury — Daventry road direction, you will need to go right through the village and turn left just before you get to the railway bridge.

There is adequate car parking space for which a small charge of 20 pence will be made.

Additionally, we would respectfully ask you to keep within the confines of the site field and not stray into the fields on either side where growing crops may be damaged.

THIS IS YOUR TICKET

OF ADMISSION TO THE CONCERT AND WILL HAVE TO BE STAMPED ON ENTRY. DON'T FORGET TO BRING EITHER THIS SECTION OR THE WHOLE PROGRAMME WITH YOU TO AVOID DISAPPOINTMENT.

THIS TICKET ADMITS ONE

4 AUG 1979

r friends

We thought you might like to know that due to popular request Fairport vention are having a re-union concert in Cropredy on Saturday August 30th

Special guests will be Ralph McTell and Richard and Linda Thompson, plus y of our favourite artists.

There will be camping facilities, a real ale bar and various food stalls

Tickets, which will be limited are £3.50 (£4 on the gate) Children under ive are admitted free. T shirts will also be available but advance orders ld be appreciated stating size

postal orders only, made payable to C. Pegg and a stamped addressed elope to:

WOODWORMS HILTON, CHAPEL ROW, CROPREDY, OXON OX17 1NS

DAVE SWARBRICK, DAVE PEGG
SIMON NICOL, BRUCE ROWLANDS.

(clockwise from top left) Ed Wallage's ticket from the 1979 Sunderland show; The Last Farewell (Stephen Brightman); ticket for 1979 (Tim Edmonds); the 1980 reunion (Nigel Schofield); how to get around Cropredy (Tim Edmonds); 'Group Disbands' sensation (Stephen Brightman); the young Chris Leslie (Tim Edmonds)

MEMORIAL HALL
1 NOVEMBER 1974, KANSAS CITY, MISSOURI

EVAN SMITH

I saw the 'Sandy rejoining' lineup, opening for Weather Report in Kansas City. Before 'Hexhamshire Lass', Sandy joked of upcoming funny lyrics 'Saiby Syke'. Before 'Jigs' she asked 'can you dance here?' Nobody replied. Peggy seemed so tall that a friend mistook him for Pat Donaldson. Later on, the band watched Weather Report quite intently.

I saw them again at the Half Moon in Putney in August 1983, with Cathy Lesurf in for the late Sandy. I almost cried upon hearing 'Come All Ye' and 90 per cent of *Liege & Lief*, with only 'The Deserter' being omitted. I loved the chronological presentation, including many 1969 cuts. Cropredy a day or so later was almost anticlimactic but extreme fun. Nicol, Hutchings and Mattacks were busy bees, doing the Albions or the Richard Thompson Big Band as well as playing with Fairport at the festival. I sat with an American tour group and couldn't believe it when one musician offered a jam session just when Fairport was to play! I was incredulous.

In February 2000 I saw the new band at Yeovil and Cambridge. They were great shows, but Swarb didn't make it as planned. I bought a *Wood and the Wire* t-shirt and remember Simon, as he was introducing a song, saying 'it may be rubbish, but it's British rubbish.'

UNIVERSITY OF SALFORD
11 NOVEMBER 1974, SALFORD, UK

JOHN BARLASS

In July 1973 I bought a bass guitar from a friend, only to find that playing it wasn't as easy as it looks. Help was, however, at hand, in the shape of a friend of a friend called Derek Austin, bass player in Bolton's top band of the day – a group called Iron Maiden (no – not *that* Iron Maiden). Derek invited me round to his flat for a few sessions of bass tuition. For my second lesson, I took along a copy of Jimi Hendrix's *Band of Gypsies* (Hendrix) album, to impress upon Derek that I was a guy who recognised good bass paying when I heard it. 'Just listen to what Billy Cox is doing,' I said. 'Never mind Billy Cox,' retorted Derek, 'listen to this.' And he placed a copy of *Morris On* onto the turntable.

I'd honestly never heard anything like it – such a clear, joyous sound; traditional tunes played on instruments like melodeons, concertinas and violins, but with a rocky accompaniment that was as solid and vibrant as anything I'd ever heard before. It transpired that three of the chaps responsible for this eye-and-mind opening noise – Ashley Hutchings, Dave Mattacks and Richard Thompson – were former members of Fairport Convention, a band I was aware of mainly from their presence on that string of Island sampler albums, including *You Can All Join In* (1968), *Nice Enough to Eat* (1969) and *El Pea* (1971). Here, indeed was something worthy of detailed examination.

It turned out, of course, that *Morris On* was just the tip of a deeply fascinating iceberg. Since he'd broken away from Fairport in 1969, Ashley had immersed himself deeply in English folk culture. He'd set up Steeleye Span and, although he'd left Maddy and Co to their own devices after the band's third album – the wonderful *Ten Man Mop, or Mr Reservoir Butler Rides Again* – Steeleye were still fully airborne and producing such treasures as *Below the Salt* and *Parcel of Rogues*. There was also the timeless *No Roses* album that Ashley produced and curated with his (then) wife, the wonderful Shirley Collins. Richard Thompson, too, was just embarking on that amazing series of albums with his wife, Linda, that opened up all kinds of new perspectives of that world we formerly knew as folk music. And all this is before we even start to think about what Fairport had been doing.

Newly confirmed as an evangelist, *Liege & Lief* was the first Fairport album I checked out, followed by the band's new album, *Nine*. I loved them both. Up until this stage, I'd grown my Fairport familiarity by the time-honoured method of borrowing and taping albums from friends, but now I decided it was time to take the plunge. I bought my first Fairport album, *Live Convention*, in August 1974 and just a couple of months later I attended my first Fairport gig.

The band's lineup that evening was the same one featured on the *Live Convention* album – Sandy, Trevor, Peggy, Swarb, Jerry D and DM. The vast Maxwell Hall at the University was packed; this was Fairport's first UK tour with Sandy back in the ranks and she was a big star. She'd won the prestigious *Melody Maker* Female Vocalist of the Year award in 1971 and, even more impressively, duetted with Robert Plant on 'The Battle of Evermore' on Led Zeppelin's fourth album. These were huge credentials… But this evening things went a bit off course.

Some bonehead in the audience thought it would be a jolly jape to throw a plastic beer glass at the stage, just as the band were making their entry, and the glass hit Sandy on her head. Trevor Lucas, her husband, was furious and threatened to deck the culprit, a sentiment that was clearly understandable, although still rather shocking to my gentle, non-violent, teenage self.

There's no doubt that this incident cast a shadow over the rest of the evening's events, and there were a few further disappointments to come. I, and – I suspect – many others in that packed hall had been drawn to Fairport by their good-time, fast-paced approach to their music, but here was a new Fairport on show. The set list was dominated by Sandy's solo material and by songs more associated with Fotheringay than with Fairport. That's all material that I love dearly and deeply now but, in November 1974 it was all totally new to me. There was some familiar stuff in the set – 'The Hexamshire Lass', 'The Hen's March', 'Who Knows Where the Time Goes' and 'Matty' were all included – but all in all, I was a bit underwhelmed.

Fairport attract the 'Fotheringport Confusion' tag during this stage of their history but nothing negative sticks long to Fairport, and I overcame my initial disappointment by taking steps to familiarise myself with the overload of new material that I'd just experienced.

UNIVERSITY OF NOTTINGHAM
27 NOVEMBER 1974, NOTTINGHAM, UK

GRAHAME BAUMBER

I first saw Fairport in the early seventies, at the time of the *Rosie* album. Dave Swarbrick had his leg in a cast and was singing harmonies and smoking simultaneously. When DM walked up to his drum kit, he paused at a microphone and said 'guess the lineup and win a prize!' They were back in Nottingham a couple of years later. Sandy was back with them and not in the best of moods. She stomped on to the stage saying 'let's get this song over with' as the band launched into 'Matty Groves'. I have not seen them open a set with this since…

STUDENT UNION HALL, OXFORD POLY
28 NOVEMBER 1974, OXFORD, UK

PHIL NIXON

One day, well before the Eagles wrote 'Hotel California', my brother came home from sixth form with a borrowed copy of the double album *History Of Fairport Convention*. Little did 13-year-old me know that I was about to check in to the 'Hotel Fairport Convention'. Despite checking out now and then in my family and career building years, it is a hotel that I find that I can never leave.

I took up playing bass guitar in 1973 at the same time as becoming intoxicated with Fairport's early recordings. Dave Pegg became one of my main influences, along with Richard Sinclair of Caravan and Chris Squire of Yes; all melodic players who weren't afraid of going up the neck to what many bass players refer to as 'the dusty end'.

I bought a Fairport songbook and took it along to my first FC gig, going backstage to get all the band's autographs: Mattacks, Swarb, Jerry, Peggy, Trevor and Sandy. I was a short-haired 16-year-old with bumfluff above my lip, but I must have said some nice things to Sandy, as she said I was such a charmer and put a kiss mark next to her autograph.

Skint, but enthusiastic, I went to Reading University Student Union a week later with my mate Nigel. We didn't have tickets for this sold out gig and were hanging around outside at the back of the hall feeling sorry for ourselves when Fairport's road manager took pity on us young lads and let us in. I was an amateur photographer, using my parent's airing cupboard as a makeshift darkroom, and when I processed my photos of the band, I couldn't find a single shot in which Dave Swarbrick wasn't smoking!

Since then, I have enjoyed dozens of live performances by the band at diverse venues in the likes of Bishops Thornton, Cropredy, Exeter, Harrogate, Leeds, Masham, Nettlebed, Oxford, and Reading. Harrogate gave me my finest heckling moment. The band had tried twice to start one of the *'Babbacombe' Lee* songs but they were getting something wrong. I couldn't resist shouting out 'you only have three chances to get it right!'

Another golden touchpoint for me was finding myself in the hallowed ground of Sound Techniques studio in Chelsea. By now, it had been renamed Olympic Chelsea. My un-signed band had been doing demos at its big brother, Olympic Barnes, using a sound engineer in his spare time. When Barnes got too busy, we shifted to Chelsea. This being the late 1970s, we were still recording on to two-inch analogue tape, just like John 'the' Wood and Joe Boyd had done between these same walls with Fairport, Nick Drake, John Martyn, and so on. Sadly, the studio is now flats, but it was a special connection for me.

Being distracted from the band in my young adult days meant I missed out on the early years of Cropredy, yet twenty years ago the fickle finger of fate brought my business life and my private music-loving life together in the fields of Cropredy. In 1994 I had founded what was to become a small group of media companies, and ten years later I used a head hunter to find us a chairperson. Along came the ideal candidate, who not only happened to live in Cropredy but was also the Chair of Governors for the local school and Chair of the parish council. He got the job on merit, but luckily my first few times at the festival were at local rates and comfortable boarding in his family's nearby cottage. The price to pay for this privilege was getting up early each day to help with cooking breakfasts for festival campers, in aid of church funds, but it was worth it. What a shame they no longer live in the village!

I have far too many memories arising from the festival to write here, but I fondly remember buying Simon Nicol a large glass of white wine at the bar. We tried to talk but Simon had to diplomatically deal with the attentions of some lovely yet well-fuelled Norwegians.

I grew out of my teenage autograph-hunting period but, during lockdown, posted photos on Facebook of the aforementioned signed songbook, lamenting that Simon Nicol, who had left the band by 1974, was pictured in the book but his signature was missing. Simon commented on my post that if I sent the songbook to him, he would duly sign and return it. This he did. Thank you, Simon!

By 2018 we were living near to Nettlebed in Oxfordshire. I turned sixty in May and Fairport were playing a sold-out show in the village hall that very night. When my wife Jill realised that neither of us had bought tickets, she contacted Dave Pegg, pleaded with him that it was my special birthday and asked whether there any way we could get in? 'Of course,' he said, and he not only put our names on the door but also gave me a shout from the stage to wish me happy birthday!

In 2022 I had severe back-pain with sciatica, and wrote to the Cropredy organisers asking if I could camp in Field 6, despite not being a blue badge holder. My request was accepted, and boy did it make a huge difference. But although I could hobble into and around the arena, I missed being able to walk in to the village for breakfast and jumble rummaging. Thankfully, I've since had an operation on my spine and I am back to normal.

In 2024 I found my interaction with the 'family' continuing. I wanted to listen to Ashley Hutchings and his son Blair Dunlop's *The Guvnor* podcasts, which started in lockdown and were unheard by me. The links to the early episodes were no longer active online. I sent a message to Blair Dunlop and he jumped on it straight away, restoring the podcast episodes and following up with a number of communications to me to make sure that all was working. They are well worth a listen!

Until I check out for good, I'll continue to be in and out of this virtual hotel. Fairport have been the soundtrack of my life, and although nostalgia plays a part in this, it's great that the band have been rejuvenated by Chris Leslie and Ric Sanders, along with their contributions to songwriting. Here's to future memories together!

TIVOLIS KONCERTHALS
3 FEBRUARY 1975, COPENHAGEN, DENMARK

HANS HENRIK FRANCKE

I first discovered FC in 1970 when I bought *Liege & Lief* off a friend who didn't really like it. I did like it and subsequently bought many of their albums as they came out. I was also buying related albums from the likes of the various Albion incarnations, Steeleye Span and some Irish folk music. The first time I saw FC in concert was in Copenhagen. It was the *Nine* lineup with the welcome addition of a certain Sandy Denny. I still recall it as a good show – everybody performing to their best, with lots of

Swarb instrumentals, Peggy and DM keeping time in the way only they can and with Trevor and Jerry. (Did I mention Sandy?)

I next saw Fairport playing a daytime show at a festival in Denmark in 1989. This was the Ric/Simon/Maart/DM/Peggy lineup, sometime after *Expletive Delighted*! came out. I don't remember much about this show apart from me wearing my usual silly grin when listening to Fairport.

The last show was in the small Musikteater in Vejle, Denmark. This must have been around 2012 with Gerry Conway perhaps and it was also a nice solid set. At the break, I was heading over to Peggy hoping to have a few words but I was beaten to it…

ORANGE 75

15 AUGUST 1975, ORANGE, FRANCE

CHRIS CHARLESWORTH, *MELODY MAKER*

Staged in a spectacular Roman amphitheatre where gladiators once fought with lions, (this festival) promised much but delivered less due to several star name no-shows, bands running late and interminable delays between sets. Coupled with the hard stone seats, it's not surprising there were outbreaks of ill-feeling amidst the crowd... I watched a set by Fairport Convention but whatever enjoyment I felt was tempered by an altercation in the backstage bar I had earlier in the day with their bass player, Dave Pegg. Pegg, not in the first flush of sobriety, had taken exception to an *MM* review of his group's last LP, and decided to vent his spleen by pouring a pint of beer over my head. I too had drink taken and this emboldened me to retaliate, not least because I wasn't the author of the review that had so inflamed him. So I bought a pint and went over to where Pegg was sitting and poured it over his head. He was restrained from thumping me by others in his party. I think we made up later.

AMAZING GRACE

12 SEPTEMBER 1975, EVANSTON, ILLINOIS

TOM DELANEY

This was a small venue where you sat on a carpeted floor. I saw in the front row, right under the edge of the grand piano they provided for Sandy.

TRENTON WAR MEMORIAL
26 SEPTEMBER 1975, TRENTON, NEW JERSEY

VINCE FARINACCIO

Unlike many of the previous year's US concerts, the 1975 Trenton War Memorial show opened with 'Dirty Linen' and 'Tam Lin'. After a performance at Philadelphia's Academy of Music five days earlier, Fairport put in an appearance on Gene Shay's folk music programme on WMMR, where the band was interviewed and Swarbrick and Pegg entertained by playing a series of instrumental traditional pieces. When asked why 'Tam Lin' had been added to the set, Sandy Denny replied, 'I just got fed up with singing 'Matty Groves'.' She explained that audiences usually requested both songs. As if to prove her right, several callers to the radio station that night solicited on-air performances of both tunes.

If concertgoers in Trenton thought the opening songs of the 1975 show signalled a trip through the band's back catalogue, they were wrong. The tour had less flexible set lists than in 1974 and leaned heavily on material from *Rising For The Moon*, interspersed with staples from the previous year, including 'The Brilliancy Medley And The Cherokee Shuffle' and 'It'll Take A Long Time'. 'Sloth' was still in the set, having evolved since the previous year with Denny's piano augmenting the arrangement and Donahue's solo segment implementing a churning groove. And there were the occasional covers, but surprises like 'Mr Lacey', 'Rosie' 'The Quiet Joys of Brotherhood' and 'Listen Listen', added to the band's Royal Albert Hall set list in June, had already been retired. The new album was on display, with the title track, 'One More Chance', 'Stranger To Himself' (featuring Swarbrick on dulcimer), 'Restless' and 'Iron Lion' chosen to represent the release. The first hour of the Trenton show was broadcast by WMMR two weeks after the concert (Caravan's opening set was also broadcast by the radio station one week after the show).

Due to cost effectiveness, the band hasn't toured the US in several decades. The 1975 US tour with Fairport would be the last time Denny performed in this country before her death three years later. Perhaps it is most fitting that Richard Thompson, now a New Jersey resident, usually includes 'Who Knows Where The Time Goes?' in his solo acoustic shows, a memorial to his former bandmate as much as a consideration for us all.

CARDIFF UNIVERSITY
6 OCTOBER 1975, CARDIFF, UK

BRIAN THOMAS PHILLIPS

I'd been absolutely besotted by Sandy since I first heard her voice some years, before when I'd bought the *Bumpers* sampler double LP from Island Records. I must have owned every recorded work of hers by the time of this gig, so it was not only Sandy's voice I was besotted by but her face. I was 17 at the time and in the full flush of teenage angst / infatuation / despair / love, etc.

It was the *Rising For The Moon* tour. The band were preparing to take the stage. I'd arrived late, and after a long journey I needed to visit the loo. I left the packed concert hall and entered a long corridor. I was dithering around wondering which way to go but there was no one at all there to ask. Then I saw Sandy, also entering the corridor about 20 or 30 yards away. Sandy approached me along the corridor, possibly thinking I was familiar with the University.

She stopped directly in front of me and asked whether I knew where the toilets were. I didn't reply apart from a strange sort of hesitant and garbled 'urrgghh!' It would have been better to be entirely speechless, but no, I was being blessed by the dribbling imbecile variety of speechlessness.

I remained petrified and stuttering, drop-jawed, and wide-eyed with every emotion imaginable coursing through my teenage, temporarily mutated brain. She might have repeated her question before giving up and turning to go but all I can remember is the turmoil in my head and heart as the angel I had worshipped for years stood so close to me. Sandy suddenly hesitated, turned back and kissed me very briefly on the cheek beforte gliding away down the corridor.

My next memory is of being back in the audience with my hand on my cheek, utterly stupefied by my encounter and by the angelic voice I was now listening to as she performed the best version of 'Who Knows Where The Time Goes' that I have ever heard.

It's not a story I'm proud to tell, even though it is a precious yet embarrassing memory. I can't say for certain whether I have fully recovered my senses yet. I'm 68 so maybe there's still time.

(clockwise from top left) Nick Skilton went to Broughton Castle on a whim rather than with a ticket; Stephen & Frances Royston in 1983; Chris Leslie with Peggy & Simon at Broughton Castle 1981 (Bob Battersby/Lodestone Publishing Ltd); RT at Broughton Castle 1981 (Bob Battersby/Lodestone Publishing Ltd); Broughton Castle 1981 (Bob Battersby/Lodestone Publishing Ltd)

Woodworms Hilton,
Chapel Row,
Cropredy,
Oxon, OX17 1NS.

January, 1981

Dear Sir/Madam,

Your name has been chosen at random, as one of one hundred, from last year's mailing list to help us arrange another Fairport re-union.

We hope you enjoyed last year's concert - despite the weather.

Below there is a list of possible Fairport combinations; would you mind listing your preference?

1. Dave Swarbrick, Dave Mattacks, Jerry Donahue, Trevor Lucas and Dave Pegg.

2. Dave Swarbrick, Bruce Rowland, Simon Nicol and Dave Pegg.

3. Dave Swarbrick, Richard Thompson, Simon Nicol, Dave Mattacks and Dave Pegg.

4. Dave Swarbrick, Dave Mattacks, Simon Nicol and Dave Pegg.

A pre-paid envelope is enclosed for your reply and your co-operation would be greatly appreciated.

Regards,

<u>Fairport</u>

P.S. Any suggestions for support acts?

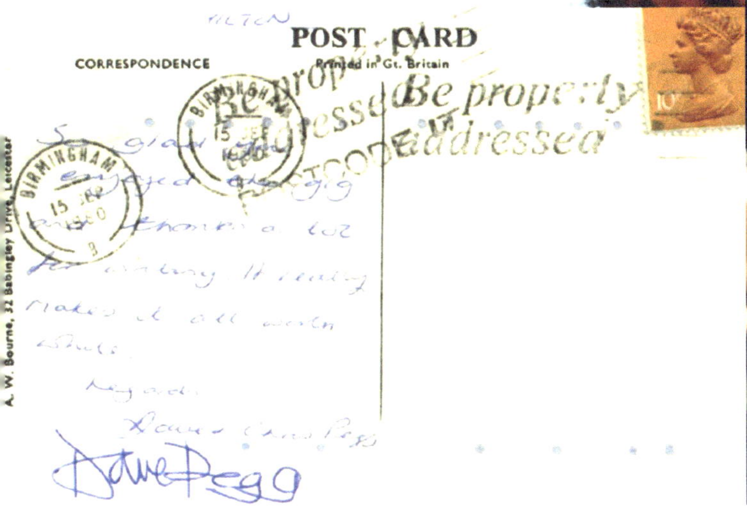

(clockwise from top left) Broughton Castle 1981 (Bob Battersby/Lodestone Publishing Ltd); Swarb, Simon & Peggy at Broughton Castle 1981 (Bob Battersby/Lodestone Publishing Ltd); Simon, Peggy & RT at Broughton Castle 1981 (Bob Battersby/Lodestone Publishing Ltd); RT at Broughton Castle 1981 (Bob Battersby/Lodestone Publishing Ltd); Nigel Schofield's 'thank you' card; Nigel Schofield's letter to 'the 100'

UMIST
11 OCTOBER 1975, MANCHESTER, UK

JOHN BARLASS

In spring 1975, I placed my advanced order for the forthcoming *Rising For The Moon* album. It was during the making of this album that DM quit the band for the second time – reportedly following disagreements with Glyn Johns, the album's producer. Bruce Rowland was drafted in to replace him on drums and it was with this lineup that Fairport made their next appearance in the Manchester area at the University of Science and Technology. This time, I was ready.

I'd fully absorbed the tunes on *Rising For The Moon* and was absolutely prepared for whatever Fairport had to offer. I wasn't disappointed. Kicking off with 'Dirty Linen', the setlist included a whole chunk of *Rising…*, with the album's title track, 'One More Chance', 'Stranger To Himself' and Trevor's magnificent 'Restless' and 'Iron Lion' all making an appearance. They raided the vaults for a few older tunes too: Sandy gave us a heart-stopping 'Tam Lin', 'Sloth' had one of its many airings and the *Nine* album was represented by 'The Hexhamshire Lass' and 'Brilliancy Medley'. I absolutely loved it and, to cap it all, I discovered for the first time what a genial, personable chap Dave Pegg really is, when I was able to chat with him in the venue's bar after the show. Our conversation was interrupted by a friend, a very attractive young lady named Sonja, who threw her arms around Peggy, kissed him passionately – and then asked him who he was!

From that night on, I've been a true devotee to the Fairport cause. The number of Fairport shows I've attended since those very early days is now well into the hundreds. More gigs in Manchester followed, including a surreal affair at the City's Royal Exchange Theatre in November 1977 – a venue that resembled a brick-bound spaceship. I surreptitiously recorded the show on a portable cassette machine and I still give the old worn tape the occasional spin. During the *Farewell* tour in 1979, flyers had been left on the seats in the various hall and auditoriums the band visited, drawing our attention to 'one final show' that would take place on 4th August at Pewitt Farm, in Cropredy, Oxfordshire. And we all know what happened next, don't we?

MUSIC HALL
20 OCTOBER 1975, ABERDEEN, UK

DAVID FRANCIS

My first time seeing Fairport was at a packed Aberdeen Music Hall. I had kind of lost touch with the band post *Full House* so wasn't sure what to expect. They played a lot of material from *Rising for the Moon* which I loved at first hearing. I went out the next morning and bought the album, which remains a favourite to this day. I was a Cropredy regular in the eighties but got out of the habit of going until finding my way back in 2017. I don't intend to get out of the habit again!

UNIVERSITY OF YORK
24 OCTOBER 1975, YORK, UK

NIGEL BANKS

The return of Sandy Denny to the fold in 1974 added another dimension and I was to see the *Rising For The Moon* lineup twice, first at the De Montfort Hall, Leicester where I was doing my teacher training year and then at York University in October '75. I had literally passed my driving test the day before, so my first proper solo journey behind the wheel was the 30 miles or so from the village of Fitzwilliam, where my digs were, to the city of York. There was no satnav in those days, of course, so it was a voyage of discovery following a map and signposts. I hadn't booked a ticket beforehand in case I failed my test but fortunately there were a few spare seats. The support act was the solo singer Bryn Haworth and this would be (thought I didn't know it at the time) the last time I would see Sandy Denny perform live and be able to hear her glorious voice. A memory to be treasured but also with a tinge of sadness.

THEATRE ROYAL DRURY LANE
26 OCTOBER 1975, LONDON, UK

PHIL COOPER

I have seen Fairport several times, starting in London in 1975. It was a great show that opened with 'Dirty Linen' and went from there. I also saw Richard and Linda Thompson at the same venue the following month. And I saw Dave Swarbrick playing with Alan Stivell at the Royal Albert Hall the night before I was to fly back to the US.

In 1982, I saw Swarb and Simon Nicol at Holstein's in Chicago. The live version of 'Sí Bheag, Sí Mhór' on the *Swarb!* Free Reed set was recorded that night. The next time I saw Fairport was at the 1987 WFMT Folk Festival in Chicago. I got to talk backstage with Dave Pegg and Maart because I was also performing there in some workshops. And I saw them again a couple years later at Biddy Mulligan's in Chicago when *Red & Gold* was released. We were at the bar, about eight feet from the band. The last time I saw them was when they played an acoustic set at Fitzgerald's in the Chicago suburbs (I forget the year).

I also saw them doing a Swarbrick remembrance workshop at the *Old Songs Folk Festival* a couple years later in upstate New York, but missed their main stage set. Along the way, I got to see Swarb and Martin Carthy in St Louis in the early 1990s. I never thought I'd see that (I loved the early albums). We drove down from Chicago to catch that.

FOLK FAIRPORT

15 DECEMBER 1975, AMSTERDAM, THE NETHERLANDS

GERARD BOUMAN

By December 1975, our little folk band was really into Fairport. We read that they were going to play the Carre Theatre in Amsterdam. In those days there was a music pub in Amsterdam located on the Prinsengracht called Folk Fairport and named after the band. Whenever Fairport played in Amsterdam, mostly at the Paradiso, they would go down to Folk Fairport for a drink after the gig and often played an acoustic set on the tiny stage there. The guys from our band wanted to see Fairport up close in this small pub. But we had a dilemma. If we went to the concert at the Carre Theatre the pub would probably be packed by the time we arrived. We decided not to go to the gig at the Carre Theatre and instead headed straight to the Folk Fairport pub, where we got a table right opposite the stage. That meant we had to sit and wait from about eight o'clock until eleven o'clock or later for the band to arrive. That was a lot of beers.

Finally, they did arrive: Sandy, Swarb, Peggy, Trevor, Jerry and Paul Warren, as Dave Mattacks had left the band by then. When Fairport took the stage they played some stuff from the *Gottle o'Geer* album that they were working on as well as some fiddle tunes, some other Fairport songs and some Fotheringay songs. I had a small cassette recorder and was recording the music as well as the people singing along and cheering. I remember Swarb saying to the guy behind the bar, 'While we're waiting for Sandy, can we have a few more beers up here, cock?'

VICTORIA PALACE
6 JUNE 1976, LONDON, UK

JOHN MCGETTIGAN

The years leading up to 1976 had been a strange time for Fairport. There had been the *Gottle O'Geer* album (no comment) and it was difficult to know who, if anyone, was in the band. Then an advert appeared in the music press announcing a gig at one of the West End theatres. I think bands played on Sunday evenings when the current production was having its day off. I duly attended and sat through a not unpleasant support band. Following the break, the lights changed and onto the stage walked Dave Swarbrick, Dave Pegg, Simon Nicol and Bruce Rowland. Apart from a change of drummer, it was the *Angel Delight* lineup. They played a great set consisting of old and new material. 'Oh joy,' I said. 'They have returned.'

PAVILION THEATRE
25 JULY 1976, TORQUAY, UK

SUSAN BASKETT

My mum and I shared the same taste in music and we were both fans. We used to go to gigs together and my dad would come to the station for us to collect us afterwards. I always liked that music going back to the seventies, bands like Steeleye Span and Fairport Convention. Mum and I used to play air fiddle to 'Walk Awhile'! We used to think Swarbrick was so agile. He was quite small in stature and he reminded me of a male version of dancers on a musical box, because he would be spinning around and dancing about. He played with absolute ease.

It was always an ambition to get to see them, but living in a village and working for low pay in catering meant I never did. But then an auntie on my mum's side went off to Torquay with her boss and they set up some holiday flatlets. We went to see her, although we didn't stay with my auntie because we wanted to be able to let our hair down a bit. Sadly, it rained most of the week and it didn't turn out to be the holiday that we had hoped for. We were about to go home at the end of the week – we were planning on going home a bit early – and we were walking around Torquay because the weather had brightened up a little bit. We just happened to pass by the Pavilion Theatre and, lo and behold, 'Oh look, Fairport Convention.' They were on that actual night, and I said, 'I've always wanted to go and see them'. That was the first time and it was absolutely marvellous.

I always fancied playing the fiddle and I bought a secondhand one at a folk festival. It was obviously in the wrong case but I restrung it. However, I live in a mid-terrace house and was afraid of upsetting the neighbours so I never really mastered it. I could only really play 'Three Blind Mice'. Life got in the way and it's been stuck in the corner ever since. A friend came round and saw it and said 'can you play it?' and I said 'not really'. 'Go on, play it. Play it!' they said. So I picked it up and started playing and I thought I did quite well and they said, 'Oh you're right. You can't play it!' So that was the end of that.

The second time I went to see them was at Warwick Folk Festival. I was living in Wales then and I was going to stay with my parents, between Stratford and Evesham, after the concert. I went to work really early to get done so I could get finished early and get on the train and go straight through from Llandrindod Wells to Warwick.

I had a front row seat at the festival, but because I'd been up since the absolute crack of dawn I was quite tired. And I was so tired that when they went into a slow number I started to drift off. They must have noticed because they played 'Matty Groves' and the bit where they go 'Get up! Get up!' was so loud I jumped up in the air! I could see by their expressions that they'd noticed that I'd nodded off.

The next time I saw them was after Dave Swarbrick had sadly passed away. They were on at the Regal Cinema in Evesham. It was a very good concert but I did miss Dave Swarbrick.

LEEDS POLYTECHNIC
5 NOVEMBER 1976, LEEDS, UK

NIGEL BANKS

In 1976, the band lineup had changed once more and FC were now a four-piece again, Simon Nicol having been enticed back into the band. Like the rest of the audience, I witnessed the baring of four pairs of FC buttocks (with four arses pressed against the window and 'FAIRPORT' spelt out letter by letter on each buttock). This being a Yorkshire audience, however, the response seemed to be a mixture of bemusement and underwhelmed-ness. So much so, that when the band returned to do an encore, Simon was forced to ask whether we had actually noticed the trouble they had gone to, or had it all been in vain. I fear that for many of the spectators, it was the latter.

CHORLEY WAKES FESTIVAL, PARK HALL
15 – 17 JULY 1977, CHARNOCK RICHARD, UK

RALPH JONES

They played twice, first in the afternoon and then following day in the evening. At the afternoon show, Dave Swarbrick told fans near the front of the stage that if they swam across the small pond near the stage, he would give them his shirt. They did this repeatedly until he was left playing the violin in just his underpants. Incredible shows, wonderful memories.

(Editor's note: Swarb offered the shirt Simon was wearing to whoever jumped into the lake, and so Simon had to partially disrobe, despite not having been consulted nor warned. At the end of the next number, he returned the favour by offering Swarb's jeans to the next aquabat: fortunately the game stopped there with honours even. Swarb had to borrow some trousers from a starnger backstage afterwards – Simon had a spare shirt for the onward journey.)

STEPHEN BRIGHTMAN

Along with a bunch of post-schoolfriends, I got into Fairport around '74 or '75. I'm not sure of the exact origin of our interest but I do remember the big part that *The History Of...* double album played in this. This was like something we'd never heard before; bright and fresh and brash and different – although it could still sit nicely alongside and complement the current wave of English prog and metal that we were also absorbing at the time (my supergroup would have been Peter Gabriel on vocals, Keith Emerson on keyboards, Jan Ackerman on guitar and Swarb on the fiddle – now there's a dream...). We worked backwards from *The History Of…* to discover all the earlier stuff we'd been missing. We'd organise discos where instead of the usual Glam or Disco stuff, you might hear 'Smoke On The Water' followed by a rollicking Status Quo bop and rounded off with 'Fiddlesticks' or 'Sir B'.

I got to see Swarb in Manchester Uni in November of '77. I was into writing poetry (OK, verse) at the time, and I had to turn down a bonfire party for my first chance to see my new hero. I remember my apology letter clearly:

...for providence dictates my hero,
mighty Swarb, tonight is turning
out to play the role of Nero
fiddling while Chorlton's burning.

We got to the Charnock Richard July Wakes Festival in '77 and that was a true blast. It was mostly incredible weather and was a mixture of all my British Isles folk heroes – Five Hand Reel, the Bothy Band – topped off by Fairport. This was the now infamous on-stage striptease gig and I still proudly show off my 'Swarb in his underpants' t-shirt that I had made from the one tiny 110 film print I'd managed to keep through the years.

Then we heard the end was nigh and luckily got word of, and tickets for, the Farewell gig in Cropredy in '79. Five or six of us hitched down, lured by the promise of not only Fairport's final gig but also a tanker of Theakston's. Others have documented the 'festival' itself, so I'll just tell one little story of my friend Josephine. I came back to our tents mid-afternoon to some kind of hubbub, which was thankfully by then dying down. It turned out a tree had fallen right on top of Josephine's tent, and there was panic for a while as her boots were poking out of it. Luckily, it turned out she wasn't attached to them. She went to the management and they said sorry and gave her 60 quid for a new tent (things were simpler in those days...).

In the following years, I moved to Ireland and really drifted apart from Fairport (though never in my musical heart). Then when I retired early, in 2011, I realised Cropredy was still going and decided to check it out. I can honestly say that from the moment I arrived in Cropredy village it was a strange feeling of déjà vu, as if I was coming home, and I knew almost instantly that this was to be my annual pilgrimage (as it has indeed been since, apart from the Covid years). I find it hard to describe to anyone who hasn't been what Cropredy is, or means, or what the attraction is, and many I've spoken to there have said the same. It just has a special secret magic of its own.

I want to thank Fairport in all their incarnations for being such a big part of my musical life, and especially to Swarb for turning me into a folkie, for which I'm eternally grateful.

CROPREDY VILLAGE FETE, PRESCOTE MANOR
23 JULY 1977, CROPREDY, UK

ANDY MACLEOD

I had just split up with my long-term girlfriend and was in the final process of converting an old VW van into a camper. I picked up the latest edition of *Melody Maker* and came across an advert in the back pages for a village fete and evening concert by Fairport Convention at a place called Cropredy in Oxfordshire. I was intrigued. A few days later I was headed off up the A34 into the unknown!

I arrived at Prescote Manor around lunchtime and was greeted at the gate by an old rustic gent sporting a very natty denim waistcoat adorned with some embroidered signatures which he proudly informed me were the members of Fairport who had signed it for him. I enquired about where I might camp and he suggested behind a large wall as there was no official camping site. I thanked him and offered to buy him a pint later and asked his name. ''Arold,' he said in a lovely old Oxfordshire accent. This turned out to be Harold Wells and we later became firm friends for many years after I often stopped at his cottage in Williamscot for a cup of tea and to skin a few rabbits. Some years later, he appeared on the band's *Gladys' Leap* album reading the intro to 'Bird From The Mountain'. A true local character and lovely bloke.

I parked up and was settling down in my van for a cup of tea when I heard voices and sat in wonderment as Peggy, Simon, Bruce and Swarb walked past with a photographer in tow, preparing for some publicity shots only few feet away. I could barely believe my eyes. What was it about this place? Maybe some of them lived around here?

Later in the afternoon, I walked up to the village and recognised the Brasenose pub from the cover of the *Nine* album and headed for the fete, where Peggy was strolling around. I think that was the first time ever that I spoke to him to say how much I was looking forward to seeing the band again that night. He was warm and friendly and seemed genuinely surprised that I had travelled up from Portsmouth to see them.

As evening approached, a couple of hundred people gathered on the lawn of the manor house where a stage had been assembled on the patio. The music started as the supporting acts got the crowd warmed up. I made my way over to the bar in search of a beer and could not quite believe it as Sandy Denny got there just before me. I was tongue-tied and only managed a quick smile as she got her drinks and disappeared off through a gate. Sadly, she did not appear on stage that night and that was the last time I ever saw her.

Fairport delivered a great performance with material mainly from the *Bonny Bunch Of Roses* album and it was great to have Simon back in the band. The beer and atmosphere were good and a brilliant night was had by a mix of Fairport fans and bemused locals. (Little did they know what was to come!)

As I packed up to leave the following morning, I saw that someone driving out had managed to demolish part of the toilet tent as a couple of Elsans lay on their side amongst the debris. Things have improved much these days, and today's festival has in my opinion the finest facilities bar none.

In the years that have followed, I have faithfully made that journey up to Cropredy each and every year, and I'm proud to say I haven't missed one festival since that day. It dawned on me on that first visit that this really was a special place indeed, and looking back now it's where life-long friendships have since been kindled. Listening to the music out in the main arena, there can often be tears mixed with laughter as we remember absent friends and soak up the camaraderie. We then wait in anticipation for the moment that our favourite band take to the stage for the big Saturday night finale and the Fairport magic is cast around the arena.

(clockwise from top left) Ragnar Søberg (right) is a Cropredy regular & here at Gregers, Hamar, 17 October 2013 with Simon Nicol (Halgrim Øistad); Ragnar Søberg's wife Kristine was very pregnant at Cropredy in 1983; VTV filming at Cropredy 1982 (Howard Johnson); 1982 Cropredy video (Ian Burgess); Ragnar Søberg (left) with 'good man' Maart; Fairport at the Half Moon (Stephen Skey); Chris & Paul Wright (centre & right) filming a gig (Howard Johnson)

(clockwise from top left) Nic Dowding still has his 1982 t-shirt; Andy Leonard was digging the record bins for Peggy; Ian Broom (right) & late wife Heather would supply Simon with Bulmer's Number Seven (Ian Broom); Tony 'Bill' Hilzbrich was a Cropredy regular until he moved abroad; William Hayter was there in 1983; Tim Romain never seemed to be in the same car twice at Cropredy: Kenneth Wexler (left) with Simon Nicol in 1983

(clockwise from top left) William Hayter (left) playing table football with Fairport; William Hayer (right) playing table football with Fairport; Cropredy 1984 (three images: Gerard Bouman); Cropredy 1983 (William Hayter)

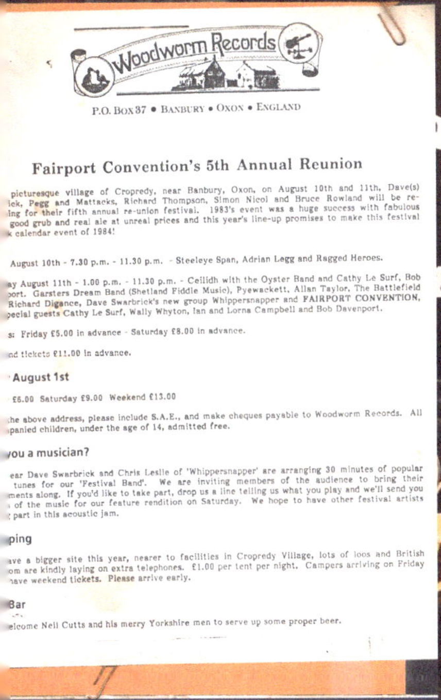

Woodworm Records

P.O. BOX 37 • BANBURY • OXON • ENGLAND

Fairport Convention's 5th Annual Reunion

picturesque village of Cropredy, near Banbury, Oxon, on August 10th and 11th, Dave(s) ick, Pegg and Mattacks, Richard Thompson, Simon Nicol and Bruce Rowland will be re- ing for their fifth annual re-union festival. 1983's event was a huge success with fabulous good grub and real ale at unreal prices and this year's line-up promises to make this festival k calendar event of 1984!

August 10th - 7.30 p.m. - 11.30 p.m. - Steeleye Span, Adrian Legg and Ragged Heroes.

ay August 11th - 1.00 p.m. - 11.30 p.m. - Ceilidh with the Oyster Band and Cathy Le Surf, Bob port. Garsters Dream Band (Shetland Fiddle Music), Pyewackett, Allan Taylor, The Battlefield Richard Digance, Dave Swarbrick's new group Whippersnapper and **FAIRPORT CONVENTION**, pecial guests Cathy Le Surf, Wally Whyton, Ian and Lorna Campbell and Bob Davenport.

s: Friday £5.00 in advance - Saturday £8.00 in advance.

nd tickets £11.00 in advance.

August 1st

£6.00 Saturday £9.00 Weekend £13.00

he above address, please include S.A.E., and make cheques payable to Woodworm Records. All panied children, under the age of 14, admitted free.

you a musician?

ear Dave Swarbrick and Chris Leslie of 'Whippersnapper' are arranging 30 minutes of popular tunes for our 'Festival Band'. We are inviting members of the audience to bring their ments along. If you'd like to take part, drop us a line telling us what you play and we'll send you of the music for our feature rendition on Saturday. We hope to have other festival artists part in this acoustic jam.

ping

ave a bigger site this year, nearer to facilities in Cropredy Village, lots of loos and British om are kindly laying on extra telephones. £1.00 per tent per night. Campers arriving on Friday have weekend tickets. Please arrive early.

Bar

elcome Neil Cutts and his merry Yorkshire men to serve up some proper beer.

(clockwise from top left) Cropredy 1984 (Gerard Bouman); Cropredy 1984 (Gerard Bouman); Cropredy 1984 (Gerard Bouman); Howard Johnson filmed several early Cropredys; Tony Rees was at Cropredy in 1982; Cropredy 1984 (Gerard Bouman)

STAFFAN WENNERLUND

Living in Sweden, I didn't get too many opportunities to see my favourite band, a band which I had been following since 1969, live. I had seen the *Live/Rising For The Moon* lineups with Sandy in 1974 and 1976 in Gothenburg, and the four-piece in Croydon while on a visit to London in 1976. So when in 1977 I read a notice in the *Melody Maker* saying that the band was going to play a concert in Cropredy in July, with all proceeds from the gig going towards a new roof for the Cropredy village hall, I immediately booked a stay in London.

On Saturday morning, July 23rd, I took the train to Banbury and hitched my way out to the then unknown (to me) village of Cropredy, only to find that the gates to the garden of the estate and gig area would not open until three o'clock. There was a nervous hour to wait until the gates opened. Would it be sold out and would I, in spite of all my efforts, not make it inside?

Finally, the entrance was manned, I paid my entrance fee and so I was one of the first to enter the area. I strolled around the garden, got myself a pint and lay down on the grass, resting my back against the hay bale. During the afternoon, I enjoyed the weather and the surroundings, watched different band members socialise in the sun, had another pint and made friends with two Daves studying in Oxford with whom I spent the rest of the evening.

It was a truly wonderful experience to watch the relaxed atmosphere and the familiarity of it all. When dusk came, I even stumbled across Sandy and Trevor, just arrived and on their way to the 'backstage area', such as it was. Neither of them joined the band on stage that night but Fairport Convention were on fire. It was a gig to remember for many reasons, and I will cherish it all my life.

FAIRFIELD HALLS
30 OCTOBER 1977, CROYDON, UK

IAN ASHLEIGH

I graduated from the glam rock of Slade and Alice Copper to Deep Purple, The Who, and Nazareth. I also dipped my toe into prog with ELP, Genesis and some Yes. Growing up in northwest London, Nicky Horne on Capital Radio was de rigueur with my schoolfriends and I, which informed our listening. Having a brother three years older than me with similar music tastes helped – until I went off at a tangent.

It was the summer of 1975 and we had completed our O levels. My friends wanted to go to the Harrow Granada to see the film *Pink Floyd: Live At Pompeii*, so peer pressure took me on the bus from Wembley to Harrow. I was bored rigid by the overrated, talentless quartet (my opinion!) but before that the cinema showed a film of Fairport Convention. I have a recollection of BJ Cole guesting on pedal steel (NB. it was Gordon Huntley), and I was captivated by the energy on stage, by the sounds, rhythms and melodies. I wanted to hear more and when my summary of the evening was the polar opposite to my friends, I thought I was going to be left stranded in Harrow with no chums at school. That didn't happen…

With the first pay from my summer job, I purchased the latest Fairport release, *Rising For The Moon*, and by the end of 1976 I had found the entire back catalogue except for *Rosie* and *Nine*. Not bad for the days before the internet. I had fallen in love with the band, and with folk music.

I passed my driving test in March 1977 and found some friends who also liked Fairport. We learned the words to 'The Eynsham Poacher' and one of them had an original pressing of 'Babbacombe' Lee. We discovered that the band were playing at the Fairfield Halls in Croydon, not exactly close to my home in Wembley. My dad agreed I could drive the family Hillman Hunter across London (pre-M25) and helped me plan the route (pre-satnav).

There we were with Simon, Peggy, Swarb and Bruce Rowland on stage in front of us. It was magic and an upbeat set. We left our seats and danced at the front of the stage with lots of others. I remember Simon sang 'Flowers Of The Forest' whilst sitting with a dulcimer on his lap, and I guess 'Matty Groves' and 'Walk Awhile' were in the set.

Alan Freeman was on Radio 1 at the time and someone asked for Fairport on his pre-Christmas request show. It was a thrill to hear 'General Taylor' on the radio.

I recall a gig for Capital Radio on a lovely evening at the Open Air Theatre in Regent's Park, a perfect setting for the band. Simon definitely sang 'Flowers Of The Forest' that night, and Bruce played bass on 'Bridge Over the River Ash'. I was left wondering if he could play bass or did Peggy teach it to him. (I had 'Bridge Over The River Ash' as the ringtone on my phone for years. It rang while I was at the Register Office registering my father's passing. How incongruous it was.

My oldest friend, Lance, was at Chelsea College where Fairport played a gig on their farewell tour gig. It was the only time my best friend saw my favourite band. Lance was summoned to 'head office' in February 2023. His wife, Sue, will be joining us at Cropredy 2024. Lance will be there in spirit, as he was in 2023 when we all sang 'Meet On The Ledge' just before midnight on his birthday (12th August).

And then there is Cropredy.

In Spring 1978 I acquired a Hillman Imp and that summer I went with my friends to the one-day Cropredy. That was the year I saw Bruce arrive in an old Austin Maxi with his drum kit in the back. (Earl Okin played that year, I think.) It was at one of those early one-day events that Bruce Lacey turned up and proceeded to undress in the middle of the field. The early events were much less formal that they are today.

From 1979 to 1982, I regularly met some university friends at Cropredy, and then had a gap until 1987. And then a very big gap until 2014, when I took my daughter for two of the three days. In 2015, my partner came with me, and it has been a fixture in our calendar ever since. Our ritual is to purchase the t-shirt as my birthday present on Thursday and I wear it on the Saturday of the festival. My birthday is on 10th August, and it is so nice of the band to invite 20,000 people to my birthday weekend.

I now live in Sussex and Fairport play regularly play at our local venue. One such evening was 13th October 2020, which is Simon's birthday. By coincidence, we had a late autumn week away in Suffolk in 2023 and went to see the band in Aldeburgh on 2nd November, which is Peggy's birthday, and he enjoyed a pre-gig pint or two of Adnam's Ghost Ship in the same pub we were in.

From a 15-year-old schoolboy to a soon-to-be 65-year-old (in August 2024) grandfather, one band has been there every step of the way. That band is called Fairport Convention.

UNIVERSITY OF NOTTINGHAM
19 NOVEMBER 1977, NOTTINGHAM, UK

MIKE BALL

I had a couple of Fairport albums in my collection but catching them live always seemed to elude me for some reason and so it wasn't until 1977, when they were promoting the *Bonny Bunch Of Roses* album, that I finally got to see them. I dragged my pal Alan along to Nottingham University. I say 'dragged' as he wasn't a fan of Fairport or the folk/rock genre at all. I'm not sure how it happened (!) but by the time Fairport appeared on stage we were both a little the worse for wear and I have very little recollection of the gig or the set list. All I remember is some crazy dancing in front of the stage to the jigs and reels.

After the guys left the stage, Alan and I decided that it was time to head home. We didn't leave by the main exit but instead headed down a corridor at the side of the stage. Who should be there to greet us as we headed down the corridor but the legendary Mr Pegg, beer in one hand and a cigarette in the other. He said hello to us and asked us if we had enjoyed the music. Of course, we said we'd had a great time, despite not being able to remember most of the set.

We were talking drunken nonsense to Peggy for a couple of minutes when Swarb poked his head around the dressing room door. Peggy told him to get us a couple of beers, as if we hadn't had enough already, but we weren't going to refuse a drink with a couple of legends like Peggy and Swarb. I remember them being very nice to us and wishing us a safe journey home. We eventually make it back home to Mansfield, although just how is a bit of a blur.

I've followed the band ever since, attending countless gigs around the country, and I've been to Cropredy a few times. I've met Peggy subsequently and told him about our drunken encounter after that Nottingham University gig. Sadly, he doesn't remember meeting us.

But it's a great memory and one I cherish as my old friend Alan, who was converted to Fairport after that night, passed away in 2022.

ALTHORP FOLK CLUB
SPRING 1978, ALTHORP, UK

DAVE CLEMO

For the next eighteen months I played very loud rock music. Our band played mainly original songs but was caught in the cusp between prog rock and the emerging punk revolution. My record purchases included *Fairport Live Convention* and the Richard Thompson double album *guitar, vocal*. I spent an inordinate amount of time listening to that and trying to figure out what he was playing. (I've since given up on that. His playing is beyond fathomable. He seems to have more than his fair share of fingers for a start.)

After the demise of my rock band, I decided to form a Top 40 covers band to play the local clubs. Our drummer turned out to be a Fairport fan as well, and one evening, either in late 1977 or early 1978, we trooped out to a pub in Althorp (a village between Northampton and Daventry) to see a performance by Dave Pegg and Trevor Lucas at the folk club based there. The room was packed. It was standing room only. I became aware of a woman behind me. It was Sandy Denny and she was drunk and heckling her husband Trevor on the stage. They lived a few miles away in a village called Byfield. A few weeks later we heard the awful news that Sandy had died from injuries caused by a fall down stairs.

Work, family and changing circumstances have meant that I rarely go to concerts these days. I remember taking a musician friend to a Fairport concert in the 2000s. We sat together, mesmerised by the incredible sounds coming from the stage. He turned to me, grinning from ear to ear. I think he got it. He got what Fairport is all about.

I've also seen RT in concert a couple of times. Once was back in 2007 when he toured the UK to promote his album *Sweet Warrior*, and the other was a concert in Northampton with Danny Thompson on double bass. The sound they made was incredible, seamless, like a single instrument. To be honest, it was too much. After over 50 years of playing catch up, I'm still just as far behind. There's only so much discouragement one can take.

SANDY DENNY DIES

21 APRIL 1978, WIMBLEDON, LONDON, UK

Sandy Denny dies without regaining consciousness after a fall two days earlier.

STATE THEATER

1978, EASTON, PENNSYLVANIA

TODD VOLPE

It was 1970 and I was a senior in high school close to graduation. There were parties wherever parents were missing for whatever reason. Many of us were smoking pot for the first time and the beer was flowing. It was at the aftermath of a party and the home was deserted except for one neighbour commandeering the stereo in the morning with the volume cranked. It was 'Walk Awhile' from the recently released *Full House*. I barged into the house and demanded to know who was this group playing on the box? My friend said, 'Fairport Convention, haven't you heard them?'

In the States there were FM radio stations that were playing the usual British Invasion stuff but only certain DJs like Michael Tearson were playing lesser-known bands like Fairport. My friend sat me down to listen to Fairport's previous albums and I was hypnotised, and bowled over. The music was sublime. I listened intensely for years but was naïve and missed the few appearances in my area over the years until my friends and I finally got tickets to see Fairport, Steeleye Span and Pentangle! We were so excited and I was so naïve that I thought I would get to see Sandy.

The day finally came and we all got fired up for the show and when we got there, there was the word in large letters across the marquee – 'cancelled'. We were stunned and soon came to find out about Sandy's passing was the reason. We drove home in stunned silence. I got married that year and had some kids and turned my daughter on at a young age to Sandy. She has been into Sandy ever since, has a nice voice and sings Sandy very well.

Over the years I have tried to glean anything Fairport I could to try and keep up. I've been hoping beyond hope that they would do a US tour and play the Sellersville Theater in Sellersville, PA. Recently I learned that the boys played in Sellersville back in 2004. I can't believe I missed it.

CROPREDY VILLAGE FETE

15 JULY 1978, CROPREDY, UK

GRAHAM WARREN

There used to be a village fete in Cropredy and I recall Ralph McTell trying to win a goldfish and several folks, who were later on stage at the back of Prescote Manor, being in the crowd – the Ian Campbell Folk Group, Earl Okin etc. And during Fairport's set a fight broke out at the front and Swarb stopped the music telling them to pack it in. 'It's not a bloody Rolling Stones concert.' Much fab music and many pints later it's still happening, which is brilliant. I've not missed a festival since 1978.

SUNDERLAND POLYTECHNIC

19 MAY 1979, SUNDERLAND, UK

ED WALLAGE

It was with a degree of sadness and sentiment that I went along to what had been announced as Fairport's farewell tour in 1979. I had been a Fairport fan since the late sixties and had seen all of the various lineups since 1970. I had grown up following them through their notoriously turbulent lineup changes. These had included the sublime *Nine* format with Sandy, and some perhaps better left glossed over… At the time, many bands were often never together for more than a few years. Fairport were relatively longstanding (in name at least) and it was therefore not unexpected that their time had come. The 1979 lineup consisted of hardcore members Simon and Daves Pegg and Swarbrick, along with Bruce Rowland.

I was a keen photographer at the time, so camera in hand I confidently wandered around the side of the stage; security was clearly not an issue at the time! I remember chatting briefly with Simon at the end and thanking him for the pleasure Fairport had given me over the years. There was a flyer advertising a forthcoming album of this farewell tour. This was to be a limited edition LP, available by mail order only. I duly sent off my cheque and received this collector's item. (I subsequently felt somewhat disappointed when it was re-released; however I know I have the real thing!)

It was sad to think it was all over, and I often wonder what became of them…

FAREWELL FAIRPORT, CROPREDY FESTIVAL
4 AUGUST 1979, CROPREDY, UK

NIGEL BANKS

Come the spring of 1979 and I was living in Cumbria. I had read that Fairport had finally decided to call it a day and were doing a farewell tour. The nearest venue on the tour was the King George's Hall in Blackburn, an hour's drive away. It took my brother and I a while to park up and find the venue and the support act had already started, so we went to the bar instead. We happened to see a flyer on a table advertising a special weekend event that August in a village called Cropredy, of which I'd never heard. As it would take place during the school summer holidays and we had relatives in Woodstock (Oxfordshire) who could put us up, I suggested on a whim that we make the pilgrimage for what was anticipated to be the band's last ever live appearance.

Little did I realise that it would be the start of a 45-year connection with a place and a festival that has gone from strength to strength and seen the revival of the band on a permanent basis from 1985 onwards, as well as giving me and thousands of others the opportunity to see a mind-bogglingly wide range of other musical acts from traditional folk, blues, country and prog rock to punk, reggae and morris dancing – to name but a few!

My memories of that first official gathering in '79 are fleeting. The weather was warm and sunny, and the stage primitive and somewhat ramshackle by today's standards. The beer was from the nearby Hook Norton brewery and the only other act I can recall playing that day was Steve Ashley, accompanied by Chris Leslie. I'm ashamed to say that I can't even remember what songs Fairport played. I know there would have been a big lump in the throat when they encored with 'Meet On The Ledge' at the end. We trudged back to the car assuming that that was it: Farewell Fairport.

Except, of course, it wasn't. Twelve months later, we were back again for more of the same. But the weather was chilly and damp, and the beer wasn't as good this time. But on the plus side Richard and Linda Thompson were there, so the familiar Strat would be lending weight to some classic stuff from the *Full House* days. I do remember that the sound system was playing up and making some very rude noises. So much so that Linda begged the techies to sort it out for the next number, 'A Heart Needs A Home'.

It was at the end of the evening that Simon uttered the now famous words 'same time next year?' We dared to hope that the spirit of FC was still alive and kicking, even if it wasn't a fully functioning band anymore.

TIM EDMONDS

In 1979 I was living and working in London, with plenty of opportunities to get to concerts by various versions of the ever-changing Fairport Convention. My parents were living just seven miles from Cropredy at Marston St Lawrence and with the news of the *Farewell* event there it was a no-brainer to visit the family for the weekend of 4th August 1979. My younger brother Andrew was living there while a student at Rycotewood College, Thame. Although a Fairport virgin, he was keen to come along too and my father kindly lent us his Hillman Imp to get there and back.

The weather was fine and there were no traffic problems as we followed the directions in our programme/admission tickets, purchased by post in advance for £2.50 each, passing through the village and down Station Road. Andrew recalls turning left and going down a lane by the railway bridge and I don't remember any problems with parking. The site used, known as Pewet or Pewet Farm (Pewet is an old form of Peewit) is on the opposite side of the canal from where the festival is now held, although it is now used as one of the car parks. There were the essentials of a bar (Theakstons) and a wine bar, plus various food and retail outlets but rather inadequate mobile toilets. Andrew comments that it was very relaxed, without lots of barriers or people in reflective jackets, and it certainly had a friendly atmosphere. The stage was basic, with scaffolding built around farm trailers and tarpaulins draped over the top, but mercifully the weather behaved so they were not tested by rain.

The music started at four o'clock with some familiar and some unfamiliar support acts to keep us entertained. Many were locally-based, including a youthful Chris Leslie playing a short set with Steve Ashley, but Fairport were late arriving since they were opening the bill at Knebworth. Their set came late in the evening and included guest slots for Ralph McTell and Maddy Prior. For Andrew, the highlight was Dave Swarbrick's solo in 'Sloth', played on his see-through electric violin, loudly amplified and with reverb. Awesome! For me it was the closing 'Meet on the Ledge'. The first and possibly the only previous time I had heard it performed was at my first ever Fairport concert back in February 1969. I thought that performance in 1979 it would be the last time – little did I know!

Despite enjoying the Theakstons, we managed to negotiate the country lanes back to Marston St Lawrence afterwards, but neither of us can remember who was driving

A DAY IN THE COUNTRY, CROPREDY FESTIVAL
30 AUGUST 1980, CROPREDY, UK

BOB BATTERSBY

I caught Fairport Convention on their last tour, but missed the 1979 'Farewell, Farewell' event at Cropredy. In 1980 I had moved to London and heard about the first reunion tour so decided to head out West. I packed a rucksack, took the Tube out to Manor Royal and stuck my thumb out into the A4. Several lifts later I got to Banbury and then had my last ride in the back of a Morris Minor pickup as far as Williamscot.

As I began to walk down the road towards Cropredy, I thought that it looked a bit quiet for a festival and thought that it must be out the other side of the village. As I reached the canal I popped into the village stores and asked where the festival was. The lady behind the counter gave me an indulgent smile and said 'it's here, next weekend.' My then girlfriend was rather surprised to see me arrive back at our flat later that afternoon.

The following weekend I repeated the journey and had a rare old time, rather too much Hooky, and spent half of the night asleep under a hedge near one of the Oxford roundabouts, where I lost a rather nice hat, before resuming my journey back to Wimbledon.

The following year I was living in Oxford and not only had I picked the right weekend but had a lift there and back from my landlady. I somehow managed to talk my way backstage (this was before Moira and her team of gate guardians!) and had nice chat with Dave Swarbrick and asked Richard Thompson, to my undying mortification, if he was still a Muslim. You can imagine the look I got. I then ended up side of stage – it was a very small one back then – taking pictures of a reunion lineup that included Richard Thompson and Judy Dyble.

I somehow missed few years (work got in the way) before returning in 1985 and seeing the inimitable Neil Innes. After that I moved away to darkest Sussex, and Cropredy and I didn't meet up again until 1997.

I had taken some pictures of the Albion Band in Tunbridge Wells and supplied one to Chris Leslie for his forthcoming solo CD. Out of the blue I got a call saying that Chris had joined Fairport and could they use my picture as a PR shot.

I can't remember the exact sequence of events, but that led to me getting a Cropredy Press Pass, which in turn got me a commission to review and photograph the festival for *Mojo* magazine, which was the start of twentyfive years standing in the pit, and occasionally on stage, taking photographs for various music magazines. Over the years I have met most of my heroes, interviewed quite a few of them, been entertained backstage by Frank Skinner, hugged by Robert Plant and got to use the nice loos with the hot water.

Sadly my attendance ended with Covid, but I still have the memories.

STEPHEN & FRANCES ROYSTON

We have been going to the Cropredy Festival almost every year since 1980. We were there when it was held at Broughton Castle. We were childless for our first few festivals. James and Emma were born in 1984 and 1988 respectively, and our grandson Idris in 2018. James has come to many Cropredy festivals with us. He once travelled overland from Hong Kong to Cropredy, via the Trans-Siberian Railway. Emma has been almost every year. Idris made his festival debut in 2022. We used to camp at the festival every year. In the mid-nineties we came to Cropredy in a hired narrowboat for a couple of years, in the days when it was relatively easy to moor close to the centre of the village. Since then, we have been lucky enough to make friends with a village family and we have stayed in their home in the centre of the village ever since.

BROUGHTON CASTLE

14 & 15 AUGUST 1981, BROUGHTON, UK

NICK SKILTON

I first became aware of Fairport Convention in the late seventies, when I was in a 'refreshed' state in a flat in Brighton, with my then girlfriend, visiting her sister. They had an album on, *Morris On*, and, as a budding drummer, I was fascinated by Dave Mattacks. I had never heard a drummer 'speak' to me in such a way. His snare work and sound in particular were the best I'd ever heard (I'm not a fan of fussy drummers). Determined to find out more, I discovered that at one time he had played with a band called Fairport Convention. A friend had *'Babbacombe' Lee* and I was instantly hooked.

I wanted to see DM live, didn't care who with and learned via *Melody Maker* about their new reunion in Cropredy. This was 1980. But when I found out where Cropredy was, I decided to give it a miss as it was (to me) a long way away. However, the urge didn't disappear, so in 1981 me and my friend Steve made plans to go to Broughton Castle. Unable to find any information in that pre-internet age, I called a Banbury record shop. 'Sorry mate,' he said, 'I don't know anything about any Fairport reunions.' Great!

We made the trip up anyway, having got the dates from somewhere. When we got there, we were sold the tickets at the entrance by a lady I now know was Chris Pegg. I already knew who Dave Pegg was, being a massive Jethro Tull fan. I could go on forever about that weekend (we forgot our tent and had to kip in the back of my small van) and how it changed my life.

I saw every *Wintour* until Maart left – fewer since – and have attended every festival from 1981 to 2023 except the Covid two and 2016 (van broke down), 2018 (didn't fancy it for some reason) and 2022 (god daughter's wedding).

I changed my style of drumming. Steve and I formed a new band in the FC style (we're still going!), I've met all the band over the years (and had some riotous evenings with Peggy, but who hasn't?) and the girlfriend I mentioned earlier went out with DM for a bit (probably best not to mention that?). I met my wife thanks to FC (28 years, and counting), and I've got hammered with Johnny Jones more than once. On buying a shirt from him: 'Will it fit me, John?' 'It would fit fucking Alfred Hitchcock!'

NIGEL BANKS

In 1981 I attended the Broughton Castle festival with my then partner. It seemed a much more ambitious and expansive affair than the Cropredys of the previous two years. It was held over two days and the grounds of the castle were properly tended, not in some farmer's field. I remember seeing the short-lived 'supergroup' The GPs (Mattacks, McTell, Pegg and Thompson) and later being able to re-live some of the highlights of Fairport's set via the *Moat On The Ledge* live album released on Woodworm Records.

I missed the next couple of reunions but was back at Cropredy for most of the rest of the decade. In all since then I've attended about twenty times – I'm not a completist, I'm afraid! I regret missing out on some of the classic acts that have graced the stage there. On the other hand, I've managed to see some memorable acts such as Steve Winwood, Procol Harum, 10cc (three times), The Strawbs (Dave Cousins' final live performance last year was magical) – and who could forget Alice Cooper?

Specific memories of golden moments include Iain Matthews, Christine Collister, Clive Gregson and Richard Thompson performing a spell-binding a capella version of 'Woodstock' in 1986, Richard Thompson's guitar string breaking in 1989 and him saying, 'Okay folks, it's community singing time,' and leading the whole field in a rousing rendition of 'Twist And Shout' whilst calmly re-stringing his guitar at the same time. And, of course the mass hankie waving at the end of Richard Digance's Saturday slot.

Over and above all the fabulous music that we Cropredeers are treated to, it's the special magical ambience that is created on that field every second weekend in August. Fairport Convention may not have achieved global commercial success in their 57-year (and counting) history but, as well as pioneering a specific genre of music and having a church bell cast with its name, the band has created a special place in the hearts of its loyal and devoted fans.

My dad once said, somewhat disparagingly, that following Fairport was my substitute for a religion. I thought that was an exaggeration, but Cropredy has definitely been a place of pilgrimage for me and thousands of other fans over the years – and long may that continue.

STEVE GERCKE

I first heard Fairport's music when I was only a young boy. My older brother would listen to BBC Radio 1 and tune into the John Peel Show which was broadcast on a Sunday afternoon. Peel always played an eclectic mix of music on his show and he really liked the sound that Fairport were making. (In those days, Fairport did a large number of radio sessions for the BBC.) My brother bought their first self-titled album when it came out. A few years later I purchased a Track Records compilation with artists including The Who, which also included Fairport's first single, 'If I Had A Ribbon Bow'. Even though I was still at primary school, I really appreciated what a great guitarist Richard Thompson was. It was not long before my brother brought their second album, *What We Did On Our Holidays*. I was always fascinated by the cover of that album.

My brother Mike loved the sound of Sandy Denny and bought all the Fairport albums she was featured on. *Unhalfbricking* was the first time I heard Dave Swarbrick and the sound he made from the fiddle was like something that I had never heard before. I was really pleased when he joined Fairport as a full-time member in August 1969.

The album which still stands up today as being the pinnacle of Fairport Convention's long career is *Liege & Lief*. I would look at the gatefold sleeve for what seemed like hours and I have never tired of playing the album from the first track, 'Come All Ye', a traditional song but arranged in such a unique way. 'The Medley – Lark In The Morning' had the hairs on the back of my neck standing on end.

My brother continued to buy Sandy Denny solo albums, but lost interest in Fairport when Sandy left. I did take him along to a Fairport gig in Guildford some years ago and Peggy announced his name from the stage as a fan from the band's early days. He really enjoyed seeing them again and acknowledged what amazing musicians they were.

I was devastated when I heard Fairport were disbanding in August 1979. I got tickets for their final tour and went to see them for what I thought would be the final time. The band were still magnificent, Peggy, Simon, Swarb and Bruce Rowland produced an amazing show. I ordered that final *Farewell, Farewell* album and was so pleased to see they hid a picture of Sandy in it.

In the early 1980s I was living in Waterloo in London and decided I would write a radio script of Fairport's history. I visited the offices of *Melody Maker* magazine and got to look up all the paper articles on the band, and album and gig reviews, I went to Islands Records to talk with staff at the label about Fairport. It was the day Bob Marley died, so the whole office was rushing around preparing and sending out press releases.

I also visited a number of record stores to purchase albums I didn't have like *Gottle O'Geer* and albums from past members including Iain Matthews, Ashley Hutchings with Steeleye Span, The Albion Band and Morris On, Richard Thompson solo and with Linda Thompson, Sandy Denny and the rock 'n' roll album The Bunch.

In 1980 I saw advertised through a Fairport newsletter that they were going to do a reunion at Cropredy. There was no stopping me from going. There was nothing like camping in a field and listening to the music from across the years of my favourite band, it was magic.

I returned a year later for another dose of Fairport medicine. There was little or no security so it was easy to go backstage and ask a member of the crew if I could interview one of the band for a radio show I was making. It was not long before I was introduced to Dave Pegg. We sat down on a couple of hay bales behind the stage and Peggy spoke to me about the history of the band for about an hour. I only had a notebook to make copious notes of everything Dave told me.

At one point, a chap walked up to us, said hello to Peggy and I was introduced to Gerry Conway who had come along to enjoy the day's music. Peggy asked Gerry if he was going to the bar, Gerry nodded and Peggy asked me if I wanted a beer, so Gerry Conway went and got Peggy and I a lovely cold beer each. I couldn't believe what was happening!

Living in London, I got the opportunity to interview Richard and Linda Thompson, prior to them releasing *Shoot Out The Lights*. They were recording a TV programme for the BBC called *A Little Night Music,* which was being recorded at the BBC's Maida Vale Studios. I went along to do the interview in their lunch break. I literally recorded the interview on cassette in the BBC canteen. The noise made it very difficult to hear and get a good recording! The Thompsons were joined on that occasion by a band made up of Peggy, Simon and DM. What a great time I had that day.

This all led to me putting together a radio script. Now living in Fareham in Hampshire, I decided to send off the script to BBC Radio Solent. Within a few days I had a call from one of their radio producers, Sibby, who presented a weekly folk programme. He asked if I had all the records I had mentioned in my script (which I did) and asked me to come into their studio in Southampton.

When I arrived, Sibby was busy in the studio. He said how impressed he was with the research and detail I had put into the script. After a few minutes he said, 'Let's do a sound check on the mic.' I looked at him and said, 'You want me to read the script? I thought you just wanted me to bring the records along.' He said, 'No, it is your show!' Fortunately, it was all being recorded and wasn't going out live. In the end we had to record it over two evenings and it was made into four programmes. And I got my name in the *Radio Times*! Sibby did offer it to BBC Radio 2 as he felt it was so good, but they decided they could do it themselves. It was many years before they did do anything on Fairport and then it was only one programme.

After this four-week stint on radio I was hooked, so I am indebted to Dave Pegg for his time and encouragement at that early Cropredy Festival. Since then, I have made many features for radio and for the last eleven years have presented my own radio show every week on Castledown FM, a local community radio station near where I live now in Wiltshire.

Over the years, I have presented a number of features on Fairport for various radio stations in the South of England. Some have been to give exposure to concerts whilst they were on tour or local festival appearances.

I heard from a fellow Fairport fan who was putting together a magazine, *The Ledge.* I wrote to Martyn offering help and he was pleased to accept articles from me about members of the band, previous members, and about albums and upcoming tours. I also carried out a number of interviews over the next couple of years and have interviewed nearly every member of Fairport: Ashley Hutchings, Simon Nicol, Richard Thompson, Judy Dyble, Iain Matthews, Dave Mattacks, Dave Swarbrick, Jerry Donahue, Trevor Lucus, Bruce Rowland, Dan Ar Bras, Ric Sanders, Maartin Allcock, Chris Leslie and Gerry Conway. It has been a pleasure to interview and talk with Ric, Chris, Peggy, Simon and DM. They are all such amazing musicians who have never taken their fans for granted.

I regret never meeting or interviewing Sandy Denny. The only time I saw her perform was with Fairport at the Fairfield Halls in Croydon in 1974, just prior to her re-joining Fairport. She came on for their encore and performed three songs, I was in heaven!

I also remember those early Winter Tours when Fairport got together again. They were being managed by Johnny Jones. He was such a lovely man and always welcomed me when I turned up at The Half Moon in London or came to see Fairport at Wimbledon Theatre. I used to also love his compering at Cropredy, where he would give all the football results in between the acts on stage.

The Cropredy Festival is a real credit to the band. They have grown it from its small beginnings under the direction of Chris and Dave Pegg to what it is today. Other artists who have appeared at Cropredy have told me they love the way that every detail is seen to, which enabled the artists to give the best possible performance on the day.

I can't imagine a day when Fairport Convention will not be performing, and it will be sad when Peggy, Simon, Chris and Ric are unable to do it anymore. However, their music will remain special forever. My hope is that future generations will listen and enjoy what this bunch of talented musicians have given us.

THE HALF MOON
10–12 AUGUST 1982, PUTNEY, LONDON, UK

STEPHEN SKEY

Friends and I went to see Swarb and Nicol do a gig at the Half Moon in Putney and had front row seats. From a previous gig, we remembered that Swarb made comment about the lack of libation and this gig was no different. So from under our chairs we produced a pint of Young's Ordinary for Simon and a large whisky for Dave. I would like to think there was a degree of laughter from the audience (it was a few years ago), but there were thanks from both Dave and Simon.

JIM BREEDS

A flustered Simon Nicol burst into the ladies toilet, to the surprise of my then girlfriend, who was in there at the time. 'Sorry about this,' he said. 'We're due back on stage and the queue for the gents is too long.'

RAGNAR SØBERG

It started with 'Si Tu Dois Partir' in 1969. I was 15, and this beautiful voice of Sandy singing an up-tempo, carefree French version of Bob Dylan's 'If You Gotta Go, Go Now' hit me full force. Then I got hold of the *History Of…* double album, four vinyl sides that made me *the* Fairport fan in my village of Rena in Norway.

My first Fairport Convention concert was at the Half Moon in Putney, one of three warm-up concerts before Cropredy 1982. My then wife and I brought over our car. We survived all the roundabouts from Newcastle to Picketts Lock in North London and headed for the pub. The small room was packed, sweaty and friendly, and we in the audience bought pints of beer and placed them on the low stage for the thirsty band to dispose of.

The next summer, 1983, I crossed the North Sea again with a bigger car, a large tent and a very pregnant wife – plus her brother. There were no folding chairs in sight, just beautiful weather, good beer, green grass and great music. Since then, I've gone to the festival numerous times either alone, with friends or with my dear wife Bente Sølvi. I've written a few reports from Cropredy in my local newspaper too.

On my 60th birthday, Fairport played the town of Hamar (15 miles from my doorstep) and somebody must have whispered something to the band. I ended up on the stage and made my first (and final) legendary performance with the band, providing backing vocals to Simon on 'Banks Of The Sweet Primroses'. A night to remember for eternity!

Thanks for all the fun and good music. Hope to see you again, lads.

CROPREDY FESTIVAL
13 & 14 AUGUST 1982, CROPREDY, UK

HOWARD JOHNSON

It's fifty years since I started my working life as a teacher and forty years since I left to set up a video production company. One of my first thoughts was to suggest to Peggy that filming an outdoor reunion concert might be a good idea. Over the years that followed, many friendships were formed and they have influenced greatly the lives of everyone that came with us to those 1980s festivals at Cropredy.

As a teacher, I always tried to find ways to encourage students to expand their horizons and the embryonic world of video production in education offered many opportunities. After meeting a like-minded colleague we set up a company (Videotech) to produce educational programmes for schools and the burgeoning corporate video market. As a musician, I also had a vision for using the technology to record performers in concert. With the prospect of Fairport 's illustrious career coming to an end in 1979, it seemed to me that recording their last performance was almost a civic duty.

However, the vision didn't match our finances or capabilities but we managed to put together a crew using a mixture of professionals and several of my former students. With unbelievable support from Fairport, we set off for Cropredy in 1980 and returned for several years after. The evidence of our early efforts can be found on YouTube thanks to various chaps who have uploaded clips from the original VHS tapes we released. What follows are accounts from two brothers (students of mine in the 1970s) who joined our crew and played crucial roles in our Cropredy experiences. We have remained friends to this day.

CHRIS WRIGHT

I can't recall whether my first Fairport reunion was in '82 or '83 and it all seems rather primitive by today's standards. At the time it was incredibly exciting with access to all areas and the opportunity to rub shoulders with greatness. Arriving a couple of days before the gig, I recall that we had to dig what seemed like hundreds of feet of cable into the ground so that the cables from the cameras wouldn't impede revelling fans or be damaged. I also recall being perched precariously on a scaffolding tower with a camera mounted on top... My kid brother and I had the onerous task of stopping fans from climbing on the tower to get better views of the stage, which whilst understandable, proved to be a nightmare from a filming perspective as all that clambering caused terrible camera-shake. We learned that asking drunken or over-enthusiastic people nicely to get down just didn't work so the occasional knuckle got trodden on and that seemed to work (sorry!). Most nerve-racking was being on stage mid-set making sure that camera cables were run out sufficiently and safely without knocking guitar stands, drum kits or posing a trip hazard to Peggy, Simon & Co.

The most bizarre occurrence I had was seeing the creative genius that was Professor Bruce Lacey (if you know, you know) dancing naked with an equally naked but much more alluring young lady in some kind of impromptu piece of performance art one afternoon, surrounded by massed fans. Backstage the following morning, the Prof had erected a 'tent' comprising some clear polythene sheeting supported by several sticks and guarded by a strategically placed ram's skull (complete with curly horns) at the entrance. Through the condensation coating the polythene you could still make out the naked couple within, when suddenly Prof Lacey uttered the immortal words... 'sorry, but what was your name again?'

Today Jonah's Oak is well known to reunion-goers. However, Jonah himself is perhaps less so except in the distant recesses of a few privileged minds. When we started filming the reunions in the early eighties, Jonah was a one man dynamo, a master of ceremonies and a project manager before they really existed. He co-ordinated and organised seemingly every aspect of the early reunions and we always looked forward to his unique brand of conversation... He'd never eaten, nor had any sleep (he said) and everything was always a bag of shit: 'Hi guys, I've barely slept this week, only managed to get two hours on a gravestone last Tuesday' sort of thing.

Jonah seemed to have a soft spot for my younger brother and myself, perhaps because we were so young or maybe because we were on leave from the military... Either way he was fun to be around and he knew everybody. Jonah also had a neat sideline in gig security and used to intimate that we'd be welcome doing work at some of his gigs... That never happened, especially after the *Daily Mail* ran a story about him running his security team (who were former Hell's Angels) up and down the country in a fleet of old ambulances. For some reason our parents weren't too keen to see us follow that career path.

On our second year at the reunion, we arrived a couple of days early to find that the stage construction was well behind schedule, with Jonah teaching anybody who'd listen a new lexicon of profanity. We were quickly pressed into helping construct the stage with minimal instruction and even less health and safety. This was all under the tutelage of a rigger who kept winching himself and equipment 30 feet into the air whilst drinking bottles of Portuguese green wine. 'An amusing bouquet. Drink too much and you'll laugh your head off...'.

Somehow everything fell into place (sometimes quite literally) and the show started on time with Jonah strutting out on stage (still telling everybody that he'd had no sleep) while introducing the likes of John Benns, Derek Brimstone, Richard Digance, etc., etc. Happy days, the memories of which have stayed with all concerned for a lifetime.

PAUL WRIGHT

It was all Howard Johnson's fault. I'd never heard of Fairport Convention. That's a good way to apportion the blame for my introduction to Fairport. Howard was my physics teacher at grammar school and we often talked about music; I was learning to play drums at the time. To cut to the story, Howard eventually left teaching to start a production company, Videotech, with a business partner named George Fretwell. Together they experimented shooting concert videos at Cropredy in 1980 and Broughton Castle in 1981. This was a massive learning curve for all concerned but it stood them in good stead for decades to come. In 1982, they set out to 'do it properly' with extra cameras and kit but they needed more crew to do it. Howard proposed to my father that my older brother, Chris, and I might enjoy a few days in the country filming a music festival. Whilst at school we had been on video filming courses with Howard so he knew that we could handle cameras and recording equipment competently.

After helping out filming several corporate videos, local fashion shows and village galas, we set out for Oxfordshire. I think I travelled down in a four-ton truck with Alan (a real cameraman) with Chris in one of the other vehicles. Arriving in Cropredy, we were instantly greeted by Johnny Jones, aka Jonah. He was large, bearded, rather imposing and not to be argued with. Jonah had just had a major falling out with the scaffolder who was supposed to build the stage; the guy wasn't following the plans and so Jonah threw him off site but kept his scaffolding. The video, lighting and sound crews then got a one-minute lesson in scaffolding and spent the day building the stage; it was all quite Wild West.

That night we were dragged down to the Brasenose Arms by Peggy and I think Simon, where a few beers and pie and chips made us all pretty happy. I got into a discussion with Simon about fiddle players and he mentioned that Swarb was one of the greatest living players but that I ought to also see Stefan Grappelli and Max Jaffa, two famous jazz fiddle players. I could then say I had seen all the great living fiddle players. I later followed this advice.

Back at the site the following day, Jonah had another falling out with a radio ham operator from the village who was threatening to turn his transmitter on and interfere with the festival sound systems. He was a bloke in his forties with a Catweazle sense of dress and a black floppy hat and came across as somewhat socially maladjusted. He had probably never seen a naked woman. (Mind you, at 17 I hadn't seen too many either.) I thought Jonah was going to remonstrate with him in a physical manner but instead he knew the guy had a car roof rack PA system and so, to avoid mischief, employed him to drive around the area passing information to the camping fields.

At the early Cropredy Festivals, Dave Mattacks and Bruce Rowland had drumkits set up side-by-side on stage and played at the same time, carefully watching each other.

For a period, I would crouch at the side of Bruce's kit just watching how they worked together and 40 years later I have still not seen percussion like it. Both Dave and Bruce sort of took me under their wings in the mornings when they came on stage to check their kits for the later sessions. I got lots of good, technical explanations of why their kits were set up as they were, especially how to mount and position cymbals. Following their advice, I have played drums on and off for forty years and have still never cracked a cymbal. They were very kind to a gobby, know-it-all teenage drummer. (I met Dave Mattacks again a couple of years ago at a drum clinic in Fareham and finally got to thank him for his guidance.)

To see Fairport as they were in the early eighties was a wonderful experience. How Peggy could play his strange, two-headed combined bass and mandolin was a mystery but really the sheer musicianship of all of them blew me away. Swarb moving effortlessly between fiddle and mandolin, Simon suddenly appearing with a viola, DM playing the keyboards set up behind his drum kit while Bruce kept the tempo going. Soon others joined, with Ric Sanders and Maartin Allcock. That changed the direction and brought a more produced, heavy sound to the band.

Going back to the festival crews, I recall that one year the sound crew had come straight back from Portugal where they had just finished the last leg of a European tour with The Stranglers. The PA had suffered, as they all do, and some of the bass bins – the really big speakers at the bottom of the PA stack – had blown up. The sound crew had ripped the guts out of the cabinets, filled the cases with Vino Verde bottles and shipped it all back. What a fantastic week that was, walking around with a wine bottle in your trouser pocket. One of them claimed it was 'an amusing bouquet, drink a bottle and laugh your head off.'

The early festivals also featured the ever-present Nicholas and Simon Theakston, from the famous Yorkshire brewery. As well as running the bar, Theakston's also provided a giant wooden keg of beer backstage. It had been carved with Fairport's logo on the front and was free for the crew and artists. Sadly, we were working and therefore opportunities to drink more than a few half pints were unrealistic, although we tried our best!

It rained heavily on the Saturday night of the 1982 festival and after the weekend the Theakston's tanker, which had been full of Best Bitter, couldn't get out of the mud. Howard had a Mk1 Range Rover, an enormous yellow beast. A towrope was found from somewhere and, with four-wheel drive selected and low ratio and diff lock in place, the Range Rover slowly hauled the articulated tanker lorry diagonally across the field until it reached firmer ground.

Backstage there used to be a large living area for crew and artists. It was a mixed bag of caravans, campers, tents and impromptu shelters for a few. I can't recall how we fed ourselves in 1982 but later festivals weren't an issue; I was in the Army by then, Chris was in the RAF and I had loads of surplus field rations as well as whatever else was on offer. There are many fleeting memories from the backstage area such as having a beer during the build up along with Peggy and his mates, including Robert Plant and Jimmy Page. It just seemed normal.

On one occasion, Swarb was getting wound up about something and was upset. He was upset at himself and Jonah explained, 'Swarb's forgotten 'is lucky jacket. We've got to send a fucking taxi to fetch it.' I can't remember whether Swarb was living in Birmingham or Oxford at the time, but four hours later he was back to his cheerful self and wearing a tan tweed jacket with an iron burn on the back.

Jonah, despite his gruff exterior, was a sort of malevolent and benevolent father figure to the crew and the bands. If you were privileged to have met him you will never forget him. The term legend is often bandied about these days but Jonah was the real deal, 'a true legend' in every sense of the word, bless him.

I missed the next Cropredy Festival as I was in the Army by then, but in 1984 I was back on site again. The Army was pretty good about this kind of thing. They had a public relations policy that they were poor at using called KAPE, 'Keep the Army in the Public Eye'. This initiative was supposed to encourage soldiers with transferrable skills to volunteer and help the community. I used the KAPE system to ensure that I got a couple of weeks off in August and headed back to Cropredy with my brother. I had trained as a combat medic by this time and tried to use my skills, knowledge and raffish good looks to charm one of the St John's Ambulance girls, who was a pretty blonde. Somehow, she managed to resist my efforts.

Under KAPE I later became a volunteer sound engineer at a local music venue. I worked with many rising (and a few sinking) careers including Gordon Giltrap, Desmond Dekker, Clive Gregson and Christine Collister, Pyewacket, The Albion Band, Martin Carthy, Stone Roses, Happy Mondays and Wilko Johnson to name a few but it was Fairport and ultimately Howard, who triggered this all.

I don't think that Videotech did any more festivals after 1986 and instead concentrated on earning a crust by doing more profitable work. I disappeared into the Army machine and eventually got married and drifted away to follow a career in the defence industry. Without the festivals, the need was for people with up-to-date video skills whereas I was becoming unfamiliar with newer cameras so my utility was more suited to hauling boxes across muddy fields and burying cables.

It was a fantastic experience working with Fairport and their friends. It opened up to me an area of music that I had previously not listened to and had a major impact on my life.

MARCUS BANKS

In the August of 1982 I was due to ship out to foreign parts for three years, so I sold my car. But within days my mate Steve suggested we go to some place called Cropredy where Fairport Convention were due to play. Its pronunciation eluded us but we managed to find it on the map. We borrowed my mum's Mini Metro and off we trundled. After an uneventful trip we pitched a threadbare old tent and immediately found the Brasenose. We already knew from Fairport's *Nine* album cover that it was a very special, famous place and we stayed within those welcoming walls rather a long time. I loved the festival site straight away, probably because I was floating on a splendid magic carpet of the finest brewer's art! That, and the feeling of being part of England's ancient landscape, coupled with a sense of freedom from everyday cares was very, very cosy.

We found out pretty quickly that the on-site 'facilities' might have been better suited to a little village fete, but since when did something like that bother a couple of lads in their mid-twenties?

I absolutely loved seeing Swarb among the sward (sorry)! Linda Thompson was a real treat and I enjoyed the inimitable Jonah keeping things moving. But Trevor Lucas stole the show with 'Marijuana Australiana'. Now there's real dude! Bob Dylan's 'Forever Young' will always stay with me as the perfect festival closer for that year. It was a real 'arms in the air and sing your lungs out' moment. That memory alone gets me right in the feels.

After the festival, Steve bought the *AT2: The Boot* cassette tape for me, to say thanks for driving. I played it to destruction, so I snapped up the CD as soon as it appeared. It remains a much loved and indispensable part of my collection. Steve and I are firm friends to this day. However, he still ribs me for – albeit only once – mistaking 4X for 6X! I know, I know. It's unforgivable but he drank it, didn't he?

It rained during the night. Of course it did. And lying awake with a nagging bladder isn't much fun. But as soon as it stopped raining, we both lurched out into the night so fast we nearly dragged the whole tent with us. Bare feet on cold wet grass – find the hedge in the dark – blessed relief!

So that was my first Cropredy. I have returned many times since, with better cars and better tents. I have also been lucky enough to have found many new friendships, which I cherish. But I can say that, without exaggeration, that first Cropredy sowed a seed which bears the most wonderful fruit every August. I will remember it with much fondness, forever.

Even if the car exhaust did fall off on the way home!

NIC DOWDING

I first discovered Fairport in the early eighties when I was going through the folk section in the local library looking for anything that looked like folk-rock and chanced upon *Nine*. I was immediately drawn to the cover and the plush gatefold sleeve. I took it out from the library, went home and expectantly put the stylus on the record. I was not to be disappointed as the rap-tap-tap of the drum was followed by Swarb's distinctive vocal and the rest of the band then kicked in. I knew I had discovered something really good, and was soon sourcing my own copy as well as looking for other Fairport albums in second hand record shops.

Shortly after this a chap I knew called Tony, who deejayed for hospital radio in Banbury, told me he had interviewed Dave Pegg about a forthcoming Fairport Reunion at a place called Cropredy near to Banbury. The generous Mr Pegg has given him a signed LP, *Moat On The Ledge*, a t-shirt for the reunion and two free tickets, all of which Tony gave to me knowing of my interest in the band. I was knocked out to see that this gig was not only going to be the last lineup but also a reunion of the *Nine* lineup.

With free tickets there was no excuse not to go so I made the journey down to Cropredy sporting the free t-shirt. If memory serves me correctly Fairport came on shortly after 7.30 and played for the rest of the night. From the minute it started I was hooked and in particular could not take my eyes off Swarb as he seemed to play like someone possessed. From that night on he would forever be one of my musical heroes.

Having been simply wowed by what had simply been my best live music experience to date, going to Cropredy was now going to be a fixture in the calendar. In 1986 I took my then girlfriend of six months, Sue, who seemed a bit nonplussed by it all. But by 1988 we were going as man and wife and with the odd exception we have been every year. A few years back, I had queued to get Swarb's autograph and was wearing my '82 t-shirt. As I approached him, he let out an expletive in his inimitable fashion and said he had still got one somewhere at home. That really made my day.

I still have my 1982 t-shirt and wear it every time I go to Cropredy. It's a bit torn and tattered now in places but it means so much. Thanks, Fairport, for all the good times and music over the years – and a belated thank you to Peggy for the album, the tickets and that t-shirt!

CROPREDY FESTIVAL

12 & 13 AUGUST 1983, CROPREDY, UK

ANDY LEONARD

I got into Fairport in the late 1970s and, thinking they were splitting up, which they were meant to be doing, I started to collect their back catalogue of LPs. I got them all apart from *Live At The LA Troubadour*, which had by this time been deleted and therefore was almost impossible to get a copy. This was pre-CDs, never mind the internet and eBay, so when I wrote off for my Cropredy tickets for the 1983 festival (remember PO Box 37, Banbury, Oxfordshire, OX16 8YN?), I asked if they knew where I could get a copy. When my tickets duly arrived, there was a note from Christine Pegg saying it had been deleted but if I posted her a blank cassette, she would get Peggy to record his copy for me. I couldn't believe such kindness from them both, and a week later I now had the album, albeit on a cassette.

Then at the festival I saw Peggy walking across the concert field so I stopped him to say 'thank you'. To my surprise, he said he was missing a Fairport LP too, *Tipplers Tales*, which had also been deleted. He had lent it to someone and it had now disappeared. Anyway, he asked me to keep an eye out for it and amazingly enough I came across a copy in a dusty old record shop in Cornwall when on holiday a few weeks later. Now I had the problem of getting it to him, because naturally I had no idea where he lived. However, in that year's Cropredy programme was an advert for Woodworm Studios with a phone number. I rang it and naively assumed it would be answered by a secretary or similar and was amazed to be speaking to Christine.

I drove up to their home in Barford St Michael and met Peggy and we've stayed in contact ever since. I've been very fortunate to stay at his and new partner Ellen's house in Brittany on more than one occasion and sampled his famous hospitality. As another friend said, 'Make sure you're not driving the next day!' I cannot believe it has been over 40 years ago. Who know where the time goes eh?

DAVE BUCKLEY

It all started in Warrington Market in 1970 when a certain spotty fifteen-year-old with exceptionally limited funds noticed a distinctive yellow double album sampler going for the very reasonable price of 29 shillings and eleven pence (in pre-decimal coinage). Happily (and unusually), I actually had this amount so purchased the record and began delving into its numerous delights once back home. *Bumpers* was an Island Records sampler displaying the stunning roster of acts on the label. I was familiar with Traffic and Free, the others not so much. But what an eye opener, and I was particularly taken by Fairport Convention's entry, 'Walk Awhile'.

In Harrogate with my parents a few weeks later, I spotted a copy of *Full House* going cheap at an outdoor market record stall. I was hooked, and weirdly my mum and dad liked it too. I was starting to play drums at the time and so tried playing along with it. WTF? This wasn't like playing along to Ringo, Charlie or Doug Clifford… What was this bloke Mattacks doing?

I began acquiring the Fairport back catalogue, each album evolving in membership and sound. My folks bought me *What We Did On Our Holidays* for Christmas in 1972. I still put that treasured LP on as we decorate the house in December and it still brings tingles down my spine.

I began investigating the wider FC world. I adored Fotheringay and Steeleye Span and bought *Henry The Human Fly*. I found lots of albums that the immortal rhythm section of Peggy, Simon and DM featured on, in particular DM's extra-curricular session work, which led me to Spirogyra, Gay and Terry Woods and beyond.

I didn't get to see Fairport at a gig till Cropredy 1983 because I couldn't find anyone to go with. Whilst I was grooving to The Band, The Flying Burrito Bros., Traffic and the chaps, my mates were lost in Yes, Hendrix, Zeppelin and Deep Purple. One of them even quite liked the Velvet Underground. I was also gigging a lot myself and hence unavailable many nights of the week.

In 1982 I decided I needed to get a proper job and started training as a mental health nurse. The gigging slackened off and I was able to get to see bands regularly, one of which was The Albion Band at Warrington's Parr Hall. It was as close as I could get to seeing Fairport, who were inactive at the time. On board were Simon (with his cornflake box guitar and reading crib sheets), Ashley and DM. It was a great gig and at the end of the night I ventured onto the stage where DM was packing his kit up and had a brief chat. He asked if I knew about Cropredy, which I didn't, but decided I would investigate. DM was my drum hero, and I've generally been a bit overwhelmed on the occasions I've met him, though he's always been engaging and happily signed a bunch of albums for me when he did a Yamaha drum clinic in our local music shop. (Despite this I still use Ludwig…)

I got married to Helen in the summer of 1983, and as part of our honeymoon we set off on a complex trek into the rustic unknowns of pre-motorway Oxfordshire, down a steep hill into the pretty village of Cropredy and a Weekend in the Country. 'Look! The Brasenose! That's on the rear cover of *Nine*! Photo opportunity…'.

Camping was random back then. We pulled up and pitched the tent in a field next to a shabby but functional shower block apparently for use by the village cricket team. We went exploring… 'Oh look! There's Dave Pegg on a quad bike!' There were dreadful ancient caravans dotted about like dead beetles containing pre-war toilets that promised unpleasantness in extremis once the crowds required servicing.

The Brasenose was quiet that Thursday night so we got a table with no problem, ate, drank and hung out with a bunch of amenable Scottish persons who over the years morphed into The McBastard Clan, and joined in their acoustic session. The weather was glorious and so was the festival. Nobody took chairs back then, but we were all a lot younger and more flexible. Blankets sufficed. You could walk right up to the stage, or indeed, right round the back as security was minimal. When I'd received the tickets

(clockwise from top left) Ric & Peggy at Errol's in Göteborg, **Sweden 1986** (Staffan Wunderlund); Will Sawers' addiction began in 1985; Martin Walker (right) with Gerry Conway in 2022; **Carl Hufton & friends** were regular attendees at Cropredy; Peggy with David Flintham's son Alex at Islington's Union Chapel; **Peter Roe** remembers Fairport being back with *Gladys' Leap!*

(clockwise from top left) Simon Frisby had a medical emergency at Cropredy; Simon & Ric at Errol's, Göteborg, Sweden 1986 (Staffan Wunderlund); Peggy at Errol's, Göteborg, Sweden 1986 (Staffan Wunderlund); Simon at Errol's, Göteborg, Sweden 1986 (Staffan Wunderlund); Heusden Festival, Belgium August 1985 (Gerard Bouman) through the post, the envelope also contained posters and a request to display them in my home locality. A cottage industry, in remarkable contrast to later years!

Fairport were wonderful. Richard Thompson had headlined the Friday night and joined them to revisit the early lineup of the band, with Cathy LeSurf standing in magnificently for Sandy Denny. Details are lost in the mists of time, but the photos I have capture a beautiful weekend complete with dray horses and a field full of happy people. Impressions remain when the fine detail is lost…

I've been to each Cropredy since. Helen and I parted ways in 1990, but we remained friends and still went every year till she passed away twenty years ago. That was a difficult Cropredy, her presence and memories were everywhere and they still are. She got a mention from the stage. A lot of us were pretty emotional. She was only small so took a beer crate with her to stand on to every Cropredy. I still had it until a few years back.

I say I've been to every Cropredy… well, almost. I remarried and had kids rather late in life. Laura went to her first Cropredy in 2006 aged three months. Dylan went to his first in 2009 aged four months. As Dylan found sleeping through quite impossible until he was eight, this temporarily curtailed our festival activities, hence I missed Little Feat and Steve Winwood and I bear a grudge to this day. Vengeance will be mine, Dylan (maybe). Since then, they've both been to every Cropredy and look forward to it every year.

Speculating who would turn up on the Saturday night FC slot was always good fun, rumours being rife in the Brasenose and Red Lion. We were informed one lubricated evening by an insider that Tull would make an appearance as Peggy and Maart were then members of both bands. And they did! We've also seen Robert Plant, Roger Hodgson, Trevor Lucas, Billy Connolly and numerous others. We have a constantly revolving lineup of numerous friends who go every year (including Rick Astley's sister). Back in the day, we generally sat in front of the mixer, the sound being best for purposes of illicit taping. Whilst waiting for Roy Harper to appear one year, our feet were trampled on by a pair of blokes leading a couple of very large dogs. I pointed out to my complaining mate Phil that he had just been slightly damaged by Robert Plant and Jimmy Page and therefore should be grateful.

We'd go to Southport Arts Theatre (or other venue) every year to see the Winter Tour, and of course the chaps were always in attendance after the gig to chat and sign things, as they were at Cropredy. I once had a long chat with Maart, who patiently asked someone to stop mithering him as he was in the middle of a conversation, which pretty much demonstrated what a lovely man he was.

The best latterday gig I think I ever saw them do was at Southport. It was probably the last tour they did before Maart left. It was quite high tech, with lights synched to synths and various effects that wouldn't have shamed a prog band. It was hugely entertaining and in no way detracted from some remarkable music.

There were also times when things got a bit shambolic over the years, with missed cues and forgotten lyrics… When the album celebrating their thirtieth anniversary was released featuring Ashley's dialogue, I'd already taped the whole evening on my trusty Sony DAT Walkman and put together a fascinating CD of the stuff that wasn't used. Considering the amount of material they had to learn, it's a wonder they got as much right as they did! And I have a curious memory of one Saturday night when the FC chaps were sitting in a row on chairs onstage tearing up newspapers. I'm not sure why, but it seemed to make perfect sense at the time...

I've still got all my Cropredy and Winter tour programmes, a drawer full of t-shirts, goodness knows how many CDs and a full run of their albums on record including a mint mono copy of their Polydor debut. I've met pretty much all the band through the years: the always convivial Peggy; Swarb signing a photocopy of his obituary; Simon photographed with my small kids on the field and my wife talking to his wife about dogs and not realising who he was; discussing with Gerry Conway one of his fills on the *Fotheringay* album; a chilled and relaxed DM with me thinking 'I am not worthy' and trying not to make a dick of myself; Jerry Donahue looking slightly freaked out that I knew who he was; Judy Dyble, a gentle, beautiful soul; Ric, looking put out when I asked him why Merry Hell hadn't been on the main stage yet.

And then there was the time a bloke came up to my friend Andy and I enquiring about something (I forget what). An hour later, we realised it was Iain Matthews as there he was up on stage. And the time I was buying a limited-edition mounted print of the Monterey Pop Festival poster, fully signed by the Country Joe Band. I returned triumphant to my partner (eventually wife) Di who was looking faintly embarrassed and trying not to grin. 'That old chap over there just fell over the dog lead.' I looked in the direction she indicated and it was Country Joe McDonald.

Only at a Fairport gig…

IAN BROOM

Back in 1983 the Cropredy 'Weekend in the Country' programme contained a comment regarding Simon's fondness for Bulmer's Number 7 cider, an excellent and very old, very dry bottled beverage that was, at the time, still being supplied to the Savoy Hotel, individually wrapped in tissue paper. As it happened, I was employed by HP Bulmer in their technical department in Hereford. My dear late wife, Heather, who held Simon in high regard from our several encounters at shows, suggested we supply some Number 7 as a gesture of our esteem. We duly pitched up at Cropredy and handed over a crate which ended up on stage that evening and elicited a between songs 'thank you' from Simon. This led to numerous reciprocal arrangements of cider for guest tickets at various venues over the years, until, sadly, Bulmer's foolishly de-listed Number 7 in a product rationalisation. Ever the gentleman, it was always a pleasure for us to sup a 20th anniversary ale with him at Cropredy, or a post-gig pint out on the road.

KEN ROSEMAN

Heaven for me has come to be a certain field in Oxfordshire, England, near the village of Cropredy. That is the site of Fairport Convention's annual festival, which I attended in 1983, 1984, 1990, 2004, 2006, 2008, and 2011. I no longer have money for overseas travel, but I fondly remember the trips I did make. So... how did a Jewish guy raised in Maryland and Massachusetts become so attached to the English folk and folk-rock community? The music itself is a great blend of grace and fire – combining medieval folkish melodies with rock 'n' roll energy. I just loved that! I had been listening avidly to Fairport Convention and Steeleye Span for about a decade and even saw both acts in person, but I wanted to get closer to the players and the music.

Finding out that Dave Mattacks was in Joan Armatrading's touring band and that she had an upcoming gig at The Cellar Door in Washington DC, I thought I should meet him. The local A&M representative, JB Brenner, put me on the guest list. The show was great, and afterwards I went backstage and introduced myself to Dave Mattacks. We got along well and he gave me his address. Thus began a long correspondence, one of the outcomes of which was that DM gave me the mailing address for Ashley Hutchings. I began writing to Hutchings, and he was very gracious with me. He arranged for me to get review copies of albums by The Albion Dance Band and The Albion Band. Both those albums, *The Prospect Before Us* and *Rise Up Like The Sun*, are now regarded as classics in the English Electric folk/folk-rock genre.

In 1983, I contacted a new English music paper about writing for them. I told the editor I was planning a trip to England and he supplied a great motivation: a press pass and backstage privileges for the Goodwood Festival. While I was backstage there, Dave Pegg turned up. I told him I was a music journalist and he gave me a ticket to the 1983 Fairport Convention festival. What a revelation that was! I saw, in person, folks I'd been listening to for years. 'Look over there. John Kirkpatrick! Look – over there! Ian Telfer from Oysterband and Fiddler's Dram. And over there – Ashley Hutchings himself! Wow!'

I attended Fairport Convention's festival six more times. Among the guest artists who most impressed me were the brilliant Home Service, with excellent original songs by Bill Caddick and John Tams and a distinctive brass section which gave the group a very regal sound. Three other acts who really stood out for me were a collaboration of June Tabor and Oysterband, Irish folk-rockers Horslips, and the all-female group The Poozies, who featured great harmony and lead vocalising. I also enjoyed the various iterations of the Albion Band and Morris On groups, and the set by progressive pop band Stackridge. Their great melodies and arrangements, well-crafted and intelligent lyrics, and excellent lead and harmony singing reminded me of both The Zombies and The Beach Boys.

Here in the 21st century, I'm pleased to report that the English folk-rock movement is still going strong. The pioneers, Fairport Convention and Steeleye Span, are still active, and there are great newish acts like Merry Hell, who bring a punky edge to their sound, and in a more classic vein, Green Diesel and The Duncan McFarlane Band. I have also enjoyed CDs by The Jon Palmer Acoustic Band, who have great lead and harmony vocals along with excellent original songs. Joshua Burnell may remind some of Richard Thompson, but he brings his own quirky spirit to English folk-rock.

Artists from outside the UK who have adapted the Fairport template to their own traditions who have appeared include Ougenweide (Germany), Malicorne (France), Folque (Norway), Alan Stivell and bands (Britanny), and Agricantus and CGS (Italy). I enjoy CDs by all of those artists.

Thanks to Fairport Convention and their associates for some of the best recordings and in person events of my life. I am proud to be a member of the English folk-rock community, who I now realise are and have been my 'family of choice' for decades. Long live Fairport Convention!

KENNETH WEXLER

The few times they played in the USA in the 1970s I missed seeing them, although I did see Swarbrick and Nicol as a duo in New York City in September 1982, on a night when they were joined by Richard Thompson and Dave Pegg. It was quite a night, but it wasn't strictly a Fairport gig. So, technically, the first time I saw Fairport was when I travelled to Cropredy in 1983. The weather that year was brilliant, which I learned was not always the case at eight subsequent Cropredys. The crowd was a lot smaller than it is these days, which gave the band a chance to show a real intimacy. The music was great, and the addition of Cathy LeSurf gave the band to perform many Sandy Denny songs which they hadn't played for a while.

TIM ROMAIN

My friends and I have been attending Cropredy since 1983, with much silliness and many adventures that would probably fail health and safety scrutiny nowadays. We've had many, many different forms of motorised transport over the years and had fun and games getting to and from the festival. I've turned up in the following: Mini City; MG Metro; Datsun Sunny; VW vans (1974 bay window and 1976 bay window – both Devon conversions); VW Golf GL; (); Peugeot 206 (hire car – the Golf GL having been written off the month before, coming out of a David Bowie concert in Milton Keynes); VW Golf GTI; Vauxhall Astra; Vauxhall Corsa (hire car – the Astra having just died); Honda Prelude MK1; Rover 100; BMW318; BMW323; Honda Prelude MK4; Vauxhall Vectra; BMW120; BMW320; Mini Countryman; Mercedes B Classe.

In 1984 we got four adults and all our camping equipment in an old-style Mini. There was so much gear in the back, stacked floor to ceiling, that we couldn't see out of the windows or see Graham and Amanda Palmer, who were buried under it all. Then there was the year that Tim Hoare-ward drove my VW Golf from the south coast to Cropredy with no brakes, which was no mean feat. Ah, the stupidity of youth.

The name Tim Stenton appears in many of these tales. He seems to have had the worst luck. Like the time in the early nineties when, after meeting in a layby on the A361, we pulled out to drive to Cropredy and he knocked the oil sump off his car, creating an instant oil slick and essentially ending the car's life. I was in the car behind him, flashing my lights and screaming at him to stop (like he could actually hear me!).

Another time Tim rode his trials bike to the festival. It was great. We rode it around the site and it certainly saved time walking to the loos. But on the Friday afternoon (when drink may have been taken) Tim had Ian Reed riding pillion and crashed on the way to the loo. Normally falling off a motorcycle travelling at about five miles an hour in a muddy field is funny, with nothing more serious than muddy knees and dented pride. But on this occasion the clutch lever broke during a slow motion wipe out. It's not easy finding a replacement clutch lever for a Kawasaki KT250 in Banbury on a Saturday morning. In the end, a tent peg-based Heath Robinson affair cobbled together with gaffer tape and cable ties got Tim home.

Then there was the year that the festival organisers put an open-air bar in Field 2. A collective decision was made that driving the 50 yards from where we were camped to get take outs would be easier and more fun than walking. Four of us bundled into Queenie's car. We pulled up parallel to the bar and, without getting out, bought a couple of pints each which were handed through the passenger windows. Then we bought two more to bring it up to a nice round number. Although it was a short drive to our camp, with three of us holding multiple pints and all the cup holders full, a significant amount of the ale was spilt on the dashboard, carpets and upholstery. Queenie reckoned that the smell took a year to fade completely but then it's widely agreed that Queenie's natural scent was eau de Smirnoff and that most people wouldn't have noticed the automotive beer chaser.

One year our friend Iain Coleman couldn't be bothered to bring a tent and slept in his car. Arriving a bit later than the rest of us, he parked near a telegraph pole with a sunken area around it on which you couldn't pitch a tent. It started raining on Friday night (the sound of raindrops hitting my tent kept me awake despite my being happily mashed) and in the morning the sunken area around the telegraph pole had turned into a small lake, with Iain's car in the middle of it and Iain happily asleep inside.

In recent years our vehicles have become more reliable and the mishaps fewer. Fingers crossed that times like when my Vauxhall Astra dumped the contents of its' radiator all over the M25 or the super-hot day when the heater exchanger lever on my VW bus jammed open, pouring hot air in to the cab, and we drove up the M40 to Cropredy with the windows and the side door wide open, are all behind us.

TONY 'BILL' HILZBRICH

In the summer of 1982, at the age of nineteen, I wasn't best pleased, during my first university summer holiday, to be summoned for jury service only months after being eligible to vote (and not even having exercised that right). When said task was done, I decided to treat myself to a record with some of the expenses provided. I stopped at a record shop and found myself holding a copy of *Unhalfbricking*, the cover of which intrigued me. Record sleeves of that era said a lot about the music and the back cover is such a homely image that seems to fit the warm, comfortable and instantly familiar feel of the songs. I knew about Fairport and had enjoyed the *Live at Maidstone* film, which had been shown at my local cinema the previous year, but hadn't bought any of their albums. When I put it on, I just loved it – and played it several times over! I later read that John Peel, in his contemporary review, had said it was an album you'd want to hear daily for a very long time and he was right. From that moment I was hooked and started purchasing other releases.

I finally got to see the band at Cropredy in 1983; I went with a university friend, who was equally as enthusiastic about Fairport. I trekked down to his home in Worcestershire from where I was staying in Northumberland and he drove us to the festival site with the lenses of his broken glasses taped over a spare pair. This gave him tunnel vision and made the journey interesting – to say the least!

The yearly bash was a lot smaller than it is nowadays, but it was a fabulous weekend. The only pity was that we only turned up for the Saturday, meaning we missed the Richard Thompson set. This was the beginning of an annual pilgrimage, which was the focal point of my yearly holiday and which in my case came to a premature end in 1988 when I moved abroad. Indeed, I've only seen the guys once since, in Lisbon in April 1995.

What sets Fairport apart from most other bands is their accessibility; their willingness to meet and greet at gigs builds a real bond between them and their fans. As time goes by and we all get older, it's almost like losing a family member when a Fairporter sadly departs this life and one harks back to the memories of happier times. More than just a great band, they are a British institution.

WILLIAM HAYTER

At the tender age of 16 I wanted to go to the 1979 Knebworth Festival to see Led Zeppelin. But I had just got a Saturday job at Marks & Spencer and wasn't allowed the day off. Not to worry, I thought, there will be other chances to see Led Zeppelin… And that would also have been my first encounter with Fairport Convention, but it was not to be.

My love affair with the Cropredy Festival began in 1983 with what was then referred to as the Annual Fairport Reunion. I originally planned to attend the 1982 reunion but as an out-of-work student, money was a bit thin on the ground and choices had to be made. My girlfriend at the time and I opted for the Cambridge Folk Festival and the Rougham Tree Fair instead. Waiting at the Waterworks Roundabout in Walthamstow and hoping to hitch a lift to the festival before dark, a ramshackle old bus zoomed around the corner, slammed the brakes on and a door popped open. 'Where are you off to?' asked a voice. It was Nik Turner of Hawkwind fame. In disbelief I said 'the same place as you, Rougham Tree Fair.' 'Hop in.' In hitchhiking terms, this was a hole-in-one. It was at Rougham that I had my first ever Fairport-related experience. Performing in the folk tent were none other than Simon Nicol and Dave Swarbrick. That was it, I was hooked.

The following year I was determined to go to the Fairport reunion. I was in a job now so could afford the train fare and, travelling alone this time, I made my way to Paddington Station and asked the ticket clerk for a weekend return to Cropredy Station. Plenty of tapping away at his machine and looking up fare directories failed to yield a destination. 'There's no Cropredy Station mate, what's it near?' 'Banbury,' I said. Banbury it was. (Turns out Cropredy Station closed in 1956!) I arrived with no information about how to get to the festival but after a few enquiries I was pointed in the direction of the road out of Banbury towards Cropredy. I started the walk with my rucksack and my six-man army tent (why didn't I take a sensible tent?). I got as far as the A423, near where the Tesco now is, when a car pulled up next to me. A sweet elderly lady opened her car door and said 'are you off to the music festival?' 'Yes,' I said. 'Hop in and I'll drive you to Cropredy. It's too far to walk with that lot.' Such a kind gesture, such a long walk!

When I got into the field, I was immediately taken with the village fête atmosphere of it all. There was a small scaffold stage with some tarpaulin-type covering and a couple of thousand people laid out on the grass. This was so laid back and nothing like the 'proper' festivals. On the Thursday evening, the night before it all started, I went into the Brasenose for a beer and sat at the bar was Dave Swarbrick. It was all so relaxed. I met a couple from Denmark in the bar, Kristian and Birgitte. We are still friends now. This set a trend for years to come. The friendly nature of the festival is such that you can easily make new friends.

Since those early beginnings, I have only missed the 1992 festival (due to a family wedding) and the two lockdown years. Cropredy is a priority in my summer planning. I never tire of the festival, even if the weather tries its best to make me call it a day, like in 1985 when the rain came down sideways and the wind was so strong it virtually blew the stage roof off. I have been scorched in the sun, soaked to the core and had my hair blown badly out of place, yet without fail I keep coming back. Great people, great music and the most relaxed festival all curated by a band that we all have a true affection for. I have seen Fairport well in excess of a hundred times. I've even beaten the band at table football in Woodworm Studio, but I'll save that and the drunken shenanigans in the George Inn at Barford St. Michael for the third edition of this book!

SOUTH LAKELAND LEISURE CENTRE
28 DECEMBER 1983, KENDAL, UK

NIGEL BANKS

Fairport played a gig at Kendal Leisure Centre when they were starting to increase their live appearances beyond Cropredy whilst not being a fully functioning outfit because Swarb had been warned by his doctor against playing electrified music. After the gig, we went back to Joyce's – a legendary local character who trained as an opera singer but was now a piano teacher. She was a fixture on the door at music event at the local arts centre but would then invite the musicians back to her place afterwards, where carousing until the wee small hours with copious amounts of alcohol would occur. Such luminaries as John Martyn, Johnny 'Jonah' Jones and even Taj Mahal had graced her humble abode. On this occasion, Messrs Nicol and Pegg arrived to enjoy Joyce's hospitality. Simon sat next to me and we had a delightful conversation including such topics as the Richard and Linda Thompson split (although I don't recall the famous 'Tour From Hell' being mentioned) and his concern about Swarb's health and nicotine consumption. HIs fears would be realised a few years later when Swarb would require a new set of bellows!

CROPREDY FESTIVAL
10 & 11 AUGUST 1984, CROPREDY, UK

SANDIE MIDDLETON

We came to Cropredy when my daughter Jo was about four or five. It was a gorgeous day, and I remember we unbolted the back seat of our Citröen 2CV and carried it over to the

(clockwise from top left) Swarb & Peggy at Cropredy 1987 (Gerard Bouman); Dave Mattacks at Cropredy 1987 (Gerard Bouman); Simon Nicol at Cropredy 1987 (Gerard Bouman); Dave Pegg at Cropredy 1987 (Gerard Bouman)

(clockwise from top left) Swarb at Cropredy 1987 (Gerard Bouman); Richard Thompson at Cropredy 1987 (Gerard Bouman); Jerry Donahue at Cropredy 1987 (Gerard Bouman); Swarb at Cropredy 1987 (Gerard Bouman) field to sit on. When walking around the stalls at lunch time, Jo spotted someone selling tin whistles and really wanted one so I bought one for her. She's lucky enough to be able to play by ear and within an hour or so she was playing tunes. That was the start of her love of music, instruments and all things folk. 40 years later, she still plays weekly for the local Morris team as well as a Ceilidh band. She even runs the Ham at The Sidmouth Folk Festival every year. She started in folk festival artists liaison when she was 16.

GERARD BOUMAN

I've remained a fan of Fairport. In the eighties, I used to trade bootlegs and radio and TV recordings with Marty Kenny. My English friend Desmond, with whom I used to play fiddle – and do still, when we meet up – took us to the Cropredy Festival in 1984. There was going to be a festival band. We got sent some sheet music in advance and at the festival people could play some tunes together with Chris Leslie and Dave Swarbrick. I took my fiddle along and was hoping to be able to play along with Swarb. Swarb didn't show up but Chris Leslie did and we played with some people from all kinds of places.

My first wife was pregnant with our eldest son then. In later years we took the ferry from Holland and went to Cropredy again with both our sons in 1996, 1997 and 1998, and I went again with Desmond in 2008. In 2017, I took my two sons and wife to Cropredy for the 50th anniversary. Thirty-three years later, my eldest son was a father himself. We had a great time at the festival.

Now, in 2024, my children have children of their own and I wouldn't be surprised if they convinced me to go to Cropredy again with the whole family. I still play music in a few bands and there is still some Fairport stuff in the repertoire. Which goes to show that Fairport, and especially Dave Swarbrick, have had a life-long influence on me. What a great band.

SIMON MORRIS

I first saw Fairport at Cropredy in 1984, but I first came across them as a friend had the 'Family Tree' (*History Of*) album. Purely by chance I mentioned I was going to see Jethro Tull to my granny and it turned out she knew Peggy's mum and dad from the OAP club. They very kindly sent me a signed tour programme and a copy of the *AT2: The Boot* cassette with Peggy's dad singing added to the end. Sadly, that tape has now been played to death!

WIMBLEDON THEATRE
6 JANUARY 1985, LONDON, UK

DEREK COLLISON

Our friends at that time were in a band called Eavesdropper and supporting them. Another few friends and myself helped load their van and travelled to Wimbledon with them, but as we had to buy our own tickets and told we would not be allowed to meet Fairport Convention, we let them do their own load in and we made our own way home after leaving them to load out on their own.

Sadly, the two Fyfe brothers have passed away but my friend tells me that Rob and Steve are still slogging on as Eavesdropper 2. I lost contact with them after I married later that year but had known them since 1981, when they played regularly at The Star pub in Broad Green, Croydon.

STUDENTS UNION
26 JANUARY 1985, SHEFFIELD, UK

WILL SAWERS

My first encounter with Fairport Convention was via a youth group leader in my late teens in the early eighties, just around the time the band were reforming. The first album I heard was the *History Of…* compilation. I was mainly listening to heavy rock bands, but this very English music drew me in and led me on to more folk-rock, back to the roots, and outwards through all the newer folk-type artists.

Once I arrived at Sheffield University in 1984, I found that Fairport were playing there, bought the *Gladys' Leap* LP from the band, and so began a lifelong addiction. Since then, I have seen the band playing live at least once almost every year in all sorts of venues, ranging from village halls to Cropredy. Some of the more memorable concerts in my early years of following them were seeing the band at the Half Moon in Putney in 1986, at a Cropredy warm-up (with the same youth leader who had first introduced me to them), and spending New Year's Eve 1988 with them, as the Fairport Ceilidh Band with Beryl and Roger Marriott, in a sports hall in Gloucester.

In 1989 I first made it to Cropredy, as a Saturday day visitor and with a university friend, and like many other people, the magic of that field seeped into my bones that day, and it has always felt like a very special place to me, one where I immediately feel at home as soon as I get there. For the next several years, family life and working overseas meant that I was only an intermittent visitor to Cropredy, but I always managed to see Fairport somewhere each year. One year, having pretty much lost touch with the friend I first visited Cropredy with, I turned round in my seat at the halfway point of Fairport's gig at the Wycombe Swan to find him sitting in the seat behind me!

I found the Talkawhile group online while working in Central Africa, which has only fuelled my addiction. Since 2012, when we moved back to the UK, I have made it to Cropredy each year, through wind, rain, extreme heat and all other weather conditions, and enjoy meeting up with online friends and others, and have discovered so much good music through Fairport's guests each year. Long may it last!

GLADYS' LEAP
RELEASED AUGUST 1985

PETER ROE

I remember seeing *Gladys' Leap* in the record shop for the first time several years after we said 'Farewell Farewell' to Fairport as a full-time band on their 'final' tour. They had met up annually for Cropredy reunions and there were the great official 'Boot' tapes that recorded these events, but we missed them as an ongoing band. Now they were back, with a classy-looking album cover with a puzzling name.

They were back with a great collection of songs including three epics; 'Honour And Praise', 'The Hiring Fair' and 'Wat Tyler'.

They were back, with no Swarb but a guest appearance from Ric Sanders who had appeared on the great Albion Band album, *Rise Up Like The Sun*.

They were back, with Simon in excellent voice and a great vocal contribution from Mr Pegg on 'Bird From The Mountain'

They were back, with a new instrumental that really rocked!

It was a long time ago now and there have been many more great albums since, but *Glady's Leap* was the album that kick-started the rebirth of our favourite band, and for that reason it means a lot.

ZECHE CLUB
5 NOVEMBER 1985, BOCHUM, GERMANY

KRZYSZTOF PRZYŚLEWICZ

In early 1970s Poland, books about rock 'n' roll were practically non-existent. Very few local music magazines dealt with anything other than mawkish and sugary eastern

European pop. And they were published in such small editions that they often could not simply be bought at a news kiosk but had to be sought out. You could ride your bike all over town hunting for a title and still come home disappointed.

Vinyl records by foreign western artists were very hard to come by. Domestic music companies did not release them. The music market, like everything else, was controlled by the regime. The music press published in countries outside the Iron Curtain were very difficult to obtain; there'd be one single copy of *New Musical Express* in the only KMPiK store in the city. The only sources of records or magazines were receiving them from family abroad, attending record fairs and, here and there, small selections of used vinyl in official state stores.

I was browsing through either a Polish or foreign magazine (I don't remember which) in 1971 or '72 when my attention was caught by a live shot with a then meaningless (to me) caption: 'Dave Swarbrick and Simon Nicol from Fairport Convention'... A short note about the guys in the picture was interesting enough for both Swarbrick and Nicol's names and the name of the group to end up in my notebook.

A few years later, I came back from the regularly and obligatorily visited record bazaar with *Unhalfbricking* under my arm. I was smitten. It was my music. And it still is after 50 years. (And my pal spent a week's salary on *What We Did On Our Holidays*.) I have since listened to FC's entire output and most of the solo works of the current and previous members of the band. The shelf in my record collection with the set of their LPs and CDs looks pretty good.

Roughly ten years after first encountering their music, I got to see Fairport in Bochum in Germany. On stage were a mix of the new and the old Fairport Convention – Simon Nicol, Dave Pegg and Dave Mattacks and two new members, Ric Sanders and Maartin Allcock. They played tracks from new studio album, *Gladys' Leap*, and their obvious classics. It was a dream come true for me, and a magical evening which I'm still reminded of by a ticket consecrated by Simon Nicol's hand.

The next piece of my Fairport story took place in Sydney, Australia on 12 May 1986, when I saw Fairport founder Richard Thompson in an acoustic concert at the famous Sydney Opera House. His performance was only a support for Loudon Wainwright III show but I couldn't pass up such an opportunity. It was again a special and remarkable event, and listening to the excellent album *Small Town Romance* years later brings the memories back.

Sometime later, looking around the music book section in one of the bookstores, I couldn't believe what my eyes were seeing: six copies of a new Patrick Humphries' publication, *Meet On The Ledge: History Of Fairport Convention*, smiling at me from the shelf for just one Australian dollar each. I bought all of them without hesitation. One of them got placed in my bookcase next to *The Woodworm Era: The Story Of Today's Fairport Convention*. It has since been blessed by the band members' autographs. And the other five copies? I gave those to family and friends.

THE INTERNATIONAL
16 JANUARY 1986, MANCHESTER, UK

MARTIN WALKER

I first saw Fairport in 1970 at the Free Trade Hall in Manchester. My friends and I saw a lot of bands there between 1969 and 1972, when we were still at school – Ten Years After, John Mayall, Deep Purple, Canned Heat, Blues Legends spring to mind – but there were many, many more. Fairport played the FTH twice in 1970 – on 6 February and 6 November – and I can't remember which concert I was at! I don't remember the lineup from 53 years ago, but it looks as if it was the *Full House* band of Simon, RT, Peggy, DM and Swarb.

During the 1970s, I lost track of Fairport, and the bands I saw most often then were Steeleye Span and Emerson, Lake & Palmer. Then in the early 1980s I bought *History Of…* in a record shop in Todmorden and realised what I'd been missing.

On 16 January 1986, I saw an advert in *The Guardian* for the reconstructed Fairport playing that evening at The International, a long-departed venue – it's now a supermarket – a mile or so south of Manchester University. I went along that evening and was hooked for the next 37 years (and counting). Apart from the music, my abiding memory of that evening was Maart wearing a hat with a fox on the front. Either Simon or Peggy introduced him, saying he had told his wife he was playing at The International that evening, and she said 'wear the fox hat' …so he did. I bought *Gladys Leap* that evening and played that vinyl hundreds of times.

I don't know how many times I have seen Fairport since then, probably 60 or 70 including gigs and festivals, at such varied venues as Burnley Mechanics, The Lowry, the Royal Northern College of Music, the Albert Halls in Bolton, the Floral Hall in New Brighton and Buxton Opera House. I have always been struck by their willingness to engage happily with their audiences off stage, before, during and after shows.

The Fairport back catalogue is huge now, and it must be frustrating for the band not to have the time, even in a three-hour Cropredy set, to be able to reach back for more of it. It's hard to list my favourite tracks, but aside from the classics I'm always happy to hear – 'Matty', 'Who Knows Where The Time Goes', 'Sloth', 'Portmeirion' and 'The Hiring Fair' – there are 'Bankruptured' (Peggy), 'Precious Time' (Ric), 'Dirty Linen' (Swarb) and 'My Love is in America' and 'Moondust and Solitude' (Chris).

The memory of Maart in those final few moments on stage at Cropredy a few weeks before his death in 2018 will stay with me for ever. The Fairport family reached out to him, and he to them, knowing we wouldn't see each other again. That shared history, built over so many years, means so much to so many of us.

ERROL'S
6 APRIL 1986, GÖTEBORG, SWEDEN

STAFFAN WENNERLUND

My favourite band was coming back to my home town! Even though I had been to England over the years and seen Fairport, visiting Cropredy (not to mention Broughton Castle) several times, this was the first time in three years that I again would hear them live. And it was ten years since I had seen a very different Fairport on my home turf, the Sandy-fronted *Live* lineup in December 1975. This time, they were going to play in the town's leading rock club, Errol's.

I had come to know another local Fairport friend, Kurt Thulin, who told me that he, together with his brother Mikael, had decided to bring a crate of beer to Errol's around soundcheck time to offer to the band, and he invited me along. That afternoon, I met up with Kurt, Mikael and the crate of beer at the venue. As I recall, there was merry post-soundcheck chat and socialising, with everybody in good spirits and anticipating a good gig. A couple of hours later we (the punters) were rewarded by a set that mixed old and new.

After the band folded in 1979, I had contacted Peggy and through him got information and also bought the last two albums, *Farewell, Farewell*, and the pretty new *Gladys' Leap*, released in 1985. So I felt well informed, knowing that the band had two new members and had only been a touring band again since October 1985. We could really feel they enjoyed it and the band sparkled. Tradition was upheld with the opening numbers, 'The Lark in The Morning' and 'Walk Awhile', and then the 'new boys', Ric and Maart, presented themselves in a new instrumental. Simon beautifully sang two new ballads, the closers of side one of *Gladys' Leap*. The band was visibly excited and happy to play in front of an enthusiastic audience, playing around on the stage. The evening's highlight was a fantastic version of 'Sloth', a song I had loved ever since the *Full House* days, and where Maart excelled with some really impressive electric guitar playing. When the gig was over and the gear packed, we invited the band along for a quiet pint in a local pub, where we had the pleasure of chatting and enjoying their company of the band members. A suitable ending to a brilliant day of Fairport Convention – music and musicians.

EXPLETIVE DELIGHTED!

RELEASED AUGUST 1986

DAVID FLINTHAM

How does *Expletive Delighted!* compare with my other Fairport favourites?

In chronological order, first is the mighty *Full House*, possibly Fairport's finest-ever album from arguably their greatest lineup. There are probably more regularly performed songs from this album than from any other, and is there a better show-starter than 'Walk Awhile'? Then there is *Full House For Sale*. Need I say more?

Next is *'Babbacombe' Lee*, a folk-rock concept album and folk-rock opera, an album that must be listened to from beginning to end. The second album after Richard Thompson's departure, this was proof that there was life after RT. That this was performed live in its entirety 40 years later is a further testimony of its class.

I'm sure the people at Island Records thought long and hard about the name for Fairport Convention's ninth album… Despite the 'Fotheringport Confusion' jibes, *Nine* came from a united band, although with a different sound: slightly less folk-rock, slightly more country-folk. What this lineup would have gone on to produce had it remained together is one of the great ifs.

Leaping forward 13 years and we come to *Expletive Delighted!* A new sound (even though Fairport Convention c1986 was three-fifths of the *Full House* one) from a line-up that would last a decade (unheard of at the time). It is an album that has rightly been described as 'fast and furious', and saw the return of Richard Thompson and Jerry Donahue for 'Hanks For The Memory'. The humorous reference to a lyric sheet was too subtle for some! And whilst it would be sacrilege to admit this at the time, I always preferred Ric Sanders over Dave Swarbrick.

Finally, nearly a quarter of a century further on, from the band's most enduring lineup came *Shuffle And Go*, released just before the pandemic and an album that helped me get through lockdown. This alone makes it noteworthy, and it is an exceptionally fine album.

CROPREDY FESTIVAL

8 & 9 AUGUST 1986, CROPREDY, UK

CARL HUFTON

Me and my mates attended Broughton Castle and thereafter Cropredy until 2013. We knew the band quite well as it was a far more relaxed event back in the eighties, especially Peggy, who was always chatty. Me and my mate Tat went to the bar in the concert field and saw Peggy with a tall, long curly-haired chap and there was a circle of space around them. We thought that was odd but we walked towards Peggy and he turned to us and said, 'Carl, Tat, you know Robert don't you?' It turned out to be Robert Plant, so we had a pint and a chat with Mr Plant and he signed a piece of paper for me, which I still have.

DAVE CHICK

I have been a Fairport fan since I heard 'Chelsea Morning' on John Peel's show in 1968 and I have attended every Cropredy from 1982 onwards, plus many gigs and a river cruise. They have been an important part of my life since I was 15 and I have many memories, from the first time I saw them, at Bath Festival in 1970, right up to March 2024, when I saw them at Dudley Town Hall on the last night of their tour.

I attended Ashley Hutchings' Cropredy fringe performance of his Cecil Sharp show at Banbury Moat House in 1986. This was on the Sunday afternoon after the festival had ended on the Saturday night. I arrived much too early and sat on my own in the bar having a drink while waiting. Gradually other people arrived. A blonde lady with a young boy came and sat near me and then a few others, talking about a camping holiday they were about to have in Ireland.

After the lady and the boy left the table, one of the girls asked, 'Where's Daddy?' The other replied, 'He's fetching Nancy's suitcase.' It dawned on me who Nancy must be and almost immediately 'Daddy' appeared. I was sitting reading the copy of the *Flypaper* fanzine that I had bought at the festival and RT looked at me with a sheepish grin. I think we were both equally embarrassed!

At the same Cropredy, 'Meet On The Ledge" had finished and everyone was departing. In those days the crowd dispersed very quickly and most of the traders closed before the music ended. My friends were going back to their tents but I desperately wanted a cup of tea. I found one place open and took my tea to a spot to one side of the stage, where I sat on a hay bale near the Samaritans' tent and contentedly watched the crew start to dismantle the stage. I became aware of a lady striding towards me in a very determined manner. She placed a hand on my shoulder and looked into my eyes, seeming very concerned about me. 'Bloody Samaritans; never there when you need them!'

EDDY MCCABE

Following on from my Cropredy (and festivals generally) debut in '85, the following year I managed to persuade an acquaintance to join me on a trip to North Oxon. I suspect my primary motivation was that he had a big enough tent and, more importantly, knew how to put one up! On arrival mid-afternoon on the Friday we (okay, he) sorted our

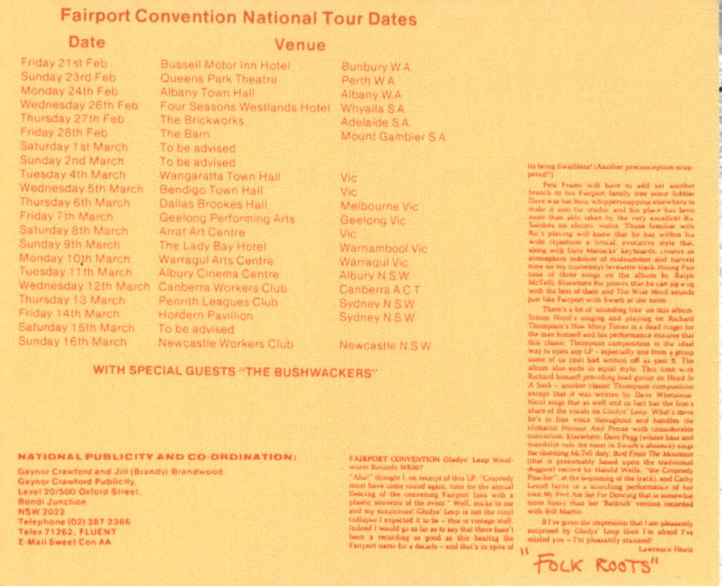

Fairport Convention National Tour Dates

Date	Venue	
Friday 21st Feb	Bussell Motor Inn Hotel	Bunbury W.A.
Sunday 23rd Feb	Queens Park Theatre	Perth W.A.
Monday 24th Feb	Albany Town Hall	Albany W.A.
Wednesday 26th Feb	Four Seasons Westlands Hotel	Whyalla S.A.
Thursday 27th Feb	The Brickworks	Adelaide S.A.
Friday 28th Feb	The Barn	Mount Gambier S.A.
Saturday 1st March	To be advised	
Sunday 2nd March	To be advised	
Tuesday 4th March	Wangaratta Town Hall	Vic
Wednesday 5th March	Bendigo Town Hall	Vic
Thursday 6th March	Dallas Brookes Hall	Melbourne Vic
Friday 7th March	Geelong Performing Arts	Geelong Vic
Saturday 8th March	Arrat Art Centre	Vic
Sunday 9th March	The Lady Bay Hotel	Warnambool Vic
Monday 10th March	Warragul Arts Centre	Warragul Vic
Tuesday 11th March	Albury Cinema Centre	Albury N.S.W.
Wednesday 12th March	Canberra Workers Club	Canberra A.C.T.
Thursday 13 March	Penrith Leagues Club	Sydney N.S.W.
Friday 14th March	Hordern Pavillion	Sydney N.S.W.
Saturday 15th March	To be advised	
Sunday 16th March	Newcastle Workers Club	Newcastle N.S.W.

WITH SPECIAL GUESTS "THE BUSHWACKERS"

NATIONAL PUBLICITY AND CO-ORDINATION:
Gaynor Crawford and Jill (Brandy) Brandwood.
Gaynor Crawford Publicity.
Level 20/500 Oxford Street.
Bondi Junction
NSW 2022
Telephone (02) 387 2366
Telex 71262, FLUENT
E-Mail Sweet Con AA

FAIRPORT CONVENTION Gladys' Leap Woodworm Records WR007

"FOLK ROOTS"

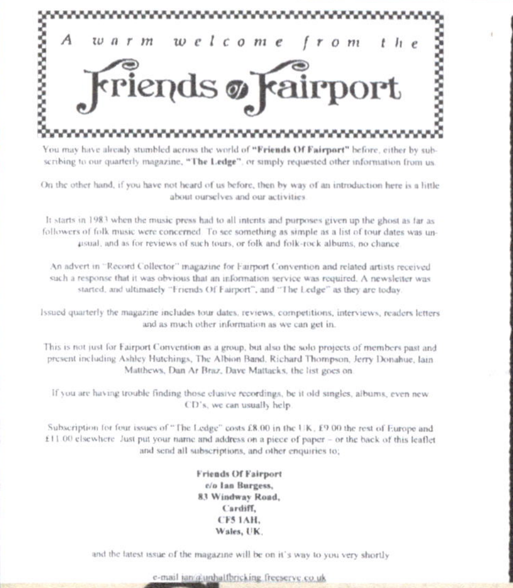

A warm welcome from the

Friends of Fairport

You may have already stumbled across the world of **"Friends Of Fairport"** before, either by subscribing to our quarterly magazine, **"The Ledge"**, or simply requested other information from us.

On the other hand, if you have not heard of us before, then by way of an introduction here is a little about ourselves and our activities.

It starts in 1983 when the music press had to all intents and purposes given up the ghost as far as followers of folk music were concerned. To see something as simple as a list of tour dates was unusual, and as for reviews of such tours, or folk and folk-rock albums, no chance.

An advert in "Record Collector" magazine for Fairport Convention and related artists received such a response that it was obvious that an information service was required. A newsletter was started, and ultimately "Friends Of Fairport", and "The Ledge" as they are today.

Issued quarterly the magazine includes tour dates, reviews, competitions, interviews, readers letters and as much other information as we can get in.

This is not just for Fairport Convention as a group, but also the solo projects of members past and present including Ashley Hutchings, The Albion Band, Richard Thompson, Jerry Donahue, Iain Matthews, Dan Ar Braz, Dave Mattacks, the list goes on.

If you are having trouble finding those elusive recordings, be it old singles, albums, even new CD's, we can usually help.

Subscription for four issues of "The Ledge" costs £8.00 in the UK, £9.00 the rest of Europe and £11.00 elsewhere. Just put your name and address on a piece of paper – or the back of this leaflet and send all subscriptions, and other enquiries to;

Friends Of Fairport
c/o Ian Burgess,
83 Windway Road,
Cardiff,
CF5 1AH,
Wales, UK.

and the latest issue of the magazine will be on it's way to you very shortly

e-mail ian@unhalfbricking.freeserve.co.uk

Fairport Convention

invite you to their 20TH Anniversary Weekend at Cropredy near Banbury, Oxfordshire, England
FRIDAY 14 AUGUST & SATURDAY 15 AUGUST 1987

FRIDAY 7.30pm – 11.30pm
JOHN MARTYN & DANNY THOMPSON
GORDON GILTRAP
and from the USA LE RUE

SATURDAY 12 noon – 11.30pm
FAIRPORT CONVENTION
Simon Nicol, Dave Pegg, Dave Mattacks, Ric Sanders, Martin Allcock with guests Ralph McTell, Richard Thompson, Dave Swarbrick, Jerry Donahue, June Tabor, Cathy Lesurf (plus surprise guests!)
RICHARD THOMPSON *solo*
WHIPPERSNAPPER
MUZSIKÁS *from Hungary*
CHICKEN SHACK *featuring Stan Webb*
MARA *from Australia*
THE STEVE ASHLEY BAND

The best in festival toilets, food and drink. Elegantly sufficient camping and car parking.

Trebles all round!

The revived Fairport Convention are celebrating their thriving cottage industry, Woodworm Records, with a 40-date tour. But it wasn't always beer and skittles . . .

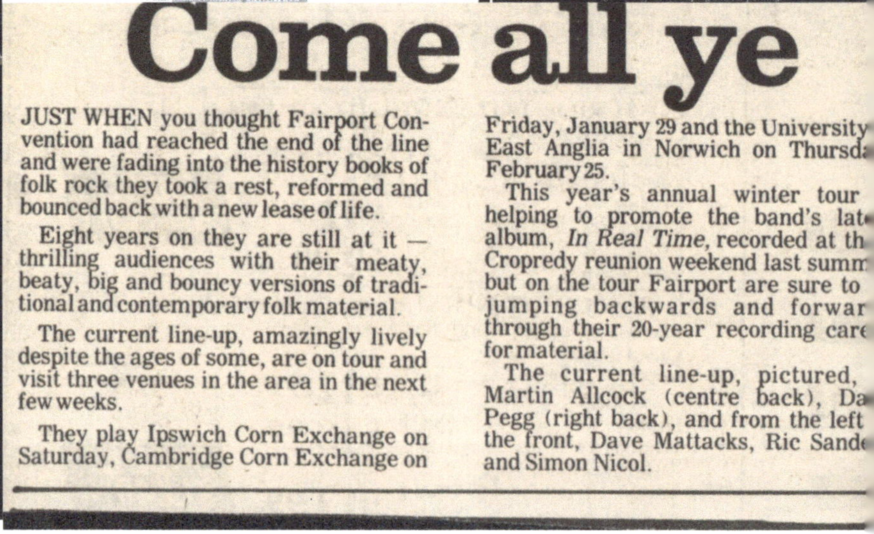

Come all ye

JUST WHEN you thought Fairport Convention had reached the end of the line and were fading into the history books of folk rock they took a rest, reformed and bounced back with a new lease of life.

Eight years on they are still at it — thrilling audiences with their meaty, beaty, big and bouncy versions of traditional and contemporary folk material.

The current line-up, amazingly lively despite the ages of some, are on tour and visit three venues in the area in the next few weeks.

They play Ipswich Corn Exchange on Saturday, Cambridge Corn Exchange on Friday, January 29 and the University East Anglia in Norwich on Thursd February 25.

This year's annual winter tour helping to promote the band's lat album, *In Real Time*, recorded at th Cropredy reunion weekend last summ but on the tour Fairport are sure to jumping backwards and forwar through their 20-year recording care for material.

The current line-up, pictured, Martin Allcock (centre back), Da Pegg (right back), and from the left the front, Dave Mattacks, Ric Sande and Simon Nicol.

(clockwise from top left) Australian tour dates 1987 (Ian Burgess); Tony Lewis proposed to wife Louisa at Cropredy; ad for Cropredy 1987 (Ian Burgess); press for *In Real Time* tour (Ian Burgess); trebles all round with Q magazine; EddieBewsher almost remembers Cropredy in 1987; a warm welcome from Friends of Fairport

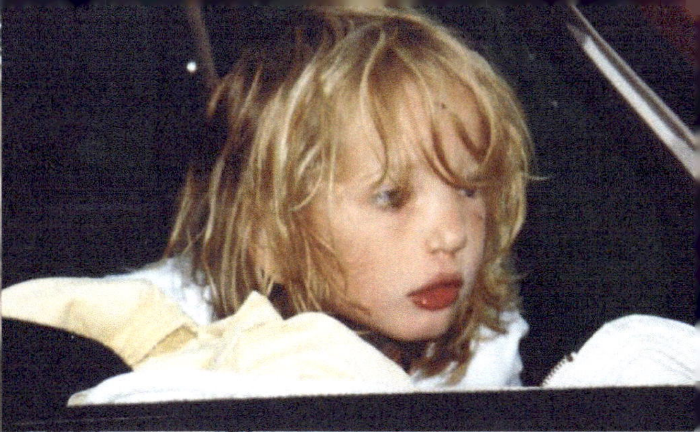

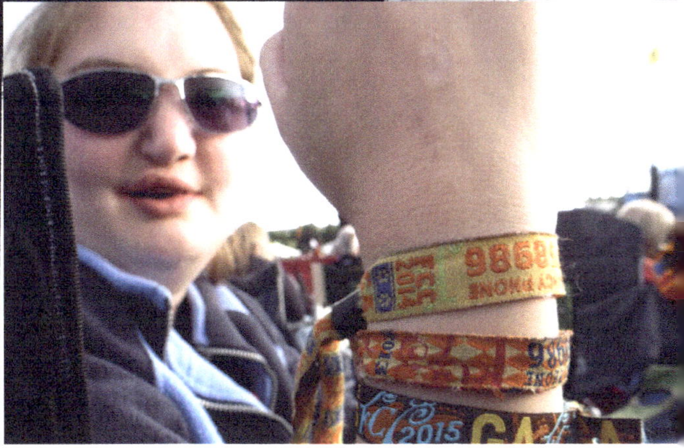

(clockwise from top left) Michael Sage with Peggy; Chris Revie about to set off for his first ever Cropredy in 1987; Emma Royston has been a lifelong Cropredy attendee; Festival Tours ad from 1987 (Ian Burgess) accommodation in double quick time, so we had some relaxation time and in short order I had struck up a conversation with our new tent-neighbours Mick and Jo, from Leeds. The chat rolled around to discussion on the various bands and artists we had seen. Needless to say, the whole thing soon degenerated into rock 'n' roll tennis' and for a little while I felt my Nice, ELP, Tull, Procol, Tir na Nog, Wings, Led Zep, etc. were just about keeping pace with Mick's Stones, Fleetwood Mac and so on. However, I caved my hand when he quite casually, and with no evidence of one-upmanship, mentioned 'the first time I saw Hendrix…'. My jaw dropped, and mustering what dignity I could manage, I suddenly felt very hungry, needing to end the conversation immediately, and get the spag bol on!

SIMON FRISBY

I've been a Cropredy veteran since '98, minus the two pesky Covid years. In 2006, I was going through some difficult moments with my mental health, but as ever I went to the best festival in the world. Late on Friday, I started suffering with breathing difficulties, and went to the excellent St John's Ambulance, where they put me on a nebuliser which seemed to sort the issue out. However, on the Saturday it got progressively worse. But being a stubborn so and so, I was determined to see Fairport, a band that has brought me much joy over my life and helped me take me away from some dark thoughts. It got to 'Matty Groves' and I couldn't breathe! Two excellent stewards rushed me to the backstage St John's where I was promptly rushed to Banbury hospital for a week's stay. My parents contacted FC High Command and informed them that I had abandoned my tent and possessions in the back packers' field. About an hour later, these items were all delivered to reception. Whatever festival would go to this length? It says everything about the festival, about the stewards, about Fairport and about Gareth. Yes, it's a business, but it's based on kindness and love, and just bringing happiness to people. As long as you host the festival I'll be there.

Fairport Convention and Cropredy. I love you.

THE NIGHT STAGE

8 OCTOBER 1986, BOSTON, MASSACHUSETTS

HARRY MCCANDLESS

When I was 19 years old and a student at the School of the Museum of Fine Arts in Boston, Massachusetts, I went to see Fairport at a club in Cambridge with my roommate, Haskell. The gig was the last on their tour of the States that fall and the band were booked for two shows that night with support by Dan Ar Braz. We only had tickets for the first show, but as it turned out, everyone was invited to stay for the second.

My impressions of the night are a bit hazy, but a few things stand out. DM was in a bad mood, and let his general displeasure come through in his deliberately lackadaisical drumming on 'Instrumental Medley '85' – we all had a chuckle at the quiet rimshots he did on the 'Riverhead' section. Peggy's bass amp had a terrible buzz that reverberated through the PA system, prompting Simon to remark, 'Nice buzz you've got there!', to which Peggy replied, 'But it's the only buzz I've had all night!'

During the interval, as the crew sorted the bass buzz, we spied Simon and DM at the bar. Simon seemed to have a different drink in his hand every five minutes, while DM bought one very flamboyant tropical cocktail complete with umbrella and set it next to his drum stool.

When the band returned to the stage, Simon announced, with a slight slur, that 'during the interval, I got drunk.' Well, things just went to pieces after that, as it became clear that Simon couldn't sing anything without laughing uncontrollably. Dan Ar Braz was called to the stage by Peggy, and it was mostly rock and roll covers for the rest of the set ('Nadine'?) with Dan on lead vocals and Simon sharing his mic for 'harmonies' mostly sung, spittle-flecked, into the side of Dan's head.

During the interval between the last number and the encore (I can't remember if they played 'Meet On The Ledge' twice, one for each show, that night), Haskell put a character sketch he had done of the band as Spinal Tap on the snare drum. From DM's smile and eagerness to show it to the rest of the chaps, he seemed, at that moment, fully cheered up.

OCTAGON THEATRE
4 FEBRUARY 1987, YEOVIL, UK

TONY LEWIS

In early 1987, I was trying desperately to engineer a situation where I could spend some time with a young lady call Louisa, who I'd admired from afar for some while. With a group of old school friends, I arranged a trip to see Fairport at The Octagon in Yeovil. Tickets were purchased and Louisa invited – I think she felt there was safety in numbers! In the event, all bar one of those friends dropped out but ex-fighter-pilot Dave drove us down there from Bristol in his mum's Mini Metro (a step down from a Tornado) and we had a fine evening. We always refer to this as an 'illicit date', as Louisa was not really aware of my designs on her.

Cropredy 1987 saw Ian Anderson and Tull take the stage. I proposed to Louisa in the middle of 'Serenade To A Cuckoo' and, thankfully, she said 'yes'! We married in

May 1988. I asked Peggy if Fairport would play at the wedding (as the Fairport Ceilidh Band) and it seemed a possibility that would happen, but I recall there was a clash with some US dates (possibly for Peggy and Maart with Tull?), so it fell through, but you did send us a lovely card on the day, signed by all the band (which I still have).

From 1987 on, we made a point of going to the Yeovil date on Fairport's Winter Tour every year, through fog, snow and all manner of weather. We managed to clock up 24 years on the trot, before Fairport decided (to our shock) to drop it from the usual itinerary. As our family grew in number, we'd bring more and more daughters to the gig (ending up with all four) and they loved that annual outing as much as we did, especially somehow getting hold of a poster from the theatre staff and getting the band to sign it in the bar after the gig. The band were always so kind to the girls and took time to talk to them – I think they recognised the girls eventually, as they met them there every year.

And it wasn't just Yeovil – our daughters were (and are) Cropredy regulars from birth. Teah, our eldest, can be seen in the early pages of the *Festival Folk* book, as a baby sat on the ground with her mum and in further pages with her sister Copper (some years later), enjoying the fun and games with Les Bicyclettes at the top of the field, both sporting Francis Dunnery t-shirts. The festival and the music just became part of them. They all learned to play (a variety of instruments) and sing, as they developed their own tastes in music, with a clear leaning towards melody and musicianship. They have forged their own friendships at Cropredy, growing up with other Fairporters' children over the years and keeping in touch beyond the festival, via social media or in person.

Now they make their own music (Teah's songs would go down a storm with a Cropredy audience, but you don't need me to tell you how hard it is to get a break as a singer-songwriter, however different or special you are). Thank you for being a huge part of *our* story and now of our four daughters' stories; for the music, the love and the 'wholesomeness' of the Fairport family. Long may these stories continue.

WINTER GARDENS
7 FEBRUARY 1987, MALVERN, UK

IAN BURGESS

I went to Malvern on the *Expletive Delighted!* tour, arriving early. I was outside the venue in the cold when Jonah saw me and invited me inside. The band had completed their soundcheck, so nothing was happening other than the crew moving some flight cases and working on the slide show that accompanied 'The Hiring Fair'. Jonah asked if I would assist a new boy on the crew in putting a flight case back in the truck. He introduced him as 'a young lad who wants to learn about sound; his name is Gareth

(Williams).' He obviously did learn, going on to tour with Fairport for some years but also Jethro Tull, Bonnie Tyler and Deacon Blue amongst others. Eventually touring with Oasis during their top years, he was also headhunted by Pink Floyd for their only reunion performance at *Live 8*. Fairport still had his phone number, so when they needed a new chief for the festival, it was him they called. I'm proud to have known him from being the junior pushing flight cases all the way to him now becoming the king of the festival.

CROPREDY FESTIVAL
14 & 15 AUGUST 1987, CROPREDY, UK

JAN & JON DIXON

In a decade far, far away, some random events happened. At Nostell Priory in 1984, Jon saw Steeleye (sorry). 'If you like that,' said Stevie, 'you'll love Fairport.' At the Oxford Apollo in 1985, Jon saw Fairport and Stevie was right. It was the final night of the tour and they had a couple of guests. Ralph McTell sang two or three songs with them, including 'White Dress' which made an immediate impression. Also, a second drummer turned up. Jon didn't know who he was but they referred to him as 'DM'.

The next event was Queen's final UK concert at Knebworth, August 1986. Jon and Jan went, decided it was a waste just being friends, and further decided they were now a couple. The gig was great, but it turned out that on the same day, not far away, Robert Plant was making a (then rare) guest appearance with Fairport at Cropredy. 'Bugger,' said Jan, reading about it in the paper the following week. 'We should check out this Fairport thing.' 'Ah yes,' said Jon, knowledgably. 'If you like Steeleye, you'll love Fairport.' They went to the Fairfield Halls in Croydon in January 1987 and Jon was right. Maart wore his fox hat and told his 'wear the fox hat' joke. The gig was great, a few people danced, lots of people sang and Fairport (wood)wormed their way into our lives. 35 Cropredys, more warm-ups and countless winter tours later, they are still there. Some highlights:

We decided to plunge straight in. In spring 1987 Jan ventured to the Half Moon in Putney to buy warm-up tickets. Our warm-up was a revelation. Stunning music in the stifling heat and we were crammed in like sardines. Someone shouted 'get up!' in 'Matty Groves' a verse early. We think about that almost every 'Matty' since. And so, possibly, does he. 'Putney's nice,' we thought, and moved in together in a flat in East Putney.

August 1987 saw our first Cropredy. We hired a car specially, the poshest one we'd ever had – a Nissan Bluebird. We drove up the A4260 feeling like celebs. In their set, Fairport backed Ian Anderson and Martin Barre on some Tull songs. 'Watch Dave

Mattacks' eyes grow stalks as he tries to read his crib sheet!' quipped Ian at the start of 'Hunting Girl'. We still use this line whenever we see a drummer grappling with something epically complicated. About two hours into Fairport's wonderful set, our feet were starting to ache. 'Never mind,' we thought, 'probably not long to go…'. We didn't know then that there were nearly three more hours to go – the longest set we've ever seen by anyone. It was so good we forgot about our feet. June Tabor sang on a brilliant 'Sailor's Life' and we have never missed a Cropredy ever again.

EDDIE BEWSHER

In 1987 there was only one way of getting round the country – hitchhiking! As some of our mates had been to Cropredy in previous years and we were fans of folk-rock and (importantly) beer, 24-year-old me decided to get down to Croppers with my mate Paul. It was not my first time of seeing Fairport – that was Leeds in 1985 on the *Gladys' Leap* tour – but Cropredy sounded like a good laugh. I was a student and Paul worked in a factory in Hull, where he found a van heading down south so we jumped in the back with the van's load. There were no windows and no seats so we bobbed around for a few hours, not knowing where we were. When the van stopped and the half-light in the back became full light as the van door was raised, we found we were at the main gate for Cropredy!

We walked in, feeling slightly seasick after the ride, and started bumping into friends we had arranged to see there. In those days you just turned up and hoped for the best or read notes pinned on trees; however, it worked. One of our mates shared a hitch from London with an Australian called Dean. He became part of our group as he had travelled solo (we still know him and I'm still in touch). Our tents were rubbish and not waterproof and we had no sleeping bags and no food. We set up the tents quickly and began drinking. Soon we were in main field. I remember La Rue. There were about ten of us now and we drank. And drank. There were lots of arms draped round peoples' shoulders.

I walked to the bar. On the way, I bumped into Gordon Giltrap. Poor Gordon. He was with a woman or two and walking along minding his own business when a drunken me put an arm over his shoulders. 'Gooordonnn! You're great, man. Hey…' I told anyone around as I propped myself up on a very patient Mr Giltrap, 'it's Gordon Giltrap.' I gave him the full drunken hugs, beer breath and over-loud speaking treatment until we parted company. Many years later, middle-aged and sober, I went up to him and apologised. Of course he didn't remember me…

The next day we started drinking by 9am. We went to the Red Lion, met loads of people and any folk-rock celeb we saw got the drunk treatment. Eventually it was back to the main field. And back to the village, back to the field, in someone's tent, all over the place. We must have staggered miles. We saw the Climax Blues Band. By the time

Fairport Convention came on, our group had expanded and we spun around, linked arms and danced like nutters to anything with a beat. In those days there was 'The Widow of Westmoreland's Daughter', Reynard The Fox' and 'Matty Groves' in the set list. It was great fun and a bit mad. We weren't the only ones; it was a big party back then. The songs the band did sounded great, and no one sat in quiet reverence wondering how the arrangement differed from the original recording. No one cared. No chairs to trip over either. We were up most of night too, talking, drinking, putting the world to rights and being silly.

At some stage the next day, me and Paul tried to hitch off site. We got no lifts all afternoon, so decided to see if we could get to Banbury and save Hull for the next day. We sat by the canal and spent hours trying to hitch a canal ride to Banbury. Again and again, people would laugh and think we were joking. We weren't!

In the early evening, we got a lift in a truck to the Banbury Cross pub. We spent the evening in the pub and after closing time wandered to a park, where we slept under a bush. We didn't bother with a tent. Neither of us realised we were next to a railway goods yard. The first shunting locomotive appeared at about 6am. Awake, and having now had no food for days, we crossed Banbury on foot, stuck a thumb out and the first lift we got was a HGV to Hull. Brilliant!

The next few Cropredys were pretty similar drink-wise, but I had a scruffy van by then and did occasionally eat something. So to Dean, Paul, Martin, Dave, Andy, Matt, Debby, Steve, Clare, Amanda and all the eighties Cropredy crew – cheers! I've not missed one since, and although I'm now sober and take my daughter, I still meet up with some of 'us lot' from those days every year. I still like to wander around, and the village and hanging out at the bar chatting is a big part of it all. I love Cropredy, although I have to admit I find all the chairs in lines these days annoying! Ah, I'm getting nostalgic…

EMMA ROYSTON

I have been a Cropredy attendee since I was in my mother's womb in 1987. My absolute favourite time of the year is when I get to stand on the Field of Dreams with 20,000 like-minded people! One of my first memories of Cropredy is of waking up on the parcel shelf of our car, our tent having flooded! Richard Thompson must have been on that year.

2018 was one of only a handful of years that I missed, because my (then) boyfriend Andrew was admitted to hospital. I was devastated to miss Brian Wilson, my musical hero, play 'God Only Knows' on that beloved field. Something good came out of it though, Andrew proposed a few weeks later and he is now my husband. He has been a Cropredy convert since his first festival in 2012.

MICHAEL MURRAY

During the early eighties, I was married with two young sons and Cropredy did not seem possible. My marriage was going through a bad time, leading to us divorcing in 1987. I lived on my own for the next two years and now there was no reason not to go. On that Friday in August 1987, I left work at 4pm and dashed home and packed. I drove the 135 miles or so, not knowing what I was going to. I was on my own but so what? I got there, pitched my tent and entered *that* field at about 9 o'clock and went 'wow!' I'd missed the first couple of acts but the magic had hit me.

Saturday was wonderful, particularly Chicken Shack, culminating in a four-hour set by Fairport. And halfway through, surprise artists Ian Anderson and Martin Barre came on for four songs. I was taken with the charisma of Ian on flute, moving round the stage. Finishing the set with 'Matty' and 'Meet On The Ledge' put the cap on a wonderful day. I was a bit flat driving home on Sunday, thinking that it would be a whole year before I could get back there.

Since that first festival, Cropredy has become a fixture each year and the highlight of the year. 2024 will span 38 years and be my 36th Cropredy, missing out the two Covid years. My younger son Neil came with me in 1988, when he was aged eleven. He's only missed two years since.

Our love of Cropredy can be exemplified by two incidents. In 1992, I was driving four of us to the festival when I ran into the back of a vehicle queuing to get onto a busy roundabout. My nearside wing was pushed back, close to the wheel. I couldn't let my passengers, who were all excited about going to Cropredy, down. I went to the front of the car and pulled the wing forward and clear of the wheel. All the lights were working, so I took a chance and we drove on. We managed to get there and back safely and enjoyed a great festival.

We normally camp but sometimes we took a caravan. In 1994, I had finished packing the caravan and Ray, our gardener, helped me move it to our gateway. I pulled from the front and he pushed from the back, unable to see me. As we reached the gateway, my left wrist hit the concrete gatepost with the full force of the caravan. The pain was agonising and I feared my wrist was broken. I went back in the house, took a couple of paracetamol and sat down.

I thought nothing was broken, and missing Cropredy was unthinkable. I decided not to ring Maria, my wife who was at work, as she would have urged me not to go. Ray helped me hitch the caravan and off I went to pick up Neil.

We got to the festival incident free. Once we got into *that* field, I went to the first aid tent. They were confident there was nothing broken. They dressed my wrist and Neil and I had a great weekend. By Sunday, my wrist was much less painful and we got home safely.

There have been numerous memories over the years, a lot of them – okay, nearly all of them – with many beers being drunk (except when I was driving). As well as 35 Cropredys, I've seen them in many places including Cleethorpes, Nottingham, Sheffield, Cheltenham, Tewkesbury, Cannock, Newark, Skegness, Aberdeen, Nairn and Inverness. And I've enjoyed every one of them.

MICHAEL SAGE

I was 'late' getting into Fairport Convention. I recall hearing 'Si Tu Dois Partir' on the radio around 1969 but really didn't get the bug then. At some point I bought *The History of Fairport Convention* double LP but didn't pay too much attention to it. My interest in folk rock started in 1975 with Steeleye Span's 'All Around My Hat' and from then I bought their back catalogue and have been a fan of Steeleye ever since. This caused me to unearth my copy of *The History of…* and I was quickly hooked on the songs and music. The chart on the front cover was my educational tool to learn the story so far, but of course it was already out of date due to the ever-changing lineup.

I didn't see either Steeleye or Fairport live for some years. I lived in Scotland from the age of 16 and moved back to England some ten years later. The first time I saw Steeleye live was with the lineup including John Kirkpatrick and the return of Martin Carthy.

In 1987, I was reading *NME* and saw a small article about Fairport's annual festival and the fact that it would be the band's 20th anniversary. I drove to Cropredy on the Saturday morning and parked in a field off a street called 'Cup and Saucer'. I bought my ticket and enjoyed the day immensely enjoyed myself. I slept in the car overnight and drove home the next day. I remember at the start of Richard Thompson's set he struck up the opening chords of 'Sgt. Pepper' and sang 'it was twenty years ago today, that Ashley Hutchings taught the band to play', much to everyone's amusement.

Since then, I have moved home and work several times but have managed to travel to Cropredy from a variety of places – Wealdstone, Kenton, Pinner, Walton-on-Thames, Shetland Islands, Orkney Islands, Faringdon, Gloucester, Malta, Glastonbury and Valencia. I now live in Ayamonte, Spain, so will fly from Faro in Portugal. I will also be going to Costa Del Folk in Portugal in October, which is only a 45-minute drive!

Since 1987, I have missed Cropredy only twice (due to work getting in the way) and of course the Covid years when it was cancelled. I think I have been about 33 times or thereabouts! Since my first solo trip, I have always gone for the full weekend and taken my wife, children and numerous friends.

Also, depending on my location at the time, I have been to gigs in various locations: Reading, Hayes, Islington's Union Chapel, The Forum, Putney, Maidstone – and several others that have slipped my mind.

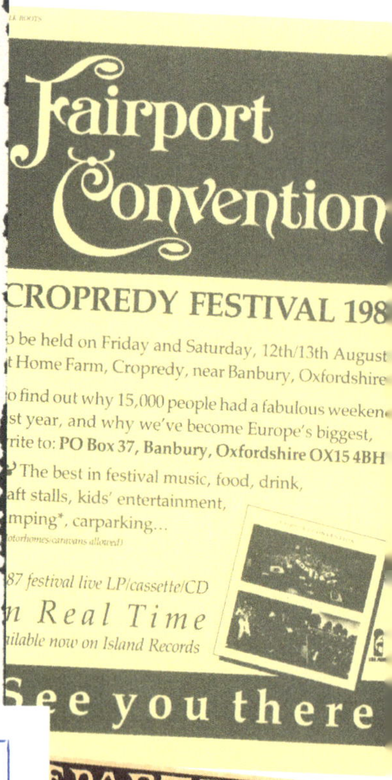

(clockwise from left) Fifth annual reunion flyer (Ian Burgess); 21st year celebration concert flyer (Ian Burgess); 1988 Cropredy flyer (Ian Burgess); US tour flyer (Ian Walton); New Year's Eve flyer (Ian Burgess); newsletter (Ian Burgess)

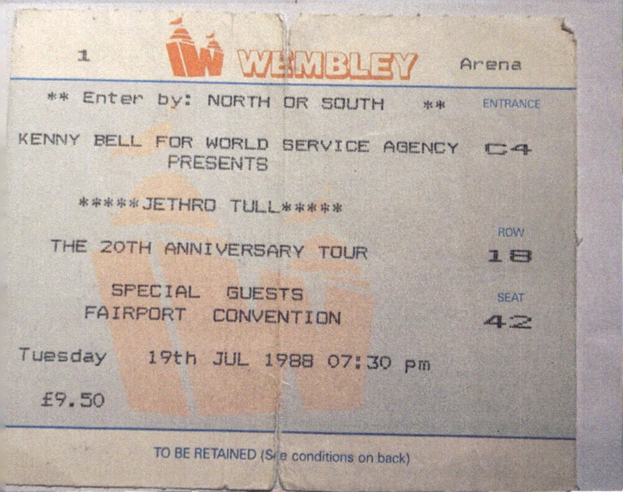

Ordered 6/2/97

30 YEARS OF Fairport Convention 1967-1997

NEWSLETTER

April 1997

Dear 'Fairporters',
Well our 35 consecutive day tour of the UK was a great success - if a little knackering. Maartin Allcocks departure on December 22nd, just before the Christmas and New Year break, left us just 7 days rehearsal with Chris Leslie. The seemingly effortless way that Chris has fitted into Fairport is a real tribute to his talent. It was a pleasure to hear the eight new songs/tunes in the repertoire develop as the gigs went by.

Cropredy Festival - August 8th and 9th

Please join us for this very special event - and tell all of your friends - we have a GREAT line up. The bar will be supplied with pub prices by The Bay Horse of Masham, Yorks. The usual friendly faces plus one or two surprises.

Friday 8th August... gates will open at **12-30pm.** Music will start at **3.00pm** with *Pressgang*, followed by *Kristina Olsen (USA), Julian Dawson Band, Osibisa, Fairport Convention* featuring: *Simon Nicol, Dave Mattacks, Richard Thompson, Dave Swarbrick, Ashley Hutchings, Judy Dyble and Vikki Clayton* and finally *The Saw Doctors* - finishing about midnight.

Saturday 9th August... gates will open at **9.30am.** Music starting at **12.00 noon** with *The Bushbury Mountain Daredevils* followed by *The Albion Band, Tempest (USA), Huw and Tony Williams, Kings of Calicutt (featuring Eliza Carthy),* and then the last ever re-union of *John Otway and Wild Willy Barrett* followed by *Fairport Convention* featuring: *Simon Nicol, Dave Pegg, Dave Mattacks, Ric Sanders, Chris Leslie, Richard Thompson, Dave Swarbrick, Jerry Donahue, Ralph McTell, Maartin Allcock, Dan ArBraz, Vikki Clayton and Cathy LeSurf* who will play until about midnight.

Ticket Prices and Camping We have done our best to keep the increase on concert ticket prices to a minimum - only £1 on 1996. However due to the stringent safety regulations now enforced, which we're sure you have noticed, the cost of camping has had to be increased. The regulations are for your safety and of course we are happy to co-operate BUT the costs are spiralling up and have to be covered by those benefiting ... ie the campers! Thanks in advance for your understanding.

Ticket Prices

Before July 1st	Weekend £35.00 Saturday £24.00
July 1st to August 1st	Weekend £38.00 Saturday £26.00
After August 1st or on the gate	Weekend £41.00 Saturday £28.00

Children under 14 admitted FREE with a paying adult

Camping:

Camping Tickets are available in advance with concert tickets.

Thursday, Friday and Saturday	£8.00 per vehicle/motor cycle
Friday and Saturday	£5.00 per vehicle/motor cycle
Saturday only	FREE
Backpackers	FREE

Accommodation details

Accommodation details in the area are available from the Tourist Information Centre, 8 Horsefair, Banbury 01295 259855 ... but you have to be quick!

Fairport Goodies

Left over from our winter tour and hence now reduced in price

T-Shirts XL or L black only	£8.00
Embroidered hats - black, blue, grey	£7.00
Programmes	£2.50

New Release

"Who Knows where the Time Goes?"

WRCD/WRC 025 - Cassette and CD

Available from us **after** July 7th ... see order form ... OR in your shops from August 11th - distributed by Pinnacle ... and of course at the Cropredy Festival record shop. Tracks will include some of the new material you may have heard on the tour - including *Sailing Boat, John Gaudie, Wishfulness Waltz, Spanish Main, Golden Glove, Bowmens' Retreat* and, of course, *"Who Knows ...?"* featuring Ric's lovely string arrangement. We also hope to have a bonus track for the UK release - *"Heard it Through the Grapevine"* featuring Richard Thompson, Roy Wood and his brass section with Fairport from Cropredy 1995.

Who Knows where the Time Goes?

(clockwise from top left) label image Dominic Duckworth (centre, back row) was a fully-fledged Goth when he attended Cropredy in 1988 & is pictured (clockwise) with family friends Leona and Oscar, daughter Jess (with Coco the pug) step grandson Casper & wife Sam; 30 years of Fairport newsletter (Ian Walton); Ian Walton enjoying the rain at Cropredy in 2015; Fairport at Wembley (Darian Nelson)

JIMMY YOUNG

Fairport's 1987 winter tour took them to the Winter Gardens, Cleethorpes where my wife, Kay, and I enjoyed a great night and welcome start to the second week of the New Year. So much so that in a post-gig queue in the Gents, I found myself next to Dave Pegg, whom I congratulated on the set. We enjoyed it that much we invited the band back to our house in Grimsby, not least as we had a bottle of Balvenie (a fine Speyside whisky) to share from our recent trip back home for Hogmanay.

The evening wore on, tracks were played and latterly talk got around to my work on fish. I'd earlier worked as a buyer in North East Scotland and then recently completed a PhD on seafood marketing. After a bit, and possibly as a ruse to get to the end of the Balvenie, Peggy suggested that I should have a chat with Ian Anderson from Jethro Tull at the forthcoming Cropredy. (At that time, Ian was a prominent entrepreneur with his Strathaird Salmon company which he ran as a very serious sideline.)

Cropredy came round and the suggested meeting was organised. I waited in a queue of journos set to interview the Tull frontman out in the artists' area of the field. Perhaps not fully trusting Peggy's recommendation, I was immediately quizzed about why he should be talking to me. I'd been a fan, like many, of *Aqualung* et al but that was no real reason to grab his attention. A brief account of my research sufficed and soon we were getting to grips with some of the then (and still) controversial issues surrounding fish utilisation and the emergent role of aquaculture. The line of journos overlooking us from the other side of a thicket fence lengthened and became increasingly impatient at the slipping PR schedule. This delay became all too much for one from *Rolling Stone*, who shouted that he'd been waiting well over an hour.

He became increasingly vocal in his indignation that a magazine such as his was being ignored. After one rant too many, Ian eventually shouted in response, 'Fuck *Rolling Stone*! This guy is talking about something far more important than rock 'n' roll – FISH!' The look of complete bemusement on the face of the guy, not to mention the other muso hacks, still brings a smile to my face. Needless to say, this added all the more to my enjoyment of that night, when Fairport were joined by effectively the full Tull line-up. Thanks Fairport – a band and many past members followed and enjoyed since 1970 and the *Full House* tour at City Halls, Glasgow.

ARENA
11 NOVEMBER 1987, BALTIMORE, MARYLAND

DAVID MCELROY

I have been listening to them since 1972 but first saw them in Baltimore, Maryland, on a very snowy Veteran's Day in 1987. Fairport were opening for Jethro Tull. I had a blast listening to them despite the eighteen inches of snow I had to plough through to get there. I saw them again in 1988 at the Merriweather Post Pavilion. Peggy was going both ways, playing for both Fairport and Tull.

The next time I saw them was at Wilbert's in Cleveland, Ohio after I had twice run the Kent State Folk Festival. Peggy suggested that I send Ian Anderson some recordings from those festivals and, as it ended up, Ian used one of the performers as an opening act for Tull. Fairport came to the Kent Stage in 2000 and I had a surprise for them. I was able to prevail upon Ian to provide an introduction for the band. They were looking for him all over, and were to later learn that he sent us a disc for the intro.

I brought the Fairports to Buffalo in 2006. The venue was dodgy, but Simon found solace in the fact that it was the only place in North America that didn't have six televisions running during their performance! Once Peggy came to Buffalo and played with a Tull knock-off band. I took him and Ellen to a hotel that he described as 'very Italian'. I knew exactly where he was staying based on this description and delivered them to their door. Three days later I discovered his merch in the back of my SUV. I tracked him down to a cruise ship and got his stuff back to him.

By far my best memory was seeing Fairport at Cropredy in the summer of 2022. The crowd was fabulous, the lineup was fantastic and the Fairport performance of *Full House* was magnificent. Just the other day, I watched the *Live at Brasenose* video and had a good joyful cry for myself. I feel fortunate to have met all the guys and to have seen them in their own element. They don't do America any longer and I don't know when I can make it back to England. May they have many more years in the fields of Oxfordshire.

BARNSLEY CIVIC
UNKNOWN DATE, BARNSLEY, UK

DAVE ALLEMBY

I have followed Fairport since 1972 when I bought the *Babbacombe Lee* and *History Of* albums. A band at my boys' grammar school played songs like 'Walk Awhile' and I wanted to hear the originals. I sort of discovered Fairport, Steeleye Span and Pentangle at the same time. I started working in 1972 and for the first time in my life I could afford albums, so I found Jethro Tull, Wishbone Ash and Prog rock as well. I still have a massive and very varied album collection. I only ever saw Fairport once, at Barnsley Civic in the late eighties. Two of my favourites, 'The Hiring Fair' and 'Portmeirion', were fairly new to the set back then. I've got all their CDs but I haven't seen them live for about 25 years!

TOWN HALL
18 FEBRUARY 1988, CHELTENHAM, UK

JEFF COOPER

I came to Fairport a little late. I was in my late twenties and the year was 1988. A work colleague was really into Fairport and a stalwart of the Cropredy Festival. Our other musical tastes overlapped so I really had to check them out. I bought the *History Of* compilation on CD. I remember my early favourites being 'Walk Awhile' and 'Angel Delight'. Not all the tracks that I now know and love so much gelled with me at first, but I persevered.

I gradually caught up on all the album releases and various lineups and now love the early Sandy (and Judy) eras as much as I love all their material. I loved collecting the back catalogue (and the forwards and sideways ones) as the music ebbed and flowed into my soul in all its differing shades and colours throughout the decades.

My first live experience was at Cheltenham Town Hall on the *In Real Time* tour. I bought a vivid light blue sweatshirt from the merch desk and wore it to subsequent Cropredys and elsewhere for many years after. It was such a fun gig and I was hooked on seeing them live again. I remember visiting the merch desk and purchasing the then recently released *Expletive Delighted!* album along with Simon's *Before Your Time* LP, both on vinyl, and getting them signed by all after the gig. I still treasure and play these today, although some of the signatures are a bit faded now.

A trip into town to buy cassette copies of *In Real Time* and *Gladys' Leap* on cassette soon followed. For a while the former was my 'go to' choice to play. With pictures from Cropredy on its cover, I had a real yearning to attend.

I lapped up the subsequent Woodworm releases – *Red & Gold* and *The Five Seasons* (my all-time favourite from this era) and eventually got to my first Cropredy in 1992. I remember Robert Plant guesting with FC and being blown away that the band were so adept at turning themselves into Led Zep for the tunes where Robert was on stage. 'Wow. These are proper musicians!' From that first festival I also remember Julianne Regan from All About Eve guesting, plus RT and Swarb with Martin Carthy were there. I was instantly hooked on Four Men And A Dog, and enjoyed Wolfstone and others too.

The discovery of new acts and old meant that I was now truly lost into my new world of folk and folk-rock in all its various guises. There are so many related artists or new bands that I have discovered thanks to Cropredy and Fairport's Wintour support slots.

I lapped up the double CD from Cropredy in '92 as a constant reminder of my first festival. It was an instant hit thanks to Maart's Pink Floyd 'Comfortably Numb' heavy metal intro to 'Matty Groves'. This version remains my favourite Matty intro and not only still knocks my socks off but turned Fairport into one of my very favourite groups to see live.

I've rarely missed a Cropredy since, although some visits have been Saturday only. The 2023 festival was particularly fabulous as I combined it with a visit to the Brasenose and met Sandy's daughter Georgia at her incredible exhibition. Other Cropredy highlights include: discovering the delights of Judy Dyble's appearances and lapping up her subsequent CD releases (with a favourite moment being watching her Band of Perfect Strangers alongside the late David Longdon of Big Big Train fame); seeing The Leningrad Cowboys – once seen never forgotten; walking up the festival field and having a lovely chat with Ashley Hutchings so I could buy a copy of his book and get it signed; and bumping into Roger Hodgson at Paddington Station on the Monday after his 2000 appearance and chatting about the weekend.

As a daily reminder of Cropredy, I have a framed art work by Jill Swarbrick hanging on the wall above my fireplace.

I snap up every Fairport album release and attend each opening night of the Wintour at the Roses Theatre in Tewkesbury. That's apart from 2015, when I was laid up with a slipped disc and gave my brother my ticket. He loved the gig and got Peggy to sign the newly released *Myths and Heroes* CD for me: 'We missed you'.

One thing I will never do is miss seeing Fairport or attending Cropredy whenever I can. I really mean it. May they always 'come round again' – and go on forever!

SPINNEY HILL HALL

26 FEBRUARY 1988, NORTHAMPTON, UK

DAVE CLEMO

By the late 1960s my finances and my guitar playing had progressed to the point where I actually owned a guitar that played in tune all the way up the neck. I'd played a few pub and club gigs (and a few folk clubs) and was intent on writing and playing my own songs and being part of the emerging underground movement. (The least said about these efforts the better.) I got together with a couple of mates and formed a group. We used to rehearse in their flat. We made room for the kit by standing the bed upright against a wall, holding it in place with my guitar amp and speaker.

In 1971 left home and moved into a bedsit in Shepherds Bush. One benefit was the ability to play my records at a respectable volume. An ever present on the turntable was *Liege & Lief*, with *Full House* close behind. One evening I paid a visit to The Duke of Clarence, a long-gone pub just off the roundabout to the east of Shepherds Bush Green. I'd played a residency there a few years earlier, but was totally unprepared for what I walked into. It was my first experience of a traditional music session. I didn't know any of the musicians, or any of the tunes, but I liked what I heard and came back the following week. A few weeks later I asked if I could bring my guitar along and sit in, and so began my involvement with a loose conglomerate of folkies who eventually adopted the name Captain Swing.

Over the next eighteen months, one night a week at The Duke of Clarence became multiple sessions and residencies in pubs across West London, appearances at folk clubs including supporting Jasper Carrott and Cyril Tawney; and appearances at the 1972 Cambridge and Chelmsford Folk Festivals where, as well as an onstage slot, we set up a session in the beer tent which continued all day and into the evening. To my eternal regret, while I was playing in the Chelmsford beer tent and getting extremely drunk, on the other side of the site Sandy Denny was playing a solo set. I never saw her play live again.

Our loose conglomeration of musicians morphed into a nucleus of five, augmented by whoever was in town that week. I was a newbie to the folk world, so the names and reputations of our co-players was lost on me. Our leader was a Scotsman called George. He had a huge ginger afro, was dressed from head to foot in denim and wore platform-soled boots. George ran a t-shirt printing company from a basement beneath a shop in Ladbroke Grove. Our guitarist was another Scot called Finn who worked for George. Concertina player Willie was an accountant and our flute player was a retired seaman called Rod Shearman. He wrote songs and we featured a number of them in our set. One was called 'London River'.

In 1974 the lure of a brand new centrally heated house in Northampton meant that we left our grotty (and cold) bedsit in Shepherds Bush for pastures new. About fifteen years later, I went to see Fairport Convention in concert at the Spinney Hill Hall in Northampton when they were promoting their new album *Red & Gold*. I was as pleased as punch to hear my favourite group play 'London River', a song that Rod had written and that we had performed countless times back in West London.

CHICAGO WFMT FOLK FESTIVAL

4 JULY 1988, CHICAGO, ILLINOIS

BRIAN O'MALLEY

This gig took place in the Patrillo Bandshell, an open-air venue in downtown Chicago's Grant Park. The lads had been in town a few months earlier, opening up for Jethro Tull, and now they were sharing a bill with Joan Baez and David Bromberg, amongst others. This wasn't just a folk festival, this was in conjunction with Chicago's 'Taste Of

Chicago', the world's largest food festival featuring dozens of local restaurants doling out their specialties. Apparently, 3.8 million people attended The Taste in the first week of July 1988. But there were only about five to six thousand people huddled around the Patrillo Bandshell!

The lineup was heavy that day, with maybe a dozen different acts on the same stage. The chaps were on around 2pm with no soundcheck. I remember it being a very short set and the out front sound was not great. They opened up with 'Reynard The Fox', then went into 'The Widow of Westmorland's Daughter' followed by 'Cat On The Mixer'/'Three Left Feet' and 'Si Bheag, Si Mhór' before finishing with 'Matty Groves'.

I went backstage as soon as their set was finished. No one was very happy with the experience. Apparently, the sound on the stage was worse than the sound out front. And Peggy and Maartin Allcock had one thing on their mind… turkey legs! While the lads were on stage, they could see people walking around carrying whole turkey legs. So we were on a mission but, as we were leaving, the stage manager insisted that we all come back for the finale.

We got our turkey legs and barbecued ribs and wandered around the festival grounds. There was also plenty of beer involved. We were all a bit hammered by the time we got back several hours later for the finale. I remember us being at the side of the stage. Joan Baez and David Bromberg were on stage. I looked out at the crowd, and there were now at least 15,000 people in the audience.

The lads were all getting ready to go on stage for the finale. I remember the stage manager coming over to them saying, 'Okay guys, get on that stage and *sing*!' As the boys were entering the stage, the stage manager then looked at me and said 'come on let's go… get out there and SING!' I remember Peggy and I sharing a mic and Joan Baez leading us off in singing 'This Land Is Your Land' and 'Michael, Row The Boat Ashore'. We were trying to sing but couldn't stop laughing… This was *A Mighty Wind* in 1988!

I remember loving the fact that hundreds of thousands of people who were at the festival that day could hear the music that I love coming from my favourite band, Fairport Convention.

As a codicil to this story, in 2004 I used to hang out at a bar called Toons in Chicago's Wrigleyville neighbourhood. I had a friend there who I only knew as David. David was a grip for *Playboy* magazine, handling lighting, cables and gear, and a big Fairport fan who also loved Jethro Tull.

I had been told by a friend that the 1988 FOLKFEST was going to be played on WFMT on Friday night at 8pm. I remember thinking 'I need to record this' so I got my cassette recorder all ready to record it. It was approaching 8pm and I had my finger on the red 'record' button when a man with a very deep voice came on the airwaves and said, 'Welcome to WFMT. We will not be broadcasting the scheduled 1988

FOLKFEST tonight. Instead, we will be bringing you *The Very Best Of Steve Goodman* to commemorate the twenty-year anniversary of his passing.' (Goodman wrote 'City Of New Orleans', made famous by Arlo Guthrie.)

I was livid. How dare they? I walked out of my apartment and over to Toons. I remember seeing David sitting at the far end of the bar. I didn't really want to talk to anybody at that moment, so I sat by myself sulking in my beer. After a few minutes, David walked over and sat next to me and said, 'What's going on with you? You okay' 'You know I'm a big Fairport Convention fan and you remember the story I told you about FOLKFEST 1988? Well, WFMT were supposed to broadcast that show tonight and I was all ready to record it when the announcer came on and said that they were playing *The Best Of Steve Goodman* instead. Can you believe it? They blew off Fairport Convention to play Steve Goodman! I wouldn't mind, but Steve Goodman's been dead for 20 years.'

To which David, in his unmistakable Chicago accent, responded, 'Brian, I'm *David* Goodman. Steve Goodman was my brother…'.

SALLY PECK

I saw them live somewhere in Chicago in the 1980s. I was into both rock and folk at the time and I also liked Irish tunes. What has stayed with me is the energy of the group and the creativity of the arrangements. I can't recall where I saw them. It was either a small theatre, a night club or a bar. I do recall quaffing a brew or two!

WEMBLEY ARENA
19 JULY 1988, LONDON, UK

DARIAN NELSON

I was 21, freshly graduated and a Jethro Tull fan with a growing awareness of folk-rock when I went to the Tull 20th anniversary concert at Wembley where Fairport were support. When they played 'Matty Groves' I was awestruck, having only ever heard Christy Moore's version, 'Little Musgrave'. To hear an old folk tune given a rocked-up interpretation hooked me. I've been a fan ever since. I quickly realised that with Maart, Peggy and DM all playing for both bands I was guaranteed brilliant musicianship whichever group I went to see.

My first Cropredy was 1989, but sadly I did not keep my ticket. The friend from university who came with me, Nigel 'Bonny' Langford, passed away early in 2013 as a result of an aggressive form of MS. I cannot hear 'Meet On The Ledge' without imagining him singing it by my side in a field in Oxfordshire that first year.

My next Cropredy was 1992. I was father to a two-year-old daughter and bought her a tie-dye t-shirt. Sineidin is now a mum herself but she still has the t-shirt and it still fits!

In 1990 I got a new job and soon discovered the boss was a fan of earlier Fairport albums and Swarb in particular. As a birthday treat, I once took him to see Swarb play in a pub in London. I left his employment in 1994 but it has become a tradition that we meet up every year to see FC on the winter tour, taking it in turns to pick venues.

Over the last 36 years, I have been to most winter tours and five further Cropredy festivals. I have introduced my daughter, my brothers and my partners to Fairport. My ex-partner and I are still friends and she will often come with me to see Fairport, most recently in 2023 at The Forum in Bath, where we both live.

I cannot think of any other band who I have followed so avidly, enjoyed so much and bought so many albums and merch of! 'Meet On The Ledge' is stipulated in my letter of wishes to be not only played at my funeral, but for lyric sheets to be given out so that everyone can join in. Recently I was forced to take early retirement on ill health grounds but I volunteer at a local radio station in Somerset and present a weekly folk, rock and Blues show. Needless to say, Fairport feature regularly along with many of the other great artists I have seen at Cropredy.

Thank you all from the bottom of my heart for so many smiles, and some tears too. Chatting to Peggy has always been a highlight before the gigs and occasionally at the intervals when we were both slaves to tobacco! Stay safe and secure in the knowledge your legacy to music will outlast us all.

CROPREDY FESTIVAL
12 & 13 AUGUST 1988, CROPREDY, UK

DOMINIC DUCKWORTH

I was 21 and had a car (that's important). I was very much into Post punk bands like The Sisters of Mercy, The Cult, Fields Of The Nephilim, The Mission and dressed accordingly i.e. black with a leather jacket. Folk-rock was not on my radar. On a visit to my local to meet up with friends Rick and Neil, they casually asked if I would like to go to a festival in August. I said 'maybe, what is it?' 'Cropredy', they said, 'it's the festival run by Fairport Convention.' Now I had heard of Fairport but knew nothing about – or by – them. My friends must have worked on me that evening because I said yes. And because of the car, of course I had to drive. I'm not sure if it was me or the car they invited!

Fast forward to the weekend of Cropredy. We had a polypin of Marston's Pedigree (coming from Burton-on-Trent, of course we did), two tents and very little else. We arrived mid-afternoon on Friday and camped on the ridged field by the main entrance

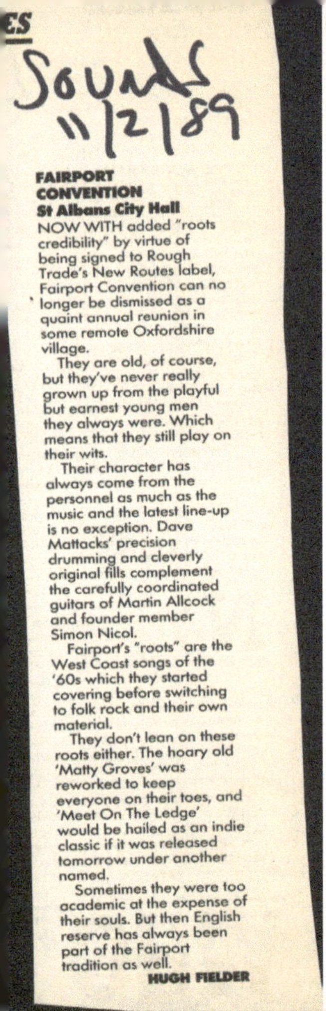

Sounds 11/2/89

FAIRPORT CONVENTION
St Albans City Hall

NOW WITH added "roots credibility" by virtue of being signed to Rough Trade's New Routes label, Fairport Convention can no longer be dismissed as a quaint annual reunion in some remote Oxfordshire village.

They are old, of course, but they've never really grown up from the playful but earnest young men they always were. Which means that they still play on their wits.

Their character has always come from the personnel as much as the music and the latest line-up is no exception. Dave Mattacks' precision drumming and cleverly original fills complement the carefully coordinated guitars of Martin Allcock and founder member Simon Nicol.

Fairport's "roots" are the West Coast songs of the '60s which they started covering before switching to folk rock and their own material.

They don't lean on these roots either. The hoary old 'Matty Groves' was reworked to keep everyone on their toes, and 'Meet On The Ledge' would be hailed as an indie classic if it was released tomorrow under another named.

Sometimes they were too academic at the expense of their souls. But then English reserve has always been part of the Fairport tradition as well.

HUGH FIELDER

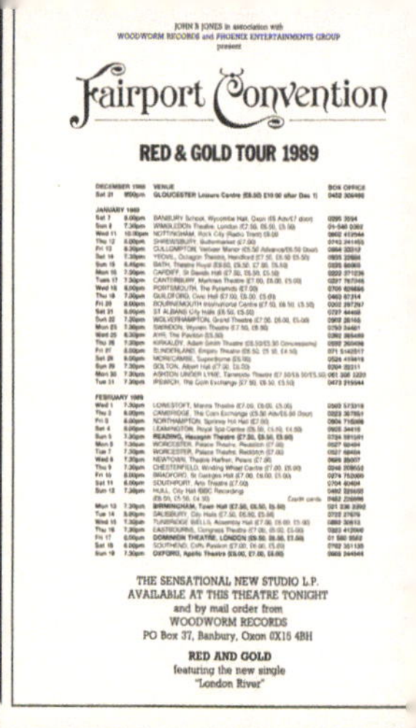

1989 gig review from *Sounds* (Ian Burgess); 1989 Cropredy ad (Ian Burgess); Burnley Traditional Song & Dance Festival ad (Ian Burgess); *Red & Gold* tour ad (Ian Burgess); Edinburgh flyer (Ian Burgess); Italian folk festival ad (Ian Burgess); Gerry Cooper was an instant fan after hearing *Unhalfbricking*; Theatre Royal Bath flyer (Ian Burgess)

FOLK AND CEILIDH
DANCE

WHATELY HALL HOTEL, BANBURY
Saturday, 25th February, 1989 at 8 p.m.

FEATURING

FAIRPORT CONVENTION
AND THE ALLSTAR BAND

AN EVENING OF
FOLK DANCE
FOLK MUSIC
AND FUN
We promise to reduce you to your knees!

A homely photograph
of Fairport Convention.

Fairport Convention need no introduction but we do provide some history about them and their friends who are joining them for the evening.

CEILIDH is a word which sums up "music, song, dance and a chat amongst friends in an informal atmosphere".

This is exactly what is planned and, for the limited number able to attend, it promises to be a night of memories which will last a very long time.

The only question would seem to be how many of our audience will last the night!

THE LATEST ALBUM AND CASSETTE FROM FAIRPORT CONVENTION WILL BE AVAILABLE FOR SALE ON THE EVENING

EVENT SPONSOR
CHEESES OF SWITZERLAND
Promoted by
THE LIONS CLUB OF BANBURY
Supported by
GENERAL FOODS

(clockwise from top left) Sophie Watson and friends always meet 'in a field'; February 1989 gig flyer (Ian Burgess); *The Ledge* fanzine (Ian Burgess); February 1989 gig flyer (Ian Burgess); Lenny (aka Leen) Hodge bumped into Peggy at a Tull gig; Rich Kinder has only missed one Cropredy since 1989, as the ever-present friend Mike likes to remind him; Darian Nelson's daughter Sineid in in her tie-dye t-shirt to the arena (used for support vehicle storage in more recent years.) We immediately met up with our friend 'Big' Ian (he was tall and robust with lots of ginger hair and beard) and his partner.

So I was at my first Cropredy with no idea what to expect. The audience was old hippies, crusties and professional weekend hippies, and the place was welcoming and the atmosphere pleasant. The field never gets more than half-full (I believe the attendance that year was about 12,000) and there were certainly no camping chairs, with everyone sat on blankets or jackets.

The music started and first up were Collaboration who I don't remember much about but who I enjoyed. Apparently, they were followed by Mike Silver and Richard Thompson but I have no recollection of either. I do remember sleeping in my car for some reason, and losing a contact lens (which I found in the dark with the help of my lighter).

On Saturday I was introduced to the Red Lion and The Brasenose. The village was full of festival goers and the bridge over the Cherwell full of buskers, artists and people selling 'stuff'. Music-wise, my memory is sketchy. I remember Sally Barker (I became a big fan over the years) and Steve Gibbons and less of the Kursaal Flyers, Filarfolket, and Dan Ar Bras.

Fairport came on and I was quite relaxed and enjoying what I was listening to. It was new to me and I was enjoying the folk-rock vibe. However, 'The Hiring Fair' really caught my attention. I can't explain why, but that song on that night single-handedly changed my musical direction and my life in general. It was a magical moment that I will never be able to convey to anyone. I became a Fairport fan right there!

After the festival, I borrowed and bought Fairport records. A cassette of *In Real Time* was played to death. I discovered the likes of Jethro Tull, Whippersnapper and Dave Swarbrick because of Fairport. My black Goth uniform went to be replaced by Fairport rugby shirts!

In 2024, I will have been to every Cropredy since 1988. My kids, now in their twenties, come every year and we plan our holidays around Cropredy. I've seen Fairport approximately 150 times since 1988. I still listen to the stuff I used to listen to, but Fairport has given me too much joy over the years. Only one of those original friends, Rick, still comes to Cropredy but he missed a few years. We have a whole new crew now that go every year, about 16 of us.

Cropredy 1988 changed my life.

RICK SHAW

I think it was a combination of the Jethro Tull link and reading an article about Cropredy in one of the Sunday supplements' that made me want to go. I'd also found *In Real Time* in the Coventry library and loved it. Dom was wise to sleep in his car as sleeping in the tent was like lying across a humped-back bridge. I had no decent sleep all weekend. I remember the polypin of Marston's very well but also don't recall too much of the music besides Fairport and Sally Barker (although she was also there in '89, so my memory of her could be from then).

In '89, I stayed in Kinsale in a caravan with Neil and our friend Sean, who may have been with us in 1988. (I can still see my Cropredy t-shirt from that year hanging on the washing line by the caravan). We were talking to the singer in the local pub who said we must get down for the annual Puck Fair festival one year, which we had just missed. The problem was that it was always scheduled for the same dates as Cropredy. I remember saying that we'd better stick with Cropredy for now, as it was unlikely to be going for much longer… How wrong was I?

IAN WALTON

My early Fairport history was a series of near misses. I heard the last song of Fotheringay's show at St Andrews University in 1970 as I walked past outside the Younger Hall on my way back from a climbing weekend. That's probably the show that produced the red undergraduate gown that features on the gatefold album cover. Then, after I moved to Santa Cruz, California in 1973, I managed to miss the 1975 Fairport show nearby. But I bought the *Rising For The Moon* album at the wonderful Logos Bookstore and I was hooked. On subsequent summer return visits to the UK, I thought Fairport were long gone until a record shop in London told me about Cropredy. I attended my first Cropredy in 1988, albeit Saturday only, by borrowing my parents' car and driving from Dumfries.

I've since travelled from California to attend 23 Cropredy weekends with assorted family and friends – surviving torrential rain with small children, the year of the mud, and the heat bubble in 2022. And I've attended many Fairport shows in California from Santa Cruz, which is my home and also the birthplace of Simon's favourite guitar. Memorable were a show in San Francisco where they opened for Jethro Tull in 1987 by announcing 'we're Herman's Hermits', my first date with my wife at the Great American Music Hall in San Francisco in 1989, a show at Espresso Gardens Café in Campbell with probably 20 other people, front row seats at the Kumbwaa Jazz Center in Santa Cruz, and even an occasion at the Rio Theater when Dave could barely remain upright for unexplained reasons… And my wife and I walked down the aisle to Ric's 'The Rosehip'. Thanks for all the great music and happy memories, including our most recent show, in Newcastle-under-Lyme in February 2023.

JAN & JON DIXON

In 1988 it rained. We stuck it out. Vin Garbutt entertained with repartee ('Of course, being from Middlesbrough, a scuffle broke out…'; we still use this line too) as well as music. Simon took the prize for best pun, introducing 'Our fan Tim, of the opera.' (Is this a reference to Tim Rice?)

JAN GALIOTTO

I started going to Cropredy in 1984. I said to my kid, 'Right, we're going camping. Somebody else's tent but we're going camping!' We went for eight or nine years. When I lived in Bristol, I stewarded at Glastonbury for about ten years. I'd met my second husband, Steve, and we moved to London. One year I said 'why don't we try working at Cropredy?' We did – and we got paid for that! (Glasto didn't pay, although you did get free entry and special fields to camp in, with better security than for other festival-goers.)

We hired an RV (camper van) for Cropredy one year so at least we had our own toilet. Even at Cropredy the toilets can be a bit hit and miss. There was a lot of boredom with being a steward because they kept shoving us on a far gate that wasn't even open to the public and there was rain and wind and hail. But we had AAA passes so we could go backstage and we jumped into Country Joe (he was Fish-less) who was appearing there and selling CDs, so we went to say hi to him. And we were walking up the ramp and bumped into Jimmy Carl Black from the Mothers of Invention. We'd met him a few years before when he was touring with a Mothers tribute act called The Muffin Men from Liverpool, so we said 'you won't remember us but…'

But my particular Cropredy memory goes back to 1988. My first husband had died in the June. John was 35 and I was 32. We used to go to Cropredy with a load of friends and all our kids. I was thinking, 'I don't know about this year.' But my friends said, 'Come on, what else are you doing? It'll be good for Phil (my son),' so I agreed to go. We got to Fairport and the last night and they were on the stage, on their own. I'd left the kids with the others in a safe space and come down to the front to get a better view, because halfway up the field you can't really see.

And I don't know if it was to my surprise or horror, but Simon started talking about my husband. I knew they did things about people that weren't there that year, but I thought they were about people they knew. But one of my friends had contacted them and said 'could you say a few words about John?'. It blew me away. I needed to be with my friends and I rushed back up, but the moment had passed. They said, 'Did you hear that?' and I said, 'Yes, I was about four people from the stage.'

Thank you to Simon for doing that. It blew me away. I was not expecting that at all.

ST GEORGE'S HALL
10 FEBRUARY 1989, BRADFORD, UK

GERRY COOPER

My earliest memories of Fairport are of seeing reports of them in the *NME*, *Melody Maker*, etc. in the late 1960s. I would probably have heard some of their early material on the radio, especially the John Peel shows, which I listened to as often as I could. Living in Newcastle-upon-Tyne, there was minimal chance to see them live.

In 1969, while at college in Liverpool, I acquired a girlfriend (whom I later married and still later divorced). She lived in Bradford and had a brother who was severely physically disabled and confined to a wheelchair. However, he had what I thought then was impeccable taste in music, meaning he liked much the same things as I did! When I visited the family at home, Stuart would often commission me to head into Bradford to buy LPs which had taken his fancy (he listened to the radio constantly, being all but blind), and one day his shopping list included an album with the unlikely title of *Unhalfbricking*. We listened to it together and to say I was amazed would be an understatement. I loved the whole LP, but two tracks stood out; 'A Sailor's Life', with its long, improvised outro, and 'Who Knows Where the Time Goes?'. For me, this recording is still the definitive version of that fabulous song. Sandy's singing intertwining with Richard's subtle but fascinating guitar work has never been bettered.

I'd been playing acoustic guitar for about five years and was a big fan of players such as Davy Graham, Bert Jansch and John Renbourn, and it was astonishing to hear RT playing on electric guitar with the same kind of fluidity and harmonic creativity as those players. (I remain a great fan of RT. He is one of the very few players who is equally at home on both acoustic and electric instruments – and a genius on both!)

Thus *Unhalfbricking* made me an instant fan, and the release of *Liege & Lief* later in 1969 confirmed that this band was here to stay, at least as far as I was concerned. So it was a major frustration that in these formative years I never got to see them live. Part of the reason was geographic: Newcastle is a fairly isolated city in UK terms and there were few bands who ventured that far north in 1970-72, which were the last years I lived in my hometown. When I married and moved to the Bradford area, the reasons became economic. I was a schoolteacher at the beginning of my career with a wife and (eventually three) children to support. Throughout the seventies and eighties, I only attended two major concert hall gigs, a wonderful Bob Dylan one in Leeds and a dreadful Neil Young one in Manchester (he was high on coke, out of tune and foul-mouthed to his audience – I left halfway through, and I was by no means the first or last).

The nearest I ever came to any form of contact with Fairport Convention was a little bizarre. My wife and I once visited some friends who lived in North London, and they took us out for lunch in Muswell Hill. As we walked along a street near the restaurant, we passed a pleasant-looking house which a nameplate by the gate. The plate read 'Fairport'...

I tried hard to keep track of Fairport during these years, but it was difficult, not least because of the constant changes in personnel and – it must be said – the very variable quality of their albums. However, I was keeping up with other members of the Fairport family such as RT, Sandy and honorary member Ralph McTell, as well as spin-offs such as The Albion Band and Steeleye Span.

The great change came in the mid-eighties when my brother-in-law had me buy an album called *Red & Gold*. Again, I was smitten. The new blood of Ric Sanders and Maartin Allcock (who used to work as a bass player with my former guitar teacher, Roger Sutcliffe) seemed to lift the band to a level not achieved since their late sixties golden years. The songs especially were superb: the title track, the glorious 'Summer Before The War' and the beautifully melancholic 'Dark Eyed Molly' were the standouts; the instrumental tracks seemed supercharged with new energy and driven by the astonishing drumming of Dave Mattacks. I wonder to this day how DM managed to get a snare-drum to sound like that! And then came *The Five Seasons* and the *Jewel in the Crown*, albums of the highest quality.

I finally succeeded in seeing the band in concert on the *Red & Gold* tour, a great night at St. George's Hall in Bradford, and I've seen them in other venues around Yorkshire, including the Victoria Hall in Saltaire, five minutes' drive from where I now live. I last saw them in March 2024 at the Harrogate Theatre, a beautiful old room in the centre of the town. They performed two storming sets, including a very long and utterly mesmerising version of 'Sloth', supported by two very dear friends of mine, Michelle Plum and Nick Hall aka Plumhall. I've known Nick since he was about 17 and introduced him to the music of Fairport back in the early nineties, so it was a very special moment to see him and his wife perform with the band, singing as they did the second verse of 'Meet On The Ledge' in superb harmonies following a fine support spot.

A dubious claim to fame (I have others!) is that I was once jabbed with his violin bow by Ric Sanders. In the summer of 1994, I was granted a schoolteacher fellowship for a term's study at Manchester College, Oxford (now Harris Manchester), just round the corner from the famous Holywell Music Room. One night there was a benefit gig there for Amnesty International, featuring a local folk group, Jez Lowe, an early appearance of Show of Hands, and at the top of the bill Simon, Nicol and Ric, totally acoustic. They simply walked onto the floor of the room, strolled around and played a blinder, just like an old-fashioned folk club gig. I was in Ric's eyeline as they came out. I was wearing a Cropredy t-shirt (although I've never yet made it to the festival, many of my friends have and one kindly brought me a 1992 t-shirt). Ric saw this and smiled, gave me a thumbs up and turned towards Simon to begin… Opposite me across the floor was a young lady wearing a t-shirt emblazoned with the name and image of Steeleye Span, so, on seeing her, naturally Ric was incensed. 'How dare you come here wearing that? Are you not ashamed?' (all with great good humour all round, of course). Then he ran across to me, jabbed me in my Cropredy-clad chest with his bow and said, 'That's what you should be wearing! This gentleman knows how to show respect!' It made my night. And then he and Simon played for about forty-five minutes and were absolutely brilliant.

PLAYHOUSE THEATRE

21 MARCH 1989, EDINBURGH, UK

LEEN HODGE

We went to see Jethro Tull at the Edinburgh Playhouse and, as we did in those days, went to the back of the Playhouse after the show to get autographs. Ian Anderson came out and sat in a car and signed programmes, etc. through the passenger window. Dave Pegg came out and started to walk past the queue at the car before stopping and asking for directions to a small venue where a guy he knew was playing in a band. The venue was a small but popular place in the Eighties. A few of us said we knew about it and so we went off with him. It wasn't far but, on the way, Peggy told us about the Cropredy Festival. We hadn't heard about it before but we went on to book. We all went for the first time in 1989 and have continued every year. (Well, just about every year.)

CROPREDY FESTIVAL

18 & 19 AUGUST 1989, CROPREDY, UK

JAN & JON DIXON

1989 gave us another catchphrase, 'doing a DM', meaning to decisively finish a song. The fantastic Steve Harley was clearly having a great time in his slot. The audience participation choruses of 'Make Me Smile' were going on and on, ricocheting round the field. But you can maybe have too much of a good thing. After (it seemed) hours, running late, and with no signs of Steve planning to stop, DM brought his sticks down in a loud, definitive, final drum fill that brooked no opposition. Steve Harley bowed out and the schedule breathed a sigh of relief. Over the years we've wished for DM on various extended solos by other acts… That year also saw the most wonderful 'Sloth', fully cosmic and the longest one we ever saw, at nearly 20 minutes.

RIC SANDERS, FAIRPORT CONVENTION

Hello folks – it's Ric here! I'm sure you've heard it said that lightning never strikes twice, but in my case, playing electric violins, it has. The first time I got to join the Family Fairport was in, I think, 1976. I might have got the year wrong because now, at the age of 71, I find I'm losing some of my short-term memory, and some of my long term memory. And, also… some of my short-term memory!

So picture the scene. I'm in the foyer of the National Theatre, where they had lunchtime foyer concerts. Well, where else would you have foyer concerts except in a foyer! I'm playing a jazz set with the late and very great pianist and composer Michael Garrick. His son, Chris Garrick, who I've known since he was born, is now one of my very favourite violinists, an amazing talent. Google him and go see one of his concerts, please! So Michael and I are playing away when The Albion Band, who were rehearsing 'The Passion Play' in The Cottesloe (now The Dorfman) Theatre, all turned up to see us. In that magical day I met John Tams, Ashley Hutchings, Simon Nicol, Michael Gregory, Graeme Taylor and Dave Mattacks. (Actually, I'm not sure if Simon and DM were there, but in my memory they were. These are, as Clive James said in the title of his autobiography, 'Unreliable Memoirs'.)

I already knew Peggy and Swarb through the Birmingham connection. We were in a gang called the Peaky Blinders! Only kidding! We were all in The Girl Guides! Only kidding! What's this got to do with lightning? Stick with me. So I joined The Albion Band, and was also in Soft Machine – it was an exciting time.

I've always called myself an electric violinist, and at this time I was using a Victorian skeleton practice violin with a Barcus Berry pickup. Worked great. I've always loved using guitar effects pedals to make the sound weird, and especially echo pedals. I was doing a solo version of 'Afro Blue', from the Albion Band album *Rise Up Like The Sun*, at a gig in London somewhere. My Roland Space Echo is on, and I'm giving it jazz rock big time. Suddenly the frame of my Victorian violin snaps, sending all the strings wildly out of tune, causing epic cacophony. The audience didn't notice, and it went down really well. 'Why bother practising?' I thought!

Years later, very late eighties, I think, and I'm at Cropredy playing 'Sloth', again with the echo device full on. At this time, I'm using Zeta electric violins, very high tech, made in California. I have two, one black, and the spare, red. This was a time when our lighting engineer was fond of using dry ice, so the stage was covered in fog. I'm giving it jazz rock big time as usual when suddenly a string breaks, causing a similar cacophony witnessed by the London audience at that Albion show. So I disappear into the fog and reappear seconds later with the spare Zeta. Nobody has ever asked me about the cacophony, only about how did I disappear for a moment and then reappear having made the violin change colour! 'Why bother practising?' I thought again. Must go now folks. Got to practise! Love, Ric.

RICH KINDER

I was 19 and there with my two best mates from school, Mike and Vince. We went for the Saturday only. (It was all we could afford). The big draw for us – apart from Fairport, of course – was All About Eve. We had seen FC for the first time the previous year at Manchester Polytechnic and were blown away. This was like nothing we'd heard in the charts, growing up.

This was our first festival of any kind so unfortunately the excitement and alcohol of the occasion meant that lasting memories of the weekend are few and far between. I do remember we had neglected to consider our overnight accommodation and the three of us slept in Vince's MG Metro. rock, paper, scissors for the right to the back seat!

Whatever occurred that weekend started an annual reunion which has lasted 34 years and seen me miss only one festival. Friends (and wives) have come and gone over the years but Mike never misses and lords that lost year over me every time.

'Same again next year?'

SOPHIE WATSON

It was my old friend Pete who introduced me to Fairport, on the *Red & Gold* tour in February 1989, just before my 20th birthday. Later that same year, he took me to my first ever Cropredy, having discovered it himself just one year previously. To give me an idea of the treat in store, he sat me down to watch *It All Comes Round Again*, the VHS video that was made to commemorate the festival's 20th anniversary in 1987. I was hooked before ever setting foot in the field. For many years thereafter, I would watch that video in the week leading up to Cropredy, and it was as much part of the preparation as packing and checking the tent. I did stop watching it in the end, round about the time when the festival went from two days to three, but I still have it.

And so Cropredy became a fixture in my life, interspersed with seeing Fairport on tour. In 1991, Simon Nicol and Ric Sanders played a gig in Ipswich, with Stowfolk (a local ceilidh band in which Pete played drums) as support. It was the only time I ever heard them do 'Ledge' other than in a full band setting. I have the gig poster in a box somewhere.

I left Pete in August 1992. I didn't have a driving licence and he was my only way of getting to Cropredy, so naturally I didn't leave him until after the festival! I didn't see him for several years, but gradually he drifted back into my life, back into the Fairport fold and back to the festival. He died in December 2015 and we sang 'Meet On The Ledge' at his funeral.

Many of my memories of Cropredy aren't of Fairport themselves but of other bands, friends, little incidents. There are some real stand-out Fairport moments too, though: the *Excalibur* set, Swarb, Maart's highly emotional final performance in 2018, individual

Saturday, 20th January

Fairport Convention

1990

WINTER TOUR

with special guest KIERAN HALPIN

Dear Fairporters,

Just writing to invite you to join us on our 1990 winter tour — into our third musical decade! Fairport will be playing a two hour set and a very good friend, KIERAN HALPIN, will start the show off each night at 7.30. Make sure you're there early — he's a dynamic singer and songwriter.

Book in advance if possible.

A big thank you to those who visited Cropredy this year — judging by your letters you had as good a time as we did. Next year's festival is on 17th and 18th August. We're all pleased and proud that the event is so popular but fear that it is becoming too big, so in 1990 we may only advertise via our mailing list. Make sure your correct address is listed in order to receive full details.

We're looking forward to re-convening in January and meanwhile wish you all a Happy New Year.

Hope to see you soon, all the best.

Peggy, Ric, Simon, D.M. and Martin.

FAIRPORT

FAIRPORT have been playing their own distinctive brand of British folk-rock for over 20 years, actually making their debut in a church hall in Golders Green the day Sgt Pepper was released.

It was only in 1970 that Fairport made their American debut, a tour which included a residency at Los Angeles' legendary Troubador Club where such notables as Los Lobos, Led Zeppelin and Linda Ronstadt trooped down to see the band in spellbinding form.

Fairport finally called it a day in 1979, but, true to form returned in 1980 with their first reunion. The reunions have subsequently become annual events. Every August the sleepy Oxfordshire village of Cropredy plays host to Fairport Convention and Friends — over one weekend Fairport run through a wide selection of their best loved material, and over the years their Friends have included Robert Plant, Billy Connelly, and Jethro Tull.

Cropredy aside, there were plenty of other commitments to keep Fairport busy — bassist Dave Pegg is also a full-time member of Jethro Tull while drummer Dave Mattacks has worked with Paul McCartney, Jimmy Page, Chris Rea and Bill Wyman.

Fairport's creative re-birth in 1985 with the release of their Glady's Leap album, which recalled their pioneering work of the late-Sixties. The line-up stabilised with 1986's instrumental Expletive Delighted, and it is this five-man-Fairport that can be heard today. Fairport Convention now consists of founder member Simon Nicol, Dave Pegg, Dave Mattacks, multi-instrumentalist Martin Allcock and violinist Ric Sanders.

Fairport Convention's impact on British rock music has been substantial; new bands such as The Pogues, The Men They Couldn't Hang, The Home Service, All About Eve and The Oyster Band owe Fairport a tremendous debt.

(clockwise from top left) Assorted items from the Ian Burgess archive: 1990 Cropredy newsletter, 1990 Winter Tour newsletter, 1990 Cropredy flyer, *Five Seasons* tour flyer; Fairport illustration (Dr Oliver Ilgner); Peter Marsh got a Fairport-themed card for his 60th birthday; Australian *Fiddlestix* fan magazine (Ian Burgess); Swarb & Martin Carthy on the cover of *Folk Roots* (Ian Burgess); *Fiddlestix* cover (Ian Burgess)

(clockwise from top left) unflattering *Telegraph* review (Ian Burgess); Simon Young had a brief chat with DM; Michael Scrivens & family bring out the best in Peggy favourite songs, and of course 'Meet On The Ledge', which is always special. I've since sung 'Ledge' at too many funerals (and one wedding) over the years, and of course belted it out at Cropredy every year, in a 20-strong group hug, the shout of 'Absent Friends' during the double drum-beat getting louder each year.

I've made so many friends in that field, including my partner of 20 years. If any of us meet elsewhere during the year, it's never 'see you at Cropredy' but 'see you in a field'. There's no need to say anything more.

PAUL MELHUISH

I'd decided Oxfordshire villages were empty, dead places. I was an adventure-hungry 19-year-old and I'd lived in one all my life. (I won't name it in case the parish council tries to sue me. Unlikely, but you never know.) Winter was bleak and isolating whilst summer brought the highlight – the annual village fete and a cricket match. Oh, and the classic car show on the village green. Very nice but I yearned for something a bit noisier, more imaginative. I wanted these villages to come alive but just couldn't imagine how it could ever happen. A mate of mine had told me about this 'hippy festival' in a village a few miles away in a place called Cropredy. He regaled me with tales of cool hippies and friendly girls and made the whole thing out to be some kind of sixties revival love-in. Hearing this, I had to go.

None of my mates were around so I went on my own and didn't really know what to expect. I naively thought that if I went to the village pub beforehand I might just bump into someone who was also going. So, one Friday in 1989 I hitched to Banbury and got there early. I decided to walk from Banbury to Cropredy. As I passed the great General Foods factory and left the main road into the countryside, I got a definitive feeling I was leaving reality behind (and, no, I hadn't taken anything).

Leaving the A423, I passed through Little Bourton and saw a lady up a ladder painting an upstairs window. She looked down at me, smiled and said hello. I took this to be a good sign. Before I knew it, I was alone in a bucolic country lane overlooking Cropredy on the far side of the valley. My reverie was spoiled by a sudden fear that I might have got the wrong weekend because things were so peaceful.

I left my quiet lane and joined the main road that runs from Great Bourton to Cropredy itself. I stopped, amazed. There were all these people walking down the hill like they were on some kind of psychedelic pilgrimage. They all had long hair and loose shirts but weren't like the headbangers or indie kids I frequented with. These people were older than me. I definitely hadn't got the wrong weekend. I can't think what it must have been like to be a folkie in the late seventies and the eighties. Laughed at by punks and derided by the mainstream but holding on to your beliefs and your music. My preconception that Fairport were just old hippies melted in a second.

If joining the pilgrimage winding down the road (to paraphrase Led Zeppelin) wasn't magical enough, entering Cropredy itself blew my mind. The place was packed with people. Cool people. Just in front of the Brasenose was a small triangle of grass. A trio of musicians were playing guitar and fiddle here. A man was sitting on a wall a few yards away playing a penny whistle. Another man was holding out his pint glass and his dog was drinking out of it. A group of new age travellers (remember them?) were begging passers-by for money. Teenagers were lounging around on the grass. Old people (in their thirties; everyone looks ancient when you're 19) were lounging about on the grass. People were sitting on the pub wall laughing and the roads and pavements seemed to be filled with amiable folk.

My earlier preconceptions of 'I might see someone in the pub who is going' were blown out of the water. Those first few impressions became one of those life-affirming moments that stay with you forever.

I'm not going to go into detail about the rest of the weekend. All I can say was I drank too much cider but had my first exposure to folk music via Steeleye Span and Fairport. There have been many subsequent Cropredys and folk-related experiences that have led me into Morris dancing and other creative avenues, but it all started here.

In photos people have put on the Fairporters website, there are clouds in the sky and not everyone has long hair and loose shirts, but in my memory, the sun was shining down and the afternoon was hazy and golden. I remember how I felt that day, and there definitely was a woman in Great Borton painting her windows. It must have been sunny.

CROPREDY FESTIVAL
17 & 18 AUGUST 1990, CROPREDY, UK

MICHAEL SCRIVENS

In the summer of 1985, at the tender age of nine, I was taken to a Whippersnapper concert in the gardens of Leicester's De Montfort Hall. Armed with a newly acquired tape recorder, I went along hoping to capture the magic of the performance. I found myself face to face with Swarb and I mustered the courage to ask for permission to record the show. To my surprise and delight, Swarb not only granted my request but also took the time to grab me a chair, sit me down and demanded I get all of it – ensuring I had the best possible experience. It was years later I learned that he was a voracious recordist of many shows himself! At that moment, Swarb became a musical hero, inspiring me to delve into finding more music which in turn led me to the Albion Band and then on to Fairport – *The History Of Fairport* album - who both blew me away.

For my tenth birthday in the same year, I was presented with the brand-new album,

Gladys' Leap, by the recently reconvened Fairport. With the new sound I had found my new favourite band, who spoke to me more than the chart music of the time. Thus began a voyage of musical discovery, friendship and to eventually finding 'that' field. This continues to be shared by my children now almost 40 years later. As I explored the albums, learning the intricacies of the lineups and the various projects each of the Fairport family were involved in, I entered my teenage years with a recurring soundtrack of folk-rock which always came back to Fairport Convention.

My standout memories are many but have to include attending my first Cropredy in 1990 as a 14-year-old with a local friend. Being left to our own devices sparked a few years of returning the festival. My first evening, with The Bootleg Beatles headlining the Friday night in the pouring rain whilst some wreckless soul climbed the PA speaker tower and then forgetting where we'd pitched the tent, was a first-rate introduction to festival life. I am not sure why I didn't come back after '95 until 2007, though since rediscovering that special field I haven't missed one since – pandemics permitting. It truly is the greatest place in the world to be for those few days of amazing music and company.

I remember the gig at Leicester Uni on the *Five Seasons* tour where maybe a maximum of 20 of us turned up and yet Fairport played a blistering set, only interrupted once when some students accidentally ended up on stage briefly having come from an upstairs bar through the wrong door… And the gigs each year, the musicianship which is unfailingly perfect and the repertoire that keeps evolving yet brings a respectful nod to the past catalogue is always a thrill to catch. The warmth and character the band extend to the audience, both from the stage and at the bar or merch stall, make each and every one of us that are lucky enough to experience it feel part of the Fairport family. Thank you to all the musicians that have been part of Fairport Convention since the beginning – for your inspirational musicianship and songwriting, for the magical moments live on tour and at Croppers, for the laughs and for the emotional moments when remembering those who have passed on.

They say you shouldn't meet your heroes. But in Fairport's case this is never true! The time the band take to engage with the audience off stage, the sharing of dedications and stories is a huge part of their magic. I also count myself particularly fortunate, as a bass player with slightly fewer follicles than most, to have had the privilege to spend time with my bass idol – I'll never forget the kindness and welcome extended to myself, and particularly my daughter Elouise, when we first stayed with Peggy and Ellen in Brittany. El's superpower, when Peggy asked her what she'd choose, was 'flower power'… a perfect response, and since then she, my son Sam and I catch up with Peggy, Ellen and the rest of the band whenever possible. It's been a joy to bring Elouise and Sam to gigs and to Cropredy and to see them catch the infectious joy of Fairport and share that with their friends. Wherever the time goes, the music of Fairport Convention will play on for generations to come!

MARC LIBRESCU

I've been to Cropredy a couple of times, back in '89 and '90. In 1990, the stage lights went out and we shone torches on the stage to illuminate Ralph McTell. I met him a few years later and got to tell him I did the lighting for one of his gigs.

PETER MARSH

It was the spring of 1990 and I was 27, living in Kidlington, Oxfordshire. I met a work friend, Darren Green, in a pub in Oxford. Darren had brought two of his mates along, who I hadn't met before, and they mentioned they were getting tickets for Cropredy Festival and asked if I was interested. I said I'd never heard of it before or any of the other bands playing and that I wasn't really into folk music. They told me how it wasn't far, near Banbury, that they'd be camping and could sort me out with a ticket if I wanted to come.

At the time, I was more into heavy rock and metal and had only heard of one Fairport Convention song called 'Crazy Man Michael'. It featured on a tape that Darren had given me, which was mainly metal and grunge, so I usually just skipped this track to get to the heavier stuff. I'd also remembered how I'd come close to seeing Fairport before, in 1979. I'd queued up at Harlequin Records in Oxford to get tickets to see Led Zeppelin at Knebworth and Fairport Convention were on the bill. My mum wouldn't let me go – I am still crushed, believe me. In the end I agreed to go to the festival, I played the tape again and listened to 'Crazy Man Michael, telling myself at least now I would know one song.

On the morning of Cropredy Festival, we met in the Black Horse pub in Kidlington and then got the bus to Banbury. All I took was the clothes I was wearing, a wallet with some money in it and a sleeping bag that was missing the case, so I had tied some string around it and looped it around my shoulder. After stopping for a drink at The Grand Union pub in Banbury, we then got a bus that took us straight to the festival.

Once we'd set up the tents, I took a look at the programme and, aside from Fairport Convention, I'd only heard of Ralph McTell, as I'd listened to the song 'Streets Of London'. But we all made an effort to see as many bands as we could, getting beers on-site in between sets. If someone from the group got lost, you were pretty stuffed. I remember at one point wandering around where the bands were performing and thinking to myself, 'I haven't seen any of my mates for about three hours.'

A few times we nipped into Cropredy to go to the pubs and had a lovely breakfast in The Red Lion in Cropredy. I have a less lovely memory of the portaloos, which by Saturday night were so terrible that nobody wanted to go anywhere near them. By Sunday morning though, I needed to go – so I found a skip, climbed inside and had a shit in there. But anyway, Cropredy was excellent, I enjoyed every second and made some great memories.

After the festival, I didn't listen to Fairport straight away or go to Cropredy the next year. I nearly went in 1992 but was going on holiday, though I met the group in a pub in Banbury just before they headed off to Cropredy. As a souvenir, I picked up two beer mats which I have kept to this day, alongside my programme from 1990.

It wasn't until 1999, when I saw a two CD box set for sale called *Meet On The Ledge: The Classic Years*, that I started listening to Fairport Convention again. I had bought it because it featured the song 'Crazy Man Michael', which I remembered from Darren's tape. It was buying and listening to *Meet On The Ledge* that got me more and more into folk and the music of Fairport. And it was 24 years later that I saw them again, in 2014.

Since then, I have seen them twelve times and all over: Banbury Mill, Banbury Trades and Labour Club, Chipping Norton, Hook Norton, Peak Cavern, Tewkesbury, Oxford Playhouse and The Stables at Milton Keynes. Further reliving memories of Cropredy, I have also seen The Dylan Project (three times), Ralph McTell, Richard Thompson and Chris Leslie. In 2023, 33 years after first attending Cropredy, I celebrated my 60th birthday there with all my family.

QUEEN'S HALL
31 JANUARY 1991, EDINBURGH, UK

CHRIS REVIE

Somehow, I've persuaded Fairport to let me – an impoverished student – promote them at the Queen's Hall in Edinburgh. The great day arrives and the crew, led by then road manager Rob Braviner, have arrived and set up the equipment. Braviner says to me, 'Right, we're off for lunch. If the band turns up, give me a ring on my mobile.' I don't have a mobile myself but there is a landline in the green room behind the stage, so of course I say 'no problem'.

A couple of hours later and DM is busy sound-checking the drums, but no Braviner and crew, so I phone him. 'Hi Rob, you told me to call when the band turned up.'

'Oh, for BLEEP's sake. Well, we've only just got our starters. We'll be at least an hour and a half. Who's actually there?'

'DM.'

'Well he can BLEEP right off! If he complains, tell him he's a BLEEP!'

Hangs up

So I go back on the stage and, in an innocent voice, DM asks 'so what did Rob say?'

And just as I'm considering how to diplomatically convey that the crew may be some time, I spot a grinning Braviner waving his mobile at me from the back of the stalls.

ZECHE
18 MARCH 1991, BOCHUM, GERMANY

DR OLIVER ILGNER

Everyone has his or her favourite Fairport lineup and mine is the one that played on the *Full House* album. The musicianship of its members is greater than the sum of its parts, they displayed their song-writing skills and a strong choice of material in what was then still a young band, and they showed such originality. 'A Sailor's Life' on *Unhalfbricking* demonstrated that a British folk song could be played in a modern electric setting, *Liege & Lief* was proof that the idea worked as a whole album concept, and *Full House* is testament to what can be done when faced with the task of creating something new within the spirit of a new age in popular music.

I was grateful to hear and see the original 1970 lineup at Cropredy in 1992 and 1997, the somewhat substitute lineup playing the material at Cropredy in 2002, the Chris Leslie-expanded *Full House* lineup at Cropredy in 2012 and all the accompanying warm-up shows at The Mill Theatre in Banbury and elsewhere. When I think about all the Fairport shows I went to between 1987 and 1996, I realise I was so fixed on nostalgia that I didn't pay enough attention to the then current lineup of the band. I remember a lot of evenings in hotel bars and pubs in the company of Peggy and Maart, probably annoying them by being a young lad always wanting to know everything about Fairport's dim and distant past.

Looking now at Peggy's hand-written setlist from a gig in Bochum, Germany early in 1991, I see that the band started with the 'Lark in the Morning Medley', ended with 'Matty Groves' and played 'Crazy Man Michael' early during their first set, but the other sixteen songs relied entirely on then new material. It was probably the wisest thing they could have done to establish a reputation as a band in its own right and avoid giving in to nostalgia freaks (like me) and becoming just a tribute act to themselves.

CLARE HALL
APRIL 1991, HAYWARD'S HEATH

JAN & JON DIXON

Casting around for something to do the evening before our wedding, we came upon a ceilidh at Clare Hall, Haywards Heath. The band was Fairport! They were kind enough to let us lead off the dancing for one of the numbers. We weren't very good. We are nearly (but not quite) over the embarrassment.

BARRYMORE'S

16 APRIL 1991, OTTOWA, CANADA

IAN MCLEISH

I had been a fan for years and couldn't wait to see them live. The Nicol-Swarbrick-Pegg-Mattacks version visited our fair town of Ottawa in April 1991. I worked for the local campus radio station and got to introduce the band on stage – my first compere job! Before the show, Swarb and I were talking about music in general and he mentioned that he liked the Swiss harpist, Andreas Vollenweider. I just happened to have a promo copy of his latest cassette in my car, so I offered it to Dave and he jumped at the chance. We walked the two blocks to where I was parked and he got his prize. I had a few words with the others, too. Nice to meet your heroes and find them down-to-earth and quite pleasant.

So I got on stage and did a big warm-up, talking a bit about the band and their history and influences and finally said, 'Ladies and gentlemen – Simon Nicol, Dave Pegg, Dave Mattacks and Dave Swarbrick – Fairport Convention!' Lots of applause, and then… nothing. Silence. The band shuffled uncomfortably, looking around. One of the amps was on the fritz and they couldn't start until it was repaired. To fill the time, each of the four told his worst joke (fortunately, none of which I can remember now) until finally they were ready to go. I taped the concert on my little cassette recorder but it turned out to be a terrible recording. Wah!

But a great evening I shall always treasure.

(Editor's note: Swarb wasn't there!)

CROPREDY FESTIVAL

16 & 17 AUGUST 1991, CROPREDY, UK

DAVID TARES

I appreciate Fairport's music but I just see them as friends really. I've been a Fairport fan since seeing Jethro Tull in concert at the Caird Hall in Dundee in August 1984. I've now seen them 111 times, and I've only missed Cropredy three times since 1991. I first saw Fairport in Dundee in 1986 and the festival was mentioned then. Because I was born with cerebral palsy, I never thought about going, but my brother suddenly announced that he was going. I said to him, 'Don't go and then come back and tell me how good it is.' I was still living with my parents and my mum saw how interested I was, so she phoned my uncle in Reading and asked how far Banbury was from his house. He said 'it's not that far' and she said, 'Could you deliver David to the festival site and pick him back up afterwards?'

I didn't have a ticket, but I had a pen friend who went to the festival on a regular basis. I phoned her and said, 'I want to go to the festival.' She said, 'Well, the best thing to do is to fax Woodworm Records and tell them what you need to know.' I phoned my cousin, who was working in Reading, and said 'could you fax this question please and give me a phone when the answer comes back?' About an hour later, the phone rang but it wasn't my cousin ringing back… it was Dave Pegg! I was so awestruck I couldn't get my words out. He said, 'I'll send a free ticket to your address in Reading and once you arrive just come and search me out backstage. And if you need anything just let me know.' My brother was at the festival with six or seven friends so we were both at the festival, but separately.

I arrived late in 1991. I was desperate to get there on the Friday night to see Richard Thompson. Towards the end of the set I thought, 'I'm at the bottom of the field in my manual wheelchair. How am I going to get up to the top of the field?' I tried to get the attention of one of the technical guys on stage and about half an hour later there was an announcement saying, 'There's a disabled gentleman down at the front of the stage here. Could anyone come down and give him a hand at the end?' It was dark and two young girls came towards me and said 'we'll help you'. They were only 16, 17, 18, and I thought 'how are they going to manage?' But they did. I was down the front the next morning and Danny Thompson was miked up and he said to me 'did you manage to get your help last night?' It was nice that he remembered.

I'm a big Richard Thompson fan as a result of liking Fairport Convention. Through that I got to know Simon Tassano, Richard's sound engineer, and then Tristan Bryant after Simon retired. Being a wheelchair user, I was next to the mixing desk and got chatting to Tristan when I went to see Richard perform in Perth. Tristan is also Fairport's road manager, and he and I had a conversation about me getting married. I thought nothing more about it until I got an email from Dave saying, 'I've asked Tristan to try and book a couple of gigs in Scotland around your wedding so that we can attend and play for you.' And Tristan said to me, 'I've been told by the band that you can choose the setlist.' I got married in October 2022 and they played for 40 minutes at my wedding. And they played in Kinross three days beforehand, so I turned that gig into my stag night!

I was on stage with Fairport at Cropredy in 2002. I was on the field with Dave and I said to him 'is there any chance that I can get up on stage and join everyone during 'Meet On The Ledge'? Because it was something I'd always wanted to do.' He looked at me and said, 'I don't see any reason why not.' At that point they'd erected a ramp for

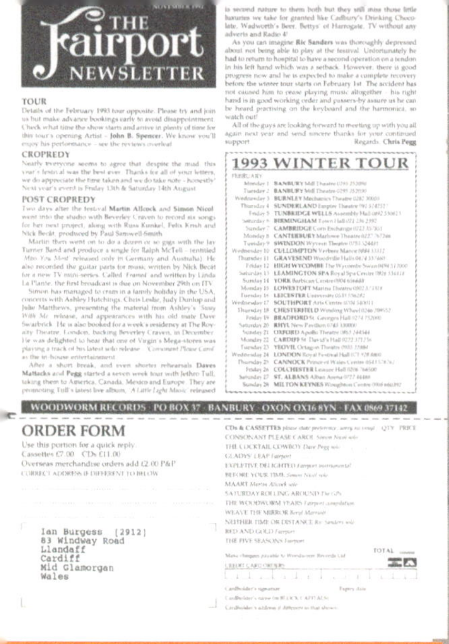

(clockwise from top left) 1993 newsletter (Ian Burgess); on the cover of *Folk Roots* magazine 1992 (Ian Burgess); Grant Nicholas at Cropredy in 2022 with his children Tess (left) and Rohan; *Fiddlestix* magazine (Ian Burgess)

(clockwise from top left) Richard Thompson on the cover of *Acoustic Guitar* (Ian Burgess); Fairport beer mat (Ian Burgess); 1993 winter tour flyer (Ian Burgess); flyer for Penyrheol Theatre (Ian Burgess)

Swarb. 'We'll get you up there.'

Swarb and I formed a very strong friendship. I was in the centre of Banbury one time, in the music shop in White Lion Walk, and he was coming the other way. We struck up a conversation and he said to me 'would you like to come and join me personally for the cricket match on Sunday?' We ended up spending three or four hours together, just observing the cricket match and talking about stuff generally.

A couple of years after his lung transplant for emphysema, I was backstage after Cropredy on the Saturday night and I came round the corner and Dave was there. He said, 'I've been asking for your address for some time. I've just released a box set that I would like to give you as a present.' He sent someone away to get it for me and, while we waited, he said, 'I'd like to tell you something. You have inspired me more than anyone else.' For Swarb to say that to me was something very, very special. You go about life and you don't know how you influence people or how you help people. But my just going about my ordinary life and doing what I did must have helped him a lot. I burst into tears when he said that.

Fairport did a couple of benefit gigs and I was at one of them, at the Symphony Hall in Birmigham. I arrived at the venue and the first person I bumped into was Dave. He came across to me in his wheelchair and he said 'I knew you'd be here, you bugger.' I recently reconnected with his widow, Jill, and she was so pleased to speak to me again. She said I meant so much to Dave. I said to her, 'It was a mutual admiration society.'

WALTER HEGER

It started in March 1991 when Fairport did the *Five Seasons* tour in Germany. I had the first album, *Liege & Lief* and *'Babbacombe' Lee* in my collection. My friend Volker from Berlin arranged for me to interview Simon and Peggy in Stuttgart at the Altes Schützenhaus (he had previously interviewed Dave Pegg for a Berlin radio station). Simon Nicol eagerly answered questions about the first two years, mentioning Ashley Hutchings as the eminence gris in North London, running different bands. He also talked about some songs from the first album and gave details about the songwriters. Dave Pegg started with the story of his legendary trip to London to audition for Fairport with a van where the steering didn't work properly: 'an everlasting left turn drive'. Then he told the whole story of Fairport up to 1991 including all the ups and downs. I was so fascinated that I decided to write a book about them, which I did – twice!

Peggy invited me to Cropredy and I brought four friend who had never heard of Fairport before. It started with a personal disaster. We arrived in Banbury early in the morning, and as our guest house was not yet ready for a check-in, we went to town for a while. Afterwards we had a sleep. When I woke up, I realised that I had left a little bag at a public telephone box with all my important things inside, including ticket, eurocheques, passport, etc. After two or three hours, the police station phoned up the B&B and told me that someone had given the bag to them. How happy I was at this moment. We came to the field in time for the first band, local heroes Freeway Jam. I was standing right in front of the stage and they started their set with Big Bill Broonzy's 'I Feel So Good'. Tears of joy were running down my face, because that was exactly how I felt then. I made friends with the Freeways afterwards, especially Ben Bennion and Mick Bullard, and was very happy when they came back to Cropredy in 2002.

Later on I talked to PJ Wright without knowing who he was. Suddenly he said, 'I have to go somewhere else now,' and minutes later I saw him on stage playing with the Steve Gibbons Band. This is an experience unique to Cropredy, the stars mingling with the crowd.

I also met Paul Smith. Through him I learned a lot about how important it is to have a sound engineer with good ears. He has worked for Fairport recently quite often recently. He's become my best friend in England.

TOWN HALL
27 JUNE 1992, MASHAM, UK

NICK HALL

Back in 1992 when I was a callow 19-year-old, the very kind Ron Gurnsey (who had been my art teacher at Middle School) got in touch and asked if I wanted tickets to a gig. 'You'll love them – it's a mixture of folk and rock, which is right up your street.'

Turns out he was a long-term fan of Fairport Convention and thought that my brother Duncan and I (having recently started gigging properly as The Hall Brothers) would benefit from seeing them live. 'No charge. Bring a couple of friends along. They're playing up in Masham at the Town Hall.'

Our poor friend Harry had been the first of us to pass his driving test so he was often drafted in to provide the wheels for these kinds of excursions. His sister Hilary came along for the ride and, on the appointed date, we hopped into Harry's red Mini and headed off to Masham. It being our first visit to the town, we popped into the closest pub to the Town Hall. Had we only known about the wonderful White Bear pub (just outside the town centre) we'd possibly have bumped into the band themselves as it is a favourite watering hole of the Fairports.

Duncan and I had heard of Fairport before and, on arriving at the venue and buying a programme, we soon realised that there were more connections between the band and the Indie/Goth music we were currently into than we could possibly have expected. The programme listed some of the favourite sessions that the band had played and we were excited to see that Maartin Allcock had played on the most recent album by The Mission and that Ric Sanders had recorded with both The Mish and our favourites, All About Eve. Suitably impressed, we installed ourselves at the front of the 'mosh pit' (it was a standing gig) and joined the large crowd in cheering on the band as they took to the stage. Duncan and I also realised straight away that we'd seen them on television. (The Birmingham Town Hall 1990 concert – remember when they used to show brilliant concerts on TV late at night? Those were the days…)

As the first set began, we were struck by a number of things. Firstly, we knew more of the songs than we expected (our dear friend Gerry Cooper had recorded many of their songs on his cassette albums, which we loved). Secondly, the musicianship of the band was outstanding. And thirdly, they were funny – really funny. We were used to rock bands who barely spoke onstage. The Fairports had the aura of a rock band while they were playing but went straight into folk mode between songs.

I can still remember hearing 'The Hiring Fair', 'Wat Tyler', 'Close To The Wind' and so many more from the 'Woodworm Era'. The band cast a musical spell over us and we loved them. At one point, the PA overloaded the venue's ageing wiring and shut down. Three-fifths of the band wandered off without fuss while Maartin and Dave Mattacks effortlessly and expertly began playing Hendrix songs, with Maart even playing his Strat with his teeth at one point! It was stunning. When the PA started working again, they continued playing brilliantly up to the break.

As soon as the band came off stage, a side door opened and down a flight of stairs came Ric Sanders. To our amazement he walked right up to us. We were used to bands hiding in their dressing rooms and never speaking to their audiences face to face. 'Hello! Young people!?! What brings you here?' He chatted happily away to us and then headed off to the merch stall. Duncan disappeared off to buy a t-shirt and came back, excited.

'I've just been chatting to the bass player – he's lovely! He says we should go along to their festival they put on every year. It's at a village in Oxfordshire with a funny name…'. And that, my friends, is how you market a band: be warm, friendly, open, approachable and who knows? You might end up turning two teenagers into lifers, still attending concerts and your festival into their late 40s and beyond.

We did go to Cropredy that year, with our lovely dad as chaperone, and it turned into a (nearly) yearly pilgrimage. We later played at Masham Town Hall and even supported Fairport themselves in Saltaire. How life can change course on the turning of a sixpence… So a huge thanks to Mr Gurnsey for being both a brilliant teacher and a very perceptive fellow!

Fast forward to 2024 and my duo Plumhall (featuring the wonderful Michelle Plum) have just finished a 30 date Winter Tour opening for… you've guessed it… Fairport Convention! How this remarkable ending to this story came about is too long to go into here, but suffice to say that, at the age of 51, it was an incredibly long-held dream came true.

I'm happy to report that Fairport are as vital as ever, with brilliant musicianship still combined with great humour. We learned so much from them and had the most incredible laughs along the way. Simon, Peggy, Ric, Chris, DM, their partners and crew have become, I hope, friends for life. It's funny how life sometimes turns out if you dream hard enough.

See you at Cropredy, where it will all come round again…

MILL THEATRE
11 AUGUST 1992, BANBURY, UK

JAN & JON DIXON

One of our favourite Fairport (or any other act) moments occurred at the first warmup in 1992 at The Mill when they brought out Robert Plant to do three Zeppelin songs plus 'Girl From The North Country'. We had no idea he was coming. Fairport proved themselves the best backing band in the world (as well as all their other talents) on 'Babe I'm Gonna Leave You'. A transcendent moment.

CROPREDY FESTIVAL
14 & 15 AUGUST 1992, CROPREDY, UK

GRANT NICHOLAS

I remember my first Cropredy festival, aged 18, as one of the most enjoyable, inspiring, life-affirming, and in some ways transformative, events of my life. My two best friends (Martin and Jon) and I had heard about the festival through the grapevine (how else did you hear about these things back then, in a world without the internet?), and being big fans of Fairport, set about making plans on how to get to this mythical place.

Martin, the one who had alerted us to the festival's existence, managed to get hold of the information for ticket ordering which, as I recall, was sent via mail order, in a stamped addressed envelope, to the band/management. The weekend ticket (Friday evening and all day Saturday) was the princely sum of £18! However, none of us owned cheque books at this time, so we had to pass our hard-earned cash (earned picking spuds at a local farm) over to Martin's father, who then duly wrote out the cheque.

Next, how to get there? A National Express bus ticket from Swansea, via (it seemed) the whole of South Wales and the Midlands to Birmingham (taking about eight hours) and then on to Banbury. I remember it being very warm at Banbury bus station and asking some long-haired fellows if they were going to see Fairport, which they were, and how to get there. They said 'follow us' and we did. We got off the bus on the green outside the legendary Brasenose Arms, with people lolling about on the green and sitting on the wall, drinking warm ale – chatting, singing and laughing. I had the unforgettable feeling that I'd come home – at least to my second, spiritual home!

On the following night, while watching Fairport, we were treated to another of my absolute favourite acts as a special, surprise guest – the great Robert Plant. Simon and Robert playing 'Girl From The North Country' that evening was a moment I'll never forget.

The following year, we were treated to another extended performance from Percy and Fairport. I actually bumped into RP in the crowd on the Saturday afternoon and said 'hello' to him, then ran back to my friends to tell them and they wouldn't believe me. They said, 'Well, there's a lot of chaps here with long curly blond hair '(that was true) and 'you've had too many Wadsworth's in the sunshine; sit back down and forget about it.' However, they believed me when he turned up on stage again that evening and were gutted they hadn't risen from their blanket to wander over and say hello to the great man themselves!

I remember chatting via Facebook Messenger to the late, great Maart Allcock about that Cropredy years later. He said it was one of the most fun and memorable experiences of his musical life – getting the opportunity to pretend to be Jimmy Page for the evening (two years in a row) and cranking out all those timeless, instantly recognisable riffs!

That first trip to Crop was inspiring, life-affirming and transformative, as it made me feel part of an extended tribe or family. I wore a cowboy hat and poncho for the whole weekend and received nothing but compliments. It was not an outfit I'd have felt comfortable wearing at many locations in 1992!

I remember walking back to the campsite a couple of years later with a monk – yes, a real monk, long robe and all. It had just started raining but he said he was prepared; lifting his habit slightly, he showed a good sturdy pair of rubber boots. I broke into a Billy Connolly song:

If it wasnae for your wellies, where would you be?
You'd be in the hospital, or infirmary
Cause you would have a dose of the flu, or even pleurisy
If you didnae have your feet in your wellies!

He enjoyed my rendition so much he gave me a flask of his monastery's mead in gratitude. Now this story may sound fanciful, but in the memorable words of the

Incredible String Band's Robin Williamson when he played solo on the Cropredy stage, 'I wouldn't waste your time telling you a pack of lies, now would I?'

I also remember waking up one morning, after having slept in my friend's grandfather's World War II canvas tent, with my head poking out the side because we hadn't pegged it down properly. Sitting mere inches away, my campsite neighbour was washing up his breakfast dish and he greeted me with, 'Good morning! What a splendito morning it is, and what a splendito evening it was last night!' 'Splendito' has been in mine and my friends' vocabulary ever since.

All three of us friends that attended that first year – Martin, Jon and myself – have gone on to be musicians of one kind or another, either semi-pro or pro. For me it was the inspiration I gleaned from Cropredy that the music we enjoyed had a home and an audience, even if it didn't appear on Radio 1, that was a motivating force to give it a try myself! Music has given us all so much over the years, both as fans and performers, though we've never made much money (in case the Inland Revenue are reading this).

I've been going to Crop ever since – with only a few years missed – and I catch the band as often as I can on the road. My wife and three children are all now fans too and have all been to the festival several times – my wife now considers Cropredy a second home too. Over the 30 plus years I've been attending, there are way too many memories to recall even a fraction of them, and as has been said before, 'I was probably very drunk at the time,' especially in the early years.

However, I vividly remember the very hot year we took our four-month-old first born son – he managed brilliantly, and my wife was a real star carrying him around most of the time in a papoose with a parasol. We also spent a portion of our honeymoon there – it poured down that year! The last really hot year, 2022, we discovered the open-air pool just down the road in Banbury and popped there every morning for a swim and shower, before returning to the field very refreshed – a great secret I can't believe it took me that long to discover, and I'm not sure I should be sharing!

Without sounding too soppy, Fairport are so much more than a folk-rock band. They are an institution, and I consider the band members as the heads of a very loyal and loving extended family – long may it all come round again!

KEVAN TAPLIN

As a council house kid, I failed the eleven plus and was sent to a technical school, where the expectation was that one should follow your father into the factories… I was dyslexic and on arrival, I was placed in the lowest form (effectively special needs, before the term was coined). I had lived through post-war austerity and I still have my ration book…

Like others, in my winkle pickers I started to listen to the Stones and The Beatles. Stevenage was a hub for London bands and I saw bands such as the Yardbirds, the

Kinks, and The Who, music based on the blues idiom of Black urban America. Even the Stones and Jimi Hendrix played in Stevenage. I started to play drums based on these rhythm patterns and attended Stevenage College of Further Education part time. Bob and Carole Pegg were lecturers there and lived in the town.

I got involved with the college band, one of whom went on to design album sleeves for Island Records (Cat Stevens, Free, Jethro Tull, etc.). His girlfriend's two brothers worked for Island Records. The bass player went on to play in Mr Fox with Bob and Carole. We also booked bands for the college gigs such as Free, Roy Harper, Chicken Shack, etc. Even the sister of Robert Plant's girlfriend/wife was at the college.

We used to visit the Fairport's pub in Essex when they played in the field. *What We Did On Our Holidays* was released and I loved 'Fotheringay' and the mix of Iain Matthews' voice. Fairport openly paid homage to the West Coast America scene in their influences as we all listened to Jefferson Airplane, Joplin, CS&N, Zappa, Beefheart, The Doors. Grateful Dead, etc. Music underpinned and supported the counter-culture. I went on to play washboard and percussion on the London folk and blues scene, supporting acoustic acts such as Dave Cousins, Jansch and Renbourn (pre- and post-Pentangle), Nick Drake, Mike Chapman and one of my all-time favourites, John Martin, and on the Blues side, Jo-Ann Kelly, Fleetwood Mac, Tony McPhee and Brett Marvin and the Thunderbolts. We listened to all genres with an open mind; jazz via Herbie Hancock and Graham Bond, Indian music via Ravi Shankar, Greek music via Cat Stevens.

Fairport had a bad year in 1969. However, *Unhalfbricking* was released and remains an all-time favourite with Richard's feel on 'Autopsy' and the socially aware 'Genesis Hall' particular favourites. Again, this was in line with my own burgeoning beliefs of social justice. Then followed *Liege & Lief* all within a year and which effectively gave birth to the folk-rock genre. I played 'Medley' until it was worn out.

At the time I freelanced for *Music Now* and worked as a 'gofer' for Island. The role was unpaid but you could take what records you wanted from 'the cupboard'. Tull's *This Was* and *Stand Up* (the cover designed by the drummer), *Full House*, *In The Court Of The Crimson King* and anything by Traffic were all purloined. I also booked Sandy for one of her first gigs after the split, and will never forget her rendition of 'Banks Of The Nile' with Richard on lead.

Fairport were threads in the amazing eclectic weave of my experience for an influential period of my life. This was a time of a very pro-active counter culture. Globally the Left Bank was in flames. There were Civil Rights and anti-Vietnam movements in the USA, and here we had Grovesnor Square, the Trials of Oz and the Night Assemblies Bill, which was designed to curb music festivals, etc. As the Chinese say, we lived in 'interesting times'. Apart from my life-long passions for music and the other art genres, it helped cement my own code founded on values such as fairness, social Justice, Integrity, tolerance etc as well as the naive idealistic premise that…we can change society as Lennon says from the bottom up. This code has stood me in good stead. My long-time lead guitarist often ruefully comments that we had a chance to really change things at this time, but didn't push hard enough.

I saw Simon years later at a gig at the Theatre Royal in Norwich. He looked over and said 'I recognise you'. As my wife stood open-mouthed, I told him that I used to visit the pub in Essex. He invited us to the 25th anniversary gig at Cropedy. My youngest son was toddler then and I had him on my shoulders at the front as we got to see Swarb play 'Medley'. My son is now a good (technical) musician who probably blames me for such conditioning.

Recently, I briefly saw Simon again. Fairport play regularly on a nearby pier and I finally managed to get him to sign my very knackered vinyl sleeve of *Liege & Lief* (Ashley had previously signed it). I thought it was a little bit of a shame that the majority of the audience were – like myself, Peggy and Simon – of the age echelon where our recreational drug of choice is a cup of tea and a digestive biscuit. However, even with Fairport's elevated degree of musicianship, transposing a Fairport classic into a 'slammed' lyrical style is probably a bridge too far.

The world today is a very different one to what we envisaged in those counter-culture days, a far cry from the peace and love ethos at its centre. As an extra in *The Rolling Stones rock and Roll Circus*, when I see 'Sir' Mick in his box at Lords, I feel that the revolution definitely failed!

SHERATON HOTEL BALLROOM
26 APRIL 1993, ANKARA, TURKEY

LEVENT VARLIK

My friend Jan worked at the British Council, who knew I was a fan of folk music, called me and told me that they were planning to invite a folk band from Britain to introduce the British music and culture to Turkish people. He asked me for a list of folk bands available for international tours. I advised him not to think too much and to call Fairport's management. I had been dreaming about seeing Fairport Convention since the summer of 1969 and now my dream was about to come true.

A few weeks later, Jan called me again and said, 'Fairport have accepted our offer to visit Turkey for a seven day tour, but nobody knows them here in Turkey, so you must provide some information about them to music fans – play their albums and write some articles and reviews, et cetera. But you need to start now and you need to hurry up!'

It was really hard to give people an idea about music they were not familiar with

Fairport Convention

1993 CROPREDY FESTIVAL

Friday 13th & Saturday 14th AUGUST

If you are interested in the above and are not already on our mailing list, but would like full details in the spring of 1993, please complete the form below and return it to:

Clapping along t
crusty favourites

MENTION the name Fairport Convention to most people and chances are they'll imagine the Sixties-vintage, folk-rock outfit fronted by the late Sandy Denny or Richard Thompson, long since departed.

If the name is somehow bigger than the sum of its extant parts, at least three members — Dave Mattacks, Dave Pegg and lead singer Simon Nicol — have endured through four decades of maudlin shanties and scratchy sweaters.

The current line-up, in-

Fairport Conventio
Royal Festival Hal
MAX BELL

Nicol's repetitive jibes
Pegg's baldness, the sar
ally carefree quintet ji
and poked their way thro
the corn fields of olde
land, cuckolding a far
here, nuzzling a breast th
issuing a few wise words
the folly of war, the fat
whales and the grimnes
Wolverhampton as they
versed, or whatever.
Crusty favourites fr
Full House — the lending

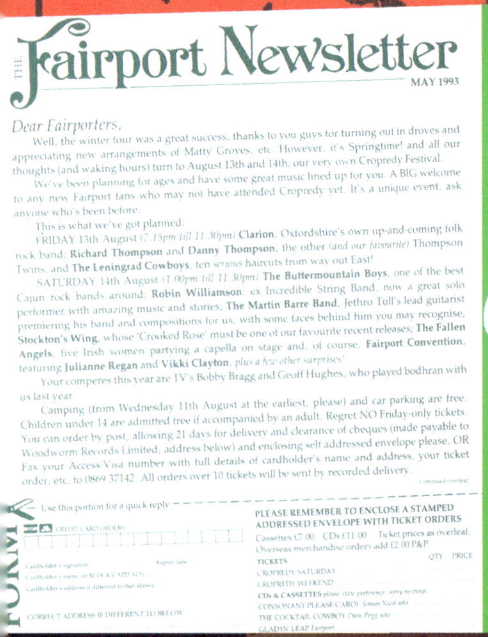
THE Fairport Newsletter

MAY 1993

Dear Fairporters,

Well, the winter tour was a great success, thanks to you guys for turning out in droves and appreciating new arrangements of Matty Groves, etc. However, it's Springtime! and all our thoughts (and waking hours) turn to August 13th and 14th; our very own Cropredy Festival.

We've been planning for ages and have some great music lined up for you. A BIG welcome to any new Fairport fans who may not have attended Cropredy yet. It's a unique event, ask anyone who's been before.

This is what we've got planned:

FRIDAY 13th August *(7.15pm till 11.30pm)* **Clarion**, Oxfordshire's own up-and-coming folk rock band; **Richard Thompson** and **Danny Thompson**, the other *(and our favourite)* Thompson Twins, and **The Leningrad Cowboys**, ten *serious* haircuts from way out East!

SATURDAY 14th August *(1.00pm till 11.30pm)* **The Buttermountain Boys**, one of the best Cajun rock bands around; **Robin Williamson**, ex Incredible String Band, now a great solo performer with amazing music and stories; **The Martin Barre Band**, Jethro Tull's lead guitarist premiering his band and compositions for us, with some faces behind him you may recognise; **Stockton's Wing**, whose 'Crooked Rose' must be one of our favourite recent releases; **The Fallen Angels**, five Irish women partying a capella on stage and, of course, **Fairport Convention**, featuring **Julianne Regan** and **Vikki Clayton**, *plus a few other surprises!*

Your comperes this year are TV's Bobby Bragg and Geoff Hughes, who played bodhran with us last year.

Camping (from Wednesday 11th August at the earliest, please) and car parking are free. Children under 14 are admitted free if accompanied by an adult. Regret NO Friday-only tickets. You can order by post, allowing 21 days for delivery and clearance of cheques (made payable to Woodworm Records Limited, address below) and enclosing self addressed envelope please. OR Fax your Access/Visa number with full details of cardholder's name and address, your ticket order, etc. to 0869 37142. All orders over 10 tickets will be sent by recorded delivery.

Use this portion for a quick reply

CREDIT CARD ORDERS

PLEASE REMEMBER TO ENCLOSE A STAMPED ADDRESSED ENVELOPE WITH TICKET ORDERS

Cassettes £7.00 CDs £11.00 Ticket prices as overleaf.

Overseas merchandise orders add £2.00 P&P

QTY PRICE

TICKETS

CROPREDY SATURDAY

CROPREDY WEEKEND

CORRECT ADDRESS IF DIFFERENT TO BELOW

(clockwise from top left) Assorted items from the Ian Burgess archive: *The Ledge* fanzine; 1993 Cropredy flyer; 1993 concert review; 1996 Cropredy flyer; for Levent Varlik, Fairport coming to Turkey was a dream come true, meeting DM & Maartin; Fairport newsletter (Ian Burgess) Cropredy flyer (Ian Burgess)

(clockwise from top left) Fairport in Turkey (Levent Varlik); Tony Soll came to Cropredy from the US, and brought his daughter Becky; Liz Hames (left) with fellow Fairport fan Stella Clarke in such a short time, but I wrote a press release about Fairport's music on behalf of the British Council. Then I organised a public performance of Fairport's CDs at the Atlantis Hi-Fi Centre, the most famous music store in Ankara. (Fairport later visited the store, signed CDs for their new fans and spent several hours taking photographs and talking with the beautiful lady manager of the store.)

I wrote a long article giving information about the past and present Fairport Convention which was published in a magazine, with photographs taken from various sources. Before Fairport came to Ankara, I sent a copy of the magazine to Dave Pegg.

At last, it was time for their visit. I was very impatient to see them and hoping I might have an opportunity to shake their hands and possibly to talk to them, but I thought it would be very hard to contact them. The first gig was in the ballroom of the Sheraton Hotel and I was there an hour before the concert started in what was an unexpectedly crowded ballroom. Everyone was looking around, hoping to see the band members. Shortly, Jan, my friend from the British Council came to me, and said, 'Levent, where the hell have you been? I've been looking for you for an hour. Dave Pegg has been showing everyone your article in the magazine. I don't know where he found it, but he's been asking to meet you!'

A few seconds later I was with Peggy. He thanked me for the article and for sending it to him. He also gave me some recent Fairport CDs as a gift (later on in the tour, he told me not to tell anybody about those gifts – sorry, Peggy!) and invited me to The Black and White Bar after the concert. The concert was unbelievable, and afterwards we went to the bar.

The band members were all there and we talked and drank beer until midnight and took lots of photographs. One characteristic of The Black and White Bar is that the walls are filled with hundreds of black-and-white photographs of famous people such as Marlon Brando, Marilyn Monroe and Bridget Bardot. If you visit the bar, you'll see that are now also three framed photographs of Fairport Convention on the wall from that night.

Ric began to ask me questions about Fairport to test my knowledge. 'Hey Levent, tell me where Maartin is from,' and I gave him the right answer later. 'Well, tell me, what is the title of our first album?' I got that one right too. 'Okay, Levent, do you know what Richard Thompson eats for his breakfast?' That I didn't know!

CROPREDY FESTIVAL

13 & 14 AUGUST 1993, CROPREDY, UK

LIZ HAMES

It was nearly half a lifetime away, but it still seems like yesterday, and the memory always makes me smile – that first step onto the journey with the wonderful Fairport

Convention and their unique Cropredy Festival. The year was 1993. Robert Plant was touring that year and he had told a friend he was appearing there, so of course we had to go! We'd seen him at another festival that year, but I found it too big and overpowering and longed for something more intimate. Arriving in the lane leading to the Cropredy Festival site, we already had a taste of the marvellous atmosphere and philosophy that the festival encompasses. Throngs of people dressed in fantastic costumes and carrying rugs and picnic hampers walked, laughing and joking, down the lane in anticipation of the delights (unknown as yet to us) to come.

Pretty much as soon as we walked onto the field my friends made a beeline for the bar – they had spotted someone they knew and wanted a photo with him. I held back. He seemed like a very nice man but I didn't know him and didn't think that either he or my friends would want me in the photo. Out of the corner of his eye he took one look at me, grabbed me around the waist and pulled me into the photo! I soon found out that his name was Dave Pegg and that he was the bass player in Fairport Convention. What a lovely introduction to the festival for this Cropredy virgin!

I have been to the festival many times since then. Apart from the amazing music on offer, there is a distinctive thread of inclusivity that is woven tenderly through everything the band work so hard to do to make the whole weekend inviting, warm and enjoyable. Thank you, Fairport, for all the years of joy you have brought and, hopefully, will continue to bring.

TONY SOLL

In the autumn of 1969, my friend David came back from summer in England (from where I had emigrated to New York, aged ten) and threw down an LP, saying something like 'here's the kind of crap you'll probably like'. It was *Unhalfbricking*. Of course, he liked them too but I became a fanatic.

In '93, we came all the way from Brooklyn to Cropredy. That summer it rained a lot, but the weather at Cropredy was great. As my wife, two teenage kids and I looked for a spot to spread a blanket, a large, shirtless, tattooed, burly guy moved some of his family aside and made a space for us, handing me a rather large can of beer. As I looked at his extensive tattoos, I must have reacted to seeing a swastika in the middle of it all (we are nominally Jewish). He noticed and reassured me that it was OK. 'Sorry mate, I used to be a biker.' We had a great time hanging out with his family for the rest of the day.

Despite being a bass and guitar player, including for John Hammond and the Neville Brothers, I've never been a fan of Zeppelin. However, I became a loyal follower of Robert Plant after seeing him that year, as well as the Leningrad Cowboys!

Many years ago, we went to see Acoustic Fairport at Joe's Pub in Manhattan. Dave Pegg is truly one of my favourite bassists and a huge influence on my playing. There I was in the men's room, standing at a urinal, when to my left who should I see but Dave P. We were both emptying out, but I said, 'Hiya. You're my favourite bass player.' To which he replied, 'We have to stop meeting like this.' I almost had an accident!

LEISURE HALL
23 JANUARY 1994, COLCHESTER, UK

TIM DIEU DE BELLEFONTAINE

In 1993 I was into racing 18-foot catamarans (called Dart 18s) and running around the boat park at Worthing Sailing Club, desperately looking for a guy named Duncan who my friend Peter Ewing had arranged to crew for me. A voice piped up and said, 'I know Duncan and he's not here.' The voice belonged to Hils, who had arranged to come and watch the fun while Duncan sailed with me. I thought 'rats', took one look at her and said to the fair maiden, 'How much do you weigh? Never mind.' (I never did get an answer to the weight question.)

There was the usual consternation with minor details like 'I don't have any kit', to which I said 'why not go into the girls' changing room and someone will sort you out?' I explained that I was desperate. Hils wandered into the changing room, explained the situation and a voice from the back said 'that's Hilary!' It was a school friend from Yorkshire where the two girls had played in an orchestra together. From Yorkshire to the south coast. Serendipity or what?

So there we were on the water, sailing around and discussing anything but where we were supposed to be going. I remember diverting to pick up cuttlefish. We found out we had a lot in common, including music, sailing, wildlife, mountain walking, camping and lots more. The race was a social success, so we sailed another race and had a great time in the bar afterwards. I was camping overnight so we raced again the next day. Hils lived near Grafham Water and wanted to sail more regularly. We got on well and agreed to go to another couple of open meetings.

I'd seen FC on a couple of occasions and had some LPs, and I knew Hils had been to Nostell Priory. Noticing that Fairport were playing in Colchester, I bought tickets to see them but kept it as a surprise. I was standing in the kitchen thinking about food when something clicked in my head and I realised that it was the day of the gig and we only had 30 minutes to get to the venue. We scraped into our front row seats just before Vikki Clayton came on. Hils leaned over to me and said 'couldn't you get me nearer the band?'

I ran an insurance agency for racing catamarans and it was a couple of months later when a Brummy voice came on the phone and said, 'I'm told I need to speak to Tim to get insurance for my boat.' I started to take down the new client's details when we got to the name: 'Dave Pegg.' I said, 'I'm really sorry and I don't normally do this. I don't think we've ever met but why do I know your name?' Dave then replied, 'Perhaps it's because I'm the bass player in a couple of bands, Fairport Convention and Jethro Tull.' My world stopped. Here was one of my music heroes, who had an unknowing part in our upcoming wedding, asking about insurance. 'So you are *that* Dave Pegg' was all I could think of.

Peggy, as he became known to me, was an exemplary client.

Time passed. Peggy phoned up to say he wanted to sell his Dart 15. He lived near our holiday house in France. There was no market in France for the type of boat he was selling, so I agreed to take it to the UK and find a buyer for him. The next time we went to France, I took him the sale proceeds. Peggy had a party in June and we turned up. And Hils finally got to play with the great man. It wasn't quite on stage with FC, but close enough.

We've had a lot more fun and games at Peggy and Ellen's over the years, like using our chainsaws and brush cutters around the substantial pond, erecting a large garden ornament and an emergency trip to Brico Depot when the water supply needed repairing before a big party. We also had some fun dismantling a yacht destined for recycling. The most rewarding episode was erecting a pergola over a decking area which hopefully will last a while. Peggy tried to tell his mates it was all his work. Well, I suppose as foreman he would say that!

Obviously, we go to see Fairport often, and we do Cropredy as it is such a great time. Health permitting, we also drop in to see Peggy and Ellen when we can.

CROPREDY FESTIVAL
12 & 13 AUGUST 1994, CROPREDY, UK

ANNE HOGG

It was during the gig at the 1994 Tyne Theatre, Newcastle-upon-Tyne (which was memorable for many things, including the fact that the hole in the roof resulted in snow falling onto the stage during the concert) that Fairport announced that local lads Lindisfarne would be their Friday night headline act at Cropredy. Being huge fans of both Fairport Convention and Lindisfarne, my husband Trevor and I decided there and then to buy tickets for that year's festival.

1994 was the start of our love affair with Fairport's Cropredy Convention and we have been to every festival since that date (minus the two which were postponed). Many important friendships have been formed on that field and we look forward to meeting up every year, or on other occasions where possible. Fairport have introduced us to many great acts over the years, many known (eg. Jethro Tull, Alice Cooper and Bellowhead), others unknown (eg. The Travelling Band, the Ukelele Orchestra of Great Britain and Legend) and a few acts that I would be happy never to see again! Whatever the weather (and I can always tell the wet years by the state of the programmes, some of which have pages stuck together), being at Cropredy is guaranteed to put a smile on our faces.

Long live Fairport and their annual reunion. Thank you for the music.

MILL THEATRE

9 AUGUST 1995, BANBURY, UK

JAN & JON DIXON

The 1995 warm-up was a very emotional one. We are both huge fans of the Grateful Dead and had heard, an hour before the gig in Banbury McDonalds, that Jerry Garcia had died. We trudged down the alleyway (now replaced by the bus station and the hip Canal Quarter) to The Mill. At the end of the show (an excellent one featuring RT and Roy Wood), Maart dedicated 'Meet On The Ledge' to Jerry.

CROPREDY FESTIVAL

12 & 13 AUGUST 1995, CROPREDY, UK

PETER CLARKE

My mate Barry and I had been day visitors to Cropredy for several years, travelling from our respective homes or dossing down with our long-suffering friend Harry in Coventry. But we felt we were missing out on a lot – a lot of beer for a start – so in 1995 (we think; it was very hot which should mean Richard Thompson wasn't playing, except he was…) we decided to try camping. 'Wot larks' we could have if we stayed over and could enjoy a few pints.

Our respective camping experiences were decades before, when tents were made of canvas, and neither of us had a tent, so a kind (if misguided) friend of Barry's lent us his for the weekend and off we went. We arrived late, ending up in the top end of Field 7, close to the railway. We thought we were out in the sticks. Wrestled from its bag, what was technically a two-person tent seemed more of a two-child tent, reaching knee height at best. We tangled with it and the various guy ropes and tent pegs for a very long time on that hot Friday afternoon, until word association possibly came into play as we hammered away at the tent pegs. Peg. Pegg. Ale…! We left the tent semi-erect (!), an essay in folds, creases and hazardous, sagging guy ropes, and headed for the bar.

After a wonderful evening, we wove our woozy way back to Field 7. It's amazing how difficult it is to spot a crumpled half-put-up knee-high tent in the dark in a field full of proper standy-up tents. We wandered around for at least half an hour until we located it by falling over the guy ropes, breaking the taller of the two poles holding the structure up. This had the effect of collapsing it even more. We then had great trouble trying to get our sleeping bags unrolled and into the tent. Barry offered to hold the broken tent pole together so we could both get in.

Eventually we got the sleeping bags in top to tail – the only way we could nearly fit in. We realised Barry couldn't sleep whilst still holding the pole together, and he was thinking it was hurting a bit as well, so he disconnected the two halves of the pole. We tried to sleep – difficult as the friendly train drivers sounded their horns each time they passed and the air was, perhaps, growing a little stale – and we couldn't understand why things were getting wet.

Things were not helped by a late-night itinerant camper who, returning from the loos, failed to spot our low-slung structure and fell full length on top of us. When he eventually got up and staggered off, all the tent pegs were out of the ground, the tent poles were collapsed at both ends and we were left to drop into an ale-induced comatose state, lying in our two cheap nylon sleeping bags inside what was by now a larger and completely collapsed nylon bag.

Next morning, the sun came up early. It was hot. It beat down on the nylon bag of a tent which, being dark blue, absorbed the heat early and effectively. At 7am we were woken by the banging in our heads and the intense heat and condensation inside our nylon bags. We were covered in dried blood. Barry had been holding the two broken ends of the tent pole together but his purlicue was trapped between them – and it hurt! Eventually these two very hungover, sweaty and – in one case – injured festival-goers got to their car and drove to Coventry to wake up Harry so we could recover a bit.

Needless to say, the tent went in the bin and Barry had to fork out to buy the owner a new one. I bought a much larger new canvas tent for 1996. Happy days!

(The purlicue is the web of skin between your thumb and forefinger.)

CHRISTINE POWELL

I don't remember much about the festival in 1995 except that it was hot, we had a great weekend as usual – and I did a watercolour sketch!

SPOTKANIA Z PIOSENKĄ ŻEGLARSKĄ I MUZYKĄ FOLK

15 DECEMBER 1996, WROCLAW, POLAND

KRZYSZTOF PRZYŚLEWICZ

Fairport Convention Acoustic were playing Wroclaw, my hometown in Poland. Thanks to my friend the musician, journalist and producer Krzysztof Opalski, I had the opportunity to spend a few hours with the band before and after the concert. Even though it was just an acoustic lineup without Dave Mattacks (which made me a little sad), it was an excellent performance. It really lowered my spirits to hear the shocking news sometime later of the ultimately fatal consequences for Maartin of the unfortunate train trip from Warsaw to Wroclaw with Simon hours before the show. Maart was an amazing musician and a lovable gentleman.

KRZYSZTOF OPALSKI

The organizers of *Spotkania z Piosenką Żeglarską i Muzyką Folk* (*The Meeting with Sailing Songs and Folk Music*), a well-known event in the Wroclaw cultural calendar, invited an international star for the first time, the legends of British folk-rock, Fairport Convention. The chance to see artists playing this kind of music in our country was rare and fans were attracted from all over Poland. The group came to Wrocław as a quartet, without drummer Dave Mattacks, with their new acoustic programme called Fairport Acoustic Convention.

The concert started late, at around 11pm, which meant that part of the audience – tired after the performances of the Polish bands Carrantouhill, Krewni i Znajomi Królika and Bumpers – did not stay to watch. Fairport's late appearance was due to the plane from Warsaw to Wrocław being full, Simon Nicol and Maartin Allcock having to travel by train and arriving at Wrocław railway station only an hour before the concert.

Fairport – Simon Nicol (vocals, acoustic guitar), Dave Pegg (bass guitar, vocals), Ric Sanders (violin) and Maartin Allcock (acoustic guitar, bouzar, vocals) – introduced the audience to the land of their folk stories with a calm ballad before more lively sounds were heard, which especially pleased the dancing part of the audience. We heard 'Widow Of Westmorland's Daughter' and 'Walk Awhile', a classic track from the 1970 album *Full House*. The band, warmly received by the Wrocław audience, were clearly slowly warming up after a rather exhausting journey from England. The most tired seemed to be Maartin Allcock, one of the brave users of the PKP (Polish National Railways) services and the Wars restaurant wagon. Lightly stroking the strings of the guitar, however, he extracted the most appropriate sounds for folk music. He also presented his abilities on the bouzar (a cross between a guitar and a bouzuki). Apparently, there are only four bouzars in the whole world and Maartin showed that he is one of the four best virtuosos on this instrument!

Ric Sanders replaced the legendary Dave Swarbrick, who was forced to give up performing folk music in a rock style due to hearing problems, in Fairport in the eighties. Here Ric proved that he is the undisputed master of the violin, giving the band a specific, even more modern sound than his predecessor. He is a versatile musician who seems comfortable in both folk and swing, as he proved in the Stépane Grappelli-inspired bravura performance of his own composition 'Woodworm Swing', from the band's latest album, entitled *Old New Borrowed Blue*.

I was also full of admiration for Simon Nicol. Instead of losing its attractiveness with age, his voice sounds more dignified and noble. Fairport's front man live gives the impression of a character from a cloak-and-dagger novel. His interpretation of one of the most beautiful ballads in the history of the band, 'Crazy Man Michael', electrified the audience. It is difficult to compare with the original version, sung years ago by the late Sandy Denny, but it caused quite a stir in Wrocław. The concert also featured dance jigs and reels, as well as ballads by Ralph McTell (composer of the famous 'Streets of London') and Loudon Wainwright III, the latter with a slightly country music arrangement, which I took as a nod to the Americans in the audience.

After an hour, the musicians played a ten-minute long final piece, the traditional 'Matty Groves' theme with the instrumental coda 'Dirty Linen' from the legendary album *Liege & Lief*, an album as important to folk-rock as The Beatles' *Sgt. Pepper* is to popular music in general. After the always great performance of 'Matty Groves', it seemed that the concert was over. However, despite the late hour the Wrocław audience demanded an encore, and Simon and Ric appeared on the stage to perform the beautiful ballad 'The Deserter' from Simon's solo album, *Before Your Time*.

Congratulations to the organisers of the first Fairport Convention concert in Poland, and I hope that the musicians visit our country again, maybe this time with a full rock lineup.

PLAYHOUSE THEATRE
11 FEBRUARY 1997, WESTON-SUPER-MARE, UK

GORDON SOLLIS

It wasn't until their 30th Anniversary tour that I saw Fairport live for the first time, at the Playhouse Theatre in Weston-super-Mare. (Great fish 'n' chips round the corner, eh Peggy?)

Woodworm Records

PRESS RELEASE – NOVEMBER 1994

Fairport Convention

'JEWEL IN THE CROWN' TOUR & ALBUM

FAIRPORT CONVENTION, the group who single handedly invented folk-rock, are out on tour again this coming January and February. The band will be bringing their enthusiastic, eclectic, unique though often imitated style of mixing traditional and contemporary folk music with an all-out rocking force which has attracted thousands of loyal fans over their long though sometimes tempestuous career.

Formed in North London in 1967 in guitarist/singer **Simon Nicol's** house (named 'Fairport'), the band, which then featured guitarist **Richard Thompson**, discovered traditional music while searching for an essentially 'British' sound. The music seemed like it was always waiting for a rhythm section, and in **Dave Pegg** (bass) and **Dave Mattacks** (drums) found one of the greatest engine-room partnerships ever to share a stage.

Although the band has been through several lineups since 1967, the new recruits have always been chosen to continue in this ground-breaking direction, and Fairport Convention is one of the rare instances of a group growing from strength to strength in spite of instability, and indeed, the band has always been greater than the sum of its parts. The current lineup dates from late 1985, when **Ric Sanders** (violin) and **Maartin Allcock** (multi-instrumentalist) came into the fold with their own unique talents. This lineup has toured extensively in UK, USA, Europe, Australia, Hong Kong and even Turkey!!

Every August Fairport Convention hold their own festival in the village of **Cropredy** in North Oxfordshire, with crowds of 17,000 people from as far away as America and Australia. One of the attractions of the festival is the surprise guest factor, and it is a testament to the band's musicianship that such names as **Robert Plant**, **Roy Wood** and **Everything But The Girl** were queuing to get up on stage with Fairport last ye

Now Fairport have re-convened to bring yo 1995 Winter Tour which starts January 20 in Le ton and finishes February 18 in Oxford with **no off**. That's how much this band love to play excellent evening is guaranteed which will ma laugh, make you cry, make you want to dance an you away happy. Special guests on the tour will b **and Tony Williams**.

JEWEL IN THE CROV

The new release on Woodworm Records, CD WR cassette WRC023. Distributed by Pinnacle.

This is Fairport's first studio album for fou and will be released on January 9th on the Woo label. There are 15 tracks including new instrum from Ric Sanders and Maartin Allcock, "The Is written by Ralph McTell and featured on The S track of Billy Connolly's Scottish travelogue progr "Travelling by Steam" from Huw Williams, L Cohen's "Closing Time" and some fine traditiona that you probably won't have heard before.

The Jewel in the Crown, incidentally, is the favourite take-away curry house and features sleeve design. Also (a first for the Fairports) a disc. Yes, it's a poppadom!

The band are very happy about this release available for interviews throughout December, J and February.

We can also offer concert ticket prizes for venues and CD prizes if your newspaper or radio wishes to organise competitions.

For more info call **Dave Pegg** on 0869 338 fax 0869 337142.

For tour dates see next sheet.

WOODWORM RECORDS • PO BOX 37 • BANBURY • OXON OX16 8YN

DAVE AND CHRIS PEGG FOR WOODWORM RECORDS PROUDLY PR

Fairport Convention

TOURETTE 1996

WITH SPECIAL GUEST JULIAN DAWSON

Date		Box Office Number
January		
Fri 12	Leamington Spa Centre	01926 334418
Sat 13	Bradford St Georges Hall	01274 752000
Sun 14	Cardiff St Davids Hall	01222 878444
Mon 15	Yeovil Octagon Theatre	01935 22884
Tues 16	Canterbury Marlowe Theatre	01227 787787
Wed 17	Worthing Pavilion Theatre	01903 820500
Thur 18	Newark Palace Theatre	01636 71156
Fri 19	High Wycombe Swan Theatre	01494 512000
Sat 20	Tunbridge Wells Assembly Hall	01892 530613
Sun 21	Burnley Mechanics	01282 30055

Date		Box Office N
January		
Mon 22	Southport Arts Centre	01704
Tues 23	Chesterfield Winding Wheel	01246
Wed 24	Chester Northgate Arena	01244
Thur 25	St Albans ARENA	01727
Fri 26	Birmingham Town Hall	0121 6
Sat 27	London Walthamstow Assembly Hall	0181 52
Sun 28	Oxford Apollo Theatre	01865
Mon 29	Keele University	01782 711411

WOODWORM RECORDS LIMITED
PO BOX 37 • BANBURY • OXON OX16 8YN • FAX 01869 3

(clockwise from top left) Assorted items from the Ian Burgess archive: *Fiddlestix* magazine, 1994 gig flyer, press release for *Jewel In The Crown*, 1996 Tourette flyer; the view into Peggy's garden (Dave Pegg)

(clockwise from top left) *Forever Young* fanzine (Ian Burgess); Anne Hogg & husband Trevor have been Cropredy regulars for 30 years; Peter Clarke (left) and his mate Barry decided to camp at Cropredy in 1996; Christine Powell was at Cropredy in 1995 & painted this watercolour

I had been aware of Fairport since their early days, mainly as a result of listening to BBC radio folk programmes but had managed to miss them whilst a student at the University of Exeter, although I can't remember why. I bought the *History Of* double LP as soon as it was released, but then lost touch with them. Life then was all about family and career, although the aforementioned record was played on a regular basis. Then in 1996 the BBC broadcast a concert promoting the *Jewel in the Crown* album. 'They're unbelievably in their 29th year,' quipped Ken Bruce, introducing the show. I taped the concert.

I was so impressed by the musicality of the then lineup that I bought the CD, filled in the 'request for a newsletter' form that came with it and waited. It was the newsletter that informed me of the tour dates and, as I was living in Bristol, it was the most convenient venue. A couple more visits to Weston-super-Mare cemented my revived and intensified interest. The accumulation of the CD version of their previous albums began. However, there was no way that the invitation to a village in Oxfordshire could be accepted as the date clashed with Bristol's Balloon Fiesta, a firm favourite with our two daughters.

My first Cropredy had to wait until 2004 after a move to Bedfordshire a couple of years earlier and after the children had well and truly flown the nest. As I write, there have been a further nine visits to the festival, all those with my wife, Grace, where various combinations of family and friends have gathered, including the aforementioned daughters, and where accommodation has variously included a house in the village, a narrow boat on the canal and a tent or caravan on the fields.

The pull of the festival survived a move to South Wales in 2007 and one year, because of a change in its date, we managed the Balloon Fiesta one weekend followed by Cropredy the next. Result!

There have been many highlights over the years including: seeing Show of Hands live for the first time that first year, 2007, along with Peggy's other band; 10cc in 2006; the *Liege & Lief* set the following year; Ade Edmonson and the Bad Shepherds in '09; just about every act in 2010 (definitely the best overall programme I've seen); the iconic Home Service in 2011; young talent in the form of Joe Broughton's Conservatoire Folk Ensemble and Blackbeard's Tea Party in 2014; and, in 2015, the pair for whom we would have walked 500 miles or even twice that amount if we had had to – The Proclaimers.

Which brings us to 2017 and the best ever Fairport set, celebrating their 50th anniversary. Watching the videos of that set was a major aid to recovering from an operation the following summer which prevented the trip to Oxfordshire.

And of course, over all those years, there have been the regulars and the appearance of the band members, past and present, in other outfits. And it was so good to be there again in 2023, for the first time since the op and amongst 20,000 people for my biggest gathering since Covid, and the chance once more to be with friends from various locations and with the younger daughter (the big hot-air balloon fan) and her husband, who, by the way, says can we have a brass band? (Well, I seem to recall we had an opera singer one year.)

So, you keep going chaps and we'll try and keep supporting.

CROPREDY FESTIVAL

8 & 9 AUGUST 1997, CROPREDY, UK

MALCOLM MACLEOD AKA BIG MAC

I'd heard of Fairport, but no more than that. A friend from work, Bob Parker, had been going to Cropredy since 1987 and was always trying to get me to go along. I always said no as it always clashed with the Knowle Hill Steam Rally. But in 1997 he suggested we go to a folk music weekend at Butlins in Minehead. I agreed, and a few of us trooped down there and saw Fairport, Pentangle, Lindisfarne, Carillion, Labi Siffre, Mick Abrahams and a few others. After seeing Fairport I was hooked, and when Bob asked if I fancied going to Cropredy that year I jumped at the chance. (The Knowle Hill Steam Rally had moved one week on that year so didn't clash.) On the Thursday night we all walked up the road to the Bell at Great Bourton and became exceedingly over refreshed. A good fry-up breakfast on the Friday morning soon got rid of any unwanted after effects of too much beer.

After that first year at Cropredy, it was obvious that I'd be back the following year and many more years after that. I was the provider of the tent for us all to kip down in. Camping was a little confusing at times as whilst my name is Mac, the other three tent residents were all called Bob. They became known as Young Bob, Old Bob (sometimes referred to as Nobby) and Bob the Butcher (as this was his trade). But it was a 'quick-erect' giant of a tent, which over the years we got off to a tee, and we all knew what we were doing regarding setting up camp. So when the tent was up and the kit was inside, we were off to the cricket club within about 15 minutes, while our neighbours were still faffing around reading assembly instructions and trying to work out which poles went where.

Each year after the music had finished, I'd prepare a music quiz for us to take part in whilst we continued to keep refreshed and ate copious amount of cheese and biscuits. Young Bob's musical knowledge was quite good and the other two Bobs fairly useless, but they all joined in.

Once I had started going to Cropredy, I felt the need to start going to other Fairport and ex-Fairporters' gigs. With it often being the first gig of the tour, the Roses Theatre at Tewkesbury became a must attend event and I've been almost every year since 1998, apart from once when it sold out and so went to Swindon's Wyvern Theatre instead. The band themselves are so accessible, happily chatting to punters before and after the show. My son-in-law was most impressed.

Cropredy is such a lovely, chilled-out, family- and dog-friendly festival, I don't see me ever stopping attending as long as it continues and my health holds out. I started going with work colleagues and friends, then family – including dogs – started coming along and we now have three generations going; me, my daughter and her husband and my grandson. Last year we met up at Cropredy with some old school friends I hadn't seen in 45 years. I was still in touch through Facebook and convinced them they would love Cropredy – they did!

Covid aside, I have been to every festival since 1997. And in 2021 my daughter organised our own little Cropredy in her garden, with t-shirts, lanyards and wristbands. We played numerous Cropredy and other Fairport DVDs in the barbecue hut and drank copious amount of cider. It felt like a proper festival, but having the real thing back for 2022 after two years without the real thing just felt so good.

THE WHARF
19 OCTOBER 1997, TAVISTOCK, UK

JERRY FORD

Some 25 years after first seeing Fairport at Fairfield Halls in Croydon (*'Babbacombe Lee'*) and a few university gigs in between, I managed to catch them again in Tavistock when the band (now with Chris Leslie and his Mandocaster) were touring with material from *Who Knows Where The Time Goes*. Who knows indeed!

The standout number for me was 'John Gaudie' with Ric and Chris duelling fiddles. The song was introduced with the 'hammer down the mine' punchline of 'A flat Minor'. A few years later (possibly 2011), with further attendances in the intervening years, I managed to catch them in York in a somewhat sticky-carpeted low-ceilinged venue. It was sort of intimate. 'John Gaudie' was introduced again, to which I questioned from the floor 'what key is it in?' The blank looks from all members of the band were somewhat disarming, and I had to supply the punchline. Regardless, the performance was still ore-some!

'T OUDE POTHUYS
22 NOVEMBER 1997, UTRECHT, THE NETHERLANDS

RICHARD HAMILTON

In February 1995, Tom Leary and I decided, on spec, to travel from our respective homes in North Oxfordshire to Chesterfield to catch Fairport at the Winding Wheel Theatre. There, Tom introduced me to Koen Hottentot, a big Fairport fan. Koen and I met again two days later, at Oxford New Theatre, for Fairport's final gig of that year's Winter tour.

Very quickly, Koen and I became friends. He invited me to stay with him at his home near Amsterdam when a late-change to the itinerary of a Fairport European excursion necessitated a venue switch from Bruges in Belgium to Utrecht in The Netherlands. On that late November 1997 evening, Koen and I took the short train ride to Utrecht. We walked to the venue where Fairport were playing that evening: 't Oude Pothuys, a canalside café restaurant at 279 Oudegracht ('Old Canal').

When we arrived, the venue was packed with diners. The food looked sumptuous but the restaurant was fully booked. We stayed in the bar area, waiting for the meals to end, the tables to be cleared and the gig to start at around 9.30pm. When Fairport Acoustic (Messrs Nicol, Pegg, Sanders and Leslie) came on, it was standing room only in the low-ceilinged audience area and it was packed. We started chatting to some locals who admitted to never having heard of Fairport Convention. They just came regularly for the 'fantastic food and music here'. It didn't take long for them to ask Koen and me multiple questions about these four virtuosi who were captivating them.

CROPREDY FESTIVAL
14 & 15 AUGUST 1998, CROPREDY, UK

GWYNETH TRY

I have been to every Cropredy that has taken place since the fourth reunion. My children have been every year since they were born, my eldest first attending aged only six weeks and my twin daughters when they were just six months. I think it must have been the summer of 1998. We were at Cropredy as usual, two adults and three children. My eldest daughter was five and the twins were two and a half. We were settled on our usual space near the sound tower and I had to do a toilet run with my eldest and one of the twins, leaving the remaining twin with her father. We made the return trip to the toilets to find my husband sitting on his own.

'Where is Tamsin?' I asked. 'I thought she went with you,' came the surprised reply.

Panic set in. A two-and-a-half-year-old little girl was somewhere amongst twenty thousand festival goers. The people around, who are still the same people we sit near these days and who we only meet at Cropredy, were wonderful, helping in the search. A search party set off to look for her, with my husband going to the Lost and Found children's area at the top of the field. Luckily, she was there, happily sitting eating a portion of chips. She had taken herself off at the same time as we went on the toilet run, heading straight for one of the food stalls to ask for chips. The people running the stall gave her some chips and took her to the top of the field to wait to be claimed.

TRON EIVIN ØVREBØ

I grew up in Stavanger on the west coast of Norway. With only one radio station, my only access to new music was via Radio Luxemburg and the local library. But we had a piano at home, my mum bought me a guitar and I had fiddle lessons. I can read musical notation but I don't have the ear for it. Neither can I sing or remember any words. So it was that I was expelled from the school choir. And my sister says Dad paid me £30 to quit playing the fiddle!

I was introduced to Fairport in August 1978 after buying a batch of vinyl via mail order from the UK. I chose albums with long titles including *The Man Who Hated Mornings* (Michael Chapman), *The Infinite Rider Of The Big Dogma* (Michael Nesmith), *If You Saw Thro' My Eyes* (Iain Matthews), *On The Other Hand, There's A Fist* (Jona Lewie), *Hark! The Village Wait* (Steeleye Span), *I Want To See The Bright Lights Tonight* (Richard and Linda Thompson) and, best of all, *The Northstar Grassman And The Ravens* (Sandy Denny). I still remember the goosebumps from first listening to 'Late November'.

At the library I listened to Fairport's back catalogue – *What We Did On Our Holidays*, *Unhalfbricking* and *Liege & Lief*. In the years that followed I listened to a lot of Richard Thompson and a lot of Sandy, both solo and with Fairport (but not the newer Fairport stuff). When RT played in Stavanger in 1987 (with his band) and in 2000 (with Danny Thompson), I was there. But I missed Fairport playing the Egersund Visefestival in 2003, and they were supposed to play at the Vikedal Rootfestival in 2013, but were 'stavangered' by a bomb threat at Heathrow. They did play the following year, but I wasn't able to attend.

I was introduced to the Cropredy Festival by another FC fan, Levent Varlik, in the early nineties and, at the age of 38, I decided to go to my first ever music festival! A friend joined me, and we booked a room at a B&B close to Banbury Cross. There was no Cropredy warm-up, but we had tickets for a Vikki Clayton show at the Mill.

The festival itself was a shock. People drinking beer in a churchyard. Four generations of family bringing their own food and drinks. People smoking whatever they wanted.

Children playing. Great music! Nice weather (RT played the year after) with hardly any police or security. I don't recall any serious drunkenness or any trouble, just lots of unpretentious and friendly people having fun.

Except for FC and Loudon Wainwight III, we had never heard of any of the artists before. Solstice were my highlight before the last act, Fairport (who were joined by another favourite, Dave Cousins). I don't remember much of the act. Did Dave sing 'Ringing Down The Years'? I have the official VHS somewhere, but even though I don't remember the details of my first Cropredy, it planted a seed for what was to come. The atmosphere and setting enchanted us. I could write my own book of experiences from twenty-plus Cropredies, but I'll save that for my memoirs. Thanks to Fairport, their team, and the friendliness of the people we have met.

LIMELIGHT
25 NOVEMBER 1998, STUTTGART, GERMANY

WALTER HEGER

I started a fanzine called *Forever Young* and wrote an extensive review of Fairport's *Jewel In The Crown* album. In March 1995, Peggy phoned me up late one evening to talk about what I had written about the song 'Home Is Where The Heart Is'. He explained that he had played the guitar solo on it ('it took me three hours to learn it') and asked if I could please correct my review. I did, and I made a special page about him in the next issue, listing songs on which he played the guitar.

In 1998, Fairport returned to Stuttgart. Knowing they liked the local Swabish food I cooked two meals for them. My schnitzels with creamy sauce and spätzle and kartoffelpuffer were very well received.

In November 1998, I was in Derby at the Flowerpot with two friends to see the Dylan Project, Peggy's Bob Dylan tribute band. It was Peggy's fifty-first birthday. We brought him a birthday present of 51 German beers. Unsurprisingly, the band tried some of them immediately, to the effect that they had to play one song without PJ Wright because he had to 'go somewhere else'. After the gig, Roy Wood (of Wizzard fame) turned up to wish Peggy a happy birthday and wanted to buy a glass of wine at the bar, but the girl answered him 'it's closing time already'. I told her who he was but she responded 'I don't care who he is'.

One year at Cropredy, I interviewed Jonah Jones on the Sunday in the bar at the cricket ground. He had very interesting stories to tell but I was tired because the night had been short and twice I almost fell asleep. Everything was recorded so there was no reason to fear that the interview had been unsuccessful. But when I listened to the tape the next day,

I was astonished to hear Jonah say 'and in the forties I worked for Al Capone!'

In 2004 there was a suggestion that Cropredy might not take place the following year. After a few beers, I told Ulla Hilger that I would cycle to Cropredy if it was going ahead. It did, and in twelve days I cycled 750 miles, raising money for a children's cancer trust in Germany, including raffling off my bicycle at the festival. My journey was mentioned in the 2006 Winter tour programme.

ARSENAALTHEATER

6 DECEMBER 1998, VLISSINGEN, THE NETHERLANDS

RICHARD HAMILTON

A year after seeing Fairport in Utrecht, I travelled on Eurostar to Brussels, and then on to Bruges to where Koen and I had arranged to convene (!) with several Dutch and English Cropredy veterans. Fairport and The Dylan Project were playing a Sunday afternoon gig at the Arsenaal Theater. On the Sunday morning, we took a pleasant ferry crossing from Zeebrugge to Vlissingen. Then, after two superb sets by our musical heroes, many of us repaired to a nearby Indonesian restaurant to feast on a never-ending rijsttafel. A veritable variation of rice dishes kept coming our way. And the beer flowed. It was no surprise that we stayed there for a lot longer than planned but I was starting to wonder whether Koen and I needed to be on a train fairly soon. The locals assured me, 'Our trains run all night over here – it's not like in England.'

Eventually, our much-missed, late friend James Aldridge (a resident in The Netherlands until shortly before his sad passing in 2015) said that he needed to head for home, and offered Koen and me a lift to the nearest mainline railway station. After Koen and I had waved James goodbye, I discovered that the assurance of all-night train services to Brussels had been erroneous. The next service was 6.30am on Monday, meaning I was going to miss my booked Eurostar back to London.

I heard French voices as two uniformed men walked past us, heading for the platform. En français, I enquired whether there were any night services to Brussels that I might have missed on the timetable displays and explained my predicament. 'Non. Mais nous pouvons vous emmener à Anvers. Nous sommes la Poste Belge.' Which is how an Englishman and a Dutchman found themselves invited by two Belgian Post Office train drivers to join them in their cab, where they took us over the border to Antwerp, from where we were able to catch a night service to Brussels.

CROPREDY FESTIVAL
13 & 14 AUGUST 1999, CROPREDY, UK

LOU FORAN

I've been a fan since very young as my mum always had one of their records playing in the house. My first proper live experience was at Cropredy in 1990, when Mum first allowed me to come to the festival. I was 12 and mesmerised by the beauty and peace of that beautiful site. One of my favourite memories is mud sliding near the stage after torrential rain in 1999. I was covered head-to-toe in mud and got back to the tent where my mum looked at me in sheer horror, saying 'you're not coming in the tent like that'. I was 21!

Another favourite memory is my final concert of 2015 before my son was born. It was at Norwich Arts Centre and it was probably the best concert I'd seen them perform up to then. Cropredy in 2016 was very warm and I had my baby with me. We had washing up bowls of cold water for him to splash in and we had a great time.

'The Hiring Fair' played just as the sun is setting above Jonah's Oak is my favourite song at Cropredy each and every year. I don't know how they manage to time it so perfectly. And 'Meet On The Ledge' has been and always will be a special moment for all my friends and family who we only see at Cropredy. We all stand together swaying on the tarpaulin, crying and singing. Just wonderful.

SALLY MAYBURY

I wanted to see the solar eclipse but thought it highly likely that Cornwall would be cloudy or rainy so I packed my three young children aged twelve, ten and six into the motorbike and sidecar and we had a lovely week in Normandy. This decision made attending Cropredy a no-brainer, as the festival opened the day after the eclipse. We caught the night ferry on the Wednesday and it was an easy ride to Cropredy and we even managed to get into the family field. I was asked if we'd come far so I could reply 'yes, France'. There were no bands playing on the Thursday (for the last time that year) but I tried to stay awake on the Thursday night as Fairport were doing their sound check. It was such a brilliant start to the festival.

TELEMARKFESTIVALEN
4 AUGUST 2000, BØ, NORWAY

TOR DYBO

My first memory of Fairport Convention goes back to the early 1970s when I was in my teens. I heard a cover version of Joni Mitchell's song 'Woodstock' on the radio,

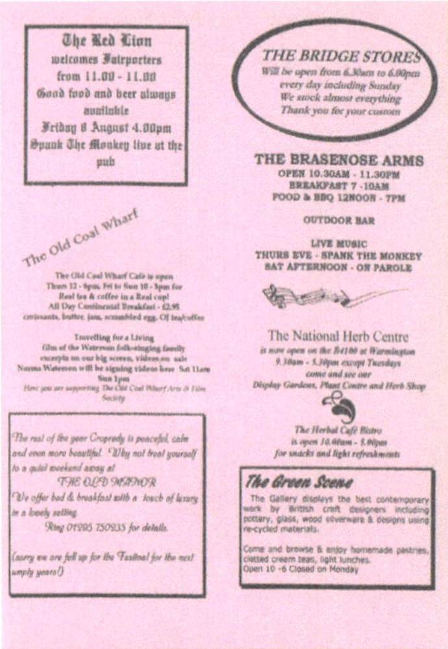

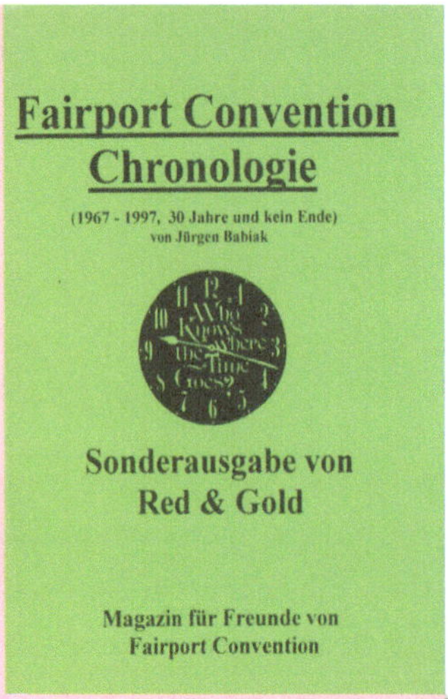

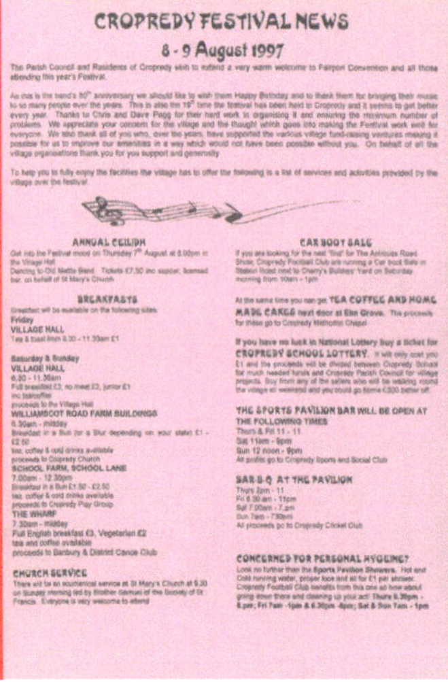

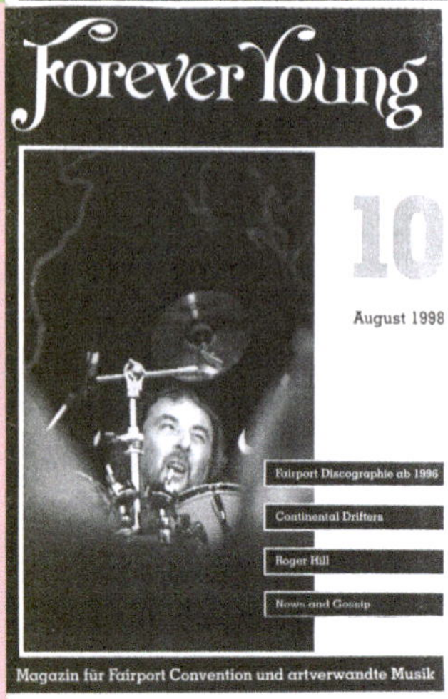

(clockwise from top left) Items from the Ian Burgess archive: Cropredy newsletter, German fanzine, April 1997 newsletter, *The Dudley Stun* reports on Peggy hitting the big 5-0, November 1997, 1998 Cropredy flyer; Malcolm MacLeod goes to Cropredy with three generations of his family, including his grandson; 30 year anniversary tour flyer (Ian Burgess); Cropredy newsletter (Ian Burgess); German fan magazine (Ian Burgess)

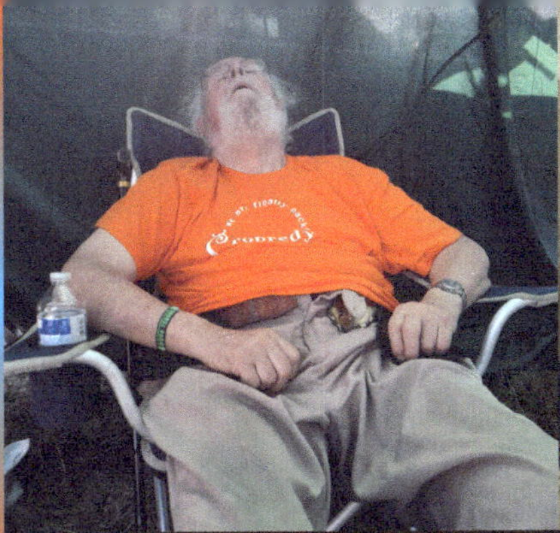

(clockwise from top left) 1998 Cropredy flyer (Ian Burgess); Malcolm Macleod enjoying himself; Walter Heger brought Peggy a beer (or 51) as a birthday present; Swarbrick, Sanders & Leslie in action at Cambridge Corn Exchange 1997 (Bob Battersby/ Lodestone Publishing Ltd); 30th anniversary concert with Vikki Clayton Cropredy (Bob Battersby - Lodestone Publishing Ltd); Malcolm Macleod's three generations of family come to Cropredy performed by former Fairport singer Iain Matthews and his band Matthews Southern Comfort. I saw the almost three-hour long documentary film of the Woodstock Festival three or four times before I turned 16. The film made an impression on me and led to an enthusiasm for the singer-songwriter traditions and particularly folk-rock.

I became aware of the burgeoning British folk-rock culture with bands such as Steeleye Span, Jack the Lad, Albion Country Band, Lindisfarne, etc. But it was Fairport Convention that especially piqued my interest, especially the *Liege & Lief* and *Full House* albums, songs from which I heard for the first time on the radio. What fascinated me was how a band such as Fairport Convention integrated British traditional folk material into rock. The double LP *The History of Fairport Convention* from 1972 was the first album I bought. And then I acquired albums like *Liege & Lief*, *Full House*, *Angel Delight*, *'Babbacombe' Lee* and *Rising For The Moon*. Today I have the band's entire catalogue in my LP and CD collection.

My first live concert experience with the Fairport Convention did not happen until the millennium year of 2000 at the Norwegian folk festival *Telemarkfestivalen*, in the village of Bø in South-Eastern Norway. The band entered the stage and Dave Pegg, Simon Nicol, Gerry Conway, Ric Sanders and Chris Leslie were getting ready to start. While this was going on, one of the festival organisers walked up to one of the microphones at the front of the stage and started to introduce Fairport Convention, by telling the audience in Norwegian in a serious way about important milestones in the band's international career and their role in international popular music history from their start-up in 1967.

Just after he started his introduction, Simon Nicol took the Norwegian language manuscript out of the presenter's hands and started to read (all the while smiling and laughing) his version of this manuscript: '…take two pounds of sugar, yeast…'. This way of jokingly presenting a recipe for making illegally distilled spirits made the audience laugh and established an informal setting, full of fun and laugher.

Since the year 2000, I have seen the band on numerous occasions in Norway, Denmark and Great Britain, including the annual festival *Fairport's Cropredy Convention* since 2006. In connection with a book project I'm completing about Fairport Convention and British folk-rock, I've met the band members from time to time throughout the years at concert venues, at Cropredy and in 2022 on the Rhine River Cruise, sometimes for interviews and sometimes just for a chat. They've always been very pleasant meetings.

When introducing 'John Gaudie' at one concert, Chris Leslie said, 'When you come to the passport checkpoint at the Shetland Airport, every man is stopped and checked that they're carrying a fiddle…' and Simon Nicol added 'and if you haven't, you get given one.' Such kinds of improvised statements from the stage create an atmosphere in which the band members do not take themselves too seriously. Simon Nicol says in this connection 'we are not shy' and that a Fairport performance would not work if they had to plan and write down in advance every chat and oral introduction of a song or statement made onstage. These moments show how important improvisational acts are to the band's performances.

CROPREDY Y2K
10, 11 & 13 AUGUST 2000, CROPREDY, UK

KRZYSZTOF OPALSKI

For the first time, Cropredy was extended to a three-day event. Over twelve thousand fans settled on specially prepared campsites and Cropredy's meadows were turned into a lively folk town for the duration of the festival, the centre of which was the stage, where concerts were held non-stop. 15 main performers performed, not counting the invited special guests. The festival began on Thursday at 7pm with a concert by local band Spank the Monkey, serving a dose of solid Rhythm and Blues. The folk highlight of the evening was the appearance of the reactivated Incredible String Band after a break of many years, with a core of the musicians from their first line-up: Mike Heron, Robin Williamson and Clive Palmer. This sincere, sometimes even clumsy music was captivating by its simplicity and the beauty of the melodic lines. Thursday's concert ended with Julianne Regan and All About Eve. This pop-rock formation played a great professional concert – the guitarist's performances and the vocal artistry of Julianne Regan herself were worthy of recognition. However, the orthodox folk music enthusiast may not have been satisfied with this concert and this style of music. But perhaps the encore of the beautiful ballad 'The Pearl Fishermen' classifies as folk?

The next day started at 1pm with Keith Donnelly, the festival's singing compere, and an acoustic set with invited guests including Eddi Reader of Fairground Attraction fame. He was followed by highly recommended folk-rock juniors Little Johnny England, who played traditional themes, interspersed with their own compositions (a composition by violinist Guy Fletcher, based on odd, almost Balkan rhythms, deserved special recognition).

After this dose of the traditional, Fairport founding member Iain Matthews appeared on stage as Plainsong, with Andy Roberts and Mark Griffiths. Iain's hit interpretation of Joni Mitchell's hippie anthem 'Woodstock' is the quintessence of Plainsong's style, with melodic themes, great-sounding acoustic guitars and great solos by Andy Roberts, and well-arranged vocals, including the outstanding, still strong and sonorous voice of Iain Matthews. This was one of the best concerts of the festival.

Plainsong were followed by American guitarist Jerry Donahue with his band The

Backroom Boys. Jerry worked with Fairport Convention and Sandy Denny for several years. But his concert oscillated around rock, showcasing his virtuosity on the Fender Telecaster, and his country-rock solos were intelligently integrated into traditional themes, giving an interesting end result.

The stage then became more folk again thanks to The Albion Band, led for years by Ashley Hutchings, co-founder of both Fairport Convention and Steeleye Span. They disappointed me a bit, despite the professionalism of their leader, both in their performance and in the choice of repertoire.

The culmination of Friday's music-making was a concert by the mysterious Priory Of Brion, which turned out to be the band accompanying Robert Plant, the former frontman of Led Zeppelin. In addition to rock and blues standards such as 'Evil Woman' and 'Baby Please Don't Go', we heard interesting versions of 'Gloria' (Van Morison), 'Darkness, Darkness' (The Young Bloods), 'If I Were A Carpenter' (Tim Hardin) and 'Season Of The Witch (Donovan), on the last of which Plant showed himself to be a pretty good guitarist. It was by far the best non-folk concert at this festival.

The final day of the festival began at 12.30pm with local band The Unprofessionals. In contrast to their name, they performed standards by The Doobie Brothers and Sly and the Family Stone. They were followed by balladeer Bob Fox, the orchestrally arranged Stackridge, noisy blues rockers The Hamsters and the folky Show of Hands.

The culmination of the whole event was the final Fairport Convention concert with invited guests, mainly ex-members of the group, including Maartin Allcock (presenting a nice sample from his solo album), Jerry Donahue with his daughter, who sang two songs from Sandy Denny's repertoire, and Ashley Hutchings and Iain Matthews, who performed a beautiful version of Leonard Cohen's Suzanne and 'Reno Nevada' by Richard Farina.

The most touching moment was the appearance of Dave Swarbrick, for many years the undisputed leader of Fairport. Recently very ill (even presumed dead by journalists) and now in a wheelchair, he bravely played as wonderfully as in the old days, electrifying the audience with 'The Hen's March'/'The Four Poster Bed' and a beautiful composition of his own, 'My Heart's In New South Wales'. 'Only Swarb could have written such a song,' said his successor in the band, Ric Sanders, who seemed touched by both the poignant sounds and the opportunity to play with an older colleague. The audience gave Swarb warm applause, happy to see him again for a few minutes in a duet with Martin Carthy. Invited guests also included Eddi Reader, Bob Fox and Roger Hodgson of Supertramp, who was accompanied by Fairport Convention on his hit song 'Breakfast in America'.

Just before midnight Simon Nicol announced the last song of the festival, addressing the audience with 'surely you know what it's going to be?' From the stage flowed a showpiece version of the traditional 'Matty Groves' with which the band always ends their concerts and which first appeared on their album *Liege & Lief* in 1969. The group said goodbye with 'Meet On The Ledge', warmly inviting the audience to the next edition of the festival. 'Thank you Cropredy, see you next year,' said Simon.

GINNY WHITE

I got together with Jerry – the man who was to become my second husband and the absolute love of my life – in 1998, when we were in our late thirties and early forties respectively and with a lot of water under our respective 'bridges'. We both found ourselves amazed and delighted to quickly realise we were falling madly in love.

What a delight it is for music lovers to be in love! As well as discovering new music together, we pored over each other's CD collections, revelling in the common ground and sharing memories and absorbing what music the other had that was new to us, some of it to become joint treasure, some of it forever to be enjoyed separately – c'est la vie!

When Jerry came across my copy of Fairport Convention's *Meet On The Ledge: The Classic Years (1967-1975)*, he became quite misty-eyed as he scoured the track listing and found what he was looking for, 'Crazy Man Michael'.

'Wow! I haven't heard any Fairport for years! I used to love this track, let's put it on!' As the opening bars filled the room, I carelessly remarked, 'Well, you've *got* to come with me to Cropredy to see them then!'

Jerry looked at me blankly and then did a double-take, as if I had taken leave of my senses. He had absolutely no idea that the band still existed (albeit with a changed line-up) let alone that they had an annual festival in Oxfordshire, the very county where we lived. Though I didn't go every year, I was a regular. I told him all about it and he looked at me in disbelief.

It was 2000 when we set off together for that Cropredy field together for the first time, just for the Saturday on what we thought would be a day trip. But we piled some bedclothes into Jerry's old van just in case we ended up the worse for wear and decided to stay. Jerry wasn't too wild about crowds and wasn't sure how long he could last in a field.

I'm sure I don't need to tell you; he was entranced. When Fairport took to the stage, I could see his old and new worlds colliding. The past rushing in on the present as he stood in the field with his 'best gal' on his arm. A Cropredy half-moon hung above us in the summer night sky. As 'Crazy Man Michael' started up, I never saw a man in quite such a reverie. He mock-pinched himself as he gazed at me, up at the moon above us and then back to the stage. It was an extraordinary moment he would not have believed possible as we clung to each other, wreathed in smiles and fragrant smoke.

We didn't make it home that night. He managed to fold his six foot four inch body around me on the diagonal in the cramped back of his van and at first light he drove home, with me still crumpled in the bedding in the back, gazing out of the rear window at the sunrise and him at the wheel, still in wonderment.

It was the enraptured first of several Fairport trips together, the next being for the whole weekend in the absolute luxury of a campervan, when I was delighted to discover friends from my past on the field who were also regulars.

Jerry and I had 15 magic years together until he died suddenly from a brain haemorrhage in 2013. I didn't go to Cropredy that year.

The following year I decided that the only thing that was worse than going to Cropredy without him was to never go to Cropredy at all. I braced myself and with a tiny pop-up tent, I made the trip alone. Except you're never alone at Cropredy, are you? I found my old friends to hook up with and made new ones. I allowed the music and the memories to enfold and sustain me, even as they tore me apart. I made it. And I've been making it ever since.

Jerry has a plaque at Jonah's Oak and I still feel him with me every year as I remember the enchantment of the first moment the opening bars of 'Crazy Man Michael' wove themselves around us under that Cropredy moon.

MARK L JOHNSON

I discovered Fairport fairly late. In college in 1986, a friend of mine introduced me to Jethro Tull via their album *Stand Up*. I was hooked. In the nineties, I got to see Tull live in Berlin a couple of times. One of the Tull programmes may have brought the Fairport Convention name to my attention, or possibly Ian Anderson mentioned that Maart and Peggy also played in another band. Whichever, and now curious about their music, I found a record shop in Berlin that had some Fairport CDs in their racks and picked up *History Of*. I loved it. Soon after I got *The Five Seasons* and *Expletive Delighted!* From there I never looked back… except to get the complete discography!

I had heard about the Cropredy Festival on the internet and thought I would like to go check it out. The problem was I either had time and no money or money and no time. But in August 2000 I finally managed to get time and money together and made the trip to my first Cropredy.

There I was, standing on the field near the bar taking it all in and happy to finally be there. At some point, I turned around and Dave Pegg walked up to me, shook my hand and asked if this was my first time at the festival. We had a nice chat and he went on his way to the bar. I knew then that I had found a home, a special place. Later that same weekend, I became friends with Maart and the rest is history...

ROB BOUSFIELD

I've only missed five Cropredy Festivals since 1995 (oh, I loved Procol Harum) and have many wonderful memories. One however does stir the old grey matter. After a fantastic weekend with All About Eve, Anna rydeR, Eddi Reader and Stackridge being just some of my favourites, it was about 11pm on Saturday. Having consumed more than six of the Xs available, I turned to my friends Graham and Karen and drunkenly said, 'I don't know whether to go to for another beer first or go to the loo.'

Then I heard from the stage 'please welcome Roger Hodgson' and I said 'bugger the loo or beer, I'll see you later.' One of my heroes had just taken to the stage alongside Fairport and off I staggered to get as near to the front as possible. Breakfast, Logical, Open the Door (his latest title track) and then a fantastic performance of Give A Little Bit. If my slightly inebriated memory serves me correctly there was about five acoustic guitars strumming away to the song, I was in my element…Then off to the loos I zig zagged or was it zag zigged?

Fairport's Cropredy Convention is the highlight of my year. Thank you, guys.

ERIC VAN MAAREN

My first encounter with Fairport Convention was in June 1979, when they were on their *Farewell* tour. Actually, there was no real encounter…

In the spring of 1979, I graduated from high school, and to celebrate I went on a camping holiday with a couple of friends. We set up some tents on a campsite near the town of Domburg, in the province of Zeeland in The Netherlands. After hearing that a Fairport concert was to be held in Zeeland (I think it was in Vlissingen, but memories are somewhat hazy on this point), I set off with two friends to see them. I was very anxious to visit the concert, having collected all their LPs so far, but had not managed to see them playing live. So this was to be the first time, albeit being their farewell tour.

When we arrived at the venue, it was all very quiet and there were no other fans to be seen. Then we caught sight of a small note glued on the door of the venue, revealing that the concert was cancelled due to lack of public interest. We were very disappointed, not least because it had been quite a long journey by motorbike from our campsite to the venue. When we got back to our campsite late in the evening, we drank away our disappointment with a few beers too many, resulting in rather severe headaches the morning after. And still not having seen Fairport playing live. Grrr…

But there is a happy ending to this little story. Since then, I have been able to see Fairport play a couple of times in Holland, and I even went to the Cropredy Festival on two occasions – in 2000 (with my friend Stan) and in 2013 (with my lovely wife Janet). I still have many fond memories of both occasions: the beautiful weather; the warm and friendly atmosphere; getting an autograph from Swarb and from Martin Carthy; seeing

Iain Matthews and Stackridge live; comparing the real Brasenose with the picture on the cover of the Fairport *Nine* LP; trying to get to talk to the Mediæval Bæbes, but to no avail because of the enormous queue; and, of course, seeing the Fairports playing their beautiful songs in the evening sun. Long may they run!

COBRA
9 DECEMBER 2000, SOLINGEN, GERMANY

DR OLIVER ILGNER

It was a Fairport gig in deepest Germany in the early 2000s. After musing on the Hanoverian origins of the melody of Fairport's version of 'John Barleycorn', Simon introduced me to a guy named Peter, telling me he was German and would be a nice partner for conversations about music in general and folk music in particular. Peter pointed out that he had played in the same venue as Fairport had played that evening and pointed at large glossy pictures on the wall next to the bar, where he was portrayed to good effect. On the way back to the car in the early morning hours, I finally came to realise that I had been talking to none other than Peter Bursch, author of one of the most famous acoustic-guitar tutorials in Austria and Germany and leader of the popular German folk, Kraut-Rock and Underground outfit, Bröselmascine.

10TH MANSFIELD BEER FESTIVAL
7 APRIL 2001, MANSFIELD, UK

DAVID PARKES

I first heard of Fairport when I was at college in Blackpool and a friend lent me a copy of *Liege & Lief*. From then I was hooked but didn't manage to see them until the 'farewell' tour when they played Nottingham Playhouse in 1979, when I went with my wife-to-be Angela. I remember Dave Swarbrick's violin cable being too short and as he moved around the stage it was frequently pulled off and silence ensuing. He also came to the front of the stage to ask an audience member for a light! Those were the days.

We didn't see them again until the 1980s, when Ric and Maart had joined, after that we saw them regularly throughout the 1990s. We had been supporting the Mansfield Beer Festival since the first one, so when we found out Fairport would be playing it couldn't have been better. By this time, Maart had left and Chris had joined. As you might expect it was standing only. Unfortunately, Angela had injured her foot so we managed to scrounge her a chair and she sat in the centre, right in front of the stage.

About halfway into the set, Angela nudged me and said, 'Look over there by the door, that chap just looks like Maartin Allcock.' I said, 'Don't be ridiculous, what would he be doing here?' About ten minutes later, the chap who looked like Maartin Allcock wandered in front of us and then jumped up on stage, picked up one of Chris Leslie's instruments and proceeded to play with the band for the rest of the set. What a brilliant night!

After they had finished, we managed to have a chat with Maart and it turned out that he was attending a family celebration in a village just outside Mansfield and had seen that the chaps were playing and had decided to surprise them. I think he succeeded in this aim.

Angela managed to have her ticket signed by the band and Maart. Before the gig, she had asked Ric to play 'Portmeirion', but he was unable to oblige. However, on the ticket he had written 'Next time, Portmeirion, Angela – I hope!' and he was as good as his word.

CROPREDY FESTIVAL
9-11 AUGUST 2001, CROPREDY, UK

KEREN NORBURY

I had been coming to Cropredy since 1998 with a group of friends, The Geriatric Hedgehogs. It was the early 2000s when what I shall refer to as the 'Blue Hand Experience' took place. We were camping in Field 4 and having a great time, as always. On the Friday evening, at the end of our post-performance party back at our tents, I locked my valuables (red wine!) in the boot of my car and set off across the field with Val and Brian for our late-night wee visit to the conveniences.

Having completed my business I arose, pulled up my shorts and – slither, slither, slither, PLOP! – my keys dropped into the toilet! I think I woke half the field with my expletive! Without a second thought, my hand dived into the dark blue murky waters and luckily retrieved the keys. Extracting my hand, I saw it was a marvellous shade of indigo. Of course, there was no water in the block I was in but Brian, gentleman that he is and worried that I had really damaged myself, had run to the bottom of the steps. He suggested that I go into the gents as there was slightly warm water there.

This I did, and I was able to change the colour of my hands to a lighter shade. Successive washes over the weekend improved the colour further, but when I got home there was still a tell-tale blue tint around my fingernails!

On the way home, we always stop for a 'clean toilet stop' and, over an orange juice, tell of a 'best and worse' moment of Cropredy for that year. Needless to say, that was the best moment for most and possibly the worst for me! This story remains in the annals of The Geriatric Hedgehogs and gets a laugh *every* year.

The Daily Epitaph

Not the late edition

Dave Swarbrick

"It's not the first time I have died in Coventry"

Swarbrick: the tributes flood in

"It is just another notch on his bedpost of notoriety" Simon Nicol

"How could he fiddle with a fag in his mouth – but he did – I wonder what Yehudi would have thought!" Michael Elphick

"He's deaf, not dead – misprint!" Barney McKenna

"This obituary notice had to be a fiddle" John Sheahan

'Evening all, thank you for coming'

Peggy's Bit

STOP PRESS: RUNNING ORDER

Fairport News

1999

dear fairporters…

ticket prices and camping

cropredy festival info…

David Taylor [2214]
103 Southend
Garsington
Oxford
OX44 9DL

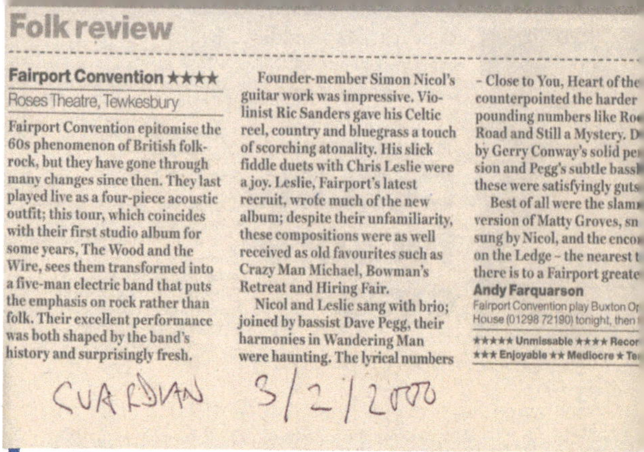

Folk review

Fairport Convention ★★★★

Roses Theatre, Tewkesbury

Fairport Convention epitomise the 60s phenomenon of British folk-rock, but they have gone through many changes since then. They last played live as a four-piece acoustic outfit; this tour, which coincides with their first studio album for some years, The Wood and the Wire, sees them transformed into a five-man electric band that puts the emphasis on rock rather than folk. Their excellent performance was both shaped by the band's history and surprisingly fresh.

Founder-member Simon Nicol's guitar work was impressive. Violinist Ric Sanders gave his Celtic reel, country and bluegrass a touch of scorching atonality. His slick fiddle duets with Chris Leslie were a joy. Leslie, Fairport's latest recruit, wrote much of the new album; despite their unfamiliarity, these compositions were as well received as old favourites such as Crazy Man Michael, Bowman's Retreat and Hiring Fair.

Nicol and Leslie sang with brio; joined by bassist Dave Pegg, their harmonies in Wandering Man were haunting. The lyrical numbers – Close to You, Heart of the … counterpointed the harder pounding numbers like Ro… Road and Still a Mystery. D… by Gerry Conway's solid pe… sion and Pegg's subtle bass… these were satisfyingly guts…

Best of all were the slam… version of Matty Groves, sn… sung by Nicol, and the enco… on the Ledge – the nearest t… there is to a Fairport greate…

Andy Farquarson

Fairport Convention play Buxton Op… House (01298 72190) tonight, then t…

★★★★★ Unmissable ★★★★ Recor… ★★★ Enjoyable ★★ Mediocre ★ Te…

GUARDIAN 3/2/2000

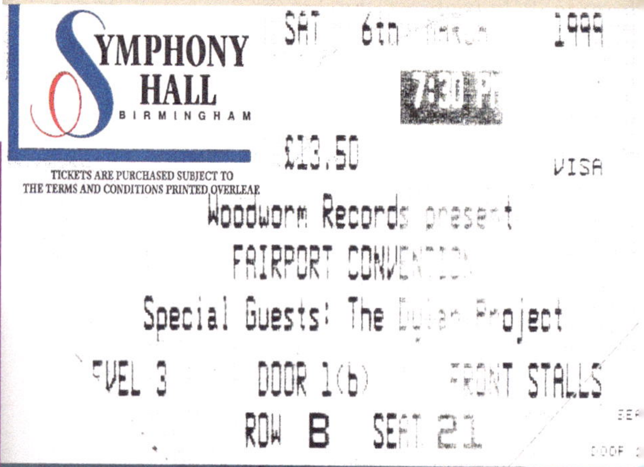

SYMPHONY HALL BIRMINGHAM

SAT 6th … 1999

£13.50 VISA

TICKETS ARE PURCHASED SUBJECT TO THE TERMS AND CONDITIONS PRINTED OVERLEAF

Woodworm Records present
FAIRPORT CONVENTION
Special Guests: The Dylan Project
LEVEL 3 DOOR 1(b) FRONT STALLS
ROW B SEAT 21

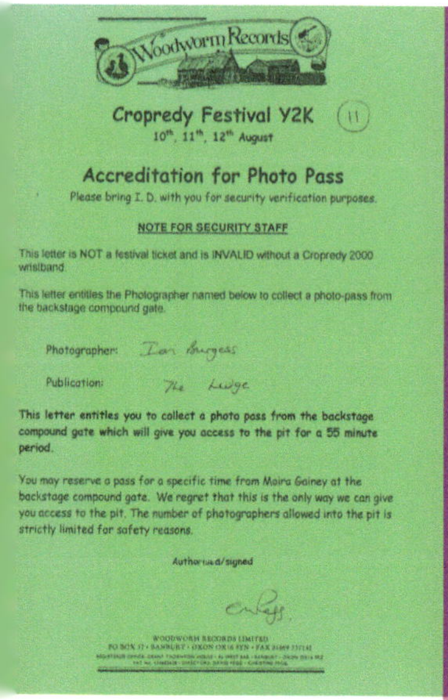

Woodworm Records

Cropredy Festival Y2K

10th, 11th, 12th August

Accreditation for Photo Pass

Please bring I. D. with you for security verification purposes.

NOTE FOR SECURITY STAFF

This letter is NOT a festival ticket and is INVALID without a Cropredy 2000 wristband.

This letter entitles the Photographer named below to collect a photo-pass from the backstage compound gate.

Photographer: Ian Burgess

Publication: The Ledge

This letter entitles you to collect a photo pass from the backstage compound gate which will give you access to the pit for a 55 minute period.

You may reserve a pass for a specific time from Moira Gainey at the backstage compound gate. We regret that this is the only way we can give you access to the pit. The number of photographers allowed into the pit is strictly limited for safety reasons.

Authorised/signed

WOODWORM RECORDS LIMITED

WOODWORM RECORDS AND CANNY CONCERTS PROUDLY PRESENT

Fairport Convention

THE WOOD AND THE WIRE TOUR 2000

with special guest BOB FOX

DATE	TOWN	VENUE	BOX OFFICE
Friday 28th January	Tewkesbury	The Roses Theatre	01684 295 074
Saturday 29th January	Tewkesbury	The Roses Theatre	01684 295 074
Sunday 30th January	Basingstoke	The Anvil	01256 844 244
featuring The Dylan Project			
Monday 31st January	Telford Oakengates	Oakengates Theatre	01952 619 020
Tuesday 1st February	Burnley	Mechanics	01282 430 055
Wednesday 2nd February	Southport	Arts Centre	01704 540 011
Thursday 3rd February	Buxton	Opera House	01298 721 90
Friday 4th February	Leicester	De Montford Hall	01162 333 111
Saturday 5th February	Croydon	Fairfield Hall	0181 688 9291
with special guest Dave Swarbrick			
Sunday 6th February	High Wycombe	The Swan	01494 512 000
Monday 7th February	Swindon	The Wyvern Theatre	01793 524 481
Tuesday 8th February	Chatham	The Central Theatre	01634 403 868
Wednesday 9th February	Bradford	St Georges Hall	01274 75 2000
Thursday 10th February	Dorking	Dorking Halls	01306 881 717
Friday 11th February	Leamington	Spa Centre	01926 334 418
Saturday 12th February	Tunbridge Wells	Assembly Hall	01892 530 613
Sunday 13th February	Canterbury	Marlowe Theatre	01227 787 787
Monday 14th February	Worthing	Pavilion Theatre	01903 820 500
Tuesday 15th February	Chesterfield	The Winding Wheel	01246 345 334
Wednesday16th February	Exeter	St Georges Hall	01392 265 866
Thursday 17th February	Weston Super Mare	The Playhouse	01934 645 544
Friday 18th February	St Albans	The Arena	01727 844 488
Saturday 19th February	Oxford	Apollo	01865 244 544
Sunday 20th February	Cambridge	Corn Exchange	01223 357 851
featuring The Dylan Project and Dave Swarbrick			
Monday 21st February	Yeovil	Octagon Theatre	01935 422 884
Tuesday 22nd February	Birmingham	Alexandra Theatre	0870 607 7544
with special guest Dave Swarbrick			

New album WRCD033 The Wood and the Wire out JANUARY 24th • Distributed by Direct

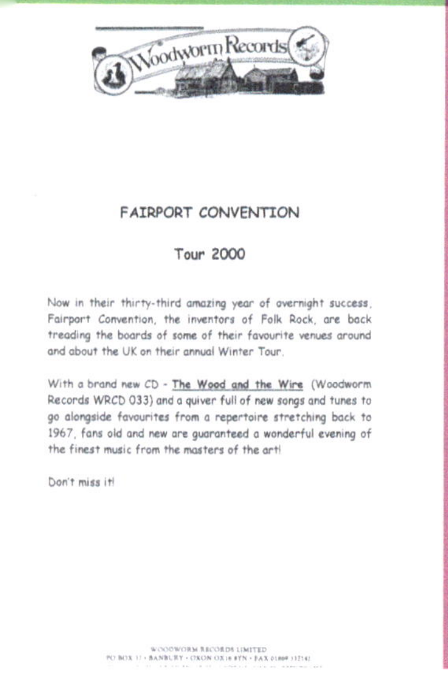

Woodworm Records

FAIRPORT CONVENTION

Tour 2000

Now in their thirty-third amazing year of overnight success, Fairport Convention, the inventors of Folk Rock, are back treading the boards of some of their favourite venues around and about the UK on their annual Winter Tour.

With a brand new CD – The Wood and the Wire (Woodworm Records WRCD 033) and a quiver full of new songs and tunes to go alongside favourites from a repertoire stretching back to 1967, fans old and new are guaranteed a wonderful evening of the finest music from the masters of the art!

Don't miss it!

WOODWORM RECORDS LIMITED

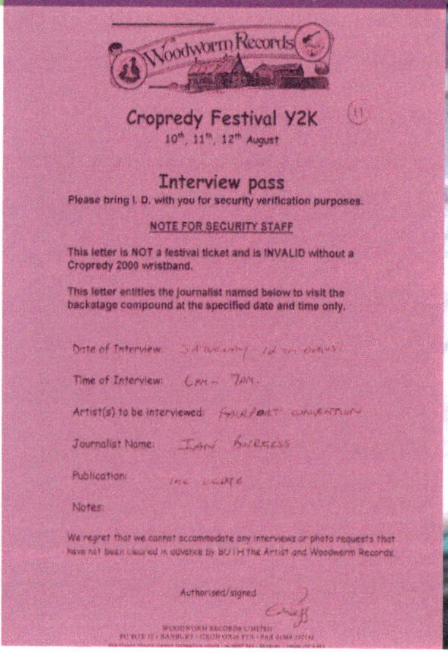

Woodworm Records

Cropredy Festival Y2K

10th, 11th, 12th August

Interview pass

Please bring I. D. with you for security verification purposes.

NOTE FOR SECURITY STAFF

This letter is NOT a festival ticket and is INVALID without a Cropredy 2000 wristband.

This letter entitles the journalist named below to visit the backstage compound at the specified date and time only.

Date of Interview:

Time of Interview:

Artist(s) to be interviewed: Fairport Convention

Journalist Name: Ian Burgess

Publication: The Ledge

Notes:

We regret that we cannot accommodate any interviews or photo requests that have not been cleared in advance by BOTH the Artist and Woodworm Records.

Authorised/signed

WOODWORM RECORDS LIMITED

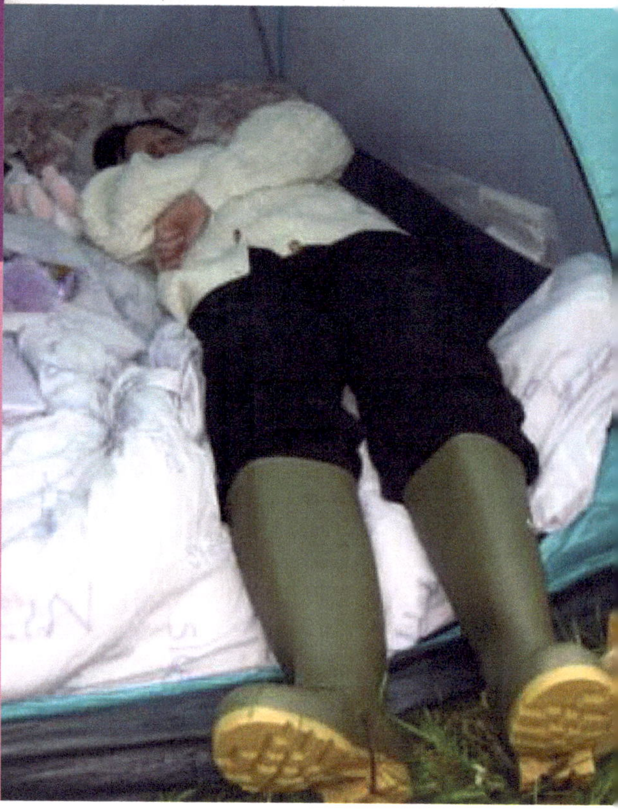

(clockwise from top left) Items from the Ian Burgess archive: *The Daily Epitaph*, 1999 newsletter, *Guardian* concert review; Terry Bidle's Winter Tour ticket; Lou Foran has been going to Cropredy since the age of 12; Y2K newsletter (Ian Burgess); 2000 tour (Ian Burgess); photo accreditation for Cropredy 2000 (Ian Burgess); *The Wood And The Wire* tour flyer (Ian Burgess)

(clockwise from top left) Tron Eivin Øvrebø was first at Cropredy in 1998; Tron has taken his wife to Cropredy; Mark L Johnson with Peggy; Lou Foran (above) remembers the mud in 1999 (*Oxford Times*); Jerry & Kristina Donahue at Cropredy 2000 (Bob Battersby/Lodestone Publishing Ltd); Sally Maybury brought her children to Cropredy via Normandy on a motorbike; Jerry Donahue & Swarb (Lou Foran); Rob Bousfield remembers Roger Hodgson's slot with Fairport; Simon Nicol (Lou Foran)

TERRY MCCRANOR

A few years ago, my starstruck friend Nigel Evans (whose ashes have since been scattered around Jonah's Oak) was amazed when Vikki Clayton approached me! She remembered I was driving her train from Tamworth to Birmingham. The very same afternoon Nigel nearly fell over when, in the CD tent, Swarb (who was signing copies of his obituary) looked up and said to me, 'Hiya – Binley Morrisons!' We both used to shop there.

SPIRIT OF 66
9 NOVEMBER 2001, VERVIERS, BELGIUM

CLAUDE CALTEUX

I had gone to see Fairport but it was the first time I had come to this place and I couldn't find it. I asked a big bald guy on the street… and Dave Pegg shows me the way! That same evening, I had a little chat with Simon. It was the first time I had seen him with short hair. He explained to me that he had cut it off because his children told him he looked like a dog!

MECHANICS THEATRE
5 FEBRUARY 2002, BURNLEY, UK

KEVAN TUCKER

I was a medical student in Leeds and saw that Fairport were playing at the Astoria Ballroom there on what I was to discover was the *Gladys' Leap* tour. I was a big Tull fan from the days of *Songs From The Wood* and so I knew about Peggy. I persuaded three or four mates to come and we were all absolutely blown away by this brilliant 'new' (to us) music. I think they started with 'How Many Times?' and I vividly remember 'Crazy Man Michael', which I instantly loved for its haunting quality. But the standout moment of a fantastic show was 'The Hiring Fair', which they played in front of a simple projector screen with a Thomas Hardyesque slideshow – very *Tess of the D'Urbevilles*!

The show was a total revelation, even to my non-Tull fan mates. We all bought the LP and posters and were amazed at meeting all the guys in the band. This started (for me) a 35 years plus total love affair with them all and a trawl through the back catalogue and exploration of former members. I love RT, have caught the Albion Band a couple of times and was even lucky enough to catch Swarb with Martin Carthy at the Lowry in Salford. Their playing was brilliant and DS was so funny. Sporting numerous tissues due to his tracheostomy, he told us the tour was sponsored by Kleenex. I bought a CD off him for £10 and he told me as a special offer I could buy two for £20!

I've seen the guys two or three times every year since and still absolutely love them to bits. For me, one story just sums up why we love them. I live near Burnley and for many years the boys played the Mechanics Theatre on the *Wintour*. I saw them on the *XXXV* tour and after the show was patiently queuing up to get my programme signed. I was behind a dad and a young lad who was maybe ten years old. They were waiting to see Ric. The little lad was obviously buzzing with excitement. I heard his dad explain to Ric that the lad had been listening to Fairport forever but this was his first gig. Well, cue lovely Ric pulling out all the stops for this lad, asking all about his favourite tracks, signing the CD and getting him to the front of the queues to see all of the other guys as well. The lad was absolutely made up and none of us minded waiting our turn. Even though the rest of us were kept waiting, nobody minded because Ric had clearly totally made this lad's day. It was really quite lovely to see. We all know Ric is a great guy but, even for him this was pretty exceptional.

I've always wanted to march up to Peggy at a gig and announce, in a theatrically loud voice, 'Thank you for pleasuring me for 35 years!' but never been brave enough!

CROPREDY FESTIVAL
8-10 AUGUST 2002, CROPREDY, UK

DAVE MONK

It's Friday 9th August 2002. My brother Mick and I have driven in the rain to Oxfordshire in my Vauxhall Vectra for our first ever Cropredy. This is billed as a special one, the thirtyfifth anniversary with an expected line-up comprising of many former members and friends of Fairport Convention.

We have high hopes and like everyone else there we pray for the rain to stop. According to the liner notes to the anniversary CD released later that year, this '…was certainly the rainiest… and it was cold.' Amen to that. Nor was it '…the sort of climate one would choose to go and stand in a field.' How true, but here we were, two intrepid Cropredy newbies joining the other 17,000 for what turned out to be an outstanding festival.

Before entering the field for the first time there's a small matter of erecting a two-man tent in a rain-soaked field behind the car, our plot. This proves beyond the expertise of Mick and I. Within a few minutes our tent is soaked inside as well as out. There's absolutely no way we're going to be spending a night under canvas, much to the amusement of the two young guys we are parked next to. They of course are veterans of this sort of thing, whereas our combined academic knowledge is clearly useless when it comes to the matter of basic camping skills. All previous experiences have been managed by people more competent than us. Our Cropredy night will be spent cramped inside the car but that comes a bit later.

Defeated but not deflated, dressed in basic rainwear, clutching a couple of brightly-coloured umbrellas courtesy of Legal & General, we make for the field. The route is of course wet, muddy and liberally adorned with cow pats. Yuck!

We make if for Mundy Turner but we have failed to come with anything dry to sit on and most other people are well equipped, sheltering under massive umbrellas. But we endure through other acts until we are rewarded with Richard Thompson's appearance, which is one of the high spots accompanied by a break in the rain. Clearly, he is blessed. His acoustic set is followed by Fairport Convention: The Early Years. As a fan of the band from the very beginning, it was great to hear old favourites from the first four albums with original members like Judy Dyble and Iain Matthews performing as well as many guests.

I remember our night in the car was uncomfortable, not improved by the underlying grim stench of cow shit which was unavoidable every time we ventured out to the nearby toilets. It was for this reason that subsequent Cropredys have been spent in one of the local Travel Lodges.

Saturday started out wet but by the time the afternoon arrived we enjoyed not just great sets by the likes of Eddi Reader and Deborah Bonham but also sun and warmth. But this afternoon was memorable for another reason. We met up with an old friend, Julian Cooper, who we hadn't seen since the late seventies. Julian worked for the Ordnance Survey, as did Mick and I for brief spells. More than that, Julian was a gig buddy, most notably the first Knebworth in '74 which featured The Allman Brothers, Tim Buckley and other great bands, and a year later the Elton John, Eagles and Beach Boys concert at Wembley Stadium. So here we were once again, at a gig together. It's a fond memory of sharing great music and new and old stories. We never met up again but we heard that Julian passed away in 2023. A powerful reason for 'Meet On The Ledge' to resonate even more when next I hear it at Cropredy.

I joined the long queue to get RT to sign a copy of the just-released Richard Thompson Band *Live Semi-Detached Mock Tudor* CD, chewing over what I would say. Something about that first encounter at the Hadham shows thirty years ago perhaps? But in the end a mumbled 'thank you Richard' was the best I could utter.

Fairport's final set was also blessed by dry weather. What made it special were the dualling guitars of Richard Thompson and Jerry Donahue on a personal favourite, 'Sloth', which had first left its mark at the second Little Hadham show in 1970. It was great for another reason too. Back in 1988 Jerry had visited Harlow College, where

I worked, to meet up with his old friend Doug Morter, who was teaching on our first ever rock music course. Back then Doug would regale me as to the brilliance and fun of Cropredy, urging me to go. But the greatest thrill was that I interviewed Jerry for the college's staff newsletter. Such a lovely man. They also played a memorable gig in our theatre, which featured Rick Kemp and Julian Dawson, to promote their album, *Brief Encounter*.

So that was the first Cropredy, full of poignant memories, none of which I was able to capture on film as my camera battery failed on the Friday and there was nowhere around Cropredy that sold replacement Canon SLR batteries. Not a mistake I have made at the other Cropredys I've attended, shared again with brother Mick and his old friend and best man Don. Two of these Cropredys were also special anniversaries, 2012, forty-five years and 2017, fifty. Long may they – Fairport and Cropredy – continue.

SPA CENTRE
14 FEBRUARY 2003, LEAMINGTON SPA, UK

IAN MCBRIDE

I came to Fairport relatively late compared to many. I'd been seriously into music since 1978 when I was eight years old but it wasn't until 1999 that I picked up a copy of *The History Of Fairport Convention* on CD. Hearing 'Meet On The Ledge', 'Matty Groves', 'Sloth', 'Walk Awhile', 'Now Be Thankful', etc. had me instantly hooked. The following year I bought a Sandy Denny compilation called *No More Sad Refrains* and from that point the obsession was cemented. I spent the next few years sourcing their back catalogue – firstly on CD and then on vinyl.

I'd known of their festival for many years prior to those first purchases – living in Nuneaton, Cropredy was only about an hour away. Plus, in the early eighties my auntie owned a pub (The Barley Mow) in the village of Stockton, just outside Southam, a stone's throw from the festival site. My auntie told me she ran a small hotdog stall at one of those early Cropredys and I have no reason to doubt her!

I finally got to see the band live in 2003 on their winter tour. That same year saw us attend our very first Cropredy after watching the previous year's festival on DVD and deciding we really must give it a go. We haven't missed a winter tour or festival since (pandemics excepted). We've also attended one of the Cropredy warmup gigs every year since 2006 and done many spring and autumn tours all over the country, from Chipping Norton to Kendal, and from Malpas to Lichfield.

The band and the festival have afforded us many friendships over the years. I'm very honoured to be able to call Peggy and Ellen friends as well as the likes of Anthony

John Clarke and Julia Porter, Anna rydeR and Marion Fleetwood. We also have a little gang of pals – pals from Ormskirk, Chorley, Pontefract and Banbury nicknamed 'the Cropredy Crew' – all of whom we met on *that* field and who have reconvened there many times over the years. And for many years we'd all meet up somewhere in the UK for a weekend away between festivals. We also have two sets of pals from the States, North Carolina and San Francisco, both of which have returned to Cropredy at least twice since their initial visits in the early 2000s.

Fairport and Cropredy have given us so much over the last two decades or more, especially those friendships, and for that we will always be eternally grateful. It really is like being in an extended family.

FITZGERALD'S
18 JUNE 2003, BERWYN, ILLINOIS

BOB HOLDSWORTH

I still have the t-shirt. I remember Simon curling up into a ball onstage as Peggy spoke about how 'most' of the band had contributed to Jethro Tull recordings. And Peggy sticking his pick to his bald pate when playing with his fingers. I also saw them some years later at the Old Town School of Folk Music shortly after Chris Leslie joined them. I had a chance to speak to him in the music shop there before the show, where I told him I was glad that his vocal range was able to let them perform songs that Swarb used to sing. I really only had *Liege & Lief* and *Full House* on LP but we have purchased several other albums on CD, as well as those two. I have seen Richard Thompson several times as he plays the States frequently, but never back when he was with Fairport. I've tried to play a few of his songs, too, but they are challenging!

CROPREDY FESTIVAL
7-9 AUGUST 2003, CROPREDY, UK

IAN HUCKIN

I went to Cropredy for the first time in 2003, mainly to see Procol Harum, Lindisfarne and Dr Hook. However, I was entranced by Fairport's tremendous music and their energy to last for almost three hours. At that time, I couldn't have named a single member of the band (ever) apart from Sandy Denny, who I only knew from Led Zeppelin and her contribution to the *Tommy* various artists album (as performed by the

London Symphony Orchestra). In the following 20 plus years, I came to realise that I did know lots, eg. Iain Matthews and Richard Thompson, but I just never associated them with FC. Needless to say, I've never missed a Cropredy since.

Now that I help run Banbury Folk Club, I've booked most of them at the club, in different guises. I've also booked acts that I've seen at the festival, based on what I've seen of them on that big stage. The many fabulous friends that I've made (and sadly a few I've lost) through the festival and folk clubs have kept me going through some really bad times. The tremendous music I've discovered has broadened my already wide range of musical tastes. I go to other festivals nowadays but Cropredy remains that special one. I honestly don't know where I'd be now, without that first venture into the world of the Fairport Convention family.

DE PUL GROTE ZAL

1 NOVEMBER 2003, UDEN, THE NETHERLANDS

RUUD VERSCHOOR

In the early seventies I was in teacher's academy in Middelburg. Some guys from the school were organising a festival in Vlissingen, and a few well-known Dutch bands were going to be playing along with a band from the UK with a singer called Sandy Denny. I read in the paper that the guitarist in this band made his guitar sing like you never heard before. Of course that was Richard Thompson. At the time, I was a fan of The Who and knew nothing about Fairport. Sandy's band was magnificent, and since then RT has become my favourite guitarist. And Sandy was the best singer ever.

From some other students, I learned that Richard and Sandy both played in Fairport Convention so I bought *Full House* and played it over and over. Not too long after, Richard and Linda Thompson came to my hometown of Goes and played in a little venue of maybe 30 or 40 people. They blew me away.

Fairport Convention have played several times in The Netherlands and I have seen them twice. The first time was in Uden in De Pul. I travelled a lot of kilometers with a friend to see the show. We had some beers (we lost count as to how many) and I had a chat and a beer with Simon Nicol while he was waiting to perform. He told me they had left England very early that morning and that it had been a very long day. The support acts were very boring but Fairport made the evening worth the wait.

The second time was in a theatre in Nieuwegein. Peggy was ill and was substituted by Vo Fletcher who did a great job. I was there with my wife and a friend. The friend is a huge fan of the *Nine* album and didn't recognise the band. (No one from that album was on the stage that night.) The band were good as always and after the show I bought a t-shirt (which I later lost) that the boys signed.

I saw the Richard Thompson Band at the Rotterdam Folk Festival and that was almost Fairport, without Swarb but with John Kirkpatrick. And when Swarb played the Matrix Club in Rotterdam, Simon and Peggy were there too, while my latest Fairport-related performance was seeing Richard Thompson in Eindhoven in 2022.

Nowadays I play in a folk-rock band called Mattick Road. We play some Fairport songs like 'Hexhamshire Lass', 'Sir Patrick Spens' and 'Tear-Stained Letter'. We got the name from an Australian reporter who wrote an article on Fairport and misspelled 'Matty Groves'; he had no idea that Matty was a person.

STEINENHAUS
6 NOVEMBER 2003, SOLINGEN, GERMANY

HANS-PETER BATTENFELD

As a fan of Creedence Clearwater Revival, The Band, Emmylou Harris, Linda Ronstadt, Little Feat and many other acts, especially Country Rock, Country and Bluegrass, I didn't care much about English Rock music until the mid-Nineties, when my interest for covers of Dylan's *Basement Tapes* songs led me to buy the *Unhalfbricking* CD at a record fair in Germany. I was pleased by what I heard and when I stumbled across *The Cropredy Box* from the 1997 festival in a shop I bought it and was enthusiastic about the fantastic music.

It wasn't until 2003 that I first saw Fairport, at a concert they gave in a pub in Solingen, Germany. By now, I had acquired almost all of Fairport's available CDs and had become addicted to their music. Just before, I had bought the Free Reed box set *Fairport unConventional* and took the accompanying book with me to get some autographs. When the pub opened, I was waiting at the door and was the first to enter. Around the still sparsely lit counter sat five shapes in the semi-darkness, who turned out to be the musicians. They were only too willing to sign my book and answer my questions. My most pressing concern was whether it would be possible to get the CDs with the Cropredy recordings from 1982/83 and 1986/87 respectively. They recommended that I look around on the world wide web, as there would surely be someone who would be willing to copy them for me. This hint proved to be true. It was a wonderful concert that evening and I drove home in an uplifted mood.

The following year, I made an unsuccessful attempt to attend the Cropredy Festival. A week before the festival started, when I had only been in England for a few days, my brother had a fatal car accident in Germany. I returned home and sent my ticket back to the organisers so that someone else might get the chance to take part. To my amazement, I got the ticket price refunded.

In 2007 for Fairport's 40th birthday, I attended my first Cropredy and have been back every year since, with the exception of 2016 when a cancer operation hindered me. During one of these visits, I met Simon Nicol at the bar and approached him about the fact that I hadn't expected to get a refund on the ticket price, and he was able to remember the concert in Solingen and replied 'we're just trying to be serious!'

Over the years I have delved deeper and deeper into the history of the band and its past and present members and have been able to add to my collection almost all the releases of Steeleye Span, the various Albion bands and Ashley Hutchings, the latter of which the guys from Talking Elephant were a great help with their stall in Cropredy during the festivals. I have made many acquaintances during the festivals, English and German, and always look forward to these visits. One of my highlights each year are Fairport's performances, and especially those where they go back into the band's history, like the 40th birthday and the performance of *Liege & Lief* in its entirety in 2007, and the 50th birthday festivities in 2017. You can usually find me at Cropredy under a German flag, at the central aisle and halfway up the festival site.

LOWDHAM VILLAGE HALL
10 MARCH 2006, LOWDHAM, UK

JENNY PARSONS

Swarb played for us several times at Farnsfield Acoustic and we always had a great night when he came. One night, as I was about to introduce him, he asked me to keep it short. I said that I would. 'Good evening, everyone. Please welcome Dave Swarbrick, you all know him, you all love him…'. As he came onto the stage and in a not very quiet voice but with a twinkle in his eye, he said 'that was the worst fucking intro I have ever had!'

Everyone here must know about Swarb's double lung transplant… which had been reported in a Grimsby newspaper as a double heart transplant! At Farnsfield Acoustic, we were privileged to host his very first gig once he was recovering. With Maart Allcock and Kevin Dempsey he had formed Swarb's Lazarus, a very appropriate band name! Swarb had worked for many years with Kevin in the fabulous Whippersnapper, but had not as far as I know played with Maart before. So that afternoon we arrived full of anticipation to set up the hall. It was only the second year that Farnsfield Acoustic had existed, so our team was still fairly new to putting on gigs.

I saw the car arrive and Jill Swarb let him out… he had the biggest smile ever… he was so happy to be gigging again after a very long time healing. He quickly sat on the stage and played… and played… and played… and played… as we were still getting

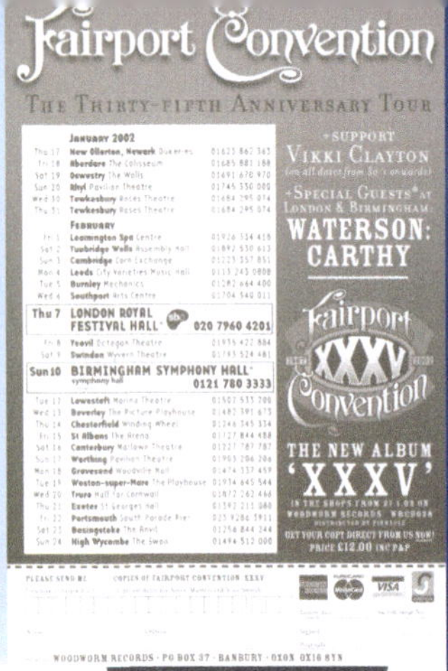

NOVEMBER 2002

The Winter Tour

Our tour this year starts of Friday, January 31st and finishes on Tuesday 25th February. We have a couple of very special nights on it. The 19th February, when our special guest will be **Dave Swarbrick**. This is at Derby Assembly Rooms and it's been organised by Neil Wayne, the hero who released the Fairport box set "Fairport Unconventional". Neil is also the President and Veterans Team Captain of Belper Rugby Club and is organising this special benefit concert to help his club out. You can get tickets from the Assembly Rooms (see our list of dates underneath) or direct from Free Reed on 01773 824157 (you then get a special money off CD voucher) or on line at www.free-reed.co.uk/concert. The other date we are doing that I don't believe we have done before is London Astoria, which is on Sunday 23rd February. Our special guest on all these dates will be **Andy Guttridge** who is a great friend of ours from Banbury and a great singer songwriter – it will be nice having him on tour.

JANUARY		
Friday 31	**Peterborough** Broadway Theatre	01733 316100
FEBRUARY		
Saturday 1	**Newport** City Live Arena	01633 213 344
Sunday 2	**Preston** Guildhall	01772 258 858
Monday 3	**Leeds** City Varieties Music Hall	0113 243 0808
Tuesday 4	**Burnley** Mechanics	01282 664 400
Wednesday 5	**Southport** Arts Centre	01704 540 011
Thursday 6	**Cheltenham** Town Hall	01242 227 979
Friday 7	**Croydon** Fairfield Hall	020 8688 9291
Saturday 8	**Yeovil** Octagon Theatre	01935 422 884
Sunday 9	**Wolverhampton** Civic Hall	01902 552 121
Tuesday 11	**Brighton** The Hove Centre	0870 900 9100
Wednesday 12	**Northampton** The Roadmender	01604 604 222
Thursday 13	**Chesterfield** The Winding Wheel	01246 345 334
Friday 14	**Leamington** Spa Centre	01926 334 418
Saturday 15	**Tunbridge Wells** Assembly Hall	01892 530 613
Sunday 16	**St. Albans** The Alban Arena	01727 844 488
Monday 17	**Weston-Super-Mare** The Playhouse	01934 645 544
Tuesday 18	**Winchester** Theatre Royal	01962 840 440
Wednesday 19	**Derby** Assembly Rooms* *plus additional guest **DAVE SWARBRICK**	01332 255 800
Thursday 20	**Dorking** Dorking Halls	01306 881 717
Friday 21	**High Wycombe** The Swan	01494 512 000
Saturday 22	**Canterbury** Marlowe Theatre	01227 787 787
Sunday 23	**LONDON** ASTORIA	020 7344 0044
Monday 24	**Hastings** White Rock Theatre	01424 78100
Tuesday 25	**Swindon** Wyvern Theatre	01793 524481

(clockwise from top left) Items from the Ian Burgess archive: *The Ledge* May 2001; 2001 Winter Tour flyer; Cropredy 2001 flyer; 2002 Winter Tour flyer

SAT 10th FEBRUARY 2001

£14.00 7:30 PM

symphony hall birmingham

Woodworm Records and Canny Concerts present

FAIRPORT CONVENTION

All About Eve

Steve Tilston

LEVEL 3 DOOR 2(d) CENT. TERRACE

ROW B SEAT 5

Tickets are purchased subject to the terms and conditions printed ov

SUN 10th FEBRUARY 2002

£15.00 7:30 PM

symphony hall birmingham

Woodworm Records & Canny Concerts present

FAIRPORT CONVENTION

support

Waterson Carthy & Vicki Clayton

LEVEL 3 DOOR 1(b) FRONT STALLS

ROW AA SEAT 24

SUN 8th FEBRUARY 2004

£16.50 7:30 PM

symphony hall birmingham

Mr T G. BIDLE

Woodworm Records & Canny Concerts present

FAIRPORT CONVENTION

Special gues s The Dylan Project

Suppor Mundy/Turner

LEVEL 3 DOOR 2(b) FRONT STALLS

ROW AA SEAT 15

£16.50 CHEQUE 8 FEB04 IE AA 15

's are purchased subject to the terms and conditions printed overleaf

Midland Box Of

North Street, Wolverhampton, WV1 1RQ

CIVIC HALL,NORTH ST,WOLVERHAMPTON

CANNY CONCERT PRODUCTIONS presents

FAIRPORT CONVENTION

in Concert

Sun, 9 Feb 03 7:30 PM Doors Open 6:30p

RIG BALC A 011

FULL £14.00 Inc VAT

10040226 Mr T Bidle

Tel: (01902) 552121

Premium Sales on the Internet: www.midlandboxoffice.com

(clockwise from top left) Terry Bidle's 2001 & 2002 tickets; Kevan Tucker with Richard Thompson; Terry Bidle's 2004 & 2003 tickets; invite to screening of the 2001 concert film (Ian Burgess)

DAVE & CHRIS PEGG FOR WOODWORM RECORDS PROUDLY PRESE

CROPREDY FESTIVAL 200

Fairport XXXV Convention 1967 2002

THURSDAY 8TH AUGUST 4.30-11.00PM
THE DUBLINERS • EIIK
THE JOYCE GANG • FREEWAY JAM Compere: JOHNNY JON

FRIDAY 9TH AUGUST 12.30-MIDNIGHT
RICHARD THOMPSON
FAIRPORT CONVENTION - 'THE EARLY YEARS'
(featuring Richard Thompson, Simon Nicol, Ashley Hutchings, Dave Swarbrick, Iain Matthews, Judy Dyble, Vikki Clayton, Gerry Conw
OYSTERBAND • MAGNA CARTA (featuring Chris & Linda Simpson and frien
SARAH JORY • BRODERICK • MUNDY-TURNER
Compere: BOB FOX

SATURDAY 10TH AUGUST 12.30-MIDNIGHT
FAIRPORT CONVENTIO
(with Dave Swarbrick, Richard Thompson, Jerry Donahue, Ralph McTell, Maartin Allcock, Vikki Clayton & surprise gues
RICHARD DIGANCE
EDDI READER with BOO HEWERDINE and COLIN REI
(from the USA) THE ALISON BROWN QUARTET
DEBORAH BONHAM • LITTLE JOHNNY ENGLAN
Compere: DANNY THOMPSON

TICKETS	THU/FRI/SAT	FRI/SAT	SATURDAY only
BEFORE JUNE 15	£52.00	£42.00	£27.00
JUNE 15 - JULY 31	£55.00	£45.00	£29.00
FROM AUGUST 1*	£58.00	£48.00	£31.00
(*OR PAY ON GATE)	CHILDREN UNDER 12 FREE IF ACCOMPANIED		
CAMPING**	£14.00	£9.00	FREE

(**CAMPING CHARGE IS PER VEHICLE-BIKERS & BACKPACKERS CAMP FREE)

INFO AND TICKETS
Send SAE to Woodworm Records
PO Box 37 Banbury OX16 8YN
Fax 01869 337142 Email faircrop@aol.com
www.fairportconvention.com

WADWORT BEER
MOJO

(clockwise from top left) Dave Monk & ?; Cropredy 2002 flyer (Ian Burgess); Bob Holdworth's US tour t-shirt

(clockwise from top left) Richard Thompson at the signing tent, Cropredy 2002 (John Barlass); Terry Bidle's signed 2003 tour poster from Wolves Civic; Ian McBride & his wife Jackie at Cropredy in 2023; Fairport in action at Wolves Civic (Terry Bidle); Ian Huckin & family at Cropredy the hall ready. After about an hour or so, Jill, Maart and Kevin had to 'persuade' him to rest in the green room.

Soon it was time to open the doors. We packed the hall with almost 200 people, many of whom had travelled a very long way to see Swarb again. The time came to introduce the trio… but I was so nervous I asked Gareth to do it. He decided not to walk back in front of the stage, so went through another door, then found he was stuck in an enclosed area of the field behind the hall. He tried to climb over the high fence as a dog walker went by. 'It's okay… I am the promoter; I've just introduced the band!'

The music was just amazing. Together the three of them played everything with such enthusiasm and professionalism, the audience clapped so loudly at the end of every piece, and at the end of the gig the standing ovation seemed to reach the roof! Swarb didn't want to leave the stage. He was grinning from ear to ear, and he was a very happy man to be back. We were all so glad that it had gone so well… we knew it would… but it had taken quite a lot of work to bring it all together. I think we all slept well that night!

Thank you Swarb, Kevin and Maart.

FAIRPORT'S CROPREDY CONVENTION

10-12 AUGUST 2006, CROPREDY, UK

PHILIP SHEPHERD

In 2006 my friends and I were lucky to get to meet with Richard Digance, Geoff Hughes, Frank Skinner and Ralph McTell. My children, although young, were and still are great fans of Richard and we still manage to get to the field for 12pm every Saturday. Anyway, in 2006 we were talking to Richard and my ten-year-old daughter Molly turned up. She had been walking around the field with one of her friends' family. Richard started talking to her and the conversation turned to pocket money. It was quickly established that I didn't give Molly regular pocket money so Richard asked those around to dig into their pockets and contribute to Molly's pocket money fund. I think about £8 was given.

Molly's younger brother Nat then showed up. Molly proudly boasted about her new found wealth and Nat started moaning about his lack of money. Another whip round was organised and the proceeds given to Nat. He wanted to spend his money straight away and he and Richard went off to make some purchases. The tale thereafter is captured by a poem Richard wrote after the festival had ended and which he emailed to one of my friends.

This epitomises the festival and why we return year after year. And here's the poem Richard wrote for our son:

Naughty Nat

Nat Shepherd, this poem is for you
Written by a man you painted blue
I will get back to you in time
But for the moment here's a little rhyme…

Naughty Nat is a little rat
I'm afraid there is no doubt of that
Instead of four legs he has two
On which he runs around to paint friends blue

He'll pretend to be your friend a while
With his freckles and his cheeky smile
But underneath the friendly face
A plan is being put in place

Richard's a special friend he met
But the special friend shall not forget
How he bought young Naughty Nat a gun
(Across a field of people, they did run)

Everything was going well
Til he chose to buy some paint as well
He never told his friend the plan
As they walked away with the gun and can

Back across the field they sped
Naughty Nat followed as Richard led
A nasty plan that Ratty had
As he ended up back with his dad,

Naughty Nat thought it was funny
Though he's used new friend's money
He could've been kind, but no instead
He painted everybody's head

Everyone was painted blue
And the special friend Richard was painted too.
What a way to thank a friend
Who on Naughty Nat three pounds did spend

One day you'll have a bright green head

Yellow face and a nose deep red
One day Richard will win the fight
And Shepherd will wash his locks by night

TOWN HALL
29 FEBRUARY 2008, BIRMINGHAM, UK

CAROLYN & MARK EVANS, RED SHOES

We'd met in 1983 and formed a band called Red Shoes, mixing rock, folk and country influences. We were signed by Mooncrest Records. In 1987 we recorded a version of Sandy Denny's 'By The Time It Gets Dark' as a single. Carolyn had been a Fairport fan from her teens, having seen them onstage a number of times. They were her favourite band and we'd been to Cropredy Festival on a few occasions through the eighties. In 1988 we got married, the band broke up in '89 and we later had two daughters. We still played at local folk club sessions, still wrote songs and, with the advent of YouTube, we put some versions of Fairport favourites online, 'Crazy Man Michael', 'Who Knows Where The Time Goes' and 'White Dress', which picked up some fans. But we thought that was it in terms of music.

In 2007 a mutual friend said we should write to Dave Pegg with our songs, with a view to him maybe producing us. It all seemed like a bit of a pipedream, but we did so and then thought nothing more of it until one morning in early 2008 we had a phone call and on the other end of the line was Mr Pegg himself! He was so friendly, and us all being Brummies, we seemed to click as we chatted. He said he was intrigued and interested and that we should meet him at Birmingham Town Hall on Fairport's Winter tour… oh, and to bring a CD with the songs on!

We duly turned up and saw the band play, enjoying the gig immensely, then waited in a long queue to speak to him at the end of the evening in the foyer. When we did finally meet and tell him who we were, his response was, 'Are you the band with the comedy drummer?' We laughed and said not. He seemed relieved, saying 'oh good!' We gave him the CD of songs, with him saying he'd take it away and have a listen and that he'd be in touch.

Good as his word, he wrote to us with an idea of us coming to Banbury, staying over, having some food and drinks, and he'd book a day in the studio and we'd see how it all went. That day in Blue Moon Studio was like a dream come true. Peggy selected the three songs we recorded. He played bass, guitar, mandolin and called Chris Leslie up to come down and play some fiddle on the tracks. We couldn't believe it!

We had an amazing time, everybody got on like a house on fire, the recordings came out so well, and later that year we went on to record what would become our debut album, *Ring Around The Land*, released in 2009.

Many years have passed since that fateful day and here we are, three Red Shoes albums later, with Peggy producing and playing on all of them plus guests from the Fairport family – Chris Leslie, Ric Sanders and Dave Swarbrick – with PJ Wright and Mick Bullard adding their talents to the mix along the way.

We've since become great friends with Peggy and shared many a happy hour along the way, playing onstage together, talking music and having fun. And a phone call every year as he and Mark share a birthday, so are Birthday Brothers – albeit with ten years between them. But the icing on the cake was when Fairport recorded our song 'Celtic Moon' for their album, *Festival Bell* – unbelievable! To hear them play it at Cropredy in front of a capacity crowd was a real 'pinch me' moment!

FAIRPORT'S CROPREDY CONVENTION
7-9 AUGUST 2008, CROPREDY, UK

JAN & JON DIXON

There was a wonderful section of Sandy's songs as a tribute 30 years after we lost her. One of them was Robert Plant and Kristina Donahue singing 'The Battle Of Evermore'. Jan was halfway back in the field with our daughter, Emily, then eight years old. Em wasn't paying attention but Jan made her stand up to watch that song, telling her she would be pleased she had seen it in later years. And she was… Now 27, she's rightfully proud to be one of the few people her age to have seen all surviving members of Zeppelin (not together sadly but, hey, what can you do?).

PHOEBE BROGDEN

My Fairport experience began when I was about six months old and my parents took me along, as any sensible parent would! I went every year for most of my childhood and fell in love with folk music so much that I made music my entire life. I have many favourite memories from making hats out of about a hundred stickers at the crafts stalls, to sitting with my grandad and listening to our favourite artists. But there is one that really sticks out in my head.

When I was about six or seven, to keep me occupied while the adults set up the tent, I was given some blue paper and a bunch of pens. I remember my parents and their friends talking about Fairport a lot, but the name that really stuck with me was Dave Pegg. They just kept saying how cool he was and I got very excited about seeing this man I barely knew but I at least knew about the extent of his 'coolness'. I drew what I thought was a highly accurate and artistically good portrait of him on a rocket with the caption: 'Dave Pegg rocks out to space.' The whole family was amused and later Dave was spotted in the field and my parent's friend took the card to him.

That night during Fairport's set, I genuinely have never felt such elation than when I saw him holding it up and showing everybody my card! He made the observation that I had drawn him with hair... How was I supposed to know he didn't have any?! Even so, to see my card up there in his hand was extremely special and I will never ever forget it. It was a completely bizarre moment that would only happen at Cropredy, where everyone is so friendly and approachable, including the artists.

I owe so much of my passion for music to Fairport and I'm so glad that those early experiences at Cropredy have led me to studying and playing the music that I love.

KURT THULIN

Having discovered Fairport in 1969, it came as a bit of a shock ten years later when I heard that they had decided to break up. Simon Nicol had rejoined two years before that and they had recorded two fine albums for the Vertigo label, but the musical scene had changed – punk and new wave were blowing up – and the group felt as though they were out of fashion. Sales of those Vertigo albums were disappointing, and Dave Swarbrick's hearing problems made him unable to safely play electric violin, which seemed another good reason to break up. One last album with the fitting title of *Farewell, Farewell* (the first on their own label Woodworm Records) was released in 1979.

However, they decided they were going to play one gig every year in the village where the two Daves, Swarbrick and Pegg, lived – Cropredy. This was good news for all of us Fairporters as we could travel to this lovely Oxfordshire village and enjoy our favourites once a year, as I would do through most of the eighties.

The festival seemed to get bigger with every outing and the band saw the addition of Ric Sanders from Albion Band to replace Swarb. In 1985 Fairport, now armed with new material, decided to record a new studio album, which they did in Dave Pegg's very own Woodworm Studios. *Gladys' Leap* was released it on their Woodworm Records label. On one occasion, I spoke to Peggy about how a small independent label could reach outside the UK. I happened to know two of the owners of a label based in Malmö in the south of Sweden called Amalthea. They had some of the country's best singer-songwriters and rock groups, but also two of Sweden's greatest folk bands, Filarfolket and Folk & Rackare, amongst their artists. I asked Amalthea if they were interested in releasing a brand new Fairport Convention album for Scandinavian distribution. I put them in touch with Dave Pegg. I was very happy to give something back to the boys on top of buying all their albums.

The following year, Fairport released their next album, the instrumental *Expletive Delighted!*, which was also released on the Amalthea label. The year after that, Amalthea celebrated ten years of business with a big concert featuring some of their artists and Fairport were invited to take part. They played a great set. At the end of the evening, I was lucky enough to be their chauffeur, taking them to their hotel in my SAAB 9000 Turbo.

As a result of their Swedish visit, Fairport invited Filarfolket to play the 1988 edition of Cropredy Festival, which was a big success for them and there are still regular Croppers who remember them. And Folk & Rackare, probably as important to the Swedish song tradition as Fairport and Steeleye Span are to the English one, got Richard Thompson to play a great solo on the Norwegian traditional song 'Inga Litimor' on their final album, *Rackbag*. I'm pleased to say that some of the people I've met on the English folk scene thanks to Fairport, like 'The Guv'nor' (Ashley Hutchings), John Kirkpatrick and his Brass Monkey bandmate Martin Brinsford have become fans of Swedish folk.

The most emotionally moving Cropredy was 2008. It was 30 years since Sandy Denny left us all too early and Fairport made a very emotional and beautiful set consisting of six of Sandy's songs and performances. Robert Plant and Kristina Donahue did a wonderful version of Led Zeppelin's 'The Battle Of Evermore', backed by Fairport. It gave me goosebumps. And during John Tams and Barry Coope's set, they introduced the beautiful song 'How High The Price' by saying, 'We would love to dedicate the next song to our dear friend Kurt all the way from Gothenburg, Sweden, because he was the one who introduced us to each other.' This was a big honour for me.

What makes Cropredy the friendliest festival on the planet? The answer is the crowd because, like me, many have met lifelong friends there. In the shower queue at 7am, after a rainy night on a muddy field, I met a wonderful Cropredy regular named Peter Rushmer from Norfolk and we had a great conversation. Some months later, I got an email from Peter who had contacted Simon Nicol and asked if he had a 'Kurt from Sweden' in his contact list. Simon replied that he had 334 UK Peters but only one 'Kurt in Sweden'. Ever since, my wife Pia and I have been close friends with Peter and his wife Felicity. To me, that's the spirit of Fairport's Cropredy Convention!

BRENDA BROWN

2008 was very muddy and, on exiting the toilets at the top of the field, I decided to try to mud slide down to where I could see my husband and his friends standing by the hot dog stand. Shouting 'oi, watch this, lads!', I ran full tilt and then locked my legs for the slide. Instead of catching me, they stepped aside and I hit the hot dog stand, slid underneath and knocked myself out on the sump. Not one of my best ideas!

Another year (again, it was raining) I decided to try some marijuana. I had given up smoking so decided to dry some homegrown leaves (given to me by a friend) and smoke them in a pipe with no tobacco, because I didn't want any nicotine. At the end of the night, and slightly merry, I walked up to the top of the field. There was a massive balloon there and a police box nearby. The police box looked warm and cosy and I was wet and cold. A very friendly policeman came out to talk to us. Evidently, I asked him if I could go into his box to get warm and said I would share my drugs and my pipe with him. Our friend who was with us was horrified, said to the policeman 'hit her on the head with your big stick' and then ran off.

I celebrated my seventieth birthday in December 2023 but I was quite old even then, so the policeman probably thought the drug was medicinal. He simply smiled, patted me on the head and told me to get a good night's sleep.

LENSOVIET
3 SEPTEMBER 2008, ST PETERSBURG, RUSSIA

BASTIAAN VAN DER PLAS

I was a fan of Fairport Convention ever since their first LP, which I bought after I read in one of the British music journals that they were the 'British answer to Jefferson Airplane'. At that time, in 1967, I collected what was then called West Coast music. My love for Fairport Convention grew when Sandy became their lead singer and I bought every LP that was released. I saw them at several concerts in the Netherlands (the country where I was born and raised) and the UK, but after I moved to St Petersburg with my Russian wife and was running my tourist agency for tourists from the Netherlands and Belgium, I had to be satisfied with ordering their new CDs over the internet.

I was walking the streets of St Petersburg with a group of my tourists in early August 2008 when I saw a poster with the words (in Russian): 'BG and DK im. Lensoveta introduce Fairport Convention (UK) and the group Akvarium in a unique joint concert. September 3.'

I accompanied my tourists back to their hotel and rushed to one of the theatre booking offices to buy two tickets for the concert. I knew the Lensoviet, we had been there before for concerts by Russian bands, and I knew the first row was not very convenient, so I had two tickets for the second row, by the gangway.

I had to be patient, but finally it was Wednesday 3 September 2008. Realising I would be witnessing a unique concert, I took my camera and iPod with microphone as we went to the Petrogradskaya metro station close to the Lensoviet concert hall. We came early, sat down and waited while the concert hall gradually filled up.

The first part of the concert was the performance by Akvarium, one of the most popular bands in Russia, with Boris Grebenshikov (better known in Russia as BG, as credited on the poster), who founded the band in 1972. After the break, BG announced Fairport Convention. He spoke of his admiration for the British band, the reason why he invited them to Russia, and then there they were on the stage: Simon, Peggy, Ric, Chris and Gerry.

'We have waited 42 years to be here,' said Peggy, and they started the concert with 'Walk Awhile'. Many more well-known songs followed as they played for over an hour. At the end, there was a short silence and I waited for what was to come and shouted 'Meet On The Ledge'; they ended the concert with an extra-long version of that legendary song, joined by Akvarium.

I took many photographs of the concert, recorded it on my iPod and after all these years I can still look back with pride at having witnessed this unique concert in the history of my favourite band.

FAIRPORT'S CROPREDY CONVENTION
13-15 AUGUST 2009, CROPREDY, UK

SIMON YOUNG

I'd been to Cropredy several times over the years but 2009 is the year I remember most. I was working as drum tech for Steve Winwood when he headlined. During the day I finally got to meet all the band plus others, including the great John Tams who I got to thank for *Rise Up Like The Sun* being my gateway album into the genre. There was a couple of beers had with Peggy and he couldn't persuade me to meet Richard Thompson. That was just too much for me.

Steve later took to the stage and I settled in after some initial drum riser monitor issues that had me faffing about in a mild panic. During 'Light Up, each band member took a solo and during Richard Bailey's turn I was aware that standing next to me and watching intently in the wings was DM.

'Is that your guvnor?' he asked.

'Yes it is.'

'He's bloody good isn't he?'

'Yes, I think so. But… so are you!'

He seemed genuinely chuffed. The rest of that weekend was a blur. Peggy had insisted I come back on the Saturday and bring my heavily pregnant partner. There was 6X to be had, Goan fish curry to enjoyed and a fantastic set by Fairport to round things off.

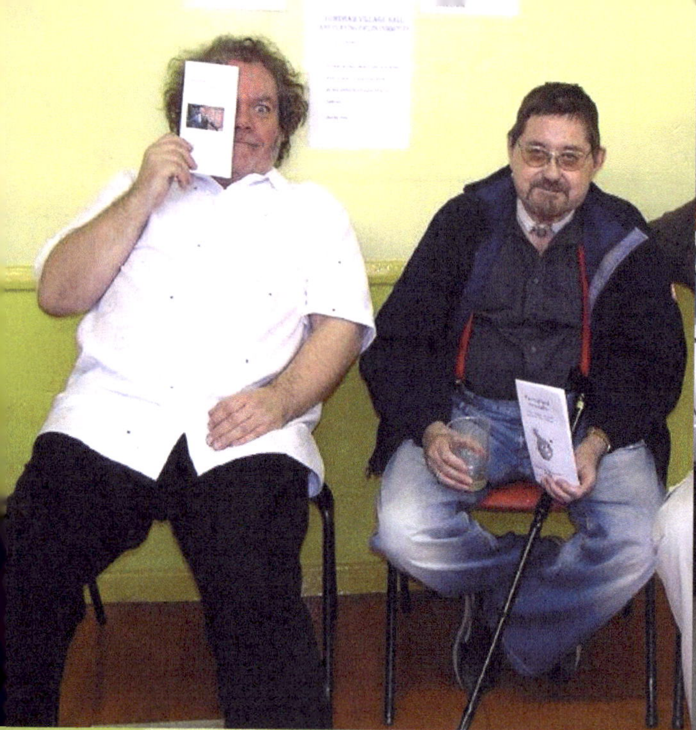

(clockwise from top left) Maart & Swarb (Jenny Parsons); Cropredy Press launch, August 2004 (Bob Battersby/Lodestone Publishing Ltd); assorted tour flyers (Ian Burgess); the 'irrepressible' Swarb with Jenny Parsons

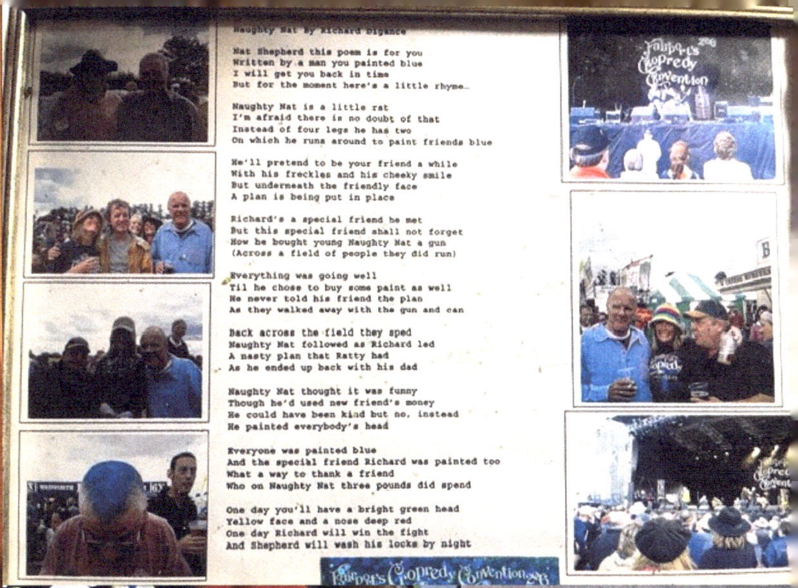

Naughty Nat By Richard Digance

Nat Shepherd this poem is for you
Written by a man you painted blue
I will get you back in time
But for the moment here's a little rhyme…

Naughty Nat is a little rat
I'm afraid there is no doubt of that
Instead of four legs he has two
On which he runs around to paint friends blue

He'll pretend to be your friend a while
With his freckles and his cheeky smile
But underneath the friendly face
A plan is being put in place

Richard's a special friend he met
But this special friend shall not forget
How he bought young Naughty Nat a gun
(Across a field of people they did run)

Everything was going well
Til he chose to buy some paint as well
He never told his friend the plan
As they walked away with the gun and can

Back across the field they sped
Naughty Nat followed as Richard led
A nasty plan that Ratty had
As he ended up back with his dad

Naughty Nat thought it was funny
Though he'd used new friend's money
He could have been kind but no, instead
He painted everybody's head

Everyone was painted blue
And the special friend Richard was painted too
What a way to thank a friend
Who on Naughty Nat three pounds did spend

One day you'll have a bright green head
Yellow face and a nose deep red
One day Richard will win the fight
And Shepherd will wash his locks by night

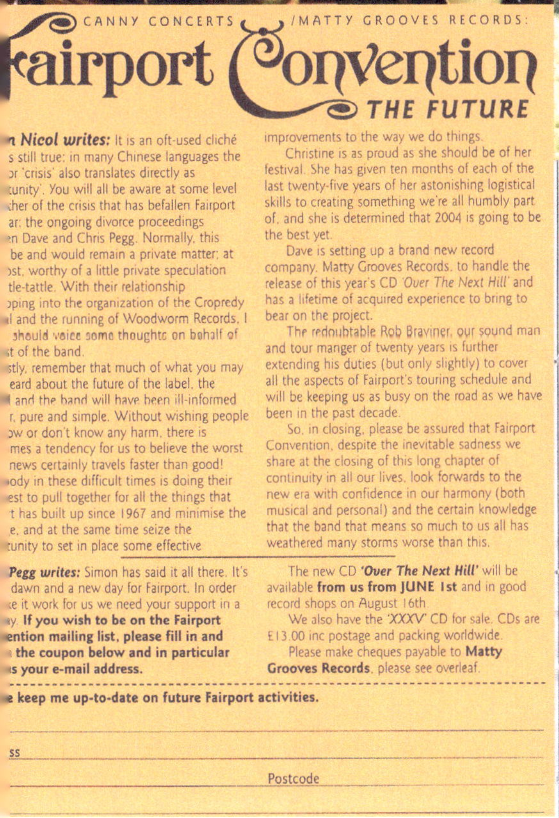

CANNY CONCERTS / MATTY GROOVES RECORDS:

Fairport Convention

THE FUTURE

…n Nicol writes: It is an oft-used cliché …s still true: in many Chinese languages the …or 'crisis' also translates directly as …tunity'. You will all be aware at some level …ther of the crisis that has befallen Fairport …ar: the ongoing divorce proceedings …en Dave and Chris Pegg. Normally, this … be and would remain a private matter; at …ost, worthy of a little private speculation …tle-tattle. With their relationship …oping into the organization of the Cropredy …l and the running of Woodworm Records, I … should voice some thoughts on behalf of …st of the band.

…stly, remember that much of what you may …eard about the future of the label, the … and the band will have been ill-informed …r, pure and simple. Without wishing people …ow or don't know any harm, there is …mes a tendency for us to believe the worst … news certainly travels faster than good! …ody in these difficult times is doing their …est to pull together for all the things that …t has built up since 1967 and minimise the …e, and at the same time seize the …tunity to set in place some effective improvements to the way we do things.

Christine is as proud as she should be of her festival. She has given ten months of each of the last twenty-five years of her astonishing logistical skills to creating something we're all humbly part of, and she is determined that 2004 is going to be the best yet.

Dave is setting up a brand new record company, Matty Grooves Records, to handle the release of this year's CD *'Over The Next Hill'* and has a lifetime of acquired experience to bring to bear on the project.

The redoubtable Rob Braviner, our sound man and tour manger of twenty years is further extending his duties (but only slightly) to cover all the aspects of Fairport's touring schedule and will be keeping us as busy on the road as we have been in the past decade.

So, in closing, please be assured that Fairport Convention, despite the inevitable sadness we share at the closing of this long chapter of continuity in all our lives, look forwards to the new era with confidence in our harmony (both musical and personal) and the certain knowledge that the band that means so much to us all has weathered many storms worse than this.

…Pegg writes: Simon has said it all there. It's … dawn and a new day for Fairport. In order …ke it work for us we need your support in a …ay. **If you wish to be on the Fairport …ention mailing list, please fill in and … the coupon below and in particular …s your e-mail address.**

The new CD ***'Over The Next Hill'*** will be available **from us from JUNE 1st** and in good record shops on August 16th.

We also have the *'XXXV'* CD for sale. CDs are £13.00 inc postage and packing worldwide.

Please make cheques payable to **Matty Grooves Records**, please see overleaf.

…e keep me up-to-date on future Fairport activities.

…ss

Postcode

Cropredy festival to go ahead

BY STEVE JOHNSON
Folk Correspondent

A FOLK ROCK festival which has become an annual pilgrimage for hundreds of thousands of music lovers over the past quarter of a century is to go ahead next year.

After months of uncertainty, Fairport Convention has announced that it will stage its annual music festival at Cropredy, near Banbury, Oxfordshire, next summer.

Fairport's Cropredy Convention will be held on August 11,12 and 13 and cater for up to 20,000 fans.

And the Evening Mail can reveal the line-up includes Country Joe McDonald and His Band, Chris While and Julie Matthews, and a possible headline appearance by Fairport founder member and now American-based singer-songwriter Richard Thompson.

“We're definitely not going corporate. There will be no selling out to big business and no huge hikes in ticket prices

The future of the hugely popular festival was thrown into doubt earlier this year because of divorce proceedings between Fairport's Brummie veteran Dave Pegg and his wife,Christine.

Question marks arose because of personnel changes which led to Fairport reorganising its business earlier this year.

But now a new festival organising team has been established and next year's event will be put together by Fairport founder member Simon Nicol, Dave Pegg, Rob Braviner and Gareth Williams.

Simon is Fairport's singer-guitarist and band co-founder and Dave, from Acocks Green, has played bass guitar in the band for 34 years and co-organised the festival for 25 years.

Rob has been Fairport's sound engineer and tour manager for well over a decade, and Gareth is a music business professional and a longstanding friend and colleague of Fairport.

Simon says: "Our intention is to make as little change as possible to this unique event.

"We want to build on the wonderful reputation Cropredy has gained over the past 25 years and the festival will remain as welcoming and friendly as ever."

Simon adds: "Keeping the lid on our plans until now may have fuelled speculation but there was no point in saying anything until everything was ready."

As in previous years, Fairport's Cropredy Convention, previously referred to as the Cropredy Festival and the Cropredy Music Festival, will occupy its long-established riverside site and will last for three days.

Dave Pegg tells me, "As always there will be a fabulous line-up of bands on stage over the three days. We've already got some ideas up our sleeves to make 2005 a really brilliant year for music.

"We're definitely not going corporate. There will be no selling out to big business and no huge hikes in ticket prices.

Village residents and Cherwell District Council have welcomed the news of the festival continuing.

Festival fans can get further information on www.fairportconvention.com.

■ *FAIRPORT CONVENTION: Upper, left to right: Chris Leslie, Simon Nicol, Dave Pegg… Lower, left to right: Ric sanders, Gerry Conway*

FOLK & COUNTY GIGS

TODAY

New Years Eve Party with Johnny B: Spangles CMC, Tascos Social Club, Hazlewell Lane, Stirchley 0121 247 1329; **Open Session:** The Royal Oak, School Rd, Tettenhall Wood, Wolverhampton 01902 754396.

TOMORROW

Campbells Country: Stirchley United Working Men's Club 0121 247 1329;

SUNDAY

Pat Brennan and The Hurling Boys, 7pm: Waxy O'Connor's, Broad Street; **Little Jimmy**, 9pm: Spotted Dog, Alcester… Digbeth 0121 772 3822; **Ca… Party:** Brian's Country Music Club, Kings Heath Cricket C… r/o 247 Alcester Rd South, Kings Heath 01564 824524.

WEDNESDAY

Crystal Folk, 8.30pm: The … in Hand, Bridge St, Audnam… Stourbridge 0121 559 8607.

THURSDAY

Claret: Cheque-Mates Folk Club @ Coton & Hopwas Social Club, School Lane, Hopwas, nr Tamworth 0121 354 4234.

(clockwise from top left) Swarb (Jenny Parsons); 'Naughty Nat' Shepherd was immortalised in verse by Richard Digance (Philip Shepherd); Keren Norbury's Cropredy posse go under the moniker The Geriatric Hedgehogs; press cutting re Cropredy 2005 (Terry Bidle); Cropredy newsletter re 'the future' (Terry Bidle); Cropredy 2005 & 'Here Comes a Beer' (John Barlass)

I may have wept a bit at some point during 'Who Knows Where The Time Goes'. (It may have been dust, of course.)

What a band, what a festival. Thanks for the memories.

FAIRPORT'S CROPREDY CONVENTION
12-14 AUGUST 2010, CROPREDY, UK

CLIVE BUTLER

I have seen the band 50 plus times. Cropredy 2010 was quite a wet one. One afternoon I nipped into the merch tent to shelter from the rain, and apart from the staff behind the counter there was only me. In walks Swarb and I thought, 'I've got to pitch this right, I can't gush or hit him with a barrage of questions.' We both said hello and ended up having a ten-minute conversation, entirely led by him, about anything and everything except music – the weather, our various health issues, etc. It's ten minutes that I will treasure.

DARREN JOHNSON

My first festival was as a fifteen-year-old metal fan in 1981, seeing AC/DC, Whitesnake, Blue Öyster Cult and Slade. I was still a baby when Fairport Convention recorded their first album and folk-rock (or at least the English variant of it) completely passed me by for most of my life. However, as I started exploring more of the bands of the sixties and seventies, I did get heavily into The Byrds and began delving into the US folk-rock scene. Eventually, I thought to myself that if I liked American folk-rock so much, maybe it was time to try out a bit of English folk-rock? I was well into my late thirties by then but I came across a live version of Fairport doing 'Meet On The Ledge' on a freebie compilation that came with a magazine and was instantly hooked. I first saw Fairport at a small festival in 2008 and remember Simon saying, just before they played 'Meet On The Ledge' right at the end, to imagine it was coming up to midnight on a glorious August evening in a field in Cropredy in Oxfordshire.

I really fancied being part of that and set about persuading my then partner that we should give Cropredy a try. A long-planned summer holiday meant it wasn't possible the following August but we got there in the August of 2010, encouraged a couple of friends to join us and (excepting the two years of Covid) I've been every year since. From my very first Cropredy in 2010 the mix of music was just perfect for me: Status Quo, Bellowhead, ahab, Rick Wakeman and Fairport! A glorious mix of retro rock and contemporary folk. I was hooked from the moment I first set foot in that field.

ROSES THEATRE
28 JANUARY 2011, TEWKESBURY, UK

DAVE GEORGE

My youngest granddaughter Millie had been bought a uke for her third birthday by her mum. I took a pic from my pocket, licked it, stuck it on her forehead and said 'there you go... a mini-Dave Pegg'. The following January, I took the picture to the opening night of Fairport's *Wintour* at the Roses Theatre in Tewkesbury. Peggy was selling merchandise and I said, 'Mr Pegg, would you mind autographing this for my granddaughter please?' He looked at it and then stared me straight in the eye and said 'not unless I can have a copy!' Well, how could I refuse?

Over the next twelve months, I tried every way possible to get that photo to Peggy but with no success. So, the following year as Tewkesbury approached, I decided I would take Millie and her mum to see Fairport so that she could give Peggy the photo herself. Unfortunately, work took me to Guernsey and I was unable to make it to the venue. I asked my middle daughter if she would be kind enough to fill my slot as she could drive.

I phoned her the following day to see how things went. She was almost speechless: 'Dad, I have never met such a wonderful group of people. I would have never thought that such famous people would be so – well – normal! Mr Pegg took the photo from Millie, gave her a hug, put the photo on his amp on stage, told the audience that this was a picture of his new friend Millie and dedicated five songs to her. And when the band came out for their meet and greet, he sat her on his knee and was saying to people, 'Sorry, I can't talk at the moment – I'm chatting to my new friend Millie.'

Since then, we have attended Tewkesbury and Cropredy whenever we have been able. One year, whilst walking through the Cropredy crowd, I heard someone shout 'Peggy... Peggy… Millie is here!' She had been spotted by Ellen amongst the crowd of 20,000!

In 2023, Millie couldn't make it to Tewkesbury or Cropredy (exams) and questions were asked! In 2024, it was a bit different. My wife, myself, Millie and her boyfriend turned up to the Roses. 'So Millie, who's this?' asked Peggy.

'This is my boyfriend, Jamie.'

'Have you ever seen us before?'

'Um... no...' was his reply.

Well, just into their set and Peggy said, 'I was talking to Millie, a long time Fairport fan, out by the merchandise table and she introduced me to her boyfriend, Jamie, who she tells me, is a Fairport virgin. I hope he doesn't hold it against her… Oh, I never meant it to come out like that!'

The whole auditorium erupted with laughter, and Jamie is now a Fairport convert as well as being a bit well known at the Roses.

Thank you, Fairport, thank you for your music, but above all, thank you for who you are and those fantastic memories.

THE VENUE
3 MARCH 2012, CHICHESTER, UK

BILL WALLACE

I have been a Fairport fan ever since I received a copy of the Full House album for my fifteenth birthday back in 1972. I must have seen them live around 100 times since then, but one particular gig stands out for me. In 2011, Fairport announced their plan to release an album of re-recorded classic songs. They ran a competition regarding the release. The idea was for fans to guess what tracks would make the final cut and whoever was closest would win signed copies of the new album, *By Popular Request*, and the live *Babbacombe Lee* album that wasreleased at the same time. I duly entered the competition and much to my surprise I was announced as the winner. My list had just one track different from those chosen for the album.

A short while later, I attended the winter tour gig at The Venue in Chichester. During the interval, my wife Claire handed a note to Chris Leslie stating that I was in the audience that evening. Before Fairport started the second set, Chris asked me to stand up, he read out the message and I rather embarrassingly received a round of applause from the audience.

Although always known as Bill, I had entered the competition under my real name of William Wallace. Simon then stated that he remembered when he was sending out the prize, he imagined that he was sending it to a Mel Gibson lookalike in full war paint! Simon also stated that as the concert was based around the songs on the new album and that they were more-or-less chosen by me, I should look on it as my personal command performance. He then dedicated the evening to me. This might have just been an off-the-cuff comment, but it meant a lot to me!

THE PLATFORM
9 MAY 2012, MORECAMBE, UK

ROGER HAYDOCK

My first experience of Fairport Convention was via John Peel in 1968 or '69, listening to his radio show on a transistor radio during my last year at university. I was hooked for the next 50 plus years. I met Dave Pegg in the bar of The Citadel in St Helens following a 'Dylan Project' gig where we duetted the Steeleye Span classic 'All Around My Hat'.

My wife Sue and I went to see Fairport at The Platform in Morecambe in 2012. It was a Saturday night show and we booked in overnight at the Travelodge. Morecambe's weather the following morning was only fit for ducks. We were waiting for the lift in the hotel before going out to get some breakfast when who should exit said lift but Chris Leslie, drenched from the rain but complete with a soggy Sunday newspaper. He asked us if we had enjoyed the previous night's concert and, having established that we were from Southport, told us of his links to and upbringing in the town. It was wonderful that he took the time to chat on that very wet morning in Morecambe.

I have particular reason for remembering that concert and the interaction with Chris, because this was the last Fairport Convention gig that my wife attended before she passed away in April 2014. Happy memories, and I'm still going to see Fairport.

FAIRPORT'S CROPREDY CONVENTION

9-11 AUGUST 2012, CROPREDY, UK

MARK GRAHAM

By any measurement, Fairport Convention must be my favourite band of all time. I've seen them perform more times than any other act, own more LPs by them than any other artist and have met the members of the band more times than all the members of other bands that I have loved put together.

And yet it's a love affair that was almost over before it had really begun. I made the mistake of seeing Fairport for the first time on the day they officially broke up. On the 4th August 1979, as a dizzy 17-year-old, I travelled from Scotland to see Led Zeppelin at Knebworth. Also on the bill were Fairport Convention, who I knew of because their late lead singer was the only 'outsider' to perform on a Led Zeppelin track.

Fairport Convention were on very early (as they were heading to Cropredy for their final, final gig as I later found out) and they were absolutely mesmerising. I'd always loved folk music (my dad was a massive fan of The Clancy Brothers) but I'd never heard anything like this before. Folk rhythms spliced with rock instruments! I thoroughly enjoyed the show but thought I'd simply been fortunate to have been there at the postscript of Britain's biggest electric folk group and left it at that.

As an avid reader of the music press, I became aware in the eighties that Fairport were a thing again but a combination of living in Scotland (to be followed by Ireland) and a focus on 'new' music throught the eighties and nineties meant that the Fairport rebirth pretty much passed me by.

And then, in 2007, the BBC award for *Liege & Lief* forced me to buy the album to finally investigate the phenomenon properly. After over 25 years of buying lots of new music, I was blown away by this music from the sixties. A couple of years later, I got the chance to see Fairport in the flesh when they finally visited Whelan's in Dublin. Desperate for some more music I went to the merch stall before the show. I told the tall bloke behind the stall it was only my second Fairport gig, that I only had one LP and asked what did he recommend? Upon learning my previous gig had been Knebworth, he suggested the 2008 live album from Cropredy as it featured Robert Plant. It was only when the band took the stage that I recognised that my salesman was the bass player of the band!

Our relationship was cemented fully when my wife bought tickets for Cropredy 2012 as a 50th birthday present for me. She was fed up with me badgering her to go over the years and finally gave in saying this would be a 'once-off'. Fortunately, she was equally smitten and we've been to every Cropredy since (Covid and illness excepting) and been on every cruise, every Irish show (there have been very few) and numerous trips across the Irish Sea, and even to Ibiza to see the guys.

Most people discover their favourite bands in their teens and stick with them all their lives. While I found Fairport in my teens, I was in my fifties before I finally discovered them and I've spent the last 15 years making up for a lot of lost time!

SIMON HARDISTY

My first Cropredy experience was in 2012. My best mate Paul had been going on about it for a few years to me, saying I needed to try a different festival as he'd been going for years. We were both in a situation where for personal reasons we both needed a break. I had recently moved into his house because of said reasons and the decision was made! We ordered the tickets and duly waited for August to come.

On the day we went, I had an open mind driving down. We got into Field 7 because of Paul's insistence on leaving later but I didn't care. We strolled into the village to the Brasenose, had a couple of pints before entering the field and that was it! I was hooked from that moment on… It turned out to be one of the best weekends I've ever had. I made a pact after that that I'd go to every one each year, and bar the Covid years I have. My family have come with me and along with Paul I have made some great friends and seen some brilliant bands and acts. It's the weekend I look forward to the most out of the year.

DEBASER SLUSSEN

19 APRIL 2013, STOCKHOLM, SWEDEN

CHRISTER HERENTZ

Fairport Convention in Stockholm! Of course we've got tickets, me and my girlfriend. The venue is Debaser Slussen, a now long-gone basement club in central Stockholm. It was nice to see members of the band, wine glass in hand, checking out the support act, Annamy. There's a short intermission and suddenly I find myself standing at the pissoir, next to Mr Dave Pegg. The main act at the public loo just before they are about to go on stage? This never happens at a Springsteen or a Stones concert!

Then… right behind Peggy's back a door slooowly opens and Mr Simon Nicol – with a mischievous smile – gives him a surprise push in the back. 'What the fuck…!' The bass player saves the situation, one hand against the wall. All smiles.

After the gig, we say hello to Peggy at the merch, buying the new CD *By Popular Request*. I don't know if it was the encounter at the pissoir that rendered the cryptic dedication 'To Lena! Good choice in men,' but we all had a laugh.

Since then, we have seen the band at Cropredy a couple of times as well as in diverse places like Uppsala and Twickenham. We also enjoyed the fabulous Albion Christmas Band in Canterbury and at Cecil Sharp House. Lovely adventures for Swedish Anglophiles, lovely folksy music and people.

FAIRPORT'S CROPREDY CONVENTION

8-10 AUGUST 2013, CROPREDY, UK

ANDREW BOTT

My first Cropredy was 1983. The first year was a one day jaunt. Years having passed, memories are hazy. However, it was great enough to encourage a repeat visit and, suffice to say, it became an annual affair for a number of years. The first thing I loved about Fairport was Swarb. I had been played the *Live Convention* album and 'Sloth' grabbed me like a vice. As a juvenile violinist, I had rarely heard violins so forward in a band. Prior to Fairport, I had only really seen ELO as a viable music for violinists who were not into playing classical, and I was a folk ignoramus. Seeing Swarb live was a major thrill. Better yet, my friends were happy to go with me. Not only that, family joined in. (My mum loved to do concerts with us boys since seeing The Who in 1979, when I had not yet turned 14.)

Over the years return visits saw us do the camping thing, Mum joining in. Every year a varied gang would venture down. Cropredy was my future wife's first festival. In 1989, she sent me off to the festival so she could prepare for our wedding unfettered by me. Within a few years, we were joined by three generations of family. In the late nineties and into the noughties, we were joined by my little kids. Then time and money started to interfere and visits were more sporadic. Nowadays, the line up dictates our visits.

In 2013, I took my dad to Cropredy as an early seventy-fifth birthday present where he braved two nights of torrential rain to see my electrician niece, his eldest granddaughter, perform with Joe Broughton's Conservatoire Ensemble.

A few years passed and we were hit with two years of waiting for Cropredy whilst Covid came and went. We had become big fans of the Slambovian Circus of Dreams, so chose Cropredy as the venue for their 2022 tour. The weather was glorious, drying up the memories of wading through muddy fields.

Over the years I have witnessed many musical heroes grace that stage: Robert Plant, Roy Wood, Jethro Tull, Lindisfarne, Roy Harper, Steve Hackett, Toyah Willcox and Robert Fripp, Nick Harper, Procol Harum, Blodwyn Pig, the Home Service, Trevor Horn, the Slambovians, and all the ex-Fairports who made the journey to the spiritual home of Fairport. And just to add extra spice my niece, Rosie Rutherford is on *50:50@50*.

You never know when you will be going back, but the welcome is always warm at Croppers!

BERGEN USF VERFTET

16 OCTOBER 2013, BERGEN, NORWAY

TRON EIVIN ØVREBØ

Fairport played at the Bergen Fest in 2009. In a radio interview, the festival organiser was asked why they invited 'oldies' like FC to the festival and he said, 'They still attract younger audiences, they are better musicians than ever, and they also seem more focused.'

My son, Morten, was studying at the University of Bergen, five hours' drive north of my home in Stavanger (but just 25 minutes by plane) so when in 2013 I discovered that FC were playing there, I decided it was time to put faces to the music that his father was listening to and I invited Morten and his friends for beer, pizza and live music. We had a chat with Peggy and Gerry and pictures were taken. The boys enjoyed it, but I'm not sure Fairport have made it onto their playlists. Later in the evening we met the sound technician, Paul Smith, at a pub and chatted over a couple of beers. I asked him why Fairport were still on the road and he said: 'They still have great fun, and I'm not sure that their pension fund is topped up.'

COSTA DEL FOLK

18 MARCH 2014, BENALMÁDENA, SPAIN

ANGIE & ANDY SCHOFIELD, COSTA FESTIVAL/HARMONY VOYAGES

Our first encounter with Fairport Convention was when they headlined the inaugural *Costa Festival* (then *Costa del Folk*) on the sunny Costa del Sol in March 2014. We were very much the new kids on the block in the UK festival scene, and the overall success of our concept of a festival holiday based within a four- or five-star Mediterranean hotel very much depended on the first one being well received.

Securing Fairport Convention to headline was a major coup for us and we were thrilled and humbled that they accepted. Sadly, Peggy hurt his hand and couldn't attend, but Simon, Ric, Chris and Gerry were all on amazing form, very ably accompanied on the bass by Peggy's son Matt.

Following the gig, we were amused when Simon said that in years gone by, his rider may have requested 'two dancing girls and a bottle of vodka' but that now he was happy with 'two bottles of water and a comfortable bed'. He also passed on some very shrewd advice as we embarked on our journey. 'Remember, baby steps.' To this day, that advice is heeded.

The guys continued to be huge supporters of the Costa Festival concept, and as our business ideas evolved so too did our relationship. We are incredibly proud to have been afforded the opportunity to get to know the band and spend time with them socially at our Costa Festivals, and more recently on our European river cruises. Who knew then that Chris's magic skills would be amazing us, or that Ric's jokes would be humouring us as we sailed the Rhine, Danube and Rhone rivers!

We even shared Covid with Simon, and whilst he was confined to his cabin with only the webcam at the front of the ship for company, Debs stood in for him, beautifully singing the lyrics to 'Meet On The Ledge' – a goosebump moment for sure.

What strikes us particularly about Fairport Convention is how utterly down to earth they all are. Being in the company of such legendary musicians, one ought to feel a sense of awe and insignificance, but we just feel that we have gained a bunch of big brothers!

It was during one of our river cruises that we recently learned of the very sad passing of Gerry Conway. The last time we saw Gerry was sailing the Rhine River and we chatted about his love of the food and the service on board. He was having such an amazing time. What an incredible gentle soul he was and may he now sleep soundly. RIP Gerry.

Cropredy is an annual pilgrimage for thousands of people, and to be able to stand at the top of 'that' field with our three meter by three metre gazebo, promoting our little Costa Festival and knowing that those amazing guys on that huge stage are our friends is an absolute privilege and one that is never taken for granted.

Fairport Convention NEWS

January 2007

Life Begins At Forty !!

Dear Fairporters,

We warmly welcome you all to the start of our fortieth year. A big cake I hear you cry! (and so do I).

Well, we are kicking off the celebrations with a brand new studio album **"Sense Of Occasion"**. We recorded it in November amongst very familiar surroundings at Woodworm Studios in the heart of Oxfordshire with our dear friend and number one pair of ears Mark Tucker at the recording desk.

It is weighing in at sixteen tracks. We had planned to record less than this, but we had great rehearsals the week before starting the recording, got excited, and put it all down!! We've had a great time and I really think it shows! There are songs from myself, Steve Ashley, Glenn Tilbrook, PJ Wright, Bill Miller, Pete Scrowther, and good old Trad. Ric has written three fabulous instrumentals. We hope you like it!

We are out on the road with "Sense Of Occasion" from the beginning of February until the middle of March with the fabulous **Tiny Tin Lady** as a support each night. We have extra special guests **Show Of Hands** as well at the Birmingham Symphony Hall on February 17th.

What a way to start our year!! Don't forget our **Fairport's Cropredy Convention** festival on 9th, 10th & 11th of August, which will also be in a celebratory mood. Check out our website at **www.fairportconvention.com** for up to date info on our other touring dates through 2007.

Love from us all,

Chris Leslie

- CANNY CONCERTS PROUDLY PRESENTS -

Forty Glorious years 1967–2007

WINTER TOUR 2007

	FEBRUARY	
Thu 1	**Tewkesbury** Roses Theatre	01684 295 074
Fri 2	**Southampton** The Brook	02380 555 366
Sat 3	**Basingstoke** The Anvil	01256 844 244
Sun 4	**Dorking** Dorking Halls	01306 881 717
Tue 6	**Worthing** Pavilion	01903 206 206
Wed 7	**Shrewsbury** Music Hall	01743 281 281
Thu 8	**Tunbridge Wells** Assembly Halls	01892 530 613
Fri 9	**Leamington** Spa Centre	01926 334 418
Sat 10	**High Wycombe** The Swan	01494 512 000
Sun 11	**Canterbury** The Marlowe Theatre	01227 787 787
Tue 13	**Lincoln** Drill Hall	01522 873 894
Wed 14	**Milton Keynes** The Stables	01908 280 800
Thu 15	**Northampton** The Derngate	01604 624 811
Fri 16	**Cambridge** Corn Exchange	01223 357 851
Sat 17	**BIRMINGHAM** Symphony Hall + very special guests **SHOW OF HANDS**	0121 780 3333
Sun 18	**Yeovil** Octagon Theatre	01935 422 884
Tue 20	**Burnley** Mechanics	01282 664 400
Wed 21	**Leeds** City Varieties Music Hall	0113 243 0808
Thu 22	**Chesterfield** Winding Wheel	01246 345 334
Fri 23	**Berwick upon Tweed** The Maltings	01289 330 999
Sat 24	**Glasgow** The Garage	0141 204 5151
Sun 25	**Edinburgh** Queens Hall	0131 668 2019
Tue 27	**Weston Super Mare** The Playhouse	01934 645 544
Wed 28	**Salisbury** City Hall	01722 434 434
	MARCH	
Thu 1	**Croydon** Fairfield Halls	0208 688 9291
Fri 2	**Peterborough** The Cresset	01733 265 705
Sat 3	**Cardiff** St David's Hall	029 2087 8444
Sun 4	**Cromer** Pavilion Theatre	01263 512 495
Tue 6	**St Albans** The Alban Arena	01727 844 488
Wed 7	**Huddersfield** Lawrence Batley Theatre	01484 430 528
Thu 8	**Southport** Arts Centre	01704 540 011
Fri 9	**Preston** Guildhall	01772 258 858
Sat 10	**LONDON** ICA Roots & Shoots	020 7930 3647
Sun 11	**Chipping Norton** Town Hall for Chipping Norton Music Festival	01608 642 350

We've been refining and streamlining our mailing list, so please make sure your details are correct and notify us of any changes. You can contact us via the website or our new email address: info@fairportconvention.com

Please also let us know your email address – that way, we can keep you bang up-to-date with all our news.

www.fairportconvention.com

Sat 17 Feb 2007

£17.50 7.30PM

symphony hall birmingham

Canny Concerts present

FAIRPORT CONVENTION

Special Guests Show of Hands & Tiny Tin Lady

Standard Type

Order #: 599204

9-Nov-06 CLees

Level 3 Door 2(b)

Front Stalls

Row C Seat 13

CLees

C 13
Front Stalls
11441842173
17 Feb 07 19:30
£17.50
Standard Type
FAI-070217-01EV

Tickets are purchased subject to the terms and conditions printed overleaf

'Sense of Occasion'

As Chris mentioned in his intro, the new Fairport studio CD is ready! Release date is 12th February and you will be able to get your copy from us via the website (see item below), from all good record shops or, of course, when you come and see us on the tour. The tracklist in full:

1 Keep On Turning the Wheel *(Chris Leslie)* / 2 Love On A Farmboy's Wages *(Andy Partridge)* / 3 The Bowman's Return *(Ric Sanders)* / 4 South Dakota To Manchester *(Chris Leslie)* / 5 Spring Song *(Chris Leslie)* / 6 Polly On The Shore *(music: Dave Pegg; lyrics: Swarbrick/Lucas)* / 7 Just Dandy *(Ric Sanders)* / 8 Tam Lin *(trad. arr. Fairport)* / 9 In Our Town *(Chris Leslie)* / 10 Edge Of The World *(Chris Leslie)* / 11 Hawkwood's Army *(Pete Scrowther)* /12 The Vision *(Bill Miller/John Flanagan)* / 13 Your Heart And Mine *(Ric Sanders)* / 14 Untouchable *(Glenn Tilbrook/Christopher Braid)* / 15 Galileo's Apology *(PJ Wright)* / 16 Best Wishes *(Steve Ashley)*.

www.fairportconvention.com

To coincide with the release of new CD, we are re-vamping our **website**. You will now be able to purchase all our merchandise and CDs direct from the website via Paypal. This method of payment proved so popular with the Cropredy tickets we have decided to extend it to our website shop.

Cropredy!

Talking of the festival, a huge thank you to everyone who came to Fairport's Cropredy Convention last August. We had a wonderful time and, according to your emails, so did you. Plans are well underway for this year's festival which will be on the **9th, 10th & 11th of August**. Alre[ady] announced (subject to contract) are **Jools Holland** [and] **his Rhythm'n'Blues Orchestra, Show of Hands**[,] **Strawbs, Kerfuffle** and **The Richard Thompson** [...] We are still finalising acts so please keep an eye on [our] website at www.fairportconvention.com

Last year, for the first time, we awarded a prize of ar[n] afternoon slot on the festival bill to the winners of th[e] Radio 2 Young Folk Award. This year's winners are a [...] called **Last Orders** and we are certain they will ma[...] the high standards set by last year's winners, **Bode**[...] were absolutely terrific and we shall be keeping a ke[...] on them for the future.

We look forward to seeing you then, if not sooner...

Love from **Chris, Gerry, Peggy, Simon, Ric** and **Rob**[...]

THE DEBUT ALBUM FR[OM]

Dave Pegg & PJ Wri[ght]

www.hedgeofsoun[...]

Take "A Night Off with Peg[gy] & PJ" at the following location[s]

March	2007	
Mon 12th	Nettlebed Village Club	[illegible]
April		
Fri 13th	Rugby Roots	[illegible]
Fri 20th	Havant Arts Centre	[illegible]
Thu 26th	Glenfarg Scotland, The Famous Bein Inn	[illegible]
Fri 27th	Glenfarg Scotland, The Famous Bein Inn	[illegible]
Sat 28th	Lichfield Guildhall	[illegible]
Mon 30th	Chester Telford's Warehouse	[illegible]
May		
Thu 3rd	Leicester The Musician,	[illegible]
Fri 4th	Swindon Arts Centre	[illegible]
Fri 11th	Cromer Folk on the Pier	[illegible]
Sat 12th	Birmingham Red Lion, Kings Heath	[illegible]
Sun 13th	Hitchin Folk Club, Sun Inn	
Thu 17th	Leek Swan Inn	[illegible]
Fri 18th	Banbury Mill Theatre	[illegible]
Sat 19th	Ebbesborne Wake Village Hall	[illegible]
June		
Fri 8th	Walthamstow Plough Inn	[illegible]
Sat 9th	Bridgwater Arts Centre	[illegible]
Tues 12th	Tewkesbury Roses Theatre	[illegible]
Thur 14th	Bury Met	[illegible]
Fri 15th	Abingdon Unicorn Theatre	
Sat 16th	Farnsfield Acoustic, Nottinghamshire	[illegible]
Fri 22nd	Wentworth S.Yorks, Rockingham Arms	[illegible]
July		
Mon 23rd	Poole Wessex Folk, The King Charles	[illegible]
Tues 24th	Southsea Eastney Cellars	[illegible]

www.fairportconvention.com

Saturday 11th Would Saturday lunchtime ever be the same without **RICHARD DIGANCE**? Richard has held this opening slot since 2002 and won't be shifted. Former winners of the BBC Radio 2 Young Folk Musicians of the Year Award, Scottish quartet **GIVE WAY**. What are the chances of finding four beautiful, talented musicians in the same family? Quite good actually, Give Way are four sisters! Next up: it's been too long! Back to Cropredy come Cornwall's finest – **THE BUCKET BOYS**. It is rumoured there may well be a guest or two joining them for this performance. Talking of rumours, although founder Fairport member **IAIN MATTHEWS** is billed as solo, what are the chances of it staying that way? The very best in English folk & rock music next from **THE STRAWBS**. Dave Cousins recently reunited the classic *'Hero & Heroine'* line-up to record and release the fabulous new *'Deja Fou'* album and we are delighted to welcome that line-up to the stage tonight. No strangers to the Cropredy stage are **BOB FOX AND BILLY MITCHELL**. These Geordie lads have gone down a storm on the folk circuit this year and it is an absolute pleasure to have them here tonight.

As always, closing the Saturday will be a marathon three and a half hour set in this, their fortieth anniversary year, from **FAIRPORT CONVENTION** – featuring a multitude of former members and even more special guests. But who? Rumours are rife!

TICKETS are still available on line from our website: **www.fairportconvention.com**, or simply send off the order form on this newsletter and remember, the earlybird price finishes at midnight on May 31st!

A Box of Peggs

SUBSCRIBE NOW! To pre-order your copy of 'A Box of Peggs', with lots of extra goodies (see below) visit the Shop at www.fairportconvention.com

Nigel Schofield of Free Reed box set fame and Dave Pegg have been working for the last eighteen months to compile this four CD box set, for 30th July 2007 release on on Matty Grooves Records. The box has a cribbage board theme and features 26 previously unreleased tracks drawn from Peggy's extensive career, featuring various Fairport Convention line ups, Jethro Tull, The GPs, The Ian Campbell Folk Group, The Dylan Project, Richard Thompson and Beth Neilsen Chapman.

Peggy has a huge discography and amongst over 72 tracks, we go from Dave playing on his first ever recording session up to a track from his recent duo album with PJ Wright. Tracks we hope to feature include rareties from Don Bilston, The Leesiders, Marc Ellington, The Exception, Excalibur, Steve Ashley, Steve Tilston, Julianne Regan, Mike Heron, Nick Drake, Dan Ar Braz, Ralph McTell, Murray Head, The Uglys, The Crawdaddys, annA rydeR, Beryl Marriott, Bob Fox, The Dave Peace Quartet and Simon Nicol.

Bonus CD via subscription

For the first 500 people who order the CD box there will be a fifth bonus CD featuring rare exclusive tracks and, as a special thank you, the subscribers' names will be included in the extensive booklet which comes with the box. Please order early to guarantee this special offer. *"A Box of Peggs"* MG4CD046

Peggy's 60th Birthday Concert

Tickets are now on sale at the Birmingham Town Hall box office (0121 780 3333) for this special evening, for which Peggy has invited many musical chums from his 43 year playing career. Definitely not to be missed – book now!

Fairport acoustic Convention **US Tour 2007**

MAY	
Fri 04	**Berkeley CA** *Freight and Salvage*
Sat 05	**Auburn CA** *Karfluki Fest www.karflukifest.com*
Sun 06	**Felton CA** *Don Quixote's Monterey Bay Celtic Society*
Wed 09	**Toulume CA** *Black Oak Casino*
Thu 10	**Altadena CA** *Coffee Gallery Backstage*
Fri 11	**San Diego CA** *Acoustic Music San Diego*
Sat 12	**San Juan Capistrano CA** *SJC Library Concert Series*
Sun 13	**Santa Monica CA** *McCabes Guitar Shop Concert*
Tue 15	**Rochester NY** *Bob Shop Series at the German House www.bopshop.com*
Thu 17	**Pittsburgh PA** *Club Cafe Live*
Fri 18	**Cleveland OH** *The Winchester*
Sat 19	**Chicago IL** *Old Town School of Music w/ Old Blind Do[gs]*
Sun 20	**Ann Arbor MI** *The Ark*
Wed 23	**Norfolk VA** *Virginia Arts Festival*
Thu 24	**Philadelphia PA** *Tin Angel*
Fri 25	**Montclair NJ** *Outpost in the Burbs*
Sat 26	**Pawling NY** *Towne Crier*
Sun 27	**Northampton MA** *Iron Horse*
Wed 30	**Wilmington DE** *Green Willow venue tba*
Thu 31	**Herndon VA** *Herndon Festival*
JUNE	
Fri 01	**Chester NY** *Bodles Opera House*
Sat 02	**Fall River MA** *Narrows Center for the Arts*
Sun 03	**New York NY** *Joe's Pub*

the DYLAN project

JUNE		
Wed 13	**Witten, Birmingham** The Barn	0121 356 5
Fri 22	**Glastonbury Festival**	

"A Night Off with Peggy & P[J]"

MAY		
Fri 11	**Cromer** Folk on the Pier	01263 512
Sat 12	**Birmingham** Kings Heath, Red Lion	0121 4416
Sun 13	**Hitchin** Folk Club, Sun Inn	01462 812
Thu 17	**Leek** Swan Inn	01538 385
Fri 18	**Banbury** Mill Theatre	01295 279
Sat 19	**Ebbesborne Wake** Village Hall	01722 780
JUNE		
Fri 8	**Walthamstow** Plough Inn	020 8503 7
Sat 9	**Bridgwater** Arts Centre	01278 422
Tue 12	**Tewkesbury** Roses Theatre	01684 295
Thu 14	**Bury** Met	01617 612
Fri 15	**Abingdon** Unicorn Theatre	01235 553
Sat 16	**Farnsfield** Acoustic Nottinghamshire	01623 870
Fri 22	**Wentworth** S.Yorks, Rockingham Arms	01226 742
JULY		
Mon 23	**Poole** Wessex Folk, The King Charles	01202 732
Tues 24	**Southsea** Eastney Cellars	02392 826
AUG		
Sat 04	**Bedford** Rhythm Festival	01234 350

We've been refining and streamlining our mailing list, so please make sure [your] details are correct and notify us of any changes. You can contact us via the [website] or our new email address: **info@fairportconvention.com** Please also let u[s know] your email address – that way, we can keep you bang up-to-date with all o[ur news.]

See you in August!

Simon, Peggy, Ric, Chris and Gerry.

www.fairportconvention.[com]

(clockwise from top left) 'Forty Glorious Years' newsletter **(Ian Burgess)**; *Sense & Occasion* newsletter (Ian Burgess); US tour details (Ian Burgess); 2007 Birmingham ticket (Terry Bidle)

Moseley Folk Festival flyer (Ian Burgess); Cropredy 2007 flyer (Ian Burgess); Peggy's 60th birthday tickets (Terry Bidle); Sandy flyer (Ian Burgess); 2007 Winter Tour flyer (Ian Burgess)

FAIRPORT'S CROPREDY CONVENTION
7-9 AUGUST 2014, CROPREDY, UK

ALLAN PICKETT

In 2014, the Cambridge Folk Festival was on the weekend before Cropredy, so we decided to make a holiday of it, and go from one to the other, with a hotel break in between. We stayed at Chipping Norton, so there wouldn't be far to go on Thursday morning, and it meant we could go to one of the warmup concerts, for the first time. I booked us in at The Crown & Cushion, without realising that it was once owned by Keith Moon, which added a bit of interest to our stay. We knew there might be guest appearances at the warmups, but were totally awestruck when Robert Plant bounced on to the stage with his harmonica. He did a few songs with Fairport, then disappeared as quickly as he came, leaving us all in a bit of a daze. We made the assumption that he would be appearing with Fairport on Saturday night, so resisted the urge to tell anyone, as we didn't want to spoil the surprise.

Saturday night arrived, and as it progressed, it slowly dawned on us that our assumption was false, and that his appearance on Tuesday, was just a random event that we were so lucky to experience. Saturday, however, did end on a good note. I always go to festivals with Brian Green, who was fifty that day, so I secretly got Fairport to sign his birthday card, and asked if they could get it announced over the PA. I wrote down the details for Ric, but I thought he might be too busy to remember as the stage was a bit hectic. He didn't disappoint though, and with half an hour to go, he announced, 'Happy birthday to 'Dangerous' Brian Green. I don't know why he's dangerous, but he's fifty today, and over by the bar, if you want to buy him a drink.' Brian was utterly gobsmacked when he heard it, and for weeks he was like a dog with two tails.

I subsequently introduced him to Ric at The Brook in Southampton, and explained that Brian wasn't actually dangerous – it was just an amusing nickname that he got landed with. It's amazing how a small gesture by the band can mean the world to a fan, so thanks to Ric and Fairport!

BETH SELF

Me and my sister Elsie have been going to Cropredy every year since before we were born, thanks to our parents, and now we are 16 and 18. Still going strong!

RICHARD HAYWARD

In the mid-eighties, friends took me to see Fairport at Hanley's Victoria Theatre, Stoke-on-Trent. I was taken then with the idea of attending the festival, but as a retail shop manager there was no chance of an August holiday. But when I retired, I went to my first one. It was so rewarding. What is fabulous is that, because everything is on one stage, the whole festival can be experienced. To me that is very important.

Thank you, Fairport, for your craft, friendship and kindness of spirit.

ST DAVID'S HALL
31 JANUARY 2016, CARDIFF, UK

STEVE PHILLIPS

Fairport have been my favourite band since I first saw them around 1978 at Cardiff University. As I approached my 65th birthday, and realising that Fairport were playing Cardiff's St David's Hall that day, I contacted Peggy and asked whether it would be possible to have a photo taken with the band. Of course, bless them, they agreed, and after the sound check, invited me onto the stage. Peggy asked me whether I played any instrument. I admitted to having struggled with the guitar since around 1971, with little in the way of progress, and was duly handed a mandolin. There I was, on the day I received my state pension, a member of Fairport Convention for a few moments. Since turning 70 I've taken up the drums, ably assisted by a pair of his signature drumsticks which Dave Mattacks so kindly gave me, I think I'm making progress!

EDEN COURT THEATRE
7 FEBRUARY 2016, INVERNESS, UK

ALEX MCMANUS

I have been a fan since the days of *Nine* and have collected most of their recordings over the years. I saw them at the Eden Court Theatre in Inverness. I remember it was a Sunday night and I travelled down by car on my own from Wick, over 100 miles away. Living so far north it's not always possible to see such icons of the music industry. The concert did not disappoint. The theatre is quite a small venue, which suited me as I was able to get up close to the band. I'm also a great fan of Iain Matthews and was naturally delighted to discover a great number of years ago that he was an FC original.

ST GEORGE'S CHURCH
4 JUNE 2016, BECKENHAM, UK

DEL CLOUTER

I discovered Fairport and had my first meeting with 'Matty Groves' in 1970 at my local record library in Kennington, South London. 'Matty' has stayed in my head until the present day! Despite not being a concert-goer, for the next 42 years I collected the vinyls whilst also adding to my Led Zep collection. As a family man, it was matrimonial separation in 2012 that changed me. This was when the Fairport connection really kicked in. An old school chum, Stephen Skey, invited me to Dartford Folk Club and within a short while I was chatting with Dave Swarbrick, who was touring with Martin Carthy. For most of the conversation, he wanted to know about my hip replacement! The following year it was the lovely Dave Pegg with A J Clarke, whose opening line to me was 'do I owe you money?' Two of my childhood heroes chatting like mates!

In 2016, I was at my lowest ebb. The divorce was ongoing and I was not in a good place. I was driving my London Bus back to the garage at the end of my duty at 12.30am when I saw a poster for Fairport playing in Beckenham in Kent. I pulled over, got the details and within an hour had booked for my very first Fairport gig. Finally, I had something to look forward to.

It was an amazing evening, and chatting to the guys after they were so friendly, and so began the Ric Sanders event; selfies whenever we meet! The only person I didn't converse with was Simon who I was in awe of, but I did learn all about Folk in the Barn, the organisers for most of Kent, and that Ric's trio were playing at the Kingston Barn a few weeks later, so I got tickets for that.

In July 2016 I arrived at the Barn early as always, and whilst walking around the car park I was approached by a guy with a big smile and a beard. It took me about two minutes to realise it was Simon. We chatted for a while and when he saw I had a copy of *Fairport by Fairport*, he asked if I wanted it signed, at which point he took me past the queue into the venue where he signed my book and let me take a photo. Legend! Over the next few months, all the guys signed the book and Folk in the Barn became a second family, including me helping Keith and Anne on the Folk in the Barn radio show on Tuesday evenings, giving me the title Offsite Research Executive – whatever that means!

Since then, I can't remember how many times I've seen the guys play. The highlight was Simon's 67th birthday in Oslo. They are still getting better, and long may it continue. They've given me a new perspective on life. They have truly been a life saver to me.

FAIRPORT'S CROPREDY CONVENTION
11–13 AUGUST 2016, CROPREDY, UK

JENNY POIRIER

My mum died on 9th August 2016 after a long illness at the age of 92. I'd been caring for her with my sister at home. Two days later we were meant to be meeting a group of friends at Cropredy as usual. I really wasn't sure if I was up to it or whether it was right to go, but the kids were looking forward to it so we decided to go ahead. Arriving to set up camp, having hugs from all my friends and it being safe to have a cry, it felt like the right decision. The familiarity and friendliness of the festival was such a comfort. Being able to sit and enjoy the music and share memories over a few beers and not have to think about anything else for a few days turned out to be just what I needed.

It was good to see The Bootleg Beatles again, who'd played at my first Cropredy. And Madness, whose *One Step Beyond* album was the first I bought on cassette, long before I got into Fairport, and which brought back early teen memories. My mum loved sunsets and I took one of the fabulous Cropredy sunsets thinking of her.

I think I shed a tear during 'Fotheringay' at:

Tomorrow at this hour she will be far away
Much farther than these islands
Or the lonely Fotheringay

'Meet On The Ledge' felt even more significant than other years, acknowledging those gone and holding those here more closely, and valuing Fairport and Cropredy festival, where we meet together each year.

BLACK BOX
27 JANUARY 2017, BELFAST, UK

DERMOT FERGUSON

Even though I've been a fan of Fairport Convention for many years it's only in recent years that I've managed to see them live, once at the Great British Folk Festival in Skegness and the other on their 50th anniversary tour in the Black Box, Belfast. They did play the Ulster Hall in Belfast in 1969, but that was before my concert going years unfortunately. I do remember the day I bought my first Fairport Convention album. It was a sunny Saturday afternoon in my favourite pub in my home town and one of my friends came in and announced that our local record shop had the reissue of *Unhalfbricking*. I rushed round and bought my copy and so started my love of the band.

ST MARY'S ARTS CENTRE
1 JUNE 2017, SANDWICH, UK

HANS HERMANN MOLL

Over 50 years ago I was on my way back from doing homework with some fellow pupils at school when I passed a shop that sold kitchen items. They also had a box of records outside the door. Whilst waiting for the bus I started to look through the LPs, which were offered for a price that suited my pocket money. I discovered a record cover with a 'framed' picture on it showing three people in front of the ruins of a burnt house, plus one looking through the remnants of a window. It was Fairport Convention's *Angel Delight.*

'Ruins as Angel's Delight?' That sounded interesting. Then I noticed that three of the musicians were named Dave. Funny! One of my fellow pupils looked over my shoulder and said, 'They are not that good anymore. The guitarist just left.' That was of course Richard Thompson who I had never heard of, and nor had I of Fairport. After much hesitation I bought the record. It was the best decision I've ever made.

When celebrating the jubilee of our school leaving examination, I started talking with an old friend about music past and present. We hadn't seen each other for quite a long time and had a lot to talk about. I told him I had recently bought Richard Thompson's *Front Parlour Ballads* and *The Old Kit Bag* and was totally excited. He asked, 'Do you know what the others do?' Remembering my copy of *Angel Delight*, I bought *Over The Next Hill*, which was very refreshing and exciting too. A few weeks later we decided to visit the Cropredy Festival.

After suffering a heart attack, I read the book that came with the *A Box Of Pegg's* box set during my recovery and we finally went to Cropredy in 2010. I felt grateful to be alive and to be able to experience the festival atmosphere, despite the heavy weather on Saturday.

We have returned every year since. In 2016, we organised a narrowboat tour on the Oxford Canal for the following year based around the festival weekend. In preparation I read a book by Steve Haywood entitled *Too Narrow To Swing A Cat*, about life on a narrowboat. Much to my surprise it had a chapter called 'The Cropredy Festival', about the festival we had missed due to my illness in 2009, when Steve Winwood headlined on the Thursday. I thought I might share it with my friends so made some annotations in German to make it easier for them to read before sending it on to the lads.

In November 2016, I had the idea that Fairport might be delighted to read it too so I erased all my annotations and my German translation and sent it to Peggy as a Christmas surprise. That was it – I thought.

I bought the 50th anniversary tour programme before crossing the English Channel to attend the spring tour concert at St Mary's Arts Centre in Sandwich, Kent, and much to my surprise found the excerpt from the book I had sent to Peggy printed in it – with two annotations I'd obviously forgotten to erase before sending it to him! I'm honoured to have been immortalised in this way.

Fairport's Cropredy Convention is always a great experience. Each year it's an opportunity to remember absent friends who have passed away over the years and to listen to a lot of artists we thought we'd never have the chance to otherwise. Thank you, Fairport, and I'll see you at Cropredy this year!

FAIRPORT'S CROPREDY CONVENTION

10-13 AUGUST 2017, CROPREDY, UK

DAN GLEDHILL

I started to get into Fairport around the mid-nineties after borrowing my mate's mother's vinyl copy of *Nine*. One day in 1997, as a 23-year-old, I was listening to Fairport when I took a phone call from my father to inform me my mother had sadly passed away. After ending the call, I went back to my room and 'Who Knows Where The Time Goes' was playing on the hi-fi. Both the lyrics and music were so poignant, I played it on repeat ten times, coming to terms with what I had just been told. I then couldn't listen to that song again for many years, except for live gigs, where each time it was played was highly emotional.

I first went to Cropredy in the late nineties and have attended most years since. I'll never forget my first Cropredy, walking into the Brasenose and, by chance, bumping into a couple of fellow Manchester City fans at the bar. That was the first time I met Dave, whose company – and stories of following Tull – were most enjoyable.

Fast forward to 2017 and my now wife Rachel and I were, I have been told, the first couple to get married at the Cropredy Festival in the Old Dairy Farm wedding venue (Field 8). Marrying on the Saturday, I suppose you could say Fairport Convention were my wedding band. It was also my then 18-month-old daughter Althea's first Cropredy – no prizes for guessing the song which inspired her name! As soon as the ceremony finished, I noticed a chap waiting to see me with a pint of ale. He told me he wanted to be the first person to buy me a beer after the marriage. It was Dave's son.

ELIZABETH PARTRIDGE

Thank you to the stage for not falling over on us in the insane winds of 2019 and letting me experience the wonders of Daphne's Flight for the first time and the nerves of standing in the merch queue to sign and meet the wonderous singers I'd just fallen in love with.

Thank you for great beer and an open equal bar where anyone feels welcome.

Thank you for sausage rolls and white wine picnics in the field on hot summer's days.

Thank you for patchwork shirts, incense and joyful self-expression.

Thank you for the surprise faces I see every few years and the people you bring back into my life, if only for the festival.

Thank you for your beautiful legacy and the community you have built over decades.

But mostly, thank you for being such a cornerstone of my relationship with my dad.

My dad is my favourite music nerd. Cropredy was my first ever festival and Richard Thompson was my first ever live gig. My first Cropredy was a blur. I was young, maybe eleven. I remember buying a silly long hat and marvelling at all the people in their colours, and hearing real live amped-up music for the first time and being immediately hooked.

I can remember my dad drumming on the steering wheel of late-night long car drives to London. The sounds of long drum solos and soaring guitar solos from Richard Thompson, Thin Lizzy or Genesis filling the air as he reminisced about gigs past.

I remember hugging him so tightly at Cropredy in 2017 just after his mum died when hearing the legendary 'Meet On The ledge' and Digance's 'We Are Searching' was so raw.

I can remember trotting along behind you, Dad, as you danced and weaved your way through the ambling late-night crowd. Pewter pint jug in hand, boogying past crowds of festival goers. I love to see you so free and full of life. Thank you for showing me that no one has to age past the point of having fun or a dance, or being nerdily enthusiastic about a band. Thank you for interrupting every conversation you can with a music reference or merrily chatting about Peggy or the posts from the Facebook group. Thank you for introducing me to a festival that you've been going to since you were in your twenties, so that I can keep going in mine.

Happy 60th birthday Dad. Here's to many more Cropredys together in that special field and with all the family.

Love you lots, Lizzie xx

HELMUT ÖLSCHLEGEL

My special Fairport memory is from 2017, when I met Peggy together with Robert Plant backstage. Peggy introduced me to Robert with very kind compliments: 'Helmut is a fabulous photographer and a very nice guy from Germany.' I will never forget this moment with two of my rock heroes and also the wonderful tiny concert with The Fairport Convention All Stars in the tent!

FOLKETS HUS
4 OCTOBER 2017, STRUER, DENMARK

JENS ANDERSEN

I have good memories of Fairport Convention on an almost daily basis, as I often listen to my 40-plus FC records and CDs. I play them all from time to time, each depending on the mood I am in. Or I hum a tune or two; I am a great hummer. Or I take my guitar and play a little. I am not a great guitar player, but I enjoy playing. I went to Fairport's concerts every time they visited Denmark and was particularly privileged to see and hear Sandy Denny twice, around the time of Rising For The Moon. *'One More Chance', which is still one of my favourite songs, blew my mind.*

On 11 August 2006, I nearly died as a result of penicillin intoxication. I was saved by the bell – and by my wife, who called 911. Thanks to her I still can listen to great music. Exactly a year later, my wife and I were in the middle of our first Cropredy festival and enjoying life. Sandy Denny was being honoured and suddenly 'One More Chance' came up. I stood there, hand-in-hand with my wife, with the best of weather in the middle of the best of crowds, crying out my gratitude for being alive and feeling the greatness of life and earth.

That what art can do to you, and that's what the music of Fairport does.

I wrote these words for the 50th anniversary tour programme. I had forgotten all about it when I went to a Fairport concert in Struer, Denmark and saw Dave Pegg enjoying a glass of red wine and selling programmes. I said hello and bought a programme. I looked in it and was talking to Dave Pegg, when I turned to the page with my story on it. I told Dave about it, and we wished each other a great concert and evening. Which it was, when suddenly during the concert Dave asked from the stage, 'Jens, where are you?' I showed them where, and then they dedicated the next song to me, which was a very nice gesture. And can you guess which song they played? 'Now Be Thankful.'

FAIRPORT'S CROPREDY CONVENTION
9-11 AUGUST 2018, CROPREDY, UK

JAN & JON DIXON

There can't have been a dry eye in the field as Maart led Fairport through 'Metal Matty' one last time. Maart is forever fixed in our minds on the Cropredy stage that night, looking out at the crowd as we sent a whole field's worth of love back to him. 'Metal Matty' is still our favourite arrangement of 'Matty'. We both remember being blown away by it the first time we heard it, at the Half Moon in Putney back in

Fairport Convention NEWS

January 2008

Happy New Year Fairporters!

What a year 2007 was! It started with a record-breaking UK Winter Tour, the longest we've done for many a year. This was followed by a trip across the pond to see our American cousins. A huge Fairport 'Thank You' to everyone who came to see us play during our fortieth anniversary celebrations.

We broke another record by selling out Fairport's Cropredy Convention in advance for the very first time in the event's long history. This meant that some people who had not booked in advance couldn't get in. The lesson is clear: book early this year to avoid disappointment.

We were very lucky with the weather, too: a few weeks before the event, the fields at Cropredy were under water but come the day we had the finest weather of the summer for our annual get-together.

As part of our *'Forty Glorious Years'* theme, we recorded highlights of the year on video. Professional television director Mike Rowbottom began filming at our winter tour gig in Birmingham's Symphony Hall and the project concluded at Cropredy 2008. As well as lots of footage of the festival itself, Mike organised a multi-camera broadcast-quality shoot of Fairport's Saturday night Cropredy set with guests including: Richard Thompson, Ashley Hutchings, Judy Dyble, Iain Matthews, Dave Mattacks and Maartin Allcock; together with Steve Ashley, Beth Gibbins, Vo Fletcher, Edmund Whitcombe and the Tommy Connolly Dancers.

The resulting footage has been professionally edited into a stunning musical documentary. As well as the great music, it features interviews with members of Fairport Convention and some of the other artists who played at Cropredy, chats with festival-goers and villagers, a trip round Cropredy hosted by Ric Sanders, and Cropredy's much-talked-about 'big screen extras' designed by Nev Bull (you must have heard about the 'Lego Matty Groves'?).

The whole documentary is now available as a fully-featured DVD release, exclusively available from Fairport's online shop – visit **www.fairportconvention.com** for full details.

If you were at Cropredy, the documentary will be a great reminder of a wonderful weekend; if you couldn't get a ticket, you can still 'be there' with this fab DVD: *Fairport@Forty*.

Fairport bassist Dave Pegg celebrated an anniversary of his own last year – his sixtieth birthday! He celebrated by releasing a four-CD boxed set covering his entire musical careeer. Titled *A Box of Pegg's*, the box set is available from our online store and from good record shops. Peggy also staged a sell-out birthday concert in Birmingham's Town Hall. With dozens of musical guests on stage>

Fairport Convention NEWS

MAY 2008

Hello Fairporters,

Summer approaches... and that means everyone's thoughts are turning to FAIRPORT'S CROPREDY CONVENTION, our annual three days of friendship, fun and great music in the glorious Oxfordshire countryside. Please make a note of the dates: 7th, 8th and 9th August 2008.

This year, we've put together one of our best-ever line-ups. On the Thursday, the headliner is **Supergrass** – Oxford's finest and one of the best live acts in the country. Friday sees **Levellers** headline with their full electric line-up, a first visit to Cropredy for this phenomenal band. It is their 20th anniversary so it's bound to be a celebration.

On Saturday, **Danny Thompson** will share the MC's duties with broadcaster **Bob Harris** who will introduce a special commemoration of the life and work of Sandy Denny. And, of course, **Fairport Convention** and their musical guests will close the festival with a stunning three and half hour set.

As always, the festival will feature a feast of fabulous acts. For a start, we've got three BBC Award Winners: **Jeana Leslie and Siobhan Miller, John Tams and Barry Coope**, and **Julie Fowl**

There will be English dance music from **Whapweasel**, a solo set from winter tour guest **Anthony John Clarke** and an all star line-up in **The Gathering** led by ex-Fairporter Jerry Donahue. **Three Daft Monkeys** and Mark Radcliffe's **Family Mahone** will liven up the pace and our very own **Peggy & PJ** will have you chuckling and singing along. Old frienc **Stackridge** will be appearing and so will sixties leger **Joe Brown**, with **Dave Edmunds** as his guest.

We've got **Paul Brady** – one of Ireland's best interpreters of traditional songs – and **Midge Ure**, bo making their first appearances at Cropredy. Fairport founder **Ashley Hutchings** will present his show base on *Lark Rise to Candleford*. **The Muffin Men**, featuring Jimmy Carl Black of The Mothers of Invention, are bac by popular demand; **Richard Digance** opens Saturday as usual, and we have some great reggae from **Legenc** You can find out more about all these fantastic acts at www.fairportconvention.com.

Every year, we make improvements to the facilities at Cropredy. This year, for example, we will be reducing the festival's carbon footprint and also increasing recycling – we'll need your help in achieving this so please watch our website for details.

Cropredy tickets are on sale now and already they're selling faster than ever before. Last year, we sold all the tickets in advance and had to turn away late-comers. So don't miss out this time – order your tickets **NOW!** You can book online or use the order form below. **And remember, if you book early you'll save money too.**

WATCH OUR CROPREDY CLIP!

We've produced a mini-documentary about Fairport's Cropredy Convention with help from TV director Mike Rowbottom. It captures the unique atmosphere of our festival through interviews and music clips. The footage was shot on the campsites, concert field and backstage. If you haven't been to Cropredy before, you can see what it's like by watching the nine-minute video on the Cropredy section of our website.

TICKETS	Weekend	Fri/Sat	Saturday
Order before June 1st	£72.00	£62.00	£42.00
June 1st – July 31st	£76.00	£66.00	£46.00
After July 31st	£80.00	£70.00	£50.00

CROPREDY TICKET ORDER FORM

Please fill in all info clearly and post this form to: Fairport Convention Ltd, PO Box 8413, Bilsthorpe, Notts NG22 8WY

www.fairportconvention.com

Guardian2

Leisure: 17-19 Job Vacancies: 20-22 Classified: 22-23 Public Notices: 23 Motors: 24-32 Thursday, July 31, 2008

Warming up for Cropredy

Folk acts prepare for festival

by Tom Gibbon

THSH Town Hall, Birmingham

Fri 29 Feb 08 7.30PM £20.00

Fairport Convention

plus support

Standard Type

Door B

Stalls

Row C Seat 11

(clockwise from top left) January 2008 newsletter (Ian Burgess); Winter Tour 2008 newsletter (Ian Burgess); May 2008 newsletter (Ian Burgess); *Banbury Guardian* front page (Ian Burgess); 2008 Birmingham ticket (Terry Bidle); Peggy has produced three albums for Carolyn & Mark Evans' band Red Shoes (Kevin Smith)

(clockwise from top left) Phoebe Brogden made a card for Peggy – and gave him hair!; Bas van der Plas caught the Fairports in the port of St Petersburg (Bastiaan Van Der Plas); Kurt Thulin (second left) with (left to right) Peter Rushmer, Pia Thulin & Simon Nicol, Cromer 2016; Keren Norbury's Geriatric Hedgehogs laugh in the face of copyright theft; Fairport in St Petersburg (Bastiaan Van Der Plas)

September 1988. It was the second of two warmups they played there in preparation for a big gig at the Barbican the following day.

MICK DONOVAN

It fell silent. Still. The stringed instruments and drumsticks put down, with the stage bathed in a blue light. The sodden Cropredy hordes gathered round and wondered what was happening. Fairport Convention had only done three or four numbers. Recorded music stirred and wafted over our field in the Oxfordshire village hosting the band's annual music festival. The sound grew and enveloped all in the post-rain fresh air. It was 'Quiet Joys Of Brotherhood' sung a capella by Sandy Denny with just a violin played by Dave Swarbrick for accompaniment. Heaven was sending the best it could send. A film was played on adjacent screens either side of the stage of the trainee nurse-turned-singer with the angel voice. We were celebrating the 40th anniversary of Sandy Denny's passing, with a nod to the more recent demise of a legendary fiddle player.

This might have been the 51st year of Fairport's existence and Sandy might have only been in the band for two spells totalling less than a handful of them, but the life-affirming effect she had on it, and on folk, folk-rock, music and me, has been incalculable. I'm sure I was not the only member of the multitude with a lump in my throat.

When the strains of Swarb's violin faded, Fairport returned to the stage to continue with an extended tribute to my favourite singer with bass player Dave Pegg insisting how 'beautiful' the performance of the Celtic tune to Richard Farina's lyrics had been.

Various singers covered Sandy songs such as PJ Wright ('Bushes And Briars'), Fish ('Solo'), It'll Take A Long, Long Time (Winter Wilson) and Sandy's vocal Fairport foil Iain Matthews ('Rising For The Moon'). Sole Fairport founder member Simon Nicol completed the tribute to the singer nonpareil with her signature song, 'Who Know Where The Time Goes'. He said how no one could do her songs enough justice and I'm sure I saw him wiping a tear away after he strummed the final note. The only pity was that Richard Thompson, who played on the recording of the song for Fairport's *Unhalfbricking* album, was absent.

All our gang were saying nothing could top the set by Brian Wilson – featuring former fellow Beach Boy Al Jardine - on the Thursday. For me, Fairport topped it with their proper tribute to a woman who I feel remains the greatest singer to draw breath.

MIKE AINSCOE

Having been on the Fairport bus for a number of years, the quiet joys of festival going in general had been always on the 'to do' list. 2018 was the year that the Cropredy cherry was finally taken. They say you always remember your first – the highlights of finding my way around the site and the village; discovering The Brasenose, the Saturday morning car boot at the cricket ground and the record stall on the canal barge, the queue stretching up the hill for the festival t-shirt and the various spots to which I'd return (as many others have done for decades before) in subsequent years.

In the rush of excitement, first stop was the signing tent, tucked away discreetly (aside from the huge queues) for Peggy's book signing before the bell rang for the Fairport acoustic curtain raiser. There followed a whirlwind that flitted between the tried, trusted and tested, with an Oysterband set before the Thursday highlight of a frail-looking Brian Wilson doing those classic Beach Boys hits with Al Jardine in the band.

Friday had Kate Rusby joining me in her first Cropredy appearance, assuring me of being in good company. This was the prelude to a Levellers sit down headline where the anticipated and typically vibrant Levs show would be sidelined for a stripped back and restrained, cabaret-curtained version. Perhaps the earlier Le Vent Du Nord frenzy was enough for the day after Fish kept up the recent strong Marillion presence and The Travelling Band and Midnight Skyracer had doubled up on some bluegrass and rocky Americana.

Saturday and another set of debutants who would wow the crowd and return a few years later were the irrepressible Bar Steward Sons Of Val Doonican. Joined by Maart Allcock, their set of barstewardised hits was a revelation for those new to the band – not me, having seen them do a couple of festivals prior – and later released in a double hit with a recording of their 2022 set. Brilliant stuff and how often do you see one the band crowdsurf into the audience in a rubber dinghy? All part of expecting the unexpected from Scott Doonican.

With the Afro Celts and Sam Kelly and The Lost Boys ('have you taken my new profile picture?' Ciaran Algar asked me) keeping the adrenaline high, 2018 was also my first experience of the revolving door of guests in the Fairport set, several taking on the 'Sandy songs' – Fish, Iain Matthews, PJ Wright, Anna Ryder – and the personal highlight being Winter Wilson coming on for 'It'll Take A Long Time'. Looking back, and with the *What We Did On Our Saturday* from 2017 to follow, it's perhaps my favourite FC Cropredy set.

The Fairport finale was tinged with the sadness of being the final time we'd see Maart Allcock. We knew his time was short and his emotional contribution in the programme was only surpassed by the incredible intro he gave to what's become known as 'Metal Matty'. There may be numerous different intros to the iconic track in existence, but for me, this will be 'the one'. Preceded by both 'Jewel In The Crown' and 'A Surfeit Of Lampreys' (I *love* that title), it was a fitting farewell and tribute for a lovely man.

RICHARD GLEAVE

I have been going to Cropredy on and off since 1977, when it was in Dick Crossman's garden. I and my wife Delia played in Beryl and Roger Marriott's ceilidh band, Watling's Treat, which shared the bill with Fairport on at least one occasion. Simon produced Beryl's 1992 CD, *Weave The Mirror*, which we appeared on, so we have got to know the band quite well.

In 2015 a very good friend, Trish Abey, sadly developed Motor Neurone Disease (MND / ALS). Before she lost her voice, I recorded her singing her favourite songs. Ric and Chris very kindly agreed to play on two songs which are available on Spotify, etc. ('It's All Over Now, Baby Blue' with Chris and 'Georgia On My Mind' with Ric.)

I have since become very much involved with the MND Association and in 2017 came to know a lovely lady, a brilliant poet named Frances White, who also had contracted MND. I discovered that she was a lifelong fan of Fairport. Frances went to the Fairport concert at Guildford in 2018 and met and was photographed with Ric, who I had told about Frances. Ric mentioned her poetry book, *Swiftscape*, was mentioned from the stage.

I suggested to Frances that she and her husband Steve come to Cropredy later that year, and I met them at the back of the field, with Frances zapping around in her electric wheelchair! Unbeknownst to them, I had been in touch with Chris and communicated with him during the afternoon, telling him where we were situated. At about 4pm, Chris duly turned up to surprise Frances, who was completely amazed and absolutely delighted. Chris stayed for about 15 minutes and they had lovely chat and pictures were taken of them all together.

I was so glad to have organised that, because sadly Frances didn't make it to 2019.

PS. I named the album *Expletive Delighted!* My name is in very small print on the album sleeve!

THE MILL
5 AUGUST 2019, BANBURY, UK

GEORGIA ROSE LUCAS

Banbury in August 2019 was a very exciting time for me. It was a long overdue visit to see many old friends of my mum, Sandy Denny, and my dad, Trevor Lucas, and to meet many new friends that I'd made online in recent times. Also, I'd not seen the guys for four or five years – well before my diagnosis of breast cancer; the ensuing operations and treatments and the huge turn around in my life. It meant the world to be re-connecting and spending time with them at this point. I felt it would be another experience in the healing process. I had been to Cropredy before but only once – back in the '90s, when I was about 15 – so this time it would be seriously different!

The evening I arrived, I went to the first warmup gig. I was greeted at the door by Cropredy and Fairport friend, Kevin Smith. Instantly, he was 'Uncle Kev' for me and still is. The whole atmosphere that night and at the next warmup gig was just amazing – such a wealth of sensations. I felt so welcomed by everyone. Ellen, Peggy's wife, took extra special care of me, so I lovingly dubbed her 'Mumma Bear'.

I was on the field the day before the festival began and heard Richard Thompson warming up – the sound stretching over the whole of Cropredy – as I walked over to see the Jonah Tree (which we put plaques on in 2023 for my mum and dad). It was so beautiful as I walked on along the canal with its narrowboats; it was lovely walking on and around the village. Visiting the Brasenose Arms was another special moment, including seeing the spot where the famous Fairport *Nine* photo (with my dad in it) was taken. Everyone was so happy and friendly – it's a special spot on Earth.

The night before the festival began, lying back and taking in the day, I had a sudden urge to write a poem to my mum. I showed it to Peggy and he asked if they could read it on stage before Fairport's acoustic set. I said 'yes' and so on the big stage Anthony John introduced me and read my poem out loud while I hung onto Peggy's arm and tried not to cry. Seeing all those people standing in front of me was totally awe-inspiring – I felt I'd come home. Out on the field over the three days, I was making friends everywhere – too many to count. It felt like all 15,000 other Croppers – plus Chalky the cockatoo! – had welcomed me with open arms. I felt truly cherished.

One stand-out memory is the Friday. There was a storm brewing during the day and I saw a double rainbow. Then, as the sun set, the storm clouds moved in. Richard Thompson was playing that night and his set included 'The Storm Won't Come' from *13 Rivers* … but it did!

I loved every single act that performed over these special days. Fairport's last night set was especially spectacular for me as they played lots of songs dedicated to me, and to my mum and my dad. Peggy sang 'Polly On The Shore' and Simon sang 'Who Knows Where the Time Goes'. There was a gorgeous tribute to Maartin Allcock. It was a very emotional set for everyone.

Being invited on stage to join in on 'Meet On The Ledge' made me feel even more a part of it all. As soon as the set finished though, the people moved out and the stage started coming down. Seeing the clearing up and dismantling of the stage, I cried in Mumma Bear's arms – I couldn't believe that something so amazing was over so quickly.

I never would have thought that, four years later, I would return with a Sandy Denny exhibition and fresh new album of Mum's unfinished work, *Songbird*.

Cropredy is like a lifeline for the folks who make their way there. It's where they recharge and find inspiration (like I did). It's a part of who they are.

Thank you, Fairport.

FAIRPORT'S CROPREDY CONVENTION
8-10 AUGUST 2019, CROPREDY, UK

BOB BRADBURY

My children were introduced to Fairport at a young age. One Cropredy Festival, maybe 1994/95, they kept asking 'when will Fairport sing 'the holiday song'?' I hadn't a clue what they were talking about and racked my brains to no avail. The band had a habit of changing the lead-in to an eternal favourite tune in those days (sorry boys, we all knew from the first bar – no, not that bar Peggy). It finally clicked with a 'dum dum bub-a-dum-dum' on the bass: 'A holiday, a holiday and the first one of the year.' It was 'Matty Groves'.

The band was playing at the Stag Theatre, Sevenoaks in 2010. I texted Peggy to offer any assistance they might need in my home town and was invited to the sound check and a beer with the band before they played. Peggy and Ellen came back to my place afterwards for a nightcap and my daughter, who was usually quite reserved, was persuaded to play piano. After a few moments, Peggy quietly picked up a guitar and played alongside her. No words were spoken, but that simple generosity was unforgettable and priceless.

After some very poor behaviour one weekday afternoon in 2003, I forswore alcohol forever and kept my word. Roll forward a few months and I was in Brittany at the same time as Peggy. He invited us to dinner and readers can imagine the rest of the story and the end to my few months of temperance… The next morning, when I was lying on a cold concrete floor unable to even raise my head, Peggy kept calling to say his boat was ready for some water-skiing and where was I? A miracle hangover cure was found in a brown bottle and we eventually hit the water.

My partner of six years, Charmaine, has never been a fan of what she considers 'folk music'. She barely remembered the name Fairport and had never even heard of Cropredy. In 2019 I dragged her to Cropredy, not quite kicking and screaming but politely reluctant. We'd only been sitting in the field for an hour or two when she said, 'Next year we'll have to bring…'. She'd already decided that we'd never miss another one.

FAIRPORT'S CROPREDY CONVENTION
13-15 AUGUST 2020, CROPREDY, UK

CRESSIDA FORD

2020 struck, and all that came with it. Sheltering in the wilds of West Wales, I received a call from Richard Pearson at what was then Radio Scarborough. I'd done an interview / documentary piece for them about the 50th anniversary of *Liege & Lief*, and hosted a folk, roots and prog show for a few months. Would I now like to help put together ten hours of radio programming to be broadcast in two parts over what would have been the Cropredy weekend, with music and interviews from all the artists on the line-up, and other notable festival regulars? Boy, would I!

So it was that I found myself chatting on the phone to the Fairport chaps and others, sharing joyful memories of Cropredies past in a series of really special conversations I shall treasure for a long time. I especially remember my call with Ric – essentially a 45-minute comedy set, full of puns, witty observations and hilarious anecdotes. He regaled me cheerfully with the tale of a time his violin string broke in the middle of a particularly expressive, wailing, effects-pedal-laden solo. He thought disaster had struck, but later, someone simply asked him how on earth he'd created such an incredible sound effect... I laughed, thinking how easy it must be for matters outside one's control to send something haywire, and finally ended the call.

The call which I hadn't recorded.

I texted him my humiliating revelation, face in my hands. What a waste of his time! How embarrassing and unprofessional of me! But I needn't have worried – he was so kind, and when I rang my own personal dial-a-standup-comedian the next day, he delivered the same wonderful repartee all over again as if for the first time. Nobody ever needed to know of my stupidity! (Until now...)

MS AMADEUS QUEEN
21-28 JUNE 2022, THE RHINE, GERMANY

JIM BORROWS

It fell about the lockdown's end, we waited for the news
To learn the cruise was finally on, two years we'd paid our dues
To join Fairport and a merry bunch, all heading up the Rhine
On a barge with food and drink for all, six days and nights, so fine

'A Beatles night', the news came through, for guests to sing along
Well 'Rocky Raccoon' it would be for me, one of my favourite Beatles songs
But the next communication, it made me frown for sure
The band would play just Beatles' hits – no 'Rocky', too obscure!

So I decided that I wouldn't join the live karaoke class
My chance to sing with Fairport, I would just let it pass
We packed our bags and caught our flight, all was okey dokey
Embarked at Amsterdam, excited; forgot about karaoke!

The ship set off, the band were great – a jazz night led by Ric
And Chris, so musically versatile, amused us with card tricks!
Then Simon went down with Covid; and was surely sorely missed
But Debs sang 'Crazy Man Michael', what a performance – bliss!

The music played, we laughed and drank beneath the sun and moon
Then came the karaoke day, and a run-through in the afternoon
But half the guests were missing, their chosen songs to sing
'Will someone sing 'Get Back'?' said Pegg, 'and 'Yellow Submarine'?'

Now here's the truth, and maybe why I avoided registration,
I'd have worried that I'd not sing well, and spoil my reputation
For I've played piano all my life, but I'm not keen on preparation
I'd rather play or sing impromptu, without audience expectation

But suddenly here was my chance, no time for a second thought
Up went my hand, 'Well if there's no-one else, I'll give it my best shot'
I must have sung half a dozen songs, that weren't meant for me
My new pal Mark, he sang some too, and the band all seemed quite pleased

So the missing guests would sing at night without their preparation
But I'd had some fun, was feeling fine, had no more expectation
But at the finish Peggy asked, 'Jim, what's your own Beatles song tonight?'
'Well Peg, I'm not down to sing at all,' I said, though now that didn't feel quite right

'Well that won't do!' came the response, 'Tonight you'll have to croon!'
And bold as brass I heard myself say, 'D'you guys know 'Rocky Raccoon'?'
'Not yet, but we can learn right now, there are only four chords in it'
Up struck the band, and off we went, me loving every minute!

So after dinner we settled down; 'Cilla' (aka Linda) led the karaoke
And some sang well – Jane, Graham, Mark, though some others were pretty croakey
A printed list was passed around, with songs and singers noted

But not me of course, for it was printed before we had all boarded

So I wasn't sure if I'd be called, and I swallowed down some bevvy
But tried not to overdo it, just in case, I'd best be ready
So they moved on down the printed list, and reached the end quite soon
'And now we've one extra number,' says Peg, 'it's Jim, with 'Rocky Raccoon'!'

Well, if you're a really nerdy Beatles fan, you might know that there's an outtake
Where Paul sings 'sminking' instead of 'stinking' – I even included that mistake!
Now I thought that was a pretty confident move, though it made me miss a beat
But the band are such true pros – they followed me seamlessly, what a treat!

And I must have performed not all that badly, for the guys said 'Stay on stage
We'd like you to lead the encore – in '63 it was all the rage!'
And we launched right into 'Twist And Shout', not even a bar of preparation
And Debs and Cilla led the dancing, gave us all excitation!

The band, they played fantastic, the crowd danced on their chairs
There was something special going on, you could just feel it in the air
So my singing career was launched right then, it couldn't have been better planned
Thrust to stardom with Fairport Convention, my all-time favourite band!

So I've written this little poem, and I swear every word is true
But it's not from the 13th century, it was 2022
And last year we did it all again, but this time down through France
The guests' night was Bob Dylan songs and I signed up early, took my chance

So for the wicked – and for me too – there was to be no rest
I didn't even get to choose! – my songs were Peggy's request
A whole year of preparation! And I sang another two
'Simple Twist Of Fate' followed by 'Tangled Up In Blue'

Now if these words don't quite pour off the page, or glow like burning coal
At least now I know the will to sing is etched upon my soul
So I'm still playing my piano, and making lots of vocal noise
And looking forward to the Danube, and hoping to be in good voice.

(clockwise from top left) newsletters from the Ian Burgess archive: April 2009; November 2009; Cropredy flyer 2009; November 2010; May 2009

E is for green

See you at Cropredy!

Simon, Peggy, Chris, Ric & Gerry

Book early!

Chiltern Railways

Mail Order buy online from www.fairportconvention.com

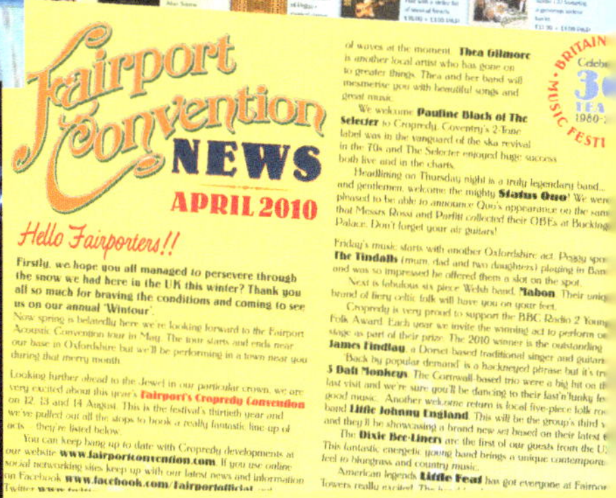
Fairport Convention NEWS

APRIL 2010

Hello Fairporters!!

Fairport acoustic Convention

MAY 2010

Sat 01	**DIDCOT, OXON** The Cornerstone	01235 515 144
Sun 02	**EBBESBOURNE WAKE** Village Hall	01722 780 717
Mon 03 / Tue 04	**SOUTH PETHERTON** David Hall Arts Centre	01460 240 340
Wed 05	**IVYBRIDGE** The Watermark	01752 892 220
Thu 06	**RAINWORTH, NOTTS** Village Hall	01623 794 700 /01623 870 668
Fri 07	**DURHAM** Gala Theatre	0191 332 4041
Sat 08	**BOSTON, LINCS** Blackfriars Theatre	01205 363 108
Sun 09	**SHIPSTON ON STOUR** Townsend Hall	01608 685 332 /07807 574 570
Tue 11	**ST. HELENS** The Theatre Royal	01744 756 000
Thu 13	**BURY** The Met	0161 761 7107
Fri 14	**HEREFORD** The Courtyard Theatre	01432 340 555
Sat 15	**SEVENOAKS** The Stag Theatre	01732 450 175
Sun 16	**BOGNOR REGIS** Alexandra Theatre	01243 861 010
Mon 17	**NETTLEBED** The Village Club	01628 636 620
Tue 18	**WORCESTER** Huntingdon Hall	01905 611 427
Wed 19	**SOUTHAMPTON** The Brook	02380 555 366
Thu 20	**LEEK** The Swan Hotel	01538 382 081
Fri 21	**LONDON** 100 CLUB	0870 264 3333
Sat 22	**ABERGAVENNY** Borough Theatre	01873 850 805
Mon 24	**SHREWSBURY** The Severn Theatre	01743 281 281
Tue 25	**WINCHESTER** The Railway	08444 771 000
Wed 26	**NORWICH** Arts Centre	01603 660 352
Thu 27	**CANTERBURY** Folk In The Barn	01227 831 493
Fri 28	**TRING** Court Theatre	01442 823 130
Sat 29	**CHIPPING NORTON** The Theatre	01608 642 350

THSH

Town Hall, Birmingham

Sat 7 Mar 09 7.30PM £21.00

Fairport Convention
Winter Tour 2009
plus special guest

Standard Type

Order #: 662441
15-Sep-08 SRock

Door E
Stalls
Row C Seat 16

C 16
Stalls
5631020498
7 Mar 09 19:30
£21.00
Standard Type
FAI-090307-01EV

(clockwise from top left) Cropredy 2009 (Ragnar Søberg); newsletters from May 2010, April 2010, May 2010 (Ian Burgess); Birmingham 2010 ticket (Terry Bidle); Cat Stevens at Cropredy (John Barlass)

ED WALLAGE

I received an email from Harmony Voyages announcing a Rhine cruise, with Fairport as the week-long entertainment. I was gutted, as we had just booked a 'standard' Rhine cruise. My wife then pointed out that the Fairport cruise was the following year, and so a second Rhine cruise was booked!

The following year Covid came to disrupt our lives and plans. I cannot recall exactly how many dates and route variations were put forward before we were eventually allowed to travel relatively normally.

One night's entertainment on the Fairport cruise was to be Beatles karaoke, with Fairport backing members of the audience. How could I resist? After over 50 years of watching Fairport perform, how good would it be to sing with them. Before the cruise, a list of the Beatles songs they would be playing was sent around for willing passengers for them to put themselves forward to sing their first or second choices. This list included the keys the songs would be played in. So out came my Beatles song book and guitar, and I worked my way through the list to determine which ones suited my vocal range. This took a little time, so I did not immediately send back my preferences.

Eventually in June 2022 the cruise left from Amsterdam to follow the original route to Basel. It was different from a normal cruise in that the passengers were keen Fairport fans (or their partners!). Mealtimes could become a bit like Fairport *Top Trumps*. When did you first see them? Did you see that line-up…? How many Cropredys have you been to?

The first night's entertainment was normal Fairport repertoire. All very good, especially in such an intimate informal setting, but I'm sure this was familiar territory for all. The following night was a swing night, and how good it was to hear them playing different music in a different style. Much credit needs to be given to Ric, the main man behind the arrangements.

Part way through the week it was announced that Simon had come down with Covid and was confined to his cabin. The previous week Richard Thompson had been performing on the same boat, and he had come down with Covid after leaving. Simon and Peggy had played with Richard on the last night of the previous cruise.

I asked Peggy when it would be announced who would be singing Beatles songs with the band. He told me songs had been allocated by Harmony Voyages on a first come, first served basis – and I was not on the list! I was downcast, but I elbowed my way onto the list as an extra by badgering Mr Pegg.

The line-up for the Beatles night was a one-off, with Gerry on drums, Chris on mandolin and harmonica, Peggy on electric guitar and Ric on ukulele bass. The chaps were resplendent in *Sgt. Pepper* jackets, although I'm not sure Peggy's shorts matched! My turn came towards the end. I like to think I acquitted myself well enough (especially as some of my fellow performers had maybe not taken the time to consider if they could sing in key, or were they just caught up in the excitement!)

The final night was back to Fairport material, but without Simon. The sound was noticeably lacking but the chaps soldiered on. Debs Earl (the future Mrs Nicol) sang a fine version of 'Crazy Man Michael' and it all ended with a mass 'Meet On The Ledge'.

On returning home I came down with Covid. From chatting to fellow travellers at Cropredy later that year, it would appear I was not alone. I blame my enthusiasm to sing with Fairport. That microphone has already been used by about a dozen people before me. But it was all worth it as I couldn't have missed that opportunity.

FAIRPORT'S CROPREDY CONVENTION
11-13 AUGUST 2022, CROPREDY, UK

TERRY HARROP

After years of reading reviews that Cropredy was the friendliest festival in Britain, I was finally going to attend. My recent conversion to all things Fairporty, after being a Sandy Denny fan for many years and the realisation that RT wasn't as bad a singer as I had originally thought, plus the promise from Peggy via email that he would buy me a pint if I saw him at the bar, was all I needed. My wife Carolann and I had booked tickets for Cropredy 2021. As we all know, it was cancelled due to Covid, but we still managed to be part of the lucky few who got to see Fairport at the Brasenose in the rain. And boy, did it rain.

Rain was certainly not going to be a problem at Cropredy 2022. In fact, it would be the sun that would be the problem. Due to work commitments and having to travel down from Scotland, we would only be attending on the Saturday. But what a line-up that was going to be.

I bought a special cool bag with wheels and packed a load of beer which I hoped would suffice for the hot day that ensued. It was so hot (as we say in Scotland, 'taps were off') that my newly acquired Jerry Donahue t-shirt was not required until at least 9.30pm that evening.

There were many highlights that day. A set from Iain Matthews and BJ Baartmans, who were joined by Richard Thompson on 'Woodstock', a set from Richard Thompson, who was joined by Iain Matthews on 'From Galway To Graceland' and The Bar-Steward Sons of Val Doonican. I've never laughed so much at a festival. Did I really see Scott Doonican crowd surfing in an inflatable dinghy with a pint in his hand shouting 'Jesus'? Or did I make it all up?

The 50th, albeit delayed, anniversary of *Full House* with the original line up, and the rather nice Mr Chris Leslie standing in for the late great Dave Swarbrick, was what most of us had been waiting for all day. We were not disappointed. Track by track was replicated live in the album's original running order, and as the final chord of the Scottish lament 'Flowers of the Forest' faded into the Cropredy evening, we knew we had all just witnessed something special.

The full band and guests ended the festival with 'Meet On The Ledge', and as Carolann and I stood up, held hands and swung them in time with everyone else, I finally experienced that wonderful sense of unison and community that only Cropredy brings. I have been to many festivals, but none like this one.

BTW, Peggy still owes me that pint.

MIKE AINSCOE

My third trip to Cropredy. No longer a virgin and some way to go to being a veteran, but feeling comfortable. It's 2022 and we were back after two fallow years due to the COVID pandemic. It was a hot one too! The line-up was looking good. Trevor Horn was packing in the hits, getting the crowd in a party mood on the opening night after Clannad have bid a fond farewell. Saturday had the progger in me in a state of bliss with Steve Hackett revisiting Genesis after a stunning set from Martyn Joseph and a blinder from the unknown quantity of The Slambovian Circus Of Dreams.

However, it's the Saturday that had me rivetted in what could have been a fantasy Cropredy line-up. There was a shift on the Earth's axis as Richard Digance was unavailable and Seth Lakeman called up from the sub's bench to open proceedings. Running into Seth in the catering tent during the morning, he confessed to being unaware of – but having heard something about – the white hanky tradition. That's not a problem though as the crowd take charge – it's the rollicking 'Change' quite appropriately that sees the tradition maintained and he loved it!

It sets the tone for a killer of a day where Holy Moly and The Crackers kept up the energy with their rock and soul and even surpassed some of the Lakeman joie de vivre with their visual spectacle. To follow, a piece of programming genius placed the returning Bar Stewards next, completing a stunning four hour sequence that might have been hard to beat. Unless you're Cropredy debutant Rosalie Cunningham, delivering something a bit on the heavier side, with her multi-coloured psychedelic rock getting a guest appearance from Ric Sanders (who'd played on her new *Two Piece Puzzle* album). Was it only the second gig for the new band she'd put together? You'd never have guessed. The sight of an Iain Matthews (with BJ Baartmans) set signalled the start of a Fairport onslaught and with Richard Thompson doing a solo acoustic set before the headliners, we were genuinely in 'can it be happening?' territory.

After a two-year delay, the 50th anniversary celebration of the *Full House* album was finally upon us (and immortalised in the CD release) with Dave Mattacks and Richard Thompson joining Peggy and Simon with Chris Leslie as 'Swarb' was truly worth the wait. All the way through to the emotional clout of 'Flowers Of The Forest' via a definitive 'Sloth' and some fiery instrumental work, the two long missing years were forgotten. How's that for an encore? Did we mention the full 16-song set that provided the warmup, where a chunk of *Shuffle And Go* mixed with Fairport classics to the extent that the time flew so quickly that even 'Matty Groves' had to take a break. 'Are we not doing the list thing?' asked Dave Pegg, realising that something had to give to hit the witching hour deadline whilst fitting in the traditional farewell?

Even without 'Matty', this had (arguably) been the perfect Cropredy day.

ROYAL HALL
14 FEBRUARY 2023, HARROGATE, UK

NIGEL SCHOFIELD

From a spellbinding 'Reynardine' to the triumphant finale of 'The Ledge' this was a joy. Highlights for me were the subtle textures and vibrant dynamics of a perfect 'Sloth' restored to its former glory, the audio-imaginatory escape to 'Portmeirion' and the blissfully Hardyesque pastoral of the timeless 'Hiring Fair'. But to select individual moments is invidious. It was simply a great show.

PETER SMITH

A very much anticipated part of my gig-going calendar is Fairport Convention on their Winter tour. I've been lucky enough to have been able to see them play at local theatres in the past. However, this year the nearest venue to me on their outing was Harrogate's Royal Hall, some 70 plus miles from home. Not to be deterred, I decided to ask my friendly taxi driver to take me on the journey down into Yorkshire. And so it was that my carer, Jackie, and I ventured south in the taxi towards the lovely town of Harrogate, leaving at around 6.40pm.

We set off on the usual familiar route but after a while it became clear that my driver's sat nav had decided to spice things up and take us via Ripon, which led us down a country road. Suddenly, fog descended and it was so thick that we could barely see the road. It was quite scary and, for a moment, I began to regret the long journey. However, we arrived safely at the Royal Hall around 8.10pm, having survived the adverse driving conditions.

To our surprise, the doors were closed and, slightly worried that we'd got the wrong date, we looked around until we eventually found one which was open. We were met by a man who led Jackie and I towards the disabled entrance. We were soon seated in a nice vantage point in the Grand Circle overlooking the stage. The Royal Hall is a wonderful, exquisite, old building. I have been there twice before, once to see Camel and on another occasion to see the Groundhogs, Martin Turner's Wishbone Ash and Focus as part of a Classic Rock package tour. When we arrived, Fairport were already on stage, just starting their first set. Sadly, we arrived too late to catch the opening act Hannah Sanders and Ben Savage. However, we did see them at the end when they joined Fairport for the encore of 'Meet On The Ledge'.

Their official website promised 'long-established Fairport favourites and some surprises from albums old and new'. This time round founding member Simon Nicol (guitar and vocals), long-time member Dave Pegg (bass guitar), Ric Sanders (violin) and Chris Leslie (fiddle, mandolin and vocals) were joined on stage by former member Dave Mattacks on drums.

Fairport always guarantee a pleasant evening with a mixture of fun stories and songs old and new. The first set was exactly that with songs from their latest album and closing with 'Sloth' from the 1970 *Full House* LP. During the interval I picked up a programme, signed by the band. Dave Pegg was, as usual, at the merchandise desk greeting fans and signing items. He kindly signed two programmes for me, one for me and one for my friend John in the USA. I also purchased a lovely little book which Peggy had produced to accompany a box set some years ago.

After a glass of red wine, we took our seats for the second half of the show. Once again, we were treated to a selection of songs old and new culminating in the traditional folk song 'Matty Groves' and the always highly anticipated encore finale 'Meet On The Ledge'. The vocals of Hannah Sanders added an extra dimension to the song which was originally sung by the sadly missed Sandy Denny.

We left via the exit and were greeted by our taxi driver. The drive north was equally scary, with a true peasouper fog that limited our speed. We eventually picked up carer number two, Elaine, close to 1am and they put me to bed just after 1.10am. It was an interesting, exciting, scary, yet completely worthwhile evening seeing the pioneers of British folk-rock.

ERIC MORECAMBE CENTRE
17 FEBRUARY 2023, HARPENDEN, UK

DEBORAH GOSDEN

February 2023 found me in the Eric Morecambe Centre in Harpenden, staring down at the *Wintour* programme and asking my parents what each of the band members were called. I was completely unaware that, a few hours later, I would have just seen what I considered the best concert of my life. My dad had introduced me to the album *50:50@50* back in 2017. It had quickly become a firm favourite, with 'Mercy Bay' and 'Eleanor's Dream' added to the playlist of my all-time top tracks. When September came around, I'd made sure that, when my dad dropped me off at uni for the first time, *50:50* was in the car.

However, in the five and a half years that followed, I confess that I hadn't actually listened to any of their other albums. Partly, I think, because I was never bored of *50:50*, and also (perhaps) because I found fifty years of discography a bit intimidating. Still, when my parents suggested I come to a *Wintour* concert with them, here was my chance to get to know other albums!

I thoroughly enjoyed my first Fairport concert, and my dad was a lot of help beside me when I wrote down the setlist in a notebook so I could find all the songs again. ('What was the last one?' I asked. "Sloth',' was the reply). To my disappointment, they did not play 'Mercy Bay', however, this sadness was pretty negligible in the face of the fact that I now had two new favourite songs, 'Cider Rain' and 'Moondust And Solitude'.

In the interval, I met Peggy, who was lovely despite my awkwardness (I'd never asked for a CD to be signed before). I now had two new signed CDs for my car – *Shuffle And Go* and *Full House For Sale*. My knowledge of the Fairport repertoire was expanding.

Next, came Cropredy. All in all, it was an absolutely amazing Saturday, and I particularly enjoyed Morganway. However, the highlight came from the fact that my mum and I unexpectedly ended up at the front for Fairport's set. It made sense, I suppose, as we'd arrived in the standing area two sets beforehand. But still! It is utter, incredible, fantastic madness to me that the second time I saw Fairport, I was right there at the front. It's definitely a memory I will treasure forever.

There was no question that we should go to see them for their acoustic tour. So, we did! It was on 3 November, in the car on the way to see the band in Saint Andrew's Church, Hertford, that I listened to 'Our Bus Rolls On' for the first time in a while and I realised how far I'd come since that first concert. I *knew* who the people in this song were, I could see where they stood on stage. Suddenly, a song which I'd previously just enjoyed became so much more special.

As I'd come to expect, Fairport's acoustic set was absolutely brilliant. What was far more surprising, was that I had the chance to talk to Chris Leslie during the interval. I'd decided to go over to the merch table, and there was Chris, coming in the other direction as he left the temporary stage. I said hello and that I was really enjoying the concert because, however shy I may be, pretending one of my favourite musicians didn't exist would have felt quite rude! After thanking me, he asked if I played anything myself, to which I admitted that while I'd stopped playing guitar years ago, listening to 'Moondust And Solitude' made me want to pick it up again, a fact that he seemed pretty delighted about.

As that interaction hadn't been disastrous, after the show I plucked up the courage to go over and ask him the name of one of the instruments he placed during 'Moses Waits'. Apparently, it's called a Kalimba! Chris was absolutely lovely – as everyone always says he is – and also once again encouraged me to pick up my guitar. And well, after that I had no choice!

I am pleased to say that, after not really remembering how to play the guitar at all, I can now play it very badly, working my way slowly through 'Moondust', 'The Hiring Fair', and 'Matty Groves' (as well as a few other non-Fairport songs).

Finally, the *Wintour* came round again!

Following a stellar performance, I again went to the merch table to pick up their new CD. This time, Peggy recognised me! This task was made easier by the fact that I'm in my twenties, and I have curly ginger hair, but still, it was pretty impressive considering I'd met him one time, a year earlier.

It was great talking to Peggy, who seems very sociable and has a real gift for making people feel welcome. Like Chris, he asked me if I played anything. This time I was able to say that I could play the guitar (badly), and Peggy – as is his fashion – suggested I take up the bass. 'It's easier and you get the same money!'

It's my hope that, by the time Cropredy comes around, my guitar (or bass!) playing skills might have moved up to mediocre.

Since February 2023, I've listened to many more albums, and have had many, many new favourite Fairport songs, too numerous to list. What's nice about having such a large discography is that I can play a song on repeat for two days (or even a week), and when it has stopped taking over my entire brain, there is another Fairport song waiting in the wings to take its place!

ATKINSON THEATRE
23 FEBRUARY 2023, SOUTHPORT, UK

MIKE AINSCOE

The choice of Ben Savage and Hannah Sanders as support for the 2023 *Wintour* was inspired, and their opening set a delight. I'd go so far as to say that they're possibly the best opening act that Fairport have had on their Wintours. 'Folk songs are like salads,' they explained. 'Nobody wants it but it's good for you.'

Having already warmed up by performing 'Reynardine' with Hannah and Ben, 'Walk Awhile' is a song that Fairport might be able to play with their hands tied behind their backs and it's a rouser. We're out of the traps and running. While once again admiring Simon's twelve-string Danelectro, it's nice to see how the set has been tweaked; with 'My Love Is In America' and Chris Leslie gets in an early claim for man of the match. It's in the same ballpark as his easy and gentle 'Moondust And Solitude', although he certainly has some rivals for the crown.

Ric Sanders appears to be revelling with a new foil – not just Ben Savage as the duo duelled away on 'Reynardine' – as the return of Dave Mattacks to the drum stool following Gerry Conway's retirement offers him a rival in the stand-up stakes and a fellow who shares the same sartorial elegance. There's a clear musical connection as, after 'Steampunkery', Ric informs us with some element of glee and sheer admiration *'that's how to play the drums!'* As well as being on form with his usual routines, Ric's pedal board and fiddle effects come into their own on a couple of songs. 'Polly On The Shore' sees his fiddle singing and soaring into the rafters, a freak out driven by some Mattacks' power. The Manchester RNCM 'Sloth' three nights later is even more potent where he coaxes out a series of sounds like a beanie-hatted fiddle magus and even indulges in some sonic experimentation with some vocal effects as he lifts the pickups toward his mouth. It's like the psychedelic 'Summer Of Love' – the fiddle Hendrix lives.

The balance of light-heartedness is restored with Simon Nicol playing his part with a carefully rehearsed humourous ad-lib up his sleeve at the start of the second half, when he follows up 1970's 'Sloth' by informing us '*we're not slaves to our past, here's one from 1971...*'. This second set is particularly strong, kicking off with (the more modern) 'Journeyman's Grace' that's a folk-rocking belter that sets the tone for the second half (and that chorus has become a personal earworm. If there were such a thing as a banger in folk-rock terms, 'Journeyman's Grace' would be it.

Another highlight comes with the romp and reel that is 'John Gaudie', another from Chris Leslie that sees him on mandolin so we're denied the terrific fiddle duet (one last experienced in the 'sit down' shows in the autumn) that often ramps up the energy even more. More evidence for those who rate young Leslie as the mainman – his 'My Love Is

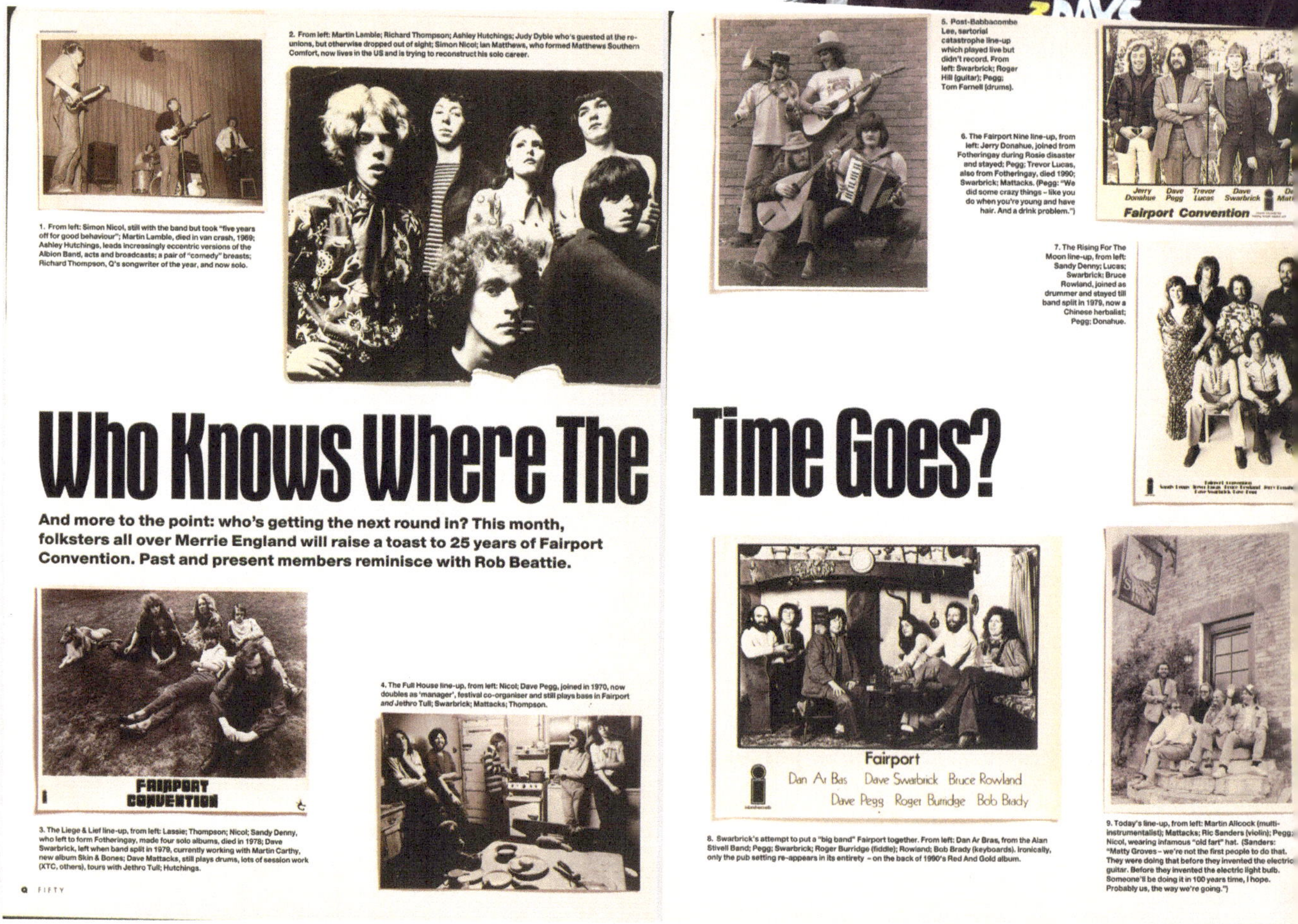

(clockwise from top left) assorted newsletters from 2011 (**Ian Burgess**); Clive Butler got a cherished ten minutes with Swarb; Q magazine wonders where the time went

(clockwise from top left) Dave George's granddaughter Millie modelled herself on Peggy; Bill Wallace got a personal command performance from Fairport; Paul Hardisty is a convert & now brings his family; Roger Haydock & his late wife Sue, who saw Fairport for the last time at the Platform in Morecambe; Gerry Conway in action at Cropredy 2011 (Bob Battersby/Lodestone Publishing Ltd)

In America', his *Shuffle And Go* songs ('Moondust…', 'Year of '59') and his all singing, all playing (not quite all dancing…) contribution. Much the same as the old-style midfield footballers like Johnny Giles and Colin Bell, who used to cover every blade of grass.

'The Hiring Fair' too has become even more statuesque; the latest incarnation with DM rolling back the years to his first instrument with a subtle keyboard part that he also plays on 'Portmeirion'. It's a song whose status places it right before 'Matty Groves', which is back and rocking, a shot of folk-rock (Peggy: *'Frock!')* adrenalin after the recent sit-down acoustic versions. It's perhaps an indication of the oomph that Dave Mattacks brings to the table. He's been called the man who invented folk-rock drumming and he seems to be channelling a bit of Bonham with his hi-hat work on 'Matty'. We're even treated to the playful *'how do you like my curtains that I bought from IKEA last week'* line at The Atkinson (perhaps saved for venues where the backdrop drapes are suitably plush).

There can really only be one possible encore farewell, where the band are joined again by Hannah 'no relation' Sanders and Ben 'not at all' Savage. Having lent on *Liege & Lief* on their latest album, even Scott and the Bar Steward Sons Of Val Doonican have resisted any temptation to do a comedy folk song about butchery called 'Meat On The Ledge'.

BECK THEATRE
28 FEBRUARY 2023, HAYES, UK

TRON EIVIN ØVREBØ

My wife and I have different musical tastes. Her favorite song is 'Knocking On Heaven's Door'. She doesn't like Sandy's voice ('why is she always so sad?') and fiddle is not her favourite instrument. To her, Cropredy is only for the men. So during a holiday in Kent and Sussex (where we were meeting friends from Cropredy), I invited her to her first Fairport gig. I was a little bit anxious, but it turned out well. She knew most of the songs. Her only comment was 'why didn't this guy with the pleasant voice sing the songs originally?' I can now listen to *What We Did On Our Saturday* in the car without protests. I like the album, perhaps because it's the only one I'm singing on. (I'm on uncredited backing vocals on Track 25, 'Meet On The Ledge'.)

When Cropredy was 'Covid cancelled' in 2021, I invited all my friends that had joined me at the festival over the years to a substitute festival at my cabin in Norway. Fairport even sent us a personal video greeting!

'BEST WISHES'

MARTIN TREVELYAN-JONES

My original encounter was with Sandy who I saw a couple of times at The Barge, moored in the Thames at Kingston. This was followed not that long after by going to a couple of Fairport gigs in the late sixties and being impressed enough to buy the first three LPs. However, I then spent the next 20 years as a geologist in Africa and rather got out of touch – in the days before the internet, it was almost impossible to follow them from locations like the Kalahari Desert. On our return to the UK, my wife Sue and I went to see them whenever we could, our favourite venue being the small Foxlowe Arts Centre in Leek. But no matter where, what makes Fairport so special – and unlike any other group – is their approachability and the fact that you really do feel part of a family.

When my wife Sue died last year, I spent some time trying to arrange the funeral service, and in particular what the music or song should be to close the service. My one thought was that I wanted the congregation to leave feeling positive and cheerful about the future, after a sad occasion. It took me a very little time to choose 'Best Wishes' by Steve Ashley as performed by Fairport. The funeral director had never heard of it, or Fairport for that matter, but I was absolutely overwhelmed by the reaction from those present and the people who have heard about it since. So many have said how fantastic and appropriate it was, and many have actually bought Fairport CDs as a result. I put a brief 'thank you' to Fairport online and had a lovely response there, including from Simon who pointed out that I had actually forgotten to thank Steve, who wrote it.

Fairport have always been special to me but even more so now. 'Best Wishes' gave just the message I wanted and will always be part of my life. I really can't say how much that song and Fairport have meant to me in the year since Sue died. So much of their repertoire not only takes me back with memories but also cheers me up if I feel a bit down.

Thank you, Fairport.

FAIRPORT'S CROPREDY CONVENTION
10-12 AUGUST 2023, CROPREDY, UK

APRIL PHILLIPS

I stay in a nearby hotel when I go to Cropredy. I was at breakfast with my friend when she noticed someone with a t-shirt with a line from a Fishermen's Friends song. I said it was possible that they were staying there. After my friend had gone to her room, another man joined this one and I noticed he had a backstage wristband on. As I went over to speak with them, they got up to leave but one of them stopped at the coffee machine. I asked the one with the wristband if he was performing at Cropredy. He said no, but he was working there. I asked what he was doing and he said 'sound'. I asked if that was for the whole event or just one band. He said just one band. I then turned to the one with the t-shirt and asked if he was working there too. He said no, he was performing. I said my friend had noticed his t-shirt and went on about Fisherman's Friends. He said he wasn't with Fisherman's Friends (though they were staying there). I asked which band he was playing with. He said 10cc. It was only Paul Burgess. A very embarrassed me gabbled away for a few minutes, much to their amusement, then I thought it best I left!

OLIVIA MARSH

This was my first time going to Cropredy Festival. As a family we all bought tickets for my dad's sixtieth birthday due to him being a huge Fairport Convention fan. Me and my boyfriend live in Bristol so we met my mum, dad, sister and her boyfriend, who all live in Oxfordshire, at the festival. This meant we missed the setting up of the tents, but it still took the six of us 40 minutes to put up one gazebo!

Aside from Fairport, I only recognised a few of the line up – Nile Rogers & Chic and 10cc, and I had seen Beans on Toast at Boomtown Festival a couple of times – but I was excited to listen to some new music. My favourite performance has got to be Nile Rogers and Chic. It seemed like they didn't even pause to take a breath between songs; it was just banger after banger! But Toyah and 10cc were awesome too. A few of the bands gained new fans – my boyfriend Sam danced down the hill to get closer to the stage after hearing Fisherman's Friends. Catherine and Connor took a shine to Beans on Toast and queued up to get their newly purchased CD signed. And I have to say, I really enjoyed both of Fairport's performances, the acoustic set on Thursday and them closing on Saturday night ('Matty Groves' is a bop). I had never really listened to folk music before, but I would definitely go to Cropredy Festival again, which I'm sure my dad will be glad to hear. It was an incredible experience all round!

RICHARD GASCOYNE

12th August 2023 was a very special day for me and two of my mates, because we were celebrating our seventieth birthdays on a very unique Oxfordshire field, aka, Fairport's Cropredy Convention. Pete, Tony and myself decided that only true way to celebrate was with all of our friends as we listened to the Saturday bands, starting with Richard Digance and finishing along with everyone else singing 'Meet On The Ledge'. We came well prepared, sparkling wine and beer purchased, and ready to celebrate. It was then that we realised that a certain Brummie bass player and Tull's first drummer and their partners were sitting alongside us. Well, it seemed churlish not to offer them a drink and so began an afternoon of storytelling, reminiscing and drinking. Jokes and smiles became the order of the day as we all became very merry. Peggy and Ellen and Clive and Ulla made us feel very welcome, so much so that when my wife, Julia, politely suggested we should leave them in peace, Peggy and Ellen insisted that we stay longer. After that, it all became a bit of a blur!

NORDEN FARM CENTRE FOR THE ARTS

11 OCTOBER 2023, MAIDENHEAD, UK

PAUL BACON

My Fairport journey starred via *ZigZag* magazine with the incredible and fascinating Pete Frame family trees. Browsing the record racks, I found the *History Of* album with the aforementioned on the cover and was completely taken by the music inside. Having a ribbon on the cover meant real care had to be taken when returning it to the shelf! I was lucky enough to work for a local independent retail group that featured record departments in each store. The record buyer, Simon Gee, guided me through the minefield that was the Fairport and family story and my collection grew. I also managed to get a copy of *The Airing Cupboard Tapes* which featured on many a journey in my car.

I first saw Fairport at The Hexagon, Reading in 1978, followed quickly by Richard and Linda, Sandy, The Albion Band and Ralph McTell that year. In 1981, I made the trek to Broughton Castle on my own, and thoroughly enjoyed the music and atmosphere. Driving home was a bit tricky as, having worked that morning, I kept nodding off at the wheel, but I managed to get home in one piece. February tours brought Fairport to Reading in 1988, 1990, 1991 and 1997, each show being wonderfully different.

My concert attending days diminished with other responsibilities but I resumed attending concerts this year, after the premature passing of my wife in 2022, and attended Norden Farm in October 2023, where I enjoyed chatting with both Dave and Simon.

QUEEN'S HALL ARTS CENTRE

27 OCTOBER 2023, HEXHAM, UK

PETER SMITH

This time it was the acoustic version of Fairport Convention, which is basically the band without a drummer. The venue was the lovely Queen's Hall Arts Centre in

Hexham. This was my first time at this venue, although I have visited Hexham many times in the past. This was the nearest that the band were appearing on their current tour, so I couldn't resist seeing them, and my friendly taxi driver was up for the challenge of taking take me to Hexham and back, an 80 plus mile round trip. We set off at 6pm, giving us what should have been enough time to arrive for the 7.30pm start. Unfortunately, there was severe delays on the roads which forced us to take a detour. This made us slightly late, and we arrived a few songs into the first set.

The Queen's Hall is set behind a park in the centre of Hexham. The staff in the venue quickly helped us up in the lift and found us some alternative seats (presumably because we were late in arriving) at the rear of the hall overlooking the stage, with actually a pretty good view of the proceedings. The staff were wonderful and helpful throughout the night, going out of their way to make sure I was safe going up and down in the lift to reach the bar during the interval.

I have seen Fairport Convention many times in recent years. Each time I enjoy them more and more. This band has a rich folk-rock heritage and a massive back catalogue of songs to draw from. Each song is preceded by a detailed and often comical explanation of the origin and meaning of the song. Each member takes a turn in explaining the songs and taking a lead role on either vocals, guitar, mandolin or violin. The first set was completed with some songs which are becoming very familiar to me now. The sound was excellent and the audience reception was very warm and friendly. At a Fairport Convention concert, I often get the feeling that it is a meeting of old friends coming together, and this gig was no exception. This band have a very strong, loyal following.

There was no new merchandise on sale, other than CDs and the recently published *Gonna See All My Friends: A People's History Of Fairport Convention* book to which I contributed and which I already have a copy of. Still, that allowed me a little more time to venture downstairs to the bar and partake in a lovely double Glenfiddich.

The second half of the concert was excellent as always. The singing troubadours delivered a set of songs, some familiar and some less so. 'Portmeirion' is based on the village where the TV series *The Prisoner* was set. I used to watch it when it was first aired in the 1960s and could not understand it then. Perhaps it is time to revisit it? I will see. Soon we were taken back in time again, to the day when, as told by Simon Nicol, they auditioned for a singer and in walked Sandy Denny, who for a few short years changed the nature, sound and destiny of the band. Simon delivered an exquisite rendition of my Fairport favourite, 'Who Knows Where the Time Goes', as magical as it ever was and always will be. I was pleased to see that particular song return to the set. Then followed the traditional song 'Matty Groves' as the closing folk tale. But we knew that wasn't the end. Fairport returned to deliver the timeless encore, 'Meet On The Ledge'. A great evening with a great band.

The journey back was another adventure. The A1 was closed for work on the road and we followed a diversion into the centre of Newcastle, through Gateshead and onward towards home. I was back home for around midnight. Roll-on next time.

QUEEN'S HALL
29 NOVEMBER 2023, EDINBURGH, UK

TERRY HARROP

My son Benjamin had been travelling and working in America and Australia for 16 months, returning to Scotland in early September. This was perfect timing to catch up with Fairport's Autumn Tour, once with Benjamin and once with my wife Carolann a few days earlier at the Old Fire Station in Carlisle. Earlier in the year at the same venue in Edinburgh, my wife and I had seen Richard Thompson, which was a wonderful night, including the Fairport number 'Genesis Hall' and only 'Dimming Of The Day' missing from the set full of classic Richard Thompson songs.

By now Fairport were now down to four in number, as Gerry Conway their drummer for 24 years and previously the drummer for Sandy Denny's Fotheringay, had called it a day after Croppers 2022. I had with me a wee present for Chris Leslie, as we share a passion for the NASA Apollo missions. I managed to grab a hold of him while he was tuning up before the set and give him a signed photo of Walt Cunningham, one of the astronauts on Apollo 7.

Peggy was on the merch desk prior to the gig. He had his granddaughter for extra company. I got a quick picture of them both with Benjamin photo bombing in the background. Peggy then signed a couple of my Fairport record sleeves and I was delighted when shortly afterwards Simon turned up and dutifully signed the same sleeves. The highlight of the set? 'Banks Of The Sweet Primroses', sung wonderfully by Chris Leslie.

TUNG AUDITORIUM, YOKO ONO CENTRE
10 FEBRUARY 2024, LIVERPOOL, UK

TEL & BENJIE HARROP

Having caught a four-piece Fairport twice on the Autumn 2023 tour, the news that DM was returning to the fold on the *Wintour* meant only one thing; 'Where can I see Fairport?' Sadly, there were no Scotland or Cumbria dates. However, it had been a while since I had been to Liverpool, so tickets were purchased for myself and my son Benjie who, like DM, spends considerable time in the States.

The drive down was fine and we had decided to make use of the trip to Liverpool to visit some of the places associated with The Beatles; Strawberry Fields, Woolton Village Hall (where Paul met John) plus St Peter's churchyard, to see the grave of one Eleanor Rigby. We moved swiftly on to various pubs and clubs in which The Beatles either played, drank or got paid in. The Beatle pub crawl started at The Jacaranda before moving on to The White Star, The Grapes and finally The Cavern itself, where we were entertained by a young Beatle tribute band for 45 minutes. A pitstop at the local Wetherspoons saw us making our way to a new venue for Fairport, The Tung Auditorium inside the Yoko Ono Centre.

As we entered, Peggy was setting up the merch desk. We got to meet Anthony John Clarke and the CD of the previous autumn tour was purchased. DM had kindly agreed to meet Benjie and I prior to the gig to sign a few of the albums he had played on, including ones by Sandy, Nick Drake and Fairport. We then moved on to the bar. After a few drinks were purchased, DM and Benjie traded Stateside stories, and we heard how it felt for DM getting to meet and work with Macca himself.

I had a new NASA t-shirt which was too big for me to wear, so prior to the bands coming on, one Chris Leslie was kind enough to take it off my hands, which resulted in a wee name check by Chris during the gig.

Benjie and I had front row seats and sat back while Fairport joined the support act, Plumhall, on their last track. Fairport then played two sets. The first started with 'Walk Awhile' and ended with a superb 'Sloth'. The second started with 'Don't Reveal' and ended (of course) with 'Meet on the Ledge', for which Plumhall joined the boys from start to finish. Chris and DM came over to say goodbye to Benjie and myself afterwards and then we headed back to Scotland, playing the autumn tour CD on repeat on the way home.

Highlights? The return of DM on the drum stool and the return of 'Polly on the Shore' to the set!

THE APEX

13 FEBRUARY 2024, BURY ST EDMUNDS, UK

GRAHAM DAY

After discovering Fairport Convention during our 'exile' in Oxfordshire, and particularly after seeing them perform at Cropredy in 1977, we have seen them on several occasions. Most recently this was at the Apex Theatre where, since early 2023, we regularly attend shows with several cousins. The current Fairport line up of Simon Nicol (guitar and vocals), Ric Sanders (violin), Dave Pegg (bass) and Chris Leslie (multi-instrumentalist) was joined on this occasion by the redoubtable Dave Mattacks on drums. Ric ambled on stage and performed a short routine as a stand-up comedian, using this as a means of eventually introducing the support act, the duo of Plumhall, who performed an excellent short set.

Fairport came on to the stage and held the capacity audience spellbound as they performed a variety of songs from their vast catalogue. They opened with 'Walk Awhile' and included two songs from their 1969 album *Liege & Lief*, 'Crazy Man Michael' and 'Matty Groves'. My other favourites on the night were 'Bankruptured' and 'Steampunkery'. There were some amusing anecdotes by band members between numbers. Dave Pegg remarked that when he joined the band, he struggled to become proficient on the guitar. He then transferred to the bass which he found easier because it involved playing fewer strings and said he was very happy once he realised he would still receive the same wages as everybody else!

The importance of Cropredy in North Oxfordshire to Fairport was emphasised by the inclusion in their set of 'Festival Bell', a track I had not heard before. In 2007 two bells – the Festival Bell and the St Mary's Bell, emphasising the connection between the village and the Cropredy Festival – were added to the ring in the church at Cropredy. The Festival Bell was always rung on the Thursday to symbolise the start of the Festival. Church bells are rung to announce joyous or sad occasions, and the joyful ringing of the Festival Bell before the annual festival is a quite unique idea which is typically Fairport.

Throughout the concert the musicianship from all was superb. Ric Sanders was a virtuoso on violin. (I remember him being introduced as the 'new' fiddler in our Banbury days.) I had not seen Chris Leslie before, but whichever instrument he used his ability was awesome. I was pleased to see Dave Mattacks again. His rhythm section with Dave Pegg provided the building blocks for all the songs. Dave's drumming was not quite as manic as when I had seen him in his younger days in 1977 at Cropredy, but it would still put other drummers in the shade. The drum kit almost became alive. And Simon Nicol's superb guitar and vocals were the icing on the cake.

The concert finished with the Cropredy anthem 'Meet On The Ledge', which was the cue for a fulsome standing ovation for Fairport. To think that continued success has come over the years for a folk-rock band who took their name from convening (meeting) for rehearsals at Simon Nicol's house in North London…

We emerged into the night air, pleased that we had seen an absorbing concert by five absolutely superb musicians performing in a really wonderful theatre.

(clockwise from top left) Robert Plant at Cropredy 2013 (**Krzysztof ?**): Ric, Simon & Peggy at Cropredy 2013 (Tim Hayes); Ric & Martin Barre from Jethro Tull at Cropredy 2013 (Tim Hayes); **Peggy & Chris** at Cropredy 2013 (Tim Hayes); Simon & Peggy at Cropredy 2013 (Tim Hayes)

(clockwise from top left) Simon Nicol at Cropredy 2013 (Tim Hayes); Peggy at Cropredy 2013 (Tim Hayes); 2013 ticket (Terry Bidle); Chris, Peggy & Christian Herentz, who met Peggy in the gents; Cropredy 2013 (Tim Hayes); Beth Self & her sister have been going to Cropredy since they were kids; violin virtuosos (Tim Hayes)

ARC STOCKTON ARTS CENTRE
28 FEBRUARY 2024, STOCKTON-ON-TEES, UK

CARL COLLINGS

At school in the late sixties, most of my friends were heavy rock fans so that's what I was into. But when I went to university in the mid-Seventies, I met a person who was to become a good friend and best man at my wedding, and vice versa. He introduced me to Fairport Convention and I never looked back. Another friend from university days was also a fan. Sadly, both these friends died (seven and four years ago respectively). I had the great pleasure of travelling from my home in Dublin to accompany their two widows to the gig in Stockton in February 2024. It was a wonderful evening and a little emotional, especially for 'Meet On The Ledge'. Thank you for a great night in memory of my friends and for all the years of great music.

UNION CHAPEL
9 MARCH 2024, ISLINGTON, LONDON, UK

COLIN RANDALL

Four elderly gentlemen, along with a hairy nipper of barely 67, strutted their hour or two upon a London stage and seemed to shave decades off their aggregate age of 362 years. Among an army of greying fans in the sell-out audience, there was even a light sprinkling of people younger than them. But far from signifying nothing, in case I do not already have William Shakespeare rotating angrily in his grave, Fairport Convention managed in the penultimate concert of a long tour to show they still matter.

My introduction to these thoughts on what was a memorably good evening is not intended to be remotely ageist. How could it be? I'm older than everyone in the band except Peggy and Dave Mattacks. All the same, Fairport's lasting qualities are a wonder to behold, even if Dylan, Jagger, Carthy, Baez and others are into their eighties. Fifty-seven years after Simon Nicol and Richard Thompson formed the band, the setting for a minor musical triumph on Saturday March 9 was one of the capital's loveliest venues, the Union Chapel, still a working church tucked in a side street across the road from Highbury and Islington Tube station.

The heights of Fairport glory were reached during the late Sandy Denny's two short stints, 1968-69 and 1974-75, but declining interest in the folk-rock genre led to the band being sidelined – though its musicians remained active – in the first half of the 1980s. Somehow, not least because of the annual Cropredy Fairport reunion festival, they have remained a fixture of the national consciousness, or at least our part of it. Not always with admiration; I recall chancing upon an episode of *The Archers* in which parental possession of Fairport albums was roundly mocked.

Nicol, now 73, is still in the band – he had a break in the 1970s – and long ago developed into a compelling lead singer whose guitar playing is also exemplary. Peggy – Dave Pegg – is at 76 the senior member of the band, still providing the solid bass work that underpins a tight, vibrant sound combining pulsating drumming (Dave Mattacks, back in the group at 75), exquisite fiddle playing by 71-year-old Ric Sanders, 67-year-old Chris Leslie's multi-instrumental flair and Nicol's adaptable rhythm guitar (he describes his style as percussive).

Saturday's repertoire included plenty of Fairport standards: 'Walk Awhile', 'Sloth', 'Crazy Man Michael', 'Genesis Hall' and – with further deference to Macbeth's soliloquy – all the sound and fury of 'Matty Groves'.

At one point, perhaps when songs less known to me were played, I did find myself wondering whether this was vintage Fairport or just a very good reminder of past triumphs. But Peggy, who lives near Lorient in southern Brittany and is a connoisseur of red wine according to Sanders, will know the French use the word *correct* when they mean 'OK but nothing special' and once they returned to more familiar territory, I knew I was indeed present at something special. I'll even acknowledge that Sanders made a decent stab at stand-up comedy, though his timing was better than the gags.

In musical terms, nothing fell short of accomplished performance, reaffirming folk-rock's status as a special genre. I wouldn't be surprised if some of those seated along the Union Chapel's pews sensed the approving, ghostly presence of departed Fairporters Denny, Dave Swarbrick, Judy Dyble, Trevor Lucas, Martin Lamble, Bruce Rowland, Maartin Allcock and David Rea (RIP one and all, and please give me a shout if I've missed someone). The very much still alive Richard Thompson was present in spirit, courtesy of key parts of the set list.

It was all preceded by an excellent husband-and-wife support duo, Plumhall, who quickly engaged the audience with the warmth of their chatter and as quickly impressed with superior songwriting and robust accompaniment. I cannot have been alone in encountering them for the first time, yet they effortlessly had the audience singing along with choruses. If I am not among those concert-goers who hog the bar until the main act is about to appear, truly memorable supports are rare indeed; only Lindisfarne (for Ralph McTell), Damien Dempsey (for Sinead O'Connor) and Show of Hands (for Fairport at the Cropredy festival that re-created each track of the renowned *Liege & Lief* album) spring instantly to mind.

One glaring omission from Fairport's two generous sets was Denny's best-known composition. Who Knows Where That Song Went? Nicol hinted at a curfew, so maybe the band simply ran out of permitted time. But in a splendid finale, Plumhall – alias Michelle Plum and Nick Hall – were summoned back on stage for a loud, lingering rendition of the anthemic 'Meet On The Ledge', helpfully bringing down the average age on stage.

Keep strutting, Fairport.

TUPELO MUSIC HALL

22 MARCH 2024, DERRY, NEW HAMPSHIRE

STEVE PUGH

I went to see Richard Thompson at a local small music venue. He was just great and even had a Vincent Black Lightning (1952?) on stage, courtesy of the local bikers. He had a girl onstage for the last third of his set while doing his new material and, for the encore, Dave Mattacks. His guitar playing was amazing and he was in good voice and fine humour, reminiscing about the Marquee Club and bands he'd seen there in his yoof. The ticket price was $70 and it was worth every cent!

MORE CROPREDY MEMORIES

OVER THE YEARS, CROPREDY, UK

ALAN BAILEY

I played briefly with Chris Leslie when he was just 15 and it was obvious even then that he was a particularly talented musician. Subsequently, I heard him several times with Whippersnapper and on tour with Kevin Dempsey, so I was not in the least surprised to find him ultimately bringing his talent to Fairport. I'd known him for almost thirty years by then. Chatting after seeing him gig with Fairport, I said that I'd always know he'd end up playing with other great musicians and suggested that 'there's still time for that to happen', whereupon Dave Pegg kicked me... More than twenty years on, I still have a small scar!

I was working behind the bar at our local venue for a Dylan Project gig. During the interval, Steve Gibbon spotted bottles of brown ale behind the bar, and reminisced that he used to drink brown and mild. I said, 'So you're a Midlander then – I hope it was Banks' Mild.' Their sound man was leaning on the end of the bar and reflected, 'My grandfather used to keep a Banks' pub . . . in Wolverhampton. I think it was called the Red Lion, near to the Ring Road.' 'When was that?' I asked. 'He retired in

1966.' I corrected him: 'I think you'll find it was called The Red House, in Zoar Street.' 'Hmmm - so it was. How do you know?' I pointed out that my grandfather retired from there in 1966, and we realised that we shared the same grandfather. I was talking to Mark Harper, a cousin I'd not met in thirty years.

A few months later, I was back in the bar for a Fairport gig when Dave Pegg walked in. He immediately apologised that he had not, to the best of his knowledge, brought me any long-lost relatives this time!

DAVE KEY

Are holograms the way forward for Fairport? A celebrity agent called Mark Roesler works predominantly with people who are no longer alive, with Albert Einstein, Neil Armstrong, Rosa Parks, Burt Reynolds, Bette Davis, Sugar Ray Robinson, Ingrid Bergman, Alan Turing and hundreds more dead celebrities, or 'delebrities' as they're sometimes called, on his books. *The Guardian* recently suggested in an article that 'the opportunities to earn a crust from beyond the grave have never been better, with holographic and AI resurrecting dead stars' voices and likenesses so that they can get back on the live circuit…'.

Could this be the way forward for Fairport? With Dave Pegg now 76 and even the newbie nippers such as Ric Sanders hitting 70 (along with myself), this could be just the job to allay the fears of many fans of a future without Fairport's annual Cropredy Convention.

Younger artists are always coming on to the folk scene, to augment the many sixties and seventies survivors that Fairport conjure every year (some of whom may soon need to access this same holographic solution themselves), so Festival organisers could still quite easily fill the bill for the three days, ending the weekend with Fairport's usual climactic set on Saturday night. But they could do so now, and forever more, with a bit of a twist, insofar as the band would not actually be there on stage in person.

ABBA have used virtual reality to stage some major shows of themselves (using avatars) at their peak whilst they're still living, with the present day versions of themselves simulating the movements of their young selves. But Roesler's holograms take this concept to a whole new level in that he is looking way past the band's demise and into a Fairport-less future – or should one say, a Fairport-filled eternity! One can imagine a time when favoured guests, who have appeared on stage in the flesh during the previous three days return for the Grand Finale (as per usual) and play alongside the Famous Five (as avatars): 'Simon', 'Dave', 'Ric', 'Chris' and 'Dave' the drummer…

This new hybrid twist would give a whole new meaning to Fairport's famous closing chorus lines from 'Meet On The Ledge':

When my time is up,
I'm gonna see all my friends again…

Perhaps not so 'closing' after all!

BOB BRADBURY

Having attended more than a few Cropredy festivals from 1979 to date, I thought that I knew the place. For the rest of each year, Cropredy village rarely came to mind except when passing the M40 exit on journeys south. But last summer, on my way to meet my daughter for lunch, she called to say that our agreed equidistant pub was closed for the day. For no reason, apart from being a similar distance for each of us at that exact moment, the word Brasenose popped into mind. Inside the Brasenose bar, there's a photo on the wall of Fairport from around the time of the first Festival.

After lunch, we wandered across the road, remembering the convenience store and finding that the shops and stalls opposite are actually open all year round. Since then, my partner has taken a hat making course there while I've found a second pub and church in the village, peeped into a garage that restores Jensens and walked along the canal to Banbury. Even in the silence of nature along the overgrown towpath, the sound of Fairport music echoes in my otherwise empty head.

APRIL PHILLIPS

I used to say I knew Dave Pegg when he had hair. Then I thought about it and realised I had known him all my life. Our mums were best friends before I was even born. Having said that, there have been various long gaps in contact over the years.

One such re-connection occurred in the late sixties when he was playing with the Ian Campbell Folk group. I used to go to the Jug o' Punch every Thursday and then Peggy started appearing and I made myself known by asking if Gospel Lane Church meant anything to him – it's where our mums went. I was to use the same line many years later.

Many years ago Gordon, my manager at work, said that he was going to see Fairport Convention that evening. He said that he and his friends knew them and often went for curry with them after a show. I wrote a letter to Peggy and asked Gordon to give it to him if he saw him. Later, I thought I would just look to see if there were any tickets left and there were. I booked for me and my daughter. At the time, my daughter was in a band and she mentioned it to one of them (Ken). He said he would get a ticket too. On the way to the gig, he said that Peggy was his all-time favourite bass player. My daughter told him that I knew him and he got really excited.

In the interval, Ken and Laurel went outside for a cigarette. I didn't smoke but went with them. Who should be leaning against a wall also having a smoke but Peggy! This is when I used my line again and he recognised me and there were hugs and chat until it was time for him to go in.

After the show we were in the bar and Peggy made his way through the crowds of well-wishers and came and sat with us. Ken was so excited at meeting him that he took over the conversation and we could hardly get a word in! Before the night ended, Peggy asked me if I knew about Cropredy. I said I hadn't heard of it and he told me all about it. It resulted in his arranging two weekend tickets and back stage passes for me and my daughter. That was to be my introduction to Cropredy for which I am so grateful. I have been to pretty much every one since (except the Covid years and a couple I had to miss due to being in hospital).

Each one has been special for various reasons. I have made new friends there, including a couple Peggy introduced me to and, as he disappeared down the field, shouted back: 'You have Birmingham in common.' It turned out that not only did we have Birmingham in common, but Pam and I had gone to the same school, had been in the same year, and the following year I took the old school photo (of the whole school) to Cropredy and we found we were standing just a few people apart! I also remember standing next to Peggy when he rang Steve Winwood to say that Pam's husband John wanted to sing 'Ging Gang Goolie' to him (he didn't, but that's Peggy!). Steve and John had been in the scouts together. Peggy asked Steve to come over but he said he couldn't as he had just become a granddad for the first time. Special, special times.

I say to people that not all the music may be to their taste, as there is such a wide variety, but it is guaranteed to be good. Many new bands have been introduced to me there and I have then gone to see those bands nearer to home. Some stand-out acts for me have been: Alice Cooper; Pierce Brothers; Petula Clarke; Status Quo; and The Bar-Steward Sons of Val Doonican (who I'm going to see again in a few weeks – at a small venue, so I don't know if they'll be able to surf the crowd!). And so, so many more.

Cropredy is the only festival I have been to but it is perfect for me. Only one field and only one stage so no decisions! I would hate the thought of missing something in one place having chosen to watch something else in another place. The organisation is tremendous and every year something has been refined. The fact that people can camp next to their cars is great (I don't camp but am impressed by this consideration). The food and drinks are all reasonably priced, not the extortionate costs you hear about at other festivals. I also like that apparently there is no backstage bar so the acts are often seen at the bar and in the field. I have met many this way. I could go on.

Here's to the best festival, definitely in the UK – probably in the world! Long may it continue.

CAT DICKERSON

I grew up knowing their music as the first time I went to the festival I was only three or four years old. I grew up local to Cropredy. My dad's best friend is Chris Leslie so it's something I've always known. My dad was the one who built Swarb's memorial bench.

CHRIS REVIE

Some Cropredy memories:

The year we put a 'No Jeans' sign on the front gate. A number of people thought it was serious.

A message over the crew radio: 'How do we feel about goats (in the concert arena)?'

One year, standing on the disability viewing platform, I looked down the access ramp at my newest team member, who was gesturing with her head slightly and giving me a face that said, 'Who is this old fart, who's been hanging around behind me for the last ten minutes?' I walked down the ramp and whispered quietly in her ear: 'That's Robert Plant.'

Watching Richard Thompson in 1989 lead a multi-part audience sing along of 'Twist And Shout' while at the same time restringing his guitar.

The first time I saw Fairport with Vikki Clayton perform 'Tam Lin'. It sent shivers down my spine.

The fiftieth anniversary concert when Fairport opened with 'Time Will Show The Wiser'!

Robin Williamson on a warm Saturday afternoon in the mid-90s, just after lunch. Just him, a harp and 20,000 people absolutely entranced by his Celtic stories.

Watching Pete Stallon wake the crew in the caravan by the top gate by vigorously shaking it back and forth: 'Morning me beauties!'

1987 and my first Cropredy. Friday night with John Martyn and Danny Thompson as the sun went down – nuff said!

My friend Ian losing the car keys in the mud on an absolutely filthy wet Friday night. Everyone else was frantically looking for them while I was thinking 'there is no point in the wet and the dark. They'll turn up tomorrow morning.' Sure enough, they had been handed into the police pod, but we only told Ian that after we'd sent him down to Lost Property at the other end of the site as a punishment.

The 2010 Friday night double header of Bellowhead followed by Little Feat.

That couple who had vigorous sex one night in their tent in Field 2 and finished to thunderous applause and cries of 'encore' from all the surrounding tents.

Somehow ending up in a Ralph McTell/Dave Pegg impromptu bar closing time chorus.

JOHN WHITING

Why go to Cropredy? Well, it's a question I get asked regularly, including by my family who see me head off on my annual pilgrimage. Actually, my family have long since accepted Dad's eccentricities in this area and accept that I'm heading off to see Fairport. And yes, that is a key part: going to see Fairport, looking forward to 'Festival Bell' at 4pm on Thursday ('JACK!') and then the wonderful Saturday set, which always comes with that tinge of Cropresse that it's the last act of the festival.

I can't remember my first Cropredy – and no that's not a rehash of 'if you can remember the sixties, you weren't there'. (Actually, I can remember a lot of the sixties – particularly my first encounter with FC!) My first Cropredy was certainly driven by wanting to see Fairport – and being bowled over both by their playing for three and a half hours on Saturday and by the profusion of guests they'd attracted. Could, and would, any other band do that?

At the end of the three days, you head home contemplating the 363 days (bother – a leap year) to the next one and that moment of Croprupture when the wristband finally goes. But at least, as in every year, I know what I'm buying myself for Christmas. Yes, my letter to Father Cropmas has only one thing on it and once the ticket arrives, with the cheerful leaflet about all the familiar features… well, it seems a long way off but it's a bit of a beacon through the dark days of winter, promising that there is a summer that is not so very far off.

But with the greatest of respect to the FFFCs (Fairport Founding Fathers of Cropredy) there is so much more to Cropredy than Fairport (and I'm sure they'd be only too ready to agree). OK, I'd come just for them, not least to see a bunch of guys of similar age to me manage to do two and a half hours plus on stage – what an example to us all! But what else is there to recommend it all? Let me think…

Is it all about the music?

Put it another way: does the line-up matter? When I first went, definitely yes. I'd think carefully about whether to go to one, two or three days (most times I've been a daily commuter). Now – and for a long time – it doesn't matter; I know there will be an eclectic Cropmixture, which, to me, is part of the point.

Every now and again there's a real Cropwow – a reason to go even if everything else got cancelled: difficult to beat Brian Wilson in this category. A bit below this level – but not much – are the acts I'm really here to see, ones who my Cropredy revolves round. Recent examples include: The Lark Rise Band, TradArrr, Lunasa, Skerryvore and the reformed Gryphon. Mabon were in that category but shame about that unfortunate car breakdown!

But in many ways the best thing about the programme is that there will be an annual Cropiscovery. Usually, it's someone who goes down a storm with the whole crowd

(clockwise from top left) Birmingham 2015 ticket (Terry Bidle); Cropredy warm up ticket for 2015 (Terry Bidle); Allan Pickett (right) got an onstage dedication for 'Dangeous' Brian (bottom left); Angela & Andy Schofield set up the Costa del Folk

(clockwise from top left) Steve Phillips (third left) was (very briefly) a member of Fairport Convention (Ian Burgess); Del Clouter has had 'Matty Groves' in his head since 1970, & was in Oslo in 2017 (two photos); Jenny Poirier had just lost her mother when she went to Cropredy in 2016; Cropredy 2016 with (left to right) Halgrim Øistad, Bente Sølvi Brænd, Aase Neset & Ragnar Søberg (Bente Sølvi Brænd); Dermot Ferguson's Great British Folk Festival t-shirt though sometimes it's just me and a subset who think 'wow, why haven't I seen them before… and when can I see them again?' In recent years I'd put Lau, Churchfitters, Blackbeard's Tea Party and Tide Lines, among others, in this category. In 2023 it was Fishermen's Friends and the Young 'Uns: though you may wonder (as do I) how I have managed not to see them before now. And how can I not include The Bar Steward Sons of Val Doonican… what an impact (and not just the hair and jumpers)!

And the others? Well, many will be 'glad I saw them but probably not going to rush to see them again' (but thanks for the Cropintro); some I'll realise (often quickly!) I can do without, so it's a good time to head off and do other things such as walk along the canal or visit the village. Just occasionally, there's an act that I turn to others and agree that was Peggy's little joke. But any disappointments or dislikes are more than compensated by those Cropriscoveries, plus the opportunity to go into the village and check out the Brasenose's Fringe programme.

And then there's Fairport – with the added bonus of the guests who join them for Saturday. Those Croprextras are really quite a tribute to FC and Cropredy: would Robert Plant really go to any other festival to sing just one song? RT and the Guv'nor of course… wondering who is dropping in really adds to the magic of Saturday evening.

What else is there to do for three days? Cropredy isn't just the music. There's a great warm, comforting Croprembrace as you enter the field having got your wristband. It's the whole set up: the stalls – food, Friends of Fairport, music store, and of course The Bar. It's great how so many are in the same place every year, with such cheerful staff who work so hard for the three days; the huge range of support staff (particular shout out to 'Ron's crew' and the Scouts); and of course the toilets which have become steadily more important as the years progressed (thank you for putting them in the same place every year but please could we have a cubicle back in the car park?).

I must mention the merch tent and another group of hard-working, unfailingly helpful people. The length of the queue for the merchandise and its speed of formation never cease to amaze me. On Thursday (well, most days actually) I try to be waiting for the field's gates to open but before I'd got my chair planted this year the queue for the merchandise seemed to be over the horizon – how do people do it? At least it means there's no queue at the bar or the tea stall… and I did get my t-shirt late on when the queue had died down.

And above all The Crowd – something annA rydeR captured so well in her seminal song. It sounds trite but you really are among friends when you go. I tend to be on my own but am never short of people to chat with, exchanging views over the act who is on, whether it's going to rain (or when it's going to stop), which of the beers to try, etc., etc. A real Croprommunity.

Maybe it's time for Cropredy to be prescribed on the NHS? The food, open air and restful nature would do more for stress relief that a year's supply of pills. Croprestful would do many more a world of good as they Crop around the clock...

I'll invariably make a pilgrimage into Cropredy village, often after deciding that a particular act is one that I can manage without. I always marvel at how the villagers cope with this descent of a small town (it's twice the size of the decent-sized place where I live, for goodness sake) that suddenly appears and disappears on their fringe. It's shades of *Brigadoon* (which was I believe also a musical) but thankfully this place appears every year (rather than every 100 years) and stays for longer than the single day of the original. But it's just as magical with, it seems, a similar risk of falling in love, given the anniversaries and births AJ recounts. How about *Croprigadoon – The Musical*?

Thankfully the villagers seem to thrive on it all; their welcome and enterprise never fails to impress and I hope they always think it's worth it when the fuss dies down and clear up starts. I keep meaning to go and visit Cropredy during one of the other eleven months of the year and have a drink in a quiet Red Lion or Brasenose. You certainly can't do that during festival time, but bouquets to the Brasenose in particular for the way they have embraced and expanded the 'fringe' – always well worth a visit. Plus, a call at the Talking Elephant stall; together with the main festival site CD tent, always a bit dangerous in terms of the numbers of new CDs I'm liable to come away with.

Any discussion of Cropredy must include some weather musings. We've all sat in pouring rain, huddled under an umbrella (if you haven't, that's a Croprexperience you must go through to be a true Cropredite). Indeed, the genius of the person who designed golf-style umbrellas (eg the Cropredy one I proudly use) only occurred to me after a few years, making it just big enough to cover me, my chair and accoutrements and still allow me to glimpse the stage through the rain, and allowing others to see over or round me.

I feel RT has been unfairly regarded as the rain god: I've certainly seen him in sunshine and many others also bring the wet stuff! A couple of Cropdeluges that stick in my mind are the extra sound effects of thunder accompanying Fairport's 'Fame & Glory' set a few years ago and barely being able to see or hear the Afro Celt Sound System, a gang I was looking forward to enjoying. But rain eventually passes, sometimes leading to an exodus to dry off and get changed. That has on occasion extended even unto the undergarments – if you commute, as I do, you have to come equipped with a full change of clothes and an ability to contort yourself into getting changed in the car...

Heat somehow seems to be less of a problem, though 2022 certainly saw the umbrellas in use for a different reason. One always packs the sunscreen but possibly this is more in hope than expectation; for example, this year applying it was very effective in preventing any sunburn as it seemed to immediately chase the sun away. Of course, one always brings a white Croperchief, which I guess could be used for sun protection once it has been my entrée to Mr Digance's community singing session.

Will I be going next year? Well, what do you think?? Croprexpectation has started and the second weekend in August is already blocked out. In the meantime, I have Fairport's autumn and winter tours to catch plus checking who is coming to The Stables, The King's Place and other nearby venues to keep the folk-rock readings in my central life systems at a safe level.

JOSEPH MARTIN

I've loved Fairport for a long time. I saw them with my family some years ago, in Philly, and a bit further north in New Jersey, but I've listened to them forever. They are the hardest working, most talented musicians ever, and wonderful human beings. I luv 'em! I dearly loved Sandy and the whole show… great music... fabulous musicians… great guys. Peggy is amazing! The entire band is amazing! I only wish they'd write more songs that sound like they were written centuries ago. I love that English folklore. Sandy had that down. I still miss her. She remains the greatest female talent anywhere. Tell them to come back to Philly!

LIZZIE ROSENFIELD

I've worked with Fairport a few times and worked back stage at Cropredy several years running. I have stored Dave Pegg's instruments under the table in my house while he went off for a few days after being at *Middlewich Folk and Boat Festival*. He came to my house with Clive Bunker and PJ Wright. Peggy asked very politely if Clive could have a guest ticket for their show. I have to be honest and say that it wasn't until I heard Peggy say Clive's name that I realised who he was. Obviously, I said yes!

KEN HUGHES

Advanced whitewater canoeing and Fairport Convention. Who would have thought they would go together? However, both are passions of mine and sit alongside each other well. Believe it or not they both evoke emotions that are aspirational. I have a responsibility to look after people on the river, keep them safe and make sure they get the best of times. Fairport do the same; they produce original music under some pressure to make sure we enjoy it. They tour so we get to see them at their best live and they organise a festival that accounts for so many variables in terms of safety and entertainment. Paddling in the winter with snow on the ground requires a resilience that some may consider verges on insanity. However, the thread that keeps you on the right side of the line is looking forward to being in the field with everyone else in August.Canoeing is one of the defining parts of my life, it offers me status and an income to exist by (albeit a very enjoyable one), but Cropredy is an experience I exist for.

How is it Cropredy has this influence?

There are many things about the Cropredy experience that people return for, but the feeling you get when your chair is set up and you have a beer in your hand for the first time early on the Thursday afternoon is one I would not swap for anything else. It is when you get that 'I've come back to the best place in the world' sensation. A safe warmth wrapping you up. When you take some time to look around you see any familiar faces. People you see each year. People of all ages sharing the joy.

If you have not chatted to the people around you, it will not be long. Everyone is experiencing what you are and are keen to share it. Remember, this is the world's friendliest festival for a good reason. Look up at the vast Cropredy sky. The cloud formations are enthralling. It is truly a big sky that adds drama to the vibe. Look around you at all the stalls with their colours and smells. What to eat is a conundrum, but you can try lots, because the food at Cropredy is excellent. You will be listening to the background music that is piped through the PA system. The selection is always carefully curated and has something for everyone. They could probably sell compilation CDs of these playlists.

All of this makes being on the field early on Thursday worth it. True there are fringe events with live music elsewhere, but this is the essence of why we are here.

We discovered Fairport through Cropredy, so the two are synonymous.

I have a lot of responsibility in my job to keep people safe. To fail in this is to see people get injured or lose more. This is not a world away from Fairport who also have that responsibility to people who go to the festival. We get frustrated and sometimes make fun of health and safety, but it is done mostly for the right reasons. At Cropredy it is very much in the background and I understand the principle of looking as though you are relaxed, but being in complete control. Organised like a group of swans gliding over the surface of the water. What we do not see is the effort of the legs below the surface.

We have become part of the Fairport family at Cropredy.

NIGEL SCHOFIELD

What makes Cropredy special? Here's a list:

- The atmosphere… they call it the friendliest festival: they can do that because it is.
- The way the whole village is involved and part of it and welcoming: at some festivals you feel the locals are hostile and resent you being there.
- You're not dashing from stage to stage and venue to venue, hoping to catch things. You find your spot, sit in your chair and it all happens before your very eyes.
- The range and variety of music… it's all different and it's all good.
- The fact there is no them and us. You bump into members of Fairport (and really big

music stars) just wandering around the field.

- It's a gathering. You meet up with friends you see once a year and the bonds are renewed and retied.
- It's almost like a shared secret.... out of the way... down unlikely country roads – the sort of old byways you forgot existed... and there it is, this unique, special magical world.
- It's become a tradition, an annual ritual, like Christmas and Bonfire Night (but a lot warmer).
- Beautiful people... beautiful music... a beautiful place.

RODDY ROGERS, CHANTER

I played with a Celtic band called Chanter (and still do, occasionally) who supported Fairport back in the late seventies. Fairport were a remarkably friendly and helpful crew. Peggy subsequently helped us record a demo in his home studio, playing brilliant bass on it. We were then looking for a bassist for our live gigs, mostly around London, and he recommended the excellent Nigel Portman-Smith. Nigel played with us for quite some time and really underpinned our sound. On one occasion, on a very wintry Saturday morning, Nigel called to let us know he was snowed in at Glasgow Airport, and wouldn't be able to make the gig. We gave Peggy a call to see if he could recommend any bass player in London who might be able to busk the gig with charts and so on. He asked us what time the gig was, and paused for a moment. Then, despite the horrible weather, he simply said, 'I should be able to get down to London in time, I'll do it.' And so he did, at the mercy of our song charts and surviving my promptings as we went through the set. Heroic! And bringing it all up to date, he recently contributed his splendid bass playing to a handful of new songs of mine. He's a top man, from a top band.

TERRY BIDLE

I have been a Fairport fan since the sixties but due to my work between 1965 and 1985 I was unable to see the band live (working away from home on cross country North Sea gas pipelines, on North Sea pipelay barges based in Scotland and Norway with related office work in France, and in Cyprus, on Teesside building an oil rig, in Iran and Cyprus again). My live experiences are only of the later versions of the band. I wrote a Fairport Odyssey for the 2017 tour programme celebrating 50 years of Fairport, which the band thanked me for by signing the Fairport eye test!

TIM HAYES

The highlight of my year is travelling to England to see Fairport Convention every August! Since they do not tour in the United States anymore, this is my only opportunity to enjoy their great music. Being lucky enough to call all the lads my friends, I have enjoyed Cropredy for over twenty years now. I love taking photos for lasting memories of my great times there. Long may Cropredy continue!

BRIAN MINSHALL

The Beatles were just about breaking up and I was looking around for more things to listen to. A friend suggested a sampler LP and I ended up buying the Island album, *Nice Enough To Eat*. There was lots of good music on it but 'Cajun Woman' blew me away. It was my introduction to Fairport, apart from the 'French-speaking' hit. I went off looking for more Fairport albums. *'Babbacombe' Lee* was just out so I bought that and then went all the way back to the rest. I've bought them ever since. I've got 60 or 70 Fairport CDs plus all the box sets. I didn't see them at the time because I got married and had children and other priorities. The year I got married, in '79, was the year they did their 'last ever concert'. But in 2005 they were playing Poynton Folk Festival and I thought 'I will go and see that.' It was around the time they brought out the *Over The Hill* album. They mentioned Cropredy at that gig, which I had no idea about, so in 2007 me, my wife Judy and the two young ones went down to Cropredy and we've been most years since. Wishbone Ash were on the first time we went, a band I loved in the seventies.

In 2008, everybody was under umbrellas with waterproofs and the wind and rain were lashing in from everywhere. Judy went up to check the tent was okay and I got a phone call about half an hour later to say the tent was flat on the floor. We couldn't get it back up so the four of us ended up in the car overnight, caked in mud. The next day, Sunday, we were driving down to Somerset to visit my aunt in Taunton and we arrived just caked in mud. We sent Judy and my daughter into Primark to buy a whole lot of new clothes. And we were booked in the Premier Inn so we walked in there caked in mud too, and they must've thought 'what the hell is going on here?'

I'll be going again this year (2024). It'll be me, my son and his eldest lad – the Three Amigos. My grandson, Jacob, had already been two or three times, and when I told him at Christmas we'd got tickets to go again this year, he was over the moon. And me? I love the place.

GEMMA TURNER

I went to see Fairport in Canterbury with my dad recently and spoke with a lovely lady who was selling merchandise. I talked to her about my childhood memories of Fairport and Cropredy. Fairport were an important part of my mum's life right up until she sadly passed in 2021. They were her favourite band. She played Fairport and Sandy Denny throughout our childhoods and took us to Cropredy Festival every year, even when she had terminal cancer and was passing away. At her funeral, her only request was that 'Meet On The Ledge' be played. We also played 'Who Knows Where The Time Goes' and she listened to this music in her final days. She was watching the last ever Cropredy Festival on TV when she passed away. She was your biggest fan!

RICHARD SINGLETON

I fell in love with Fairport Convention's music in '71 when a friend was playing the LPs *Full House* and *Liege & Lief*. I chose 'Tamlin' as my coven name when my ex and I joined a Wiccan group – and I still use it over 50 years later at age 71! I was a big fan of American folk in my teen years but had already discovered Pentangle and had seen them live in New York City. My ex-wife and I got to see Sandy Denny at a local college on her solo tour. We both loved the *Sandy* album and my ex looked a little like the cover photo of that album. In November '74 we got to see the reunited Fairport Convention in Berkeley, California, which was fantastic!

After an amicable divorce in 1983 I married again in 1985. Shellie and I had our first date at the Towne Crier Café in Beacon, New York and enjoyed many shows together there over the years including Fairport, RT, Swarb with Martin Carthy and lots of American folk and Irish and Scottish traditional music. In '85 we got to see Fairport, Steeleye and Renaissance in NYC on a triple bill. We put off our honeymoon for a year but in 1986 we went with Nancy Covey's 'Festival Tours' on an England, Scotland, Wales and Ireland music tour. This was the trip and event of a lifetime. The centrepiece of the tour was Fairport's seventh annual Cropredy reunion festival, during which Simon read our names out from the stage as the 'Festival Tours' honeymooners!

Shellie had absorbed from me a love of Fairport but especially liked the *Gladys' Leap* album. 'The Hiring Fair' had become 'our song'. At Cropredy, I was wandering around near the stage while Shellie relaxed on a blanket further back, and when Fairport began playing 'The Hiring Fair'. I made a beeline back to her so we could hold hands and enjoy that song together. This is a happy memory that brings me a smile after all these years and the painful memories of losing her to cancer in 2011. Nowadays, the song 'The Crowd' brings to my mind what it felt like during that evening at Cropredy.

We not only saw Fairport (including the pre-festival warmup at the Half Moon), the Richard Thompson Band, Battlefield Band, De Dannan, Mary Black, Kathryn Tickell and Alistair Anderson, but I got to sit down at lunch with Nancy Covey and she introduced me to Ashley Hutchings! We and our fellow tour members played the game of 'Aunt Sally' with Peggy and others at the post festival barbecue. Alec Finn (of De Dannan) and his wife put on a show for our group at Oranmore Castle that included some other band members, and Dolores Keane, John Faulkner, Sarah and Rita Keane. Shellie was of Irish ancestry and thrilled to the Irish traditional music, seeing the Cliffs of Moher and meeting two of her Irish cousins during the trip. Our daughter Michaela has the same long red hair as her mother and also loves Irish traditional music.

I'm now happily ten years into my third and hopefully final marriage, to Sandi, an old friend and new love. She is a Pentangle and Steeleye Span fan who is becoming more familiar with Fairport. Sandi knows that I want 'Meet On The Ledge' played at my memorial service!

POSTSCRIPT

DAVE PEGG, FAIRPORT CONVENTION

I consider myself extremely lucky to still be playing music at the age of 76. 54 years of that have been spent in Fairport Convention. When I first heard Fairport at Mothers, a club in Birmingham on my twenty-second birthday, I knew it was the band I wanted to play with. Of course, on that November evening I didn't envisage that I would still be providing the 'bottom end' to the band all those years later.

When Fairport split up in 1979, my ex-wife Christine and I were living in Cropredy and decided to create an annual band reunion. We were still all chums who loved getting together with our former band members once a year in that lovely village, to have a bit of fun and keep in touch. Our audience picked up on this, and the event has grown in popularity over the years. Three generations of Fairport fans now travel from the world over to join us at what we consider to be the friendliest, comfiest environment for our friends.

I have made many chums through Fairport and Cropredy and some of the tales in this book reflect the joy and camaraderie that we all experience at concerts and at the Cropredy Convention, so a huge thanks is due to all who have contributed to this tome.

Now I've written this on June 18th at our house in Brittany, I can either practise diminished arpeggios (only three) across the fingerboard all the way up the neck or have a beer. What d'you reckon?

Cheers to all the contributors to – and readers of – this book and see you down along the road.

Rock on!

Peggy

Brittany, France
June 2024

ACKNOWLEDGEMENTS

Simon, Peggy and Richard would like to thank everyone who submitted stories and images, and particularly the following for their help in compiling this book:

Simon Hendy, for permission to reproduce his father John's photographs of the 1979 *Farewell* concert at Cropredy; Colin Randall, for permission to reproduce his March 2024 review of Fairport at the Union Chapel in London from his site salutlive.com; Chris Charlesworth for permission to quote from his book *Just Backdated – Melody Maker: Seven Years In The Seventies* (Spenwood Books, 2024); Gareth Williams at Fairport HQ; Eric Hayes, for permission to reproduce his story behind the cover image for *Unhalfbricking* (erichayes.ca); Mike Ainscoe & Dom Walsh from *At The Barrier*; Nigel Schofield; Walter Heger; Tor Dybo; Krzysztof Przyślewicz, whose review of Spotkania z Piosenką Żeglarską i Muzyką Folk in December 1996 was originally published in *Tylko Rock* magazine, April 1997; Ian Burgess, without whose immense archive of Fairport images this book would be so much poorer; Peter Smith, whose blog myvintagerock.com contains details of over 2,000 concerts he has attended since 1969; Tristan Bryant; Bob Battersby & Lodestone Publishing Ltd for permission to use selected images as credited; Chris Leslie & Ric Sanders for each taking the time out from making music to write a few words about it.

Richard would also like to thank his wife, Kate, and his pomapoo, Sid, for keeping him fed and walked and (almost) sane.

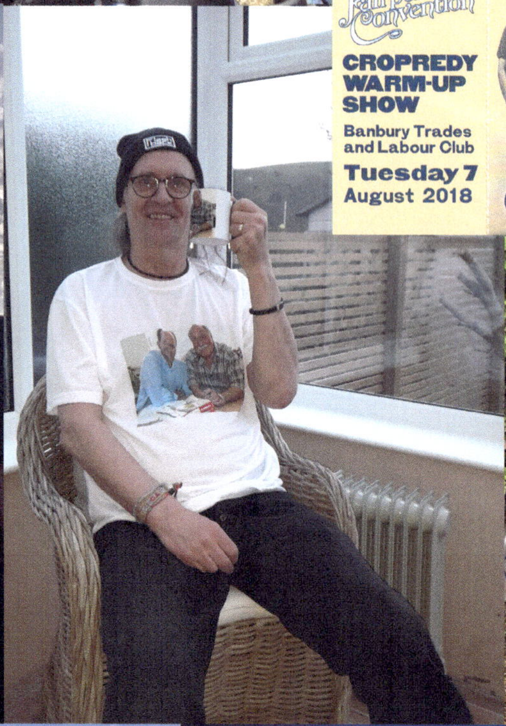

(clockwise from top left) Chris Leslie met with MND sufferer Frances White at Cropredy 2018; Cropredy 2018 (John Barlass); warm up show ticket (Terry Bidle); Mike Ainscoe was looking for records in the rain; Georgia Rose Lucas singing 'Meet On The Ledge' at Cropredy; Georgia Rose meeting Chalky the cockatoo; Mike Ainscoe at Cropredy 2019; Mick Donovan was captivated by the 2018 tribute to Sandy Denny

(clockwise from top left) Ginny White & her late husband Jerry first went to Cropredy in 2000; Maartin Allcock at Cropredy 2018 (Mike Ainscoe); Bob Bradbury's kids at Cropredy; 'Band on the Run', Cropredy 2018 (John Barlass); Cropredy 2018 (Mike Ainscoe); Jeff Cooper with Georgia Rose Lucas; Cropredy warmup ticket 2018 (Terry Bidle)

(clockwise from top left) The Bar-Stewards at Cropredy 2022 (Mike Ainscoe); Cropredy 2022 (Mike Ainscoe); Fairport Acoustic at Cropredy 2022 (Mike Ainscoe); Ric & Simon, Cropredy 2022 (Mike Ainscoe); Cropredy 2022 (Mike Ainscoe); Terry Harrop at Cropredy

RT at Cropredy 2022 (Mike Ainscoe); Seth Lakeman at Cropredy 2022 (Mike Ainscoe); Fairport played at David Tares' wedding; Jim Borrows singing The Beatles' 'Rocky Raccoon' on the Rhine; Ric & Simon at Cropredy 2022 (Tim Hayes); Darren Johnson has been hooked since 2010

(clockwise from top left) Fairport in action 2023 (Deborah Gosden); Deborah Gosden has been playing catch up with Fairport's back catalogue since 2023; Alan Bailey with Chris Leslie; Ric Sanders at Cropredy 2023 (Tim Hayes); Chris Leslie at Cropredy 2023 (Tim Hayes); Tron Eivin Øvrebø and friends at Cropredy; Fairport with Plumhall in Manchester 2023 (Mike Ainscoe)

(clockwise from top left) Ken Hughes is part of the Fairport family; Ric Sanders & Ben Savage 2023 (Tim Hayes); Peggy 2023 (Tim Hayes); Fairport in Manchester 2023 (Tim Hayes); Peggy & Chris Leslie 2023 (Tim Hayes)

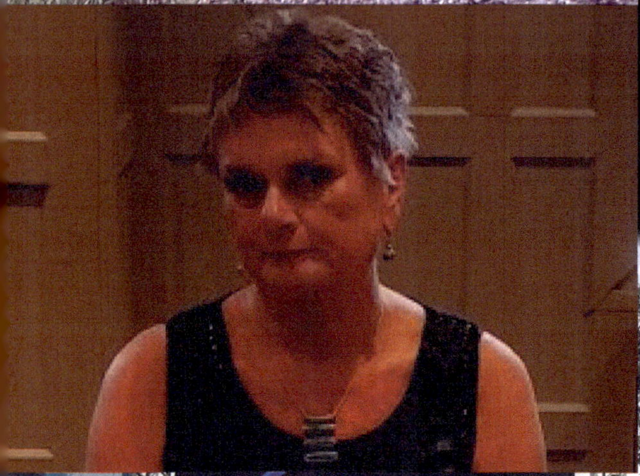

(clockwise from top left) Martin Trevelyan-Jones chose **Fairport's interpretation** of 'Best Wishes' to be played at his wife Sue's funeral; It was Olivia Marsh's first time at Cropredy 2023; **Olivia Marsh** was at Cropredy with her family; Catherine Marsh at Cropredy 2023; April Phillips embarrassed herself slightly over breakfast

(clockwise from top left) Richard Gascoyne & his wife Julia spent the afternoon with Peggy but the details are blurry; Paul Bacon discovered Fairport via *ZigZag* magazine; Plumhall in acrion (Viceversarobbi); Alan Bailey (right) was reunited with his long-lost cousin Mick at a Fairport show; Tel & Benjie caught up with DM on the 2024 Wintour; Terry Harrop's family raise a glass with Peggy

SPECIAL THANKS

John McGettigan; Jop Vlaskamp; Frank Vlaskamp; Dave Monk; Robert Osman; Darran Kellett; Bill Rintz; Andrew Morton; Christopher & Steven Harding; Martin Walker; John Whiting; Richard Kinder; Brian & Jill New; Halgrim Öistad; Graham Hawkins; Jeff Cooper; Alan Flugdate; Greg Borgartz; Dave George; Peter Clarke; Sophie Watson; Peter Roe; Anne Collins; Gillian Bonner; Oz Hardwick; Martin Driver; Joss Mullinger; Phil Lambert; Max & Wendy Bradley (Cleethorpes); Robert Bousfield; Mark Salisbury; Lee Soden; Andrew Leonard; Marcus Banks; KJC Hughes; Mike Ainscoe; Bill Sandalls; Martin & Lilian Abernethy; William Hayter; Oddbjørn Wessel; Andrew Bott; Mick Donovan; Stephen, Frances, James & Emma Royston; Martin Trevelyan-Jones; Peter Marsh & Tracy Marsh; John Barlass; Tron Eivin Øvrebø; Stephen Skey; Frazer Wylie (Cropredy legend); Martin Smith; Telandbenjie; Andrew Hooper; Christer Herentz; Nigel Chitty; Jens Andersen; Tim & Hil Dieu de Bellefontaine; Louise Foran; David Francis; Patrick McGuirk; Ian Huckin; Nat & Molly Shepherd (love Dad); Carl Hufton-Straw; Peter Turner; Dave Chick; Ian McLeish; Ian Johnson; Roddy Rogers; Dr Oliver Ilgner; Susanne Bley; Tim Hayes; Bob Mackreth; Andy Meagher & Karen Mallard; Paul Bond; Anthony & Louisa Lewis; David McElroy; Terry Bidle & Paul Bidle; Roger Haydock; James DeGaetano; Keren Norbury; John Lester; Michael Murphy; Mick Monk; David Key; Edmund Whitcombe; David, Nicola & Alex Flintham; Tim Edmonds; Brian, Christopher & Jacob Minshall; Steve Cook; Bo Ehnsio; Bob Bradbury; Sim Hardisty; Will Sawers; Marshall Blankenship; Michael Pietsch; Steve G (Director of Castledown FM); David S George; Graham Somers; Keith Whittington; Pat Thomas; Nic & Sue Dowding; Bill Wallace; April Phillips; Kevan Tucker; Ian Ashleigh; Ian Walton; Bryan O'Malley; Peter Smith; Ann Tulacz; Stephen Phillips; Sally & Jim Farmer; Glyn Parry; Hans Hermann Moll (in memory of Michael Botho); Richard John Hayward; Cynthia McCandless; Edwin Wallage; Christopher Caldecott; Rich & Julia Gascoyne; Dom Duckworth; Lt Col Mike Stephens MBE; Jamie Pipe; Jimmy & Kay Young (Nairn, Highland); Graham Ley; Roger Averill; Richard Lewis; S John Dawson; Jerry Ford; John G & friends; Denyse Anger; Paul Sampson; Graham Day; Paul Bacon; Grace (Morris) Palmer; Peter Buckley; Malcolm Howes; Jane Elizabeth Howes; Angela & David Parkes; Julie & Carl Southwell; Jane & Roger Mercer; Jan & Jon Dixon; Mac Macleod; Christopher Ellis; Vivienne Prout; Peter George; Mark Johnson; Mark Salisbury; Howard Johnson; Richard Whitehead; Mark Salt; Peter Hoskings; Mark Graham; John Farrar; Lee Perry; Chris Bates; Frits Wielens; James Borrows; Jenny Parsons; Bastiaan Van Der Plas; Graham Warren, Peter Soffe & Rosie Langan; James & Elizabeth Franey; Christian Globisch; Martin Cropp; Nick Skilton; Gwyneth Try, Rebecca Try, Robyn Try, Tamsin Try; Simon Young; Tim Romain; Russell Allan; Rob Pirrie; Grahame Baumber; Mike Dillon; Larry & Maureen Bode; Graham Law; Dermot Ferguson; Kevan Taplin; Richard Hamilton; Sally Maybury; Brigt Einar Bø; Ginny White & in memory of Jerry White; Paul Turner; Richard Singleton; Tor Dybo; Deryck Clouter; John Woods; Charlie Monck; Darren Johnson; Michael Murray; Neil Murray; Evan Smith; Steve, Clare & Hannah Patrick; Andy & Deb Mahon; Marc Breslav; Alison Hinds; Diane Langley; Charles Wilcox; Derek Cauldwell; Malcolm Garrett; David James; Jackie Thomson; Ian Close; Paul Taylor; Mark Evans; Stephen Brightman, Anne Kavanagh, Josephine Kavanagh; Eddy McCabe, in memory of Keith Stanton (1962-2024); Richard & Alison Buxton; Richard Gleave; Alan Banks; Nigel & Heather Banks; Brian Green; Kenny Kemp; Eric van Maaren; Kurt Thulin.

Listen, Listen
The complete works of Sandy Denny on CD
Join Fairport...
LEDGE
FOLKTASTIC
FAIRPORT CONVENTION
CELEBRATING 40 YEARS OF FAIRPORT WITH TALKING ELEPHANTS FAIRPORT AND FAIRPORT RELATED GOODIES - FOLKTASTIC!
THE ALBION DANCE BAND
Dancing Days Are Here Again
25TH ANNIVERSARY CONCERT
Fairport Convention's 25th Anniversary Concert was recorded live at the Cropredy Festival, 14/15th August 1992, with their special guests Robert Plant, Richard Thompson, Chris Leslie, Dave Swarbrick, Jerry Donahue, Ashley Hutchings, Ralph McTell, Julianne Regan, Vikki Clayton, Bruce Rowland, Geoff Hughes, and compere Danny Thompson. £ 13.99
OLD NEW BORROWED BLUE
6 NEWly recorded songs recorded in 1995/6. The next bunch of songs were all recorded at the Mill Arts Centre in Banbury on the penultimate day of 1995 and represent the OLD and the BORROWED. (Our picture's BLUE on the cover even if we're not...).
£ 12.99
The G.P.'s
Saturday Rolling Around £ 9.99
Richard Thompson, Ralph McTell, Peggy and Dave Mattacks
WISHBONE ASH
First Light - The band's earliest known recordings. Catch them at Cropredy on Thursday this year. £ 12.99
THE WOOD & THE WIRE £ 9.99
MANY EARS TO PLEASE £12.99
WHO KNOWS £ 9.99
ACOUSTICALLY DOWN UNDER £ 9.99
Judy Dyble
FAIRPORT'S 1ST SINGER
"Does not disappoint" Record Collector
SPINDLE £ 10.99
THE WHORL £ 10.99
ENCHANTED GARDEN £ 8.99
or buy any 2 for £ 16.99
POSTAGE
BBC RADIO OXFORD
95.2 FM | BBC One | bbc.co.uk/oxford
Relive the magic...
of Fairport's Cropredy Convention
with BBC Radio Oxford 95.2 FM
Live highlights from backstage
Saturday 6pm-1am. And all next week (6-10am) with Phil Gayle & Friends at breakfast
WHAT'S ON
JULY / AUG
IN THE THEATRE
IN THE MILLERS
Sat.6 July £2.50/2
NATIONS IN DUB
Fri.12 July £2.50/2
THE BUNNY STAPLES
Fri.19 July £4/3
ALLAN TAYLOR
Fri.26 July £4/3
KEITH HANCOCK
Sat.27 July £2.50/2
4 IN A FISH TANK
Sat.10 August
SPLIT THE REED
Sat.10 August 11am & 2.30pm
CAPTAIN CRAB £2
The All Electric Puppet Theatre
Children's Theatre for all ages
Tues/Wed 13/14 August 7.30pm
FAIRPORT CONVENTION £10
Coming soon...
Sat.7 Sept
Fri.20 Sept
Sun.22 Sept
JOHN RENBOURN AND ISAAC GUILLORY
Sat.5 Oct
more details inside.....
THE LEDGE
A Great NEW Vide
For Children
Singing Games For Children
Includes Free Songsheet
Enjoy learning and singing along to such timeless favourites as Banbury Cross, Looby Loo and Oranges and Lemons.
Music arranged and produced by Simon Nicol